THE CASE OF THE WASHED-UP CORPSE

TAM MAY

The Case of the Washed-Up Corpse

Grave Sisters Mysteries: Book 1

Tam May

Published by Dreambook Press.

Click or visit:
https://www.tammayauthor.com

ISBN: 9781734671476

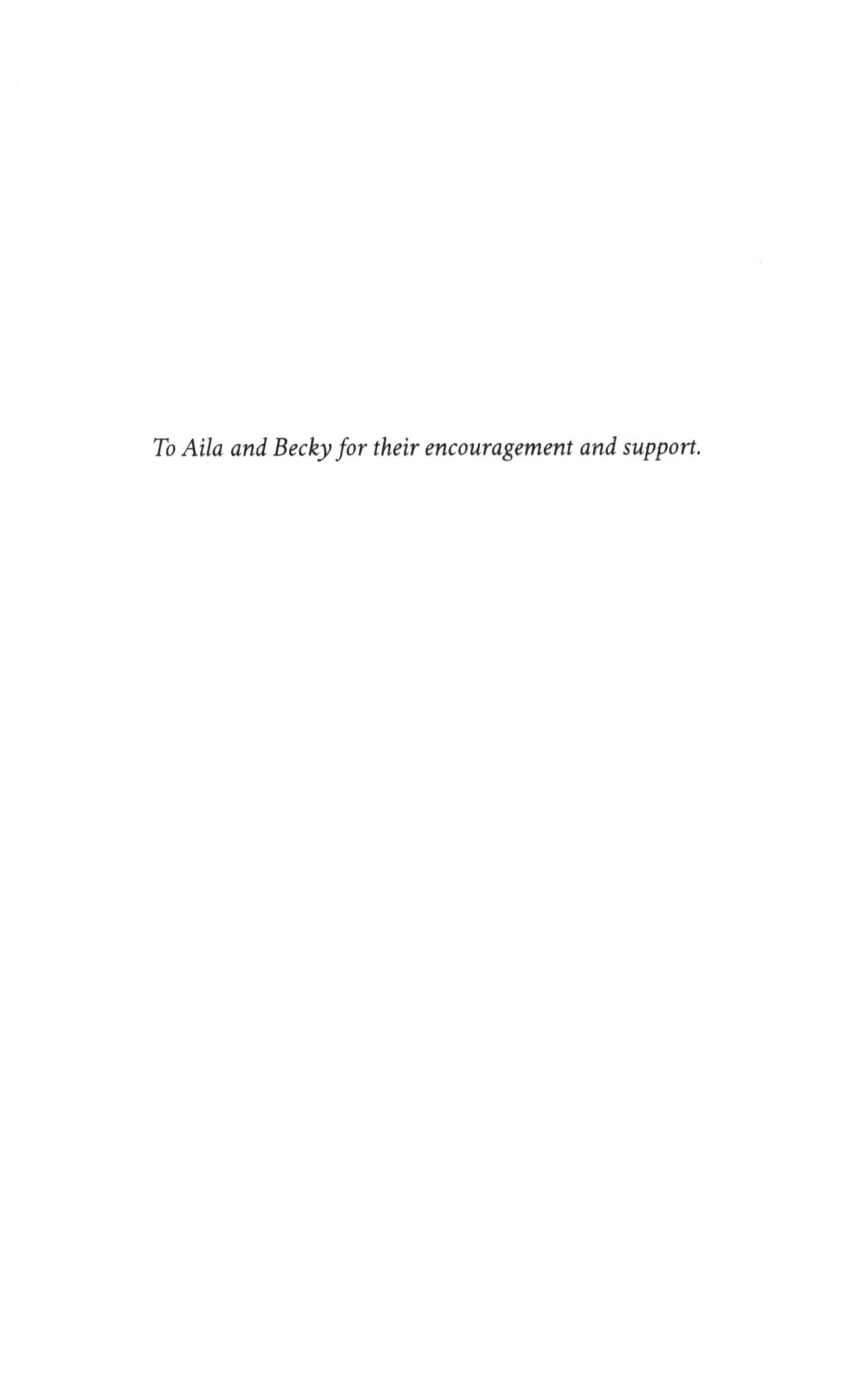

To Aila and Becky for their encouragement and support.

CHAPTER 1

They followed Oliver's Dodge, driving along the river walk which had ample lights and was not entirely deserted of lovers. They reached the edge of town where the river walk ended and the road grew rougher.

"Quite a distance from downtown." Eve shivered as they drove along the part of the river that bent like an arm with no walk, no lights, and an overgrowth of grass and shrubs.

"You don't expect a dead woman to be found washed up near the city center do you?" Helena asked.

Eve was relieved to see the police car shining its headlights as Oliver came to a stop.

"What are Mr. And Mrs. Whitman doing here?" Helena asked as they joined Oliver.

The two small gray-haired figures stood near the police car. Mr. Whitman's shoulders was wrapped around his wife's, and they both looked pale even under the dim glare.

"They discovered the body," said the district attorney. "Sheriff! Can't we get these people a cup of coffee?"

"Where from?" came the brusque response.

"From the diner up the road," Helena snapped back.

"And send someone to get Dot," Eve added. "She'll want to be with her parents."

Sheriff Warner appeared under the headlights. He was a sandy-haired man with a large frame and a belly that always seemed to strain against the buttons of his coat. His face was missing a clean shave.

"What's going on, Mr. Clarke?" He glanced at Eve and Helena.

"Give Mr. and Mrs. Whitman a seat in the car with the blanket," Oliver said. "You *do* have a blanket, don't you?"

"I got a blanket," the sheriff grunted.

"And send one of your men to get the coffee," Oliver added. "And Dot too."

"I ain't got enough men," Sheriff Warner grumbled. "Now, if the county would —"

"I told you I would deal with the county," Oliver said. "Right now, we have a dead girl on our hands."

The sheriff glared at him. "I know my job just well as you do, Mr. Clarke."

"I never thought otherwise, Sheriff." Oliver's tone softened. "Send one of your men for the coffee and the daughter, if you please. We want the Whitmans calm when they give us their evidence, don't we?"

"All right, all right." Sheriff Warner waved at him. "What's going on?" he repeated, glaring at the two women now.

"I thought Eve and Helena might be able to shed some light as to who the woman is since none of us could identify her," said Oliver. "And as Helena has medical knowledge, I thought she could tell us something about the body while we wait for Dr. Myers."

The sheriff's cigar almost fell out of his mouth. "This ain't no place for women!"

"We're not just women," Helena said. "We're professionals when it comes to the dead."

"But not this kind of dead!"

"You forget, Sheriff, we're no strangers to corpses," Eve said.

"We know them better than you do," her sister added.

"I got the coroner breathing down my neck, and Parks with his damn Kodak blinding everybody and now women!" the man grumbled.

"Parks is here because I called him," Oliver said in a gruff tone. "Maybe you haven't heard, Sheriff, but the police take photographs of the crime scene these days."

"Maybe they do in the city where you was, but not here."

"As long as I'm district attorney, we'll have photographs," Oliver said.

"And fingerprinting?" The sheriff eyed him. "I don't see no fingerprint man here."

"That's to come," Oliver promised. "I'll get the whole thing down here. Measurements, fingerprinting, everything."

"A real specialist, eh?" Sheriff Warner grumbled. "Seems to me Zak got along pretty well without all this newfangled stuff."

"Well, I'm district attorney now. And tell your men this isn't a peep show! Get out of there!" The roar made the men scatter like deer fleeing a hungry tiger. "Did you talk to Peterson?"

Sheriff Warner nodded. "He'll be down soon."

"Good."

"He thinks we ought to get Dan Frazer and Grover Mathis here." The sheriff led them carefully down the slippery incline that separated the road from the river. "Might turn out to be a Moody County case."

"The girl's on our side of the river," Oliver insisted.

"That don't mean she didn't get killed in Nevada," Sheriff Warner said. "If she did, it's their case, not ours."

"Until we find out who she is, we're going on the assumption she's our case."

Sheriff Warner's eyes narrowed a bit. "It's your decision, Mr. Clarke."

Oliver helped Helena down the last muddy piece of the

incline. Eve could see the overgrowth had been stripped away, probably by the police. Now that the officers had cleared the way, the figure of a girl was in view.

"Poor thing," she murmured.

"I told you this ain't no place for women," the sheriff growled.

"Better our sympathy than your men's gawking." Helena took her sister's arm. "Come on, Eve."

They walked carefully along to the edge of the river, as the chalky dirt had turned into mud. Oliver followed, holding his flashlight to illuminate the way.

"Evening, George." He nodded at the wiry young man with the camera as he crouched at the feet of the body lying on the ground "Getting much?"

"How can I when the sheriff won't keep the flashlight here?" he grumbled. "I'm trying my best, Mr. Clarke, but there's only so much I can do with the flash lamp."

"Well, get as many photographs as you can," said Oliver. "Don't worry about the cost. I'll see to it the county pays you back." He glanced around. "I don't see Frances here yet."

"Franki Decker?" Eve stared.

George grinned. "She's been appointed police sketch artist just as I've been appointed police photographer."

"Is that really necessary?" she asked, fidgeting a little as she thought of another woman subjected to the crime scene.

"It's how they do things now, Eve," her sister explained. "Photographs and sketches of the crime scene."

"And suspects, if there are any," Oliver threw in.

"I agree with Miss Grace," the sheriff said. "There ain't no need for all this, Mr. Clarke. We want as few people here as possible."

"We don't know what we're going to find yet," Oliver argued. "I'd just as soon err on the side of caution and have too much information rather than too little."

A young woman of about Helena's age appeared, her owl-like

face encased with a frame of wild short hair as she saluted Oliver. "Sorry I'm late, Mr. Clarke. I had a time getting down that hill." She glanced behind her with reproach.

"You ever done this sort of thing before, Miss Decker?"

She gave him a cool stare. "I think I can handle it, Sheriff."

"Just get what you can in this pitch black and give it to George," Oliver instructed. "I don't want to keep you here longer than I have to."

"Franki can stand it as much as we can," Helena insisted, pressing the girls' shoulder. "She was making drawings of the deceased for families when she was a teenager."

"Well, there's one over there now." Oliver jerked his head toward the river. Franki nodded and disappeared into the darkness.

"Golly." George gulped. "Wait until the Shane brothers hear about this!"

"You're not to give them any photographs or sketches without my release," Oliver commanded. "There may be things we don't want the public to know yet."

"Of course, Mr. Clarke," George promised. He grinned at the sisters. "Giving the corpse the full treatment, eh?"

"Eve and Helena are here is see if they know who the girl is," said Oliver.

He nodded with approval. "They know the new additions even before they're born."

"I assume that's a compliment?" Helena eyed him. He tipped his hat in response.

"With all due respect, Mr. Clarke, I can't see why Miss Grave and Mrs. Wright would know the girl if I don't," said the sheriff. "Warners have been around here at least as long as Graves have."

"People don't slink away from them like they do you, Sheriff," George said with a chuckle. "Not to mention Eve has a way of getting people to talk to her for hours and hours."

"Yes, I noticed that." Oliver smiled.

"Talking ain't knowing," the sheriff mumbled.

A whistle sounded through the darkness. "Peterson's here."

Mr. Peterson, the county coroner, was a man with an impressive crown of red hair and an outdated red beard. "Evening, all. What do we have here?"

"A dead body, obviously," Helena said.

"I realize that, Mrs. Wright." He glanced at the district attorney as if waiting for an explanation. "You sure she's ours?"

"She's lying here, isn't she?" Oliver asked.

"That doesn't mean she's ours," Mr. Peterson said. "If we got Frazer and Mathis to come down —"

"And if they did?" Oliver challenged. "They would say the same thing I am. Even if we find out she was from Nevada, she ended up in California. It's our case, not theirs."

"I'm just saying —"

Oliver squared his shoulders. "I was elected to do a job and I'm doing it."

The man backed down. "I'm not questioning your judgment, Mr. Clarke."

"Somebody give me a flashlight!" Oliver shouted. "Give the ladies one too."

A cold metal tube was placed in Eve's hand. She held it close to her side, staring down at the body.

"Oh, for pity's sake," grumbled her younger sister as she took the light and aimed it at the girl's face.

Eve felt a wave of sickness. It was like she was a child again seeing her first corpse in the mortuary. Her father had prepared the bodies then, and she remembered his soothing words: *It's only the shell of the spirit, honey. Nothing to fear from a spirit shell.*

She chided herself for being so childish and knelt down beside her sister, looking carefully at the face.

"What do you think Eve?" her sister asked.

Eve studied the milky skin under the beacon. The eyes were

closed and the lips were a thin line. The girl had a simple, solid kind of prettiness.

"I don't think I know her," Eve said softly.

"It's what I said," Sheriff Warner mumbled. "Miss Grave don't know everyone."

"I don't recognize her either," Helena admitted.

"Maybe she just arrived in town," Oliver said.

"Not many who 'just arrive' in Gyver, Mr. Clarke," Sheriff Warner said. "And when they do, we make sure to know about it."

"You're a regular watchdog," Helena snapped.

Eve brushed mud off her Oxford shoes. "Maybe when we see the poor child's face in daylight, we'll know who she is."

"I don't think she's much of a child," Helena said. "I'd guess her to be older than Vi."

"And not much tamer, by the looks of her," Sheriff Warner said with a snort.

Eve's anger rose. "There's nothing wrong with our sister!"

"That's enough, Sheriff," Oliver said.

"You think suicide, Mr. Clarke?" Mr. Peterson rubbed his long beard.

"That'd be my guess," the sheriff said. "It's that damned amendment. Women's rights!" He spit out the last words.

"What has that got to do with it?" Helena asked sharply.

"It's obvious, ain't it?" he asked. "She's young. She's not ugly. Young girls think they got the right now to run around raising hell, smoking, drinking, putting on more lipstick than is good for them, and messing around with boys."

Eve's rage rose again. "Are you insinuating —"

"Now, now, Miss Grave, I wasn't talking about anyone in particular."

"You'd better not be," Helena said. "There is such a thing as defamation of character, Sheriff." She then added, "Not to mention Vi knows just where to kick a man so it hurts, and she's not afraid to use those high heels of hers."

Oliver roared with laughter. "You'd better watch yourself, Sheriff."

The man sniffed. "As I was saying, girls nowadays get a taste of freedom and get themselves in trouble. Only way out for them is suicide."

"I'm not convinced we have a suicide on our hands," Oliver said. "If the girl really was in trouble, as you say, and wanted to do herself in, there are easier ways."

"Not to mention more permanent ones," Mr. Peterson remarked. "Drowning oneself is a mighty risky thing."

"It worked, didn't it?" Sheriff Warner growled.

"Please!" Eve felt the nausea return.

"I'm sorry, Eve," Oliver said. "I guess we shouldn't be talking like this, knowing what you do."

"It's because of what we do that we have strong stomachs, Oliver," Helena said.

Eve sighed. "I just wish we could have been more helpful."

"It was a long shot anyway," he said with a sigh.

"I'm sure we'll know her in daylight." With more resolve, she added, "I'm sure of it."

"She ought to come with us," said Helena. "To the morgue, I mean. It's where she belongs."

"Nobody's taking this body anywhere until the medical examiner gets here," Mr. Peterson insisted. "Where is that damn doctor?"

"He's been called," said Sheriff Warner. "You know Doc. He ain't one to interrupt his evening pipe even for a corpse."

"Well, he's going to," Oliver said in a vicious tone. "It's time we got some brains into that small-town mind of ours."

"Yourself included?" The sheriff eyed him.

The district attorney gave him a hard stare. "Myself included. I asked Helena to do a preliminary examination in the meantime."

"She ain't no doctor," the sheriff protested.

"I have to agree, Mr. Clarke." Mr. Peterson gave Helena an uneasy glance. "I respect Mrs. Wright's profession but the county medical examiner is the one who ought to do that."

"We've established Eve and Helena know more about dead bodies than any of us here," Oliver said. "As the medical examiner doesn't see fit to hurry with his pipe, I don't want any more delays in getting this case underway."

"She might tamper with evidence and not realize it," Sheriff Warner grumbled.

"I know all about evidence," Helena snapped. "I have some intelligence, Sheriff."

"No disrespect, ma'am —"

"Helena also studied with Mrs. Zadie Hummer in Pasadena," Eve said. "She knows more about criminal investigations than you think."

"Ain't that the eccentric millionaire's daughter who toys with the police?" Sheriff Warner narrowed his eyes.

"Mrs. Hummer has helped lawmen on more than one occasion," Helena said stiffly.

"And she taught you everything she knows, eh?"

"I trust Helena's knowledge and expertise," Oliver said. "What do you say, Mr. Peterson?"

The coroner shrugged. "I guess it's better than standing around here just looking at it while we wait."

"Looking at *her*," Eve said in a hollow tone. "She's a person, Mr. Peterson."

"Yes, miss," he mumbled.

Helena inspected the woman from head to foot. Eve noted she was very gentle and slow with her examination.

"She's a well-dressed corpse," Eve remarked.

"Not so well-dressed," her sister said. "The fabric is rayon."

"We'll search for labels later," Oliver said. "That might tell us something."

Helena glanced at him. "May I turn the body over?"

"Is that wise?" Mr. Peterson looked uncomfortable.

"Do anything you think is necessary," Oliver said.

With the help of two policemen, they got the body turned over without disturbing much of the ground underneath. As they moved the dead woman to her side, Eve gasped. "My God, her head is almost to her chest!"

"Her neck's broken," Helena confirmed.

"There ain't nothing but skin holding it up," Warner said.

"There's no need to be vulgar, Sheriff," Helena snapped. "Eve and I both know what a broken neck looks like."

"It could have broken in the current if the body came from down the river," Mr. Peterson suggested. "Lots of rocks and debris at that end."

Helena shook her head. "This was something different. Something more brutal and deliberate."

"That settles the question of suicide at least," Oliver said. "She could hardly have broken her own neck."

"It settles nothing," Sheriff Warner insisted. "Not until Doc gets here and does his official examination. He's the expert, after all."

Helena glared at him.

"The autopsy should tell us more," Mr. Peterson agreed.

"It won't tell you whether she died from the broken neck," Helena argued. "It will only tell you whether she's been in the water. Drowning is a tricky death."

Eve pulled her coat closer to her. "Why would someone try to drown her if he already broke her neck?"

"Maybe he didn't mean to break it," Oliver said. "It could have been an accident. He was holding her head down in the water, like this." He grabbed the back of a policeman's neck and pushed his head forward, making the young man gasp. "He just held too hard, and the neck broke."

"Mr. Clarke, I'd appreciate it if you wouldn't use one of my men to entertain the ladies." Sheriff Warner's face was slick with anger.

"Murder is not entertaining for us, Sheriff," Eve said in a hard voice. "My sister and I take death very seriously."

"I think you'd better apologize, Sheriff." Oliver's tone was uncompromising.

The sheriff removed his hat and bowed his head. "I'm sorry, Miss Grave. I had the deepest respect for your father."

Eve turned away, as the mention of her father always made a lump form in her chest.

CHAPTER 2

They followed Oliver's Dodge, driving along the river walk which had ample lights and was not entirely deserted of lovers. They reached the middle of town where the river walk ended and the road grew rougher.

"Quite a distance from downtown." Eve shivered as they drove along the part of the river that bent like an arm with no walk, no lights, and an overgrowth of grass and shrubs.

"You don't expect a dead woman to be found washed up near the city center do you?" Helena asked.

Eve was relieved to see the police car shining its headlights as Oliver came to a stop.

"What are Mr. And Mrs. Whitman doing here?" Helena asked as they joined Oliver.

The two small gray-haired figures stood near the police car. Mr. Whitman's shoulders was wrapped around his wife's, and they both looked pale even under the dim glare.

"They discovered the body," said the district attorney. "Sheriff! Can't we get these people a cup of coffee?"

"Where from?" came the brusque response.

"From the diner up the road," Helena snapped back.

"And send someone to get Dot," Eve added. "She'll want to be with her parents."

Sheriff Warner appeared under the headlights. He was a sandy-haired man with a large frame and a belly that always seemed to strain against the buttons of his coat. His face was missing a clean shave.

"What's going on, Mr. Clarke?" He glanced at Eve and Helena.

"Give Mr. and Mrs. Whitman a seat in the car with the blanket," Oliver said. "You *do* have a blanket, don't you?"

"I got a blanket," the sheriff grunted.

"And send one of your men to get the coffee," Oliver added. "And Dot too."

"I ain't got enough men," Sheriff Warner grumbled. "Now, if the county would —"

"I told you I would deal with the county," Oliver said. "Right now, we have a dead girl on our hands."

The sheriff glared at him. "I know my job just well as you do, Mr. Clarke."

"I never thought otherwise, Sheriff." Oliver's tone softened. "Send one of your men for the coffee and the daughter, if you please. We want the Whitmans calm when they give us their evidence, don't we?"

"All right, all right." Sheriff Warner waved at him. "What's going on?" he repeated, glaring at the two women now.

"I thought Eve and Helena might be able to shed some light as to who the woman is since none of us could identify her," said Oliver. "And as Helena has medical knowledge, I thought she could tell us something about the body while we wait for Dr. Myers."

The sheriff's cigar almost fell out of his mouth. "This ain't no place for women!"

"We're not just women," Helena said. "We're professionals when it comes to the dead."

"But not this kind of dead!"

"You forget, Sheriff, we're no strangers to corpses," Eve said.

"We know them better than you do," her sister added.

"I got the coroner breathing down my neck, and Parks with his damn Kodak blinding everybody and now women!" the man grumbled.

"Parks is here because I called him," Oliver said in a gruff tone. "Maybe you haven't heard, Sheriff, but the police take photographs of the crime scene these days."

"Maybe they do in the city where you was, but not here."

"As long as I'm district attorney, we'll have photographs," Oliver said.

"And fingerprinting?" The sheriff eyed him. "I don't see no fingerprint man here."

"That's to come," Oliver promised. "I'll get the whole thing down here. Measurements, fingerprinting, everything."

"A real specialist, eh?" Sheriff Warner grumbled. "Seems to me Zak got along pretty well without all this newfangled stuff."

"Well, I'm district attorney now. And tell your men this isn't a peep show! Get out of there!" The roar made the men scatter like deer fleeing a hungry tiger. "Did you talk to Peterson?"

Sheriff Warner nodded. "He'll be down soon."

"Good."

"He thinks we ought to get Dan Frazer and Grover Mathis here." The sheriff led them carefully down the slippery incline that separated the road from the river. "Might turn out to be a Moody County case."

"The girl's on our side of the river," Oliver insisted.

"That don't mean she didn't get killed in Nevada," Sheriff Warner said. "If she did, it's their case, not ours."

"Until we find out who she is, we're going on the assumption she's our case."

Sheriff Warner's eyes narrowed a bit. "It's your decision, Mr. Clarke."

Oliver helped Helena down the last muddy piece of the

incline. Eve could see the overgrowth had been stripped away, probably by the police. Now that the officers had cleared the way, the figure of a girl was in view.

"Poor thing," she murmured.

"I told you this ain't no place for women," the sheriff growled.

"Better our sympathy than your men's gawking." Helena took her sister's arm. "Come on, Eve."

They walked carefully along to the edge of the river, as the chalky dirt had turned into mud. Oliver followed, holding his flashlight to illuminate the way.

"Evening, George." He nodded at the wiry young man with the camera as he crouched at the feet of the body lying on the ground "Getting much?"

"How can I when the sheriff won't keep the flashlight here?" he grumbled. "I'm trying my best, Mr. Clarke, but there's only so much I can do with the flash lamp."

"Well, get as many photographs as you can," said Oliver. "Don't worry about the cost. I'll see to it the county pays you back." He glanced around. "I don't see Frances here yet."

"Franki Decker?" Eve stared.

George grinned. "She's been appointed police sketch artist just as I've been appointed police photographer."

"Is that really necessary?" she asked, fidgeting a little as she thought of another woman subjected to the crime scene.

"It's how they do things now, Eve," her sister explained. "Photographs and sketches of the crime scene."

"And suspects, if there are any," Oliver threw in.

"I agree with Miss Grace," the sheriff said. "There ain't no need for all this, Mr. Clarke. We want as few people here as possible."

"We don't know what we're going to find yet," Oliver argued. "I'd just as soon err on the side of caution and have too much information rather than too little."

A young woman of about Helena's age appeared, her owl-like

face encased with a frame of wild short hair as she saluted Oliver. "Sorry I'm late, Mr. Clarke. I had a time getting down that hill." She glanced behind her with reproach.

"You ever done this sort of thing before, Miss Decker?"

She gave him a cool stare. "I think I can handle it, Sheriff."

"Just get what you can in this pitch black and give it to George," Oliver instructed. "I don't want to keep you here longer than I have to."

"Franki can stand it as much as we can," Helena insisted, pressing the girls' shoulder. "She was making drawings of the deceased for families when she was a teenager."

"Well, there's one over there now." Oliver jerked his head toward the river. Franki nodded and disappeared into the darkness.

"Golly." George gulped. "Wait until the Shane brothers hear about this!"

"You're not to give them any photographs or sketches without my release," Oliver commanded. "There may be things we don't want the public to know yet."

"Of course, Mr. Clarke," George promised. He grinned at the sisters. "Giving the corpse the full treatment, eh?"

"Eve and Helena are here is see if they know who the girl is," said Oliver.

He nodded with approval. "They know the new additions even before they're born."

"I assume that's a compliment?" Helena eyed him. He tipped his hat in response.

"With all due respect, Mr. Clarke, I can't see why Miss Grave and Mrs. Wright would know the girl if I don't," said the sheriff. "Warners have been around here at least as long as Graves have."

"People don't slink away from them like they do you, Sheriff," George said with a chuckle. "Not to mention Eve has a way of getting people to talk to her for hours and hours."

"Yes, I noticed that." Oliver smiled.

"Talking ain't knowing," the sheriff mumbled.

A whistle sounded through the darkness. "Peterson's here."

Mr. Peterson, the county coroner, was a man with an impressive crown of red hair and an outdated red beard. "Evening, all. What do we have here?"

"A dead body, obviously," Helena said.

"I realize that, Mrs. Wright." He glanced at the district attorney as if waiting for an explanation. "You sure she's ours?"

"She's lying here, isn't she?" Oliver asked.

"That doesn't mean she's ours," Mr. Peterson said. "If we got Frazer and Mathis to come down —"

"And if they did?" Oliver challenged. "They would say the same thing I am. Even if we find out she was from Nevada, she ended up in California. It's our case, not theirs."

"I'm just saying —"

Oliver squared his shoulders. "I was elected to do a job and I'm doing it."

The man backed down. "I'm not questioning your judgment, Mr. Clarke."

"Somebody give me a flashlight!" Oliver shouted. "Give the ladies one too."

A cold metal tube was placed in Eve's hand. She held it close to her side, staring down at the body.

"Oh, for pity's sake," grumbled her younger sister as she took the light and aimed it at the girl's face.

Eve felt a wave of sickness. It was like she was a child again seeing her first corpse in the mortuary. Her father had prepared the bodies then, and she remembered his soothing words: *It's only the shell of the spirit, honey. Nothing to fear from a spirit shell.*

She chided herself for being so childish and knelt down beside her sister, looking carefully at the face.

"What do you think Eve?" her sister asked.

Eve studied the milky skin under the beacon. The eyes were

closed and the lips were a thin line. The girl had a simple, solid kind of prettiness.

"I don't think I know her," Eve said softly.

"It's what I said," Sheriff Warner mumbled. "Miss Grave don't know everyone."

"I don't recognize her either," Helena admitted.

"Maybe she just arrived in town," Oliver said.

"Not many who 'just arrive' in Gyver, Mr. Clarke," Sheriff Warner said. "And when they do, we make sure to know about it."

"You're a regular watchdog," Helena snapped.

Eve brushed mud off her Oxford shoes. "Maybe when we see the poor child's face in daylight, we'll know who she is."

"I don't think she's much of a child," Helena said. "I'd guess her to be older than Vi."

"And not much tamer, by the looks of her," Sheriff Warner said with a snort.

Eve's anger rose. "There's nothing wrong with our sister!"

"That's enough, Sheriff," Oliver said.

"You think suicide, Mr. Clarke?" Mr. Peterson rubbed his long beard.

"That'd be my guess," the sheriff said. "It's that damned amendment. Women's rights!" He spit out the last words.

"What has that got to do with it?" Helena asked sharply.

"It's obvious, ain't it?" he asked. "She's young. She's not ugly. Young girls think they got the right now to run around raising hell, smoking, drinking, putting on more lipstick than is good for them, and messing around with boys."

Eve's rage rose again. "Are you insinuating —"

"Now, now, Miss Grave, I wasn't talking about anyone in particular."

"You'd better not be," Helena said. "There is such a thing as defamation of character, Sheriff." She then added, "Not to mention Vi knows just where to kick a man so it hurts, and she's not afraid to use those high heels of hers."

Oliver roared with laughter. "You'd better watch yourself, Sheriff."

The man sniffed. "As I was saying, girls nowadays get a taste of freedom and get themselves in trouble. Only way out for them is suicide."

"I'm not convinced we have a suicide on our hands," Oliver said. "If the girl really was in trouble, as you say, and wanted to do herself in, there are easier ways."

"Not to mention more permanent ones," Mr. Peterson remarked. "Drowning oneself is a mighty risky thing."

"It worked, didn't it?" Sheriff Warner growled.

"Please!" Eve felt the nausea return.

"I'm sorry, Eve," Oliver said. "I guess we shouldn't be talking like this, knowing what you do."

"It's because of what we do that we have strong stomachs, Oliver," Helena said.

Eve sighed. "I just wish we could have been more helpful."

"It was a long shot anyway," he said with a sigh.

"I'm sure we'll know her in daylight." With more resolve, she added, "I'm sure of it."

"She ought to come with us," said Helena. "To the morgue, I mean. It's where she belongs."

"Nobody's taking this body anywhere until the medical examiner gets here," Mr. Peterson insisted. "Where is that damn doctor?"

"He's been called," said Sheriff Warner. "You know Doc. He ain't one to interrupt his evening pipe even for a corpse."

"Well, he's going to," Oliver said in a vicious tone. "It's time we got some brains into that small-town mind of ours."

"Yourself included?" The sheriff eyed him.

The district attorney gave him a hard stare. "Myself included. I asked Helena to do a preliminary examination in the meantime."

"She ain't no doctor," the sheriff protested.

"I have to agree, Mr. Clarke." Mr. Peterson gave Helena an uneasy glance. "I respect Mrs. Wright's profession but the county medical examiner is the one who ought to do that."

"We've established Eve and Helena know more about dead bodies than any of us here," Oliver said. "As the medical examiner doesn't see fit to hurry with his pipe, I don't want any more delays in getting this case underway."

"She might tamper with evidence and not realize it," Sheriff Warner grumbled.

"I know all about evidence," Helena snapped. "I have some intelligence, Sheriff."

"No disrespect, ma'am —"

"Helena also studied with Mrs. Zadie Hummer in Pasadena," Eve said. "She knows more about criminal investigations than you think."

"Ain't that the eccentric millionaire's daughter who toys with the police?" Sheriff Warner narrowed his eyes.

"Mrs. Hummer has helped lawmen on more than one occasion," Helena said stiffly.

"And she taught you everything she knows, eh?"

"I trust Helena's knowledge and expertise," Oliver said. "What do you say, Mr. Peterson?"

The coroner shrugged. "I guess it's better than standing around here just looking at it while we wait."

"Looking at *her*," Eve said in a hollow tone. "She's a person, Mr. Peterson."

"Yes, miss," he mumbled.

Helena inspected the woman from head to foot. Eve noted she was very gentle and slow with her examination.

"She's a well-dressed corpse," Eve remarked.

"Not so well-dressed," her sister said. "The fabric is rayon."

"We'll search for labels later," Oliver said. "That might tell us something."

Helena glanced at him. "May I turn the body over?"

"Is that wise?" Mr. Peterson looked uncomfortable.

"Do anything you think is necessary," Oliver said.

With the help of two policemen, they got the body turned over without disturbing much of the ground underneath. As they moved the dead woman to her side, Eve gasped. "My God, her head is almost to her chest!"

"Her neck's broken," Helena confirmed.

"There ain't nothing but skin holding it up," Warner said.

"There's no need to be vulgar, Sheriff," Helena snapped. "Eve and I both know what a broken neck looks like."

"It could have broken in the current if the body came from down the river," Mr. Peterson suggested. "Lots of rocks and debris at that end."

Helena shook her head. "This was something different. Something more brutal and deliberate."

"That settles the question of suicide at least," Oliver said. "She could hardly have broken her own neck."

"It settles nothing," Sheriff Warner insisted. "Not until Doc gets here and does his official examination. He's the expert, after all."

Helena glared at him.

"The autopsy should tell us more," Mr. Peterson agreed.

"It won't tell you whether she died from the broken neck," Helena argued. "It will only tell you whether she's been in the water. Drowning is a tricky death."

Eve pulled her coat closer to her. "Why would someone try to drown her if he already broke her neck?"

"Maybe he didn't mean to break it," Oliver said. "It could have been an accident. He was holding her head down in the water, like this." He grabbed the back of a policeman's neck and pushed his head forward, making the young man gasp. "He just held too hard, and the neck broke."

"Mr. Clarke, I'd appreciate it if you wouldn't use one of my men to entertain the ladies." Sheriff Warner's face was slick with anger.

"Murder is not entertaining for us, Sheriff," Eve said in a hard voice. "My sister and I take death very seriously."

"I think you'd better apologize, Sheriff." Oliver's tone was uncompromising.

The sheriff removed his hat and bowed his head. "I'm sorry, Miss Grave. I had the deepest respect for your father."

Eve turned away, as the mention of her father always made a lump form in her chest.

CHAPTER 3

A little while later, Dr. Myers, the medical examiner, joined them. He was a small man with a bald head and glasses who carried his medical bag like a shield.

"Shame." He shook his head at the young woman lying on the ground. "Why they take their own lives like this is beyond me."

"Mrs. Wright doesn't think it's suicide," said Sheriff Warner.

"Is that right?" He looked at Helena.

"You *do* remember she has medical training, don't you, Dr. Myers?" Eve asked in a tight voice.

"I asked Helena to examine the body so we could get an idea of what happened," Oliver said.

"You took your sweet time getting here," Sheriff Warner growled.

"Yes, well, that couldn't be helped." The doctor bent down, opening his bag.

Helena turned to the district attorney. "There's something else I think you should know, Oliver."

"Any light you can shed," he said kindly.

"Her ankles were tied together at some point."

"Tied together!" Sheriff Warner stared at her. "That don't make any sense."

"I know what rope burns look like, Sheriff," she said with a sniff. "There are grooves around her ankles. One place in particular has an indentation where the killer must have tied some kind of knot."

"A sailor's knot, maybe," Oliver said.

Eve shivered. "Wouldn't she stay down in the water once she —"

"Not once the stomach filled with gas," said her sister. "She would have bobbed right up like a balloon."

"Nice imagination you have," Sheriff Warner said sourly.

"Not imagination, Sheriff," Helena snapped. "Medical fact."

"The killer wanted to make the body stay down even with the current," Oliver said. He glanced at the coroner. "Any more doubts, Mr. Peterson?"

The man shook his head and adjusted his hat. "I think we can rule this a murder and proceed."

"I haven't done an autopsy yet," Dr. Myers protested.

"We'll wait for the official report, naturally," Mr. Peterson assured him. "But I'm satisfied we can look at this as a crime of murder by person or persons unknown." He took out his handkerchief and wiped the back of his neck. "Awful damp here. Mr. Clarke, you get me the official report by tomorrow morning."

The district attorney nodded. Mr. Peterson saluted the sheriff and made his way back to the road.

"If she was tied down in the river, why did they find her here?" Eve asked.

"Someone ain't good with knots," Sheriff Warner said with a chuckle.

Oliver glared at him. "I told you before, Sheriff, I don't tolerate vulgarity in front of ladies."

"This ain't no tea party, Mr. Clarke," the lawman said with equal force. "If we got a murder on our hands — and I personally prefer to wait for the medical examiner's report — that broken neck means the person or persons unknown meant business."

"As the sheriff insists on an official report," Oliver bent down toward the doctor, "what do you say, Dr. Myers?"

The man lowered his stethoscope. "Well, I don't think she was in the water for very long. Probably bobbed right up." Eve covered her mouth. "That makes me think she's been in this mud probably about twenty-four hours, maybe thirty-six."

Oliver glanced up at Helena. "Do you concur, Helena?"

"I'm the official doctor here," Dr. Myers said.

"Helena knows more about it than you think, Doctor," Eve said. "She's been estimating time of death in the mortuary since her days at Fieldstone."

"Bah!" The doctor sniffed.

"It just so happens I agree with Dr. Myers," Helena said in a quiet voice.

"Why, thank you, Mrs. Wright." Dr. Myers made a mocking gesture. "And I happen to agree with *you* that the neck's been broken." He motioned toward the dead woman. "Probably thrown in the water to try and hide the crime. That's my guess, anyway."

"Your guess is wrong." All the men stared at Helena. "The killer broke her neck while drowning her."

"And just how did he do that?" Sheriff Warner demanded.

"We keep referring to the killer as 'he,'" Oliver said. "But this could have been done by a woman, couldn't it?" He glanced at Dr. Myers for confirmation and the man nodded, his glasses bobbing up and down his nose.

"You would know that more than we would, Sheriff," Eve said. "We only care for the bodies once they're dead. We rarely have knowledge of how they got that way."

"I think I know how," her sister said. "The killer — he or she —held the poor girl's head down into the water by forcing it forward from the back of her head and neck."

"I think it unlikely," the doctor insisted.

"Criminals often do the most unlikely things," Oliver said.

"Unlikely, maybe, but not downright far-fetched," the sheriff growled. "I would appreciate it, Mrs. Wright, if you and your sister left the investigating to us."

"We're not investigating anything," Eve insisted.

"I think you'll find water in her lungs, Dr. Myers," Helena said. "Enough to have drowned her."

"We'll see with the autopsy." The doctor closed his bag and rose, shaking the dirt off his coat sleeves. "I'll send the ambulance out here right away."

"We brought the hearse," Helena said.

"Such cases require an ambulance, Mrs. Wright, not a hearse," Dr. Myers said. "Not until the autopsy is complete, that is." To the district attorney, he said, "We'll get the orderlies to help carry the girl up that hill."

"My men can do it," Sheriff Warner offered.

"I trust your men even less than I trust the orderlies," said the doctor. "They're liable to rough her up. Unintentionally, of course."

"It's all right, Sheriff," Oliver said. "We still need to examine her and the crime scene."

"I trust you won't mind if we store the body in your mortuary?" The doctor glanced at Helena. "Not that I expect you to have the sort of equipment necessary for this kind of examination."

Helena gave him a sly look. "I think you'll find our mortuary more equipped than your office for an autopsy."

"That might be," he admitted. "And it might be Gyver Hospital is more equipped than your mortuary."

"I prefer you use the Grave Funeral Home," Oliver said. "We want to keep this under wraps for the time being."

"Whatever you say, Mr. Clarke." The doctor shrugged. "I assume I may return to my fire and brandy now? It's gotten rather chilly." He sniffed at the damp air with distaste. "Wouldn't want to catch pneumonia."

"Pneumonia!" Helena snorted as the man made his way back to the road. "He's afraid to take his own medicines!"

Oliver chuckled. "I don't doubt it." He turned to the sheriff. "At least we know what we're looking for. Someone killed the girl yesterday night."

Eve glanced at the road and was relieved to see her friend Dot had arrived. Towering above both her fragile parents, she had an arm wrapped around each of their shoulders. Dr. Myers was talking to them, clearly eager to spill the details, as his hands waved around. Mrs. Whitman covered her mouth with her handkerchief and Mr. Whitman pressed his lips together.

"Oliver, can't we send the Whitmans home?" she asked.

"We don't even know who she is yet," the sheriff said.

"We're not going to find out standing around here." Oliver made a gesture of annoyance. "Eve's right. We need to get the Whitmans out of here."

"This ain't the place for them," the sheriff agreed. "Nice people, even if their daughter's a little bookish."

"You mean intelligent, don't you, Sheriff?" Eve snapped. "I know how much intelligent women bother you." He glared at her in response.

The party made their way back up to the road. Mrs. Whitman was sobbing while her husband offered kind words.

"Eve, what in the world are you doing here?" Dot took her arm. "And what's all this about a drowned woman?"

"That doctor had no business upsetting your mother." Helena bent down. "It'll be all right, Myrtle." With a stern look toward the sheriff, she added, "You ought to have told him to keep his mouth shut."

"It's my fault," Oliver said. "I'll have a word with him."

"Town's going to know soon anyway," Sheriff Warner said. "Don't make no difference if it's now or later."

"Then the girl is dead?" Mr. Whitman asked in a trembling voice.

Eve nodded. "We couldn't identify her." She looked at Dot. "That's why we're here."

Oliver touched Mrs. Whitman's arm. "I'm sorry, ma'am."

"We thought the doctor would —" the woman could barely speak. "Oh, the poor dear!"

"Horrible to think she drowned in that river," Mr. Whitman said. "Suicide, is it?"

Eve saw Oliver give Sheriff Warner a look. "We're still trying to get the facts," he said. "Could you tell us how you discovered her?"

"It's hard to tell." The man blinked.

"Just tell it like you saw it, Papa," Dot said with affection.

"We were taking an evening stroll," he began.

"Kind of late for a stroll, isn't it?" Sheriff Warner interrupted.

"It's not a crime to walk by the river," Helena snapped.

"Oh, I'm sure we didn't break the law." Mrs. Whitman looked up, alarmed.

"It's all right, Mama," Dot said. "The sheriff didn't mean anything by it. It's just his way."

"I got a job to do, ma'am," the sheriff mumbled.

"You don't have to do it so boorishly," Eve snarled.

"I'll ask the questions, Sheriff." Oliver gave him a fierce look. "Why don't you gather your men together and wait for me down by the river?" He flicked his head toward the place where the body had been found. "We still have some work to do."

Sheriff Warner nodded. Eve breathed a sigh of relief when he was gone.

"Now, sir." Oliver turned back to Mr. Whitman. "You were walking along the river —"

"Myrtle and I like to take a walk here when we can't sleep," Mr. Whitman said. "Nice and quiet-like. We've been doing it since we first got married." His tone sounded almost defensive.

"A nice sentiment." Oliver smiled. "Go on."

"We saw some of the brush down there disturbed," he said. "We thought it was a ball or something the kids left lying around. Kids sometimes play out here after dinner."

"So I've been told," said Oliver. "We're trying to get the county to approve a fence."

"Oh, you must, Mr. Clarke!" Mrs. Whitman said. "I couldn't bear to think of a child ending up like that poor girl." Her eyes filled with tears. "But then, she was a child herself, wasn't she?"

"She was very young," Eve echoed.

"We didn't want someone stumbling over the ball and falling into the river," Mr. Whitman continued. "We're not the only ones who go walking here at night and then there's men coming off the boats who don't have the money to spend the night at the hotel and just sort of settle here."

"They do no harm," Dot said quickly as the district attorney's face darkened. "Mama and Papa give them some food from the store."

"I'll see to it they have a place to sleep from now on," Oliver said quietly.

"Oh, we're so glad you're district attorney now, Mr. Clarke." Mrs. Whitman smiled for the first time that night. "Zak always said you were as good as gold and you'd do a lot for this town someday."

"I do my best, ma'am." Oliver promised clearly humbled.

"Tell Mr. Clarke the rest of the story, Papa," Dot said.

"Well, there isn't much to tell," he said. "We thought it was a ball so we came to see and we found the girl lying there."

"We thought she fainted," Mrs. Whitman said. "Had we known —"

"You did the right thing, Myrtle," Helena said gently. "If she had fainted, she would have needed medical attention right away."

"I wish it had been that!" Mrs. Whitman sobbed.

"We all share that sentiment, ma'am," said Oliver. "You didn't touch anything?" He glanced at Mr. Whitman.

"Certainly not, Mr. Clarke," said the man. "We don't know anything about this, of course, but we've seen enough moving pictures to know not to touch anything."

"Heaven help us, the moving pictures," Oliver said with rolling eyes and Eve suppressed a giggle. "Did you recognize the girl?"

"Never seen her before." Mr. Whitman shook his head.

Eve saw his wife looked hesitant. "Did you know her, Myrtle?"

"Well, I —"

"We didn't find anything to identify her," Oliver said. "It would help us a great deal to know *something*."

"Mother said she thinks she's seen her around the school," Dot supplied.

"What school?" asked Oliver.

"Well, I don't really know," mused the woman. "You see, we deliver produce to all the schools in town here for their school lunches."

"That's where you think you saw her?" Eve asked. "At one of the schools while delivering your produce?"

"I think so," she said. "Of course, I can't be sure, but somehow when I saw her, I thought of schools."

"Thank you, Mrs. Whitman, Mr. Whitman." Oliver patted the elderly woman's hand. "You can go home now."

"I can't imagine what her mother will think," Mrs. Whitman mumbled as Dot led them to her car.

"First we have to find her mother," Eve remarked.

"First we have to find her name," Oliver said with a sigh.

CHAPTER 4

"**I** think we ought to go down there too," Helena said as she watched the district attorney turn toward the group of lawmen down the hill.

"What good would it do?" Eve asked.

"We're taking the body to the mortuary, aren't we?" Helena asked.

"But Dr. Myers is sending the ambulance for that," her sister pointed out.

"Ambulance!" Helena scoffed. "By the time he finishes telling every doctor and nurse at the hospital everything that happened, we'll have the girl properly stored."

"There might be a lot of blood," Eve said with a shiver.

Helena took her arm. "She was drowned, Eve. There's no blood."

"It's all so gruesome," Eve said.

Her sister laughed. "That's a funny thing for a funeral director to say."

"That's different," Eve said. "We guide the soul to heaven. We don't look into the cause of death."

"You don't, but I do," Helena said. "I saw bodies dead from

31

bullet wounds and knife cuts in Pasadena. You can't guide the soul until you know the state of the body."

"I don't want to disturb Oliver," Eve said.

Helena gave her a sly smile. "I somehow think Oliver would much rather have you there than Sheriff Warner."

Eve glanced at her watch, a delicate thing with a gold band that had belonged to their mother. "Vi ought to be home by now."

Helena pulled at her arm. "Vi won't be home for hours yet and you know it."

Eve sighed. "Yes, I suppose that's true."

"Let's go down there," Helena said. "It's a hell of a lot more interesting."

"Helena!" Her sister stared at her.

"Medical students used that kind of language and no one turned a hair," her sister protested.

"They were all men," Eve pointed out.

"I thought you believed in women's emancipation." Helena led her to the hill.

"Vulgarity does not emancipate anybody," Eve protested. However, she said no more and let her sister lead her to the bank of the river.

Eve thought the policemen looked like large water beetles, crouched down and spread along the river, their heads bent. Sheriff Warner threw them a wary glance but Oliver came to meet them.

"You've both been a great help," he said in an almost absent-minded way.

"You don't mind us staying for a bit?" Helena asked. "We'll be taking the body away anyway."

George ambled up to them, the Kodak lens fully unfolded. "Do you want me to stay, Mr. Clarke?"

"Where's your partner?" the district attorney asked.

"Franki? She went home but said she'd send over the sketches to your office tomorrow."

"I was hoping to get them tonight," Oliver growled.

"Franki does things her own way," Helena said. "If she says she'll get them to you tomorrow, they'll be on your desk the first thing tomorrow morning."

Oliver nodded. "You still got film in that camera?"

"Got one roll left," George said.

"Then you stay," said the district attorney. "We've still got the crime scene to work over and there's no telling what we'll find. We might need you."

"I don't think the sheriff is very appreciative of me," George said.

"Sheriff Warner has his faults," Oliver said, "but he and his men are determined when it comes to solving crimes, and he knows he's got to accept all the help he can get."

"You've never seen them on a big crime like this," Eve said. "I don't think I remember there ever being a murder quite like this in Gyver."

"I hope I haven't brought bad luck with me," Oliver said with a sheepish grin. "My wife accuses me of carrying a streak of morose. She thinks it's because I'm part Irish."

The mention of Oliver's wife made Eve look down.

Sheriff Warner motioned toward them. "I was right, Mr. Clarke. Josh Kepler's got his shack just up the river buried in those trees over there."

"Josh Kepler, eh?" Oliver repeated. "I heard something about him when I first came here. Never met the man, of course."

"He's one of our local legends," Eve said with a laugh.

"Tells lots of stories, most of them untrue, I dare say," Helena added. "Vi used to love listening to his tales when she was a child."

"What's his business?" Oliver asked.

"Does some fishing and takes people out on the river in his boat," Sheriff Warner said. "And it's his shack?" Oliver eyed the cluster of trees. "Fishing, eh? He must have some rope there."

"He's up and down this river all the time," George added. "Maybe he saw something."

"Then we'll definitely need to talk to him," Oliver said.

"That won't be easy," Sheriff Warner snorted. "He's not that eager to talk to the police. Had some run-ins with the law in Southern California a while back."

"We'll have to tread lightly, then." Oliver turned to the sisters, speaking in a softer tone. "I'm afraid I have another job for you."

"Anything we can do," Eve said.

"It's rather embarrassing." He laughed a little.

"Don't be wishy-washy, Oliver," Helena said in an irritated tone.

"We need someone to examine the girl's clothes for identification," he said. "Examine them thoroughly."

"You want us to strip the body?" Eve asked.

"We've done it before," Helena reminded her.

"Well, yes, but never a girl murdered like that!"

"We've stripped women soaking in their own blood," Helena said, taking her sister's arm. "Remember that girl a few years back in that motor accident —"

"I remember," Eve said quickly. "All right. If it will help you, Oliver."

"I don't want his men to do it." Oliver jerked his head at the crouching beetles. "You know how young men are."

"We know how young men are," Helena said dryly. "And the girl's not bad-looking."

Oliver hung the blanket that the sheriff had given the Whitmans between some of the shrubs to act as a shield. Under the light of the lanterns sitting near the woman's head and feet, Eve examined the dress closely. It was indeed rayon, as Helena had said, with a rose print against a light pink background.

"Not exactly the cat's pajamas, as Vi would say, is it?" Helena remarked.

"But not what you would expect a schoolteacher to wear either," Eve said. "Mrs. Hanes once told me she had to wear long dresses with high collars and lace-up boots everywhere. If someone caught her in a dress above her calf, she risked getting fired."

"Then maybe Mrs. Whitman was wrong about her being a schoolteacher," Helena said. "Even Vi would approve of those shoes."

They examined the clothes, including unzipping the girl's dress and unbuttoning her jacket.

"Anything?" Oliver called from behind the blanket shield.

"You wouldn't call her fashionable, though it's clear she tried to be," Helena said. "And not exactly the uniform of a schoolteacher, though I imagine schoolteachers didn't always wear their petticoats outside of class."

"They ought to," the sheriff mumbled.

"No labels on the clothes either," Eve said.

"Laundry marks?" Sheriff Warner asked.

"Nothing."

"That's strange," Oliver said. "There should at least be something."

"Maybe the killer ripped the labels off before he did his deed," the sheriff offered. "And, well, I suppose there are people who do their laundry at home."

"There are indeed," Eve said in a rueful tone, thinking of the laundry hanging in their backyard, which was almost certainly still damp from yesterday's rain.

"These don't have any thread marks," said Helena. "It wasn't the labels he was interested in ripping."

"What do you mean by that?" her sister inquired.

"Look at her jacket, Eve."

Eve lowered her eyes. "You mean the lapel!" She removed it from the dead girl with care and held it out to Oliver.

He glanced at the sheriff. "It's been ripped all right."

"I knew it!" Sheriff Warner whistled. "A crime of unlawful carnal knowledge."

"It was *not* a rape," Helena said in a forceful tone.

"I would refrain from using such strong language in the presence of a lady like your sister." Sheriff Warner sniffed.

"Helena is a lady too," Eve insisted. "And neither of us are innocent young things, Sheriff. Your assistant deputies are more squeamish than we are." She noticed two young men flinch when Helena said the word "rape."

"How do you know it wasn't?" the sheriff asked.

"Because I saw no bruising when I examined the body earlier," Helena said.

"Well, ma'am." The sheriff shifted from one foot to the other. "There are places —"

"I examined those too." Helena eyed him with a half-smile. "I was very thorough."

Oliver chuckled. "Helena knows what she's saying, Sheriff."

"Well, I guess if she had been —" He glanced back at the two young men who had blushed. "— the doctor would have told us."

"She might have been wearing a pin or a brooch," Eve offered.

Helena nodded. "The killer didn't have time to unpin it properly."

"Robbery seems unlikely, given this woman isn't exactly wearing the latest fashion," Oliver said.

"It may have been a valuable heirloom," Sheriff Warner said.

"Steal a pin and not steal this?" Helena held up the woman's limp wrist weighed down with a heavy gold bracelet.

"He might not have seen it in the dark, Helena," her sister said.

"I agree with Helena." Oliver bent down to the dead girl. "I don't think robbery was the motive."

"That means the pin or whatever it was on her lapel was taken for a reason," said Sheriff Warner. "And a very personal reason for someone to have ripped a hole through her clothes like that."

"Which makes this a very personal crime," Oliver remarked.

"Mr. Clarke!" The call came from George Parks.

"What is it, son?" Oliver asked.

"I found this, sir." The young man handed him a square handbag with a chain handle. The bag was smeared with mud.

"How do we know it's hers?" Helena asked.

"It's the same color as the dress," Eve said.

Oliver laid the bag on the ground and turned it over. Nothing came out. He glanced at the sheriff. "You ever know a woman to take a purse without putting something in it?"

"All at the bottom of the river, I'll bet," Sheriff Warner growled.

"Why not the bag too?" Eve asked.

"Maybe the killer thought it wouldn't sink to the bottom," Oliver said. "We're certainly not dealing with a professional." He rose. "So we know she had a purse. We can search the river in the morning."

"Whatever for?" The sheriff stared at him.

"If the killer threw the contents in the river, they might still be around," Oliver argued. "We might find something to help identify her."

"But that's crazy, Mr. Clarke," the sheriff said.

"The chances of finding something might not be as bad as you think, Sheriff," Oliver said. "We'll look around here too."

"Maybe the killer dropped something in his haste," George agreed, taking hold of his camera.

The men wandered off. Eve helped Helena straighten the woman's clothes. As she lifted the lifeless arm to straighten the sleeve, she noticed a pearly thing half-buried in the mud. She absently dug it out and put it in her pocket.

The lawmen were now farther away, and Eve could see a flicker of flashlights. Sheriff Warner called, "Nothing here, Mr. Clarke."

Oliver sighed. "Well, I think we've gotten all we can."

"Alright, men, that's enough for tonight!" the sheriff yelled.

"What about me, Mr. Clarke?" George asked.

Oliver patted him on the shoulder. "You did good work, son. Get those photographs to me as soon as you can."

George grinned. "Wish Zak had asked me to take photographs like you do. Golly!" He went off, grasping his camera with both hands.

"Well, Mr. Clarke, what next?" The sheriff looked at him expectedly with his hands on his hips.

"Here's what I want you to do, Sheriff." Oliver ticked off on his fingers. "First, get a description circulating with a photo of the girl. You can get that from George once he gets the pictures developed. Get those to all the police stations in the area. We've got to find out who this girl is."

"Ain't much good trying to solve a murder when you don't know who the murder victim is," Sheriff Warner agreed.

"Then, check the local shops about those clothes," Oliver said. "They might know who bought them."

"Homemade, most likely, Oliver," Helena said. "Otherwise, they would have had labels."

"Possibly," he admitted. "But we have to check everything."

"The shoes have labels," Sheriff Warner pointed out.

"Not any I've seen in the shops around here," Eve said.

"Well, if you'll beg my pardon, miss, you can't know all of them." He stared down at her plain Oxfords.

"That's enough of that, Sheriff," Oliver commanded. "Third, check all the jewelry shops in the area. If there was some kind of pin or brooch on her, they might remember the young lady buying it."

"Unless it was a gift from a beau," Sheriff Warner said.

"Then we have another possibility for this case," Oliver said. "If she had a beau, we want to know that too."

"You don't really think —" Eve shuddered.

"Things like that do happen, Eve," her sister said.

"Anything else?" The sheriff looked at the district attorney.

"Yes," he said. "Check with all the schools."

"What for?" The sheriff sniffed.

"Mrs. Whitman told us she thought she saw her at a school," Eve said.

Oliver nodded. "She might be a teacher. It's a start, at least."

"A wild goose chase, if you ask me," Sheriff Warner snorted.

"Well, nobody asked you," Helena snapped.

"Whatever you say, Mr. Clarke." The sheriff tipped his hat as he left to gather up the rest of his men.

"What about us, Oliver?" Eve asked.

He glanced up the hill. "I see the ambulance is here."

"You mean we can take the body to the mortuary?" Helena asked. "It's about time!"

"Will they help us carry her to the hearse?" Eve glanced at the two young men cautiously making their way down the hill.

"They'll help," Oliver said firmly.

Helena grinned and moved toward the young men who greeted her with approving glances because of her beauty.

"Oliver," Eve ventured, "don't you think it's strange someone would go to all the trouble to tie something down in the river but neglect to tie it securely enough?"

"You mean the rope tied to the woman's ankles, don't you?" asked Oliver.

She nodded. "I noticed the burns just now when we were looking for the labels."

"It is indeed very strange," he agreed.

"The mark of the knot," Eve continued. "You said before it might be a sailor's knot."

"That's right."

"Wouldn't someone who knows how to tie a sailor's knot make sure it was secure?"

"What are you getting at, Eve?" Oliver eyed her.

"Whoever killed the girl wasn't a professional killer, just as the sheriff said," Eve pointed out. "And yet, they knew how to tie that kind of knot."

"It could be the current last night was so strong that it undid the rope," Oliver offered. "The rain was mighty bad yesterday."

"I suppose that could be," Eve murmured.

"But you don't think so?"

"I don't know about these things, naturally," said Eve.

"But you make a good point," he said. "We'll certainly consider it."

"Where d'you want the dead girl, Mrs. Wright?" one of the orderlies called out.

"In our car," Eve said.

The boy stared at her. "A hearse?"

"You know a better place for a dead body?" Helena asked sharply.

"Who said she can go with you?" Sheriff Warner appeared with the rest of his men.

"I'm glad to hear you're referring to the body as 'she' and not 'it,'" Helena said dryly. "That shows some humanity at least."

He snorted but said nothing.

"They have my permission to store it overnight," Oliver said.

"We intend to keep her more than overnight," Eve said.

"Murdered or not, she still deserves a decent burial," Helena added. "And we'll give it to her."

"Suppose the family don't want that?" Sheriff Warner challenged.

"We have to find the family first," said Oliver. "Then we can worry about what they want or don't want."

"Women in a murder case!" the sheriff grumbled, pushing the hair out of his eyes. But he shouted orders to a few more of his men to help move the young woman to the back of the hearse.

CHAPTER 5

*I*t was well past eleven when Helena pulled the hearse into the garage that connected to the mortuary. The house was quiet and still, and Eve had seen no light from any of the windows.

"I suppose Vi's gone to bed," she lamented as she and her sister wheeled the gurney they used to transport bodies into the morgue.

"Don't fool yourself, Eve," said Helena. "She and those friends of hers have probably barely gotten started at the drugstore."

Eve nodded reluctantly. "I'll speak to Oliver about getting Sudie to send them home by ten in the future."

"You know you can't do that," Helena said as they maneuvered the gurney carefully into the examining room. "She has a right to run her business as she pleases."

"She does *not* have the right to serve children like Vi bootleg beer!" Eve growled. "I think we ought to put her on the cooling board table right away. There should be enough ice in the ice box."

"We're going to put her right here." Helena nodded toward the examining table.

"We can't leave her there all night, honey," Eve said.

"I don't intend to," she said. "Now, are you going to help me or not?"

They managed to get the woman on the table without too much trouble, as she was of medium height and not very heavy. Eve watched as her sister put on the crisp linen coat she used when preparing the corpses.

"What are you going to do?"

"I'm going to get a more thorough look at her before the doctor does," said her sister.

"Helena!" She stared at her. "You can't do that."

"Who says I can't?" Helena snapped. "She's our property until tomorrow morning. We can do what we like."

"But Dr. Myers —"

"Dr. Myers is an ignorant pig," Helena grumbled. "He'll put a few slices in her, say she drowned, and that's all."

"But you said yourself she drowned."

"I want to take a closer look." Helena's light tone grew stubborn. "There's something about her that's bothering me, and I couldn't see anything with all those men hovering around her."

"What do you mean, something not right?" Eve eyed her.

"I won't know until I look her over, will I?" Helena took her sister's hands. "I'm not going to do anything to her, Eve. I'm just going to look her over."

Eve took off her coat. "You'll need help undressing her."

"I knew you would stay." Her sister smiled. "You're as intrigued as I am."

"But don't treat her like one of your experiments," Eve warned. "She's not that white squirrel you caught that one time."

"I wanted to see what made him white," Helena protested.

"But you didn't, did you?" Eve asked.

"If I would have had that microscope, I might have." Helena made a face and they both laughed.

"You want me to call Charlie Eaton?" Eve asked. Charlie was Helena's assistant.

Her sister shook her head. "Let him sleep. He'd turn as red as a tomato anyway if he saw the girl naked."

"He's seen naked corpses before," Eve reminded her.

"Not like this one," her sister said. "I've a feeling about her."

They undressed the dead woman again, this time stripping her of her undergarments. "Get all the lights on, Eve," Helena instructed. The woman's clothes were even brighter than Eve had first thought, and she noticed the stockings for the first time. The face had a high reddish tone and showed the peacefulness of death.

"I still don't recognize her. Do you?" Helena turned to her sister.

"She isn't familiar," Eve agreed. "But something about the way her brows are set and the roundness of her chin remind me of someone."

"Oh, don't be silly," Helena said. "Didn't Dad once say all corpses begin to look like family?"

"Yes, he did," Eve said softly. "All the same —"

Helena lifted the head very gently and peered underneath. "I was right. Look."

Though they were very faint, the back of the girl's neck showed some oval shapes.

"Those are fingerprints?" Eve gasped.

"He held her head down in the water," Helena confirmed.

Eve held on to the edge of the table. "But if someone wanted to drown a person, wouldn't they hold down the back of the person's head?"

"I think he did both," said Helena. "See how her hair is gathered in batches at the roots? He grabbed her by the hair and the neck and held her down."

"God help us," Eve murmured.

"God can only help her now," Helena agreed in a sad voice.

"Her face is so gray!" Eve said.

"What's the matter with you?" her sister asked sharply. "You've seen hundreds of dead bodies on this table. You were Dad's special helper since you were fourteen."

"This one is different," Eve insisted. "She didn't die because of God's will. She died because of someone else's will."

"Someone who had no business exercising his will on her," Helena agreed.

"We keep saying 'he,' but Oliver said it could have easily been a woman," Eve reminded her.

"I doubt it was," said her sister. "It takes a persevering strength to hold someone's head down in water. They're fighting every inch of the way."

"Do you think that's why she's bruised under the eyes?" Eve asked. "She was fighting and the killer punched her?"

Helena touched the contours of the woman's face with her gloved hand. "I don't think these are bruises," she said as she held up her finger. "They look like stains of some kind."

"Did someone mention stains? A stain on my reputation, perhaps?" Violet appeared in the doorway leading from the house, holding her coat to her chin.

"Do you know what time it is?" Eve snapped.

"Do you?" Violet challenged.

Helena laughed. "You know better than to ask her a question, Eve. She always answers with a question."

"It's eleven-forty-three," Violet said. "I'm only forty-three minutes late."

"Much too late," Eve said.

"I'm not a baby," her sister sulked. "Plenty of girls like me are already middle-aisled. And with a kid or two even."

"Heaven help us if that were you." Helena rolled her eyes.

"Is that the murdered girl?" Violet's eyes widened as she neared the table.

"That's not for you to see." Eve threw a sheet over the woman.

"Oh, rats!" Violet sneered. "I've seen the dead ones ever since I was a kid, remember?"

"This is different," Eve said. "She might have been you."

"Fat chance you'd catch me drowning myself in the river." Violet smirked.

"Who told you she drowned herself?" Helena asked.

"Joe Savage," Violet said. "Or, rather, Assistant Deputy Savage." She swept down with a bow, her coat dragging the floor. "He keeps bragging about how it was him who found her purse even though George Parks is taking the credit."

"He shouldn't be shooting his mouth off," Helena growled. "We don't even know what happened yet."

"He's sweet on me." Violet grinned. "I think it would be nice to have a police officer for a fellow. Much better than a district attorney for a brother-in-law." She eyed her eldest sister.

"Don't insinuate, Vi," Helena snapped. "Besides, the man is married."

"To a high-hatter," Violet snorted, setting her silver-plated purse on the edge of the table. "Can't I see her?"

"Absolutely not!" Eve grabbed the sheet.

"Oh, let her see the girl," Helena said. "Maybe Vi knows who she is."

"You mean nobody knows?" Violet's eyes widened.

"Didn't Big Mouth Joe tell you that?" Helena asked.

"No. He didn't." Violet studied the woman. "I think I've seen her!"

"Where?" Helena asked.

"Down by the school."

"The high school?"

Violet sniffed. "You two keep forgetting I've graduated."

"This is important, Vi," Eve said. "We've got to find out who she is."

"The elementary school," said her younger sister.

"You mean Brookline Elementary?" Eve glanced at Helena.

"I saw her there with the kids a few times," said Violet. "Not in those clothes, of course. Gads, what an awful pleat to that skirt."

"In what clothes did you see her?" Helena asked.

"Some plain ugly dress that hung on her like a sack with lots of pockets." Violet yawned.

"Was she a teacher, then?" Helena asked.

"How should I know?" Violet continued to stare down at the girl. "She looks so peaceful."

"She didn't die peacefully," Helena said. "Not with those bruises on the back of her neck."

"And her hair disheveled," Eve added with a shudder.

"You mean nearly torn at the roots." Violet pointed to a clump of hair on the left side that, when Helena lifted it with a gloved finger, was indeed hiding a small bald patch where the hair had been torn.

"Oh, Lord!" Eve covered her face.

"She must have been sobbing like the devil," Violet said softly. "Begging for her life."

"Aren't you being a little melodramatic?" Helena asked, amused.

"What do you think those patches under her eyes are?" Violet demanded.

"What do *you* think they are?" her sister countered.

"Mascara, of course."

"Impossible," said Eve. "Makeup would have washed off in the river."

"The exclusive stores sell waterproof mascara that doesn't wash off so easily," Violet insisted. "Not that either of you would know about that." She looked at both her plain-faced sisters with amusement.

"It doesn't add up," Eve said. "If she was a schoolteacher, she wouldn't be wearing high heels and makeup, would she?"

"Unless she no longer was a schoolteacher or was going to resign," Helena pointed out.

"Even so, where would someone who sewed her own clothes get the money to buy makeup from an exclusive boutique?"

"Maybe she had a rich sheik," Violet offered.

"And what, pray, is a sheik?" Eve asked.

"A boyfriend, of course." Violet grinned. "She's not bad-looking."

"I'm sure she would be thrilled to know you think so," Helena said dryly.

Violet wrinkled her nose at her "We ought to at least clean her up."

"Not yet!" Helena said. "Dr. Myers has to do the autopsy."

"Aren't you doing that?"

"Not officially," said her sister.

Violet shook her finger at her. "Naughty, naughty. You know how Dr. Myers feels about women and medicine."

"Which is why you're not going to say anything," Helena snapped.

Violet fluttered her eyelashes. "I wouldn't breathe a word. It's worth it to have one up on that toad." Her face grew solemn. "Can't we at least dress her?"

"Helena and I will do that." Eve reached for her clothes.

"I want to help." Violet's face lost its whimsical look and became serious. "I don't like to see her this way. Let me help."

Eve was touched by the deep lines in her younger sister's face. She gave her shoulders a squeeze. "All right, honey."

The sisters arranged the clothes in order, starting with the undergarments and down to the jacket.

"Not bad for a schoolteacher, I suppose," Violet remarked. "At least the skirt is just below the knee like it ought to be."

"I think you were right, Eve," said Helena. "These look like they were sewn by hand."

Eve nodded. "If she was a teacher, she wouldn't have much money for the latest fashions, even if she was allowed to wear them."

"The shoes are nice all the same," Violet said.

"I'm sure she would have been flattered you thought so," Helena said dryly.

"These might have been her best clothes," Eve added.

"If she were meeting a man by the river, she would have come in her best," Helena said.

"Do the police think that's who killed her?" Violet asked.

"The police don't think anything at the moment," Eve said.

"The police don't think at all," Helena snorted. "Not with that bull sheriff."

Violet unfolded the jacket. "Oh, the beast!"

"It's not what you think." Eve put her arm around her.

"I wasn't thinking anything!" Violet glared at her. "I know more about hanky-panky than you do, Eve."

"I don't want to hear it!" Eve's voice shook.

"I'm sure you don't," said Helena in a soft tone.

"I only meant it was a ghastly thing to do." Violet laid the jacket on the counter so the arms didn't touch the sides. "Look at that big rip!"

"It's a strangely shaped rip," Helena said. "It looks almost like a tree."

"Perhaps the pin was of a tree," Eve suggested.

"That might help the police narrow down where it was bought," her sister said.

"I wonder where her rouge and powder are," Violet said. "There was nothing in the bag, was there?"

"Didn't Big Mouth Joe tell you that too?" Helena eyed her.

"He said it was empty and they couldn't find anything."

Eve put her hand in her pocket and felt for the pearl-smooth object she had rescued from the river bed. "I may have found something." She took it out and put it on the table. All three sisters stared at the tube of lipstick in its shiny silver case against the severe white tabletop.

"Gosh!" Violet said. "She certainly was letting loose, wasn't she?"

"Don't be vulgar, Vi," Eve snapped.

Helena glanced at her. "You didn't tell Oliver about this, did you?"

"I didn't think at the time," her sister said. "I thought some silly girl dropped it. But when Vi mentioned the makeup —"

"You're not very observant, Eve," said Violet with some authority. "No girl would drop that and not come back for it."

"Why wouldn't she?" Helena asked. "Aren't you always coming home without one thing or another in your bag?"

"Mine are the cheap Maybelline, darling," her sister snapped. "This is the elegant kind from La Belle Fille."

"That exclusive shop in Moody?" Helena inquired.

Violet raised her eyebrows. "So you do know it. Don't tell me you've been there."

"Of course I haven't been there," her sister said.

"These lipsticks cost two dollars a tube." Violet sighed. "Wish I could afford one. Maybe when I get a job —"

"If it did come from there," Helena said slowly, "Maybe Vi is right that the smeared face is expensive makeup."

"Vi, are you sure that's where this lipstick came from?" Eve asked.

"Of course I'm sure," Violet insisted. "The peacock with the 'B' and 'F' is her emblem."

"Her?" Helena asked.

"Virginia Arton, the owner," said Violet. "She comes to see Sudie sometimes."

The two older sisters exchanged a look. They had never liked Sudie Markie. She boasted about having been a member of the Bohemian Club in San Francisco with Mark Twain and Brett Harte and had the town raising eyebrows when she took up with a man twenty years her junior. It was bad enough that her grand-daughter Kitty was so chummy with their younger sister.

"If she really is a schoolteacher, what would she be doing with such elegant things?" Eve murmured.

"Maybe she didn't intend to be a schoolteacher much longer," Violet said.

"It might be worth giving it to Oliver now," Helena said.

"We don't know for sure it was hers," Eve protested. "In fact, it's highly unlikely, if both Vi and Mrs. Whitman are right and she's a schoolteacher."

Violet examined the tube. "Pretty color. I wouldn't mind having it if Oliver doesn't want it."

"Vi!" Eve glared at her sister. "I didn't think we taught you to be callous when a dead girl is concerned."

"I wasn't trying to be," her sister sulked. But she dropped the lipstick on the table as if her fingers were burning.

"Let's get her dressed," Helena said. "I don't want her away from the cooling board table much longer or Dr. Myers will notice."

They finished putting on the girl's skirt and blouse. As Eve was buttoning the last of the pearl buttons, she remarked, "She must have gained some weight recently."

"Why do you say that?" Helena asked.

"Look here." Her sister showed her some folds and strings on the lining of the button holes. "The blouse has been let out."

"So has the skirt," Helena observed as she zipped up the back. "The pleats here are straight."

"Maybe she was going to have a baby," Violet said with a smirk.

"Really, honey, that Kitty Markie has been a bad influence on you," Eve snarled. "Just last week she was hinting about Dot being indiscreet."

"She was just teasing," Violet said. "Dot has been seeing a lot of Aaron Dove lately."

"She's taking care of some stocks and things for her parents," Eve retorted as they carried the dead body to the cart.

"Didn't she used to be sweet on him in high school?" Helena asked.

"Don't you start," Eve said as they all lifted the woman with delicacy onto the cooling board table. They began taking out the blocks of ice from the metal ice box Helena had once picked up from a closing factory.

"There!" Helena said with a sigh as she covered the girl with a quilt. "Safe and sound."

"Awful to say that about someone who won't see daylight again," Violet said, wrapping her coat around her shoulders with a shiver.

Eve put her arm around her. "We'll have her soul safe and sound too before long."

CHAPTER 6

The next day was Sunday and although a veil of calmness covered their quiet neighborhood on the Lord's Day, Eve couldn't help but feel a buzz of anxiety in the air. When they went to church, she could hear whispers from the community women headed by Mrs. Beaton who occupied the pews in front of them.

As she sat next to Helena and her husband and a fidgeting Violet, the reverend droning on with the sermon, she couldn't help but glance at the capped silk heads of the women around her. It seemed when the reverend's voice rose to fill the entire church, the women's whispering began just as quickly as it hushed when his voice lowered.

When they came out of the church, the same women were huddled in the curve of the stairs, their voices no longer whispering. But Eve had no interest in what they had to say, nor did they seem inclined to invite her to join, though the ladies knew the Grave sisters well enough. They had been volunteering to dress and prepare the bodies for burial for years. Eve nodded at them with a smile and was surprised to be rewarded with a critical look that seemed to stretch around the circle of women. She heard snippets of words as they climbed into the car: *river, clothes, hearse.*

"I think they know," she said quietly as she squeezed in beside Helena with Violet and Felix arguing in the back seat.

"Know what?" Helena glanced at the ladies still huddled on the steps.

"That we were with the police when they found the dead girl," Eve said.

"We weren't with the police when they found her," her sister reminded her. "Oliver asked us to come afterward."

"It would amount to the same thing for them." Eve felt her chest heavy with dread.

"Oh, Eve, who cares?" Helena patted her hand. "Since when did we need their approval to do anything?"

"They'll be gossiping around town before long," she said.

"Not if the Shane brothers get there first," Helena said. "Felix said he saw them talking to George when he came home this morning."

~~~~~

On Monday morning, the *Gyver Bee* had published the news of the young woman found at the edge of the river. Eve was the first to arrive at the breakfast table and her stomach turned as she read it.

Helena came down a few minutes later.

"Vi still in bed?" Eve asked. Her sister nodded. "Good. Let her stay there for a while." She handed her the paper.

Helena's reaction was more sedate than her sister's. In fact, she was more preoccupied with getting the sugar in her coffee than reading the article, though her eyes never left it. She tossed the paper on the table. "Yellow journalistic tomfoolery."

"Maybe so," Eve said, "but it's tomfoolery like that which encourages people to talk."

"I can't see it makes much difference." Helena shrugged. "The woman's dead. It's not as if her reputation could be ruined."
~~~~~

"What gets me is where they got all those details about the way she was found." Eve put her chin in her hand. "And the fact that there were no labels on her clothes."

Her sister eyed her. "Where do you think they got it?"

"One of the assistant deputies?" Eve offered.

"I think it more likely our dear medical examiner went tattling again," growled Helena, diving into the oatmeal Agnes put in front of her. The housekeeper's smile turned grim as she glanced at Eve's half-touched bacon and eggs.

"But he wasn't there when we examined the clothes," Eve pointed out.

"That doesn't mean he didn't find out about it later on," Helena said.

"That man is worse than the town gossips," Eve mumbled.

"I'd have Oliver put a lid on him if I were you," said Helena.

"Why me?" Eve stared at her. "What can I do?"

Helena grinned. "From the way he was looking at you yesterday, I'd say you can do plenty."

"Oh, nonsense!" Her sister blushed.

"He ought to put a lid on it." Helena shook out the pages of the book she had brought down with her. "Especially that part about the girl meeting a sweetheart. No one knows that for sure."

"You just said it can't hurt the poor girl's reputation," Eve remarked.

"That's not the point, Eve." Her sister regarded her with an almost superior look. "It's about facts, not her reputation. There are no facts to prove she was meeting a beau. If they're going to print something in the paper, let them have facts to back it up."

"Oh, but insinuations are much more intriguing," Eve said in a mocking tone. Just then, the sound of hard feet slapping the wooden stairs echoed from the hallway, and she crushed the paper in her hands. "Agnes, take this away. If Vi asks about the paper, tell her the boy left it in the mud, and we had to throw it away."

"You bet I will," said the housekeeper with a satisfied look on her face.

Oliver arrived later with Dr. Myers, who made a show of placing two medical bags filled with tools on the examining table. Helena raised an eyebrow, looking pointedly at the neatly arranged medical equipment in the corner of the lab as if to drop him a hint. But the doctor's stony expression showed he was just as pointedly ignoring it.

To further annoy them, Dr. Myers shooed Helena and Eve out of the examining room.

"He has no right!" Helena stomped around the living room as she and Eve waited for Oliver to come upstairs. "He's acting like he's doing *us* a favor."

"Never mind, honey," said Eve. "It's a good thing you did your own examination last night."

"We know a whole lot more than what he'll find," Helena snapped.

The doctor's examination was, if showy, very thorough. He and Oliver came up the back stairs some three hours later. Violet had already gone. Eve was glad, as her conscience had been bothering her ever since she let Violet help with the corpse.

"Young girl ought not to see things like that," she mumbled as Agnes brought a tray of coffee into the living room, setting it down on the table with a thud. She shot glares at both Oliver and the doctor.

The two men accepted the coffee graciously. Dr. Myers removed his apron but remained in his shirtsleeves. Oliver loosened his tie and unbuttoned his waistcoat. He wiped at his damp forehead, apologizing with a small laugh. "It's a good thing I decided to go into police work instead of being a doctor!"

"It wasn't a pleasant job," Dr. Myers admitted as he helped himself to a few gingerbread cookies. "Examining dead bodies rarely is."

"I'm sure Miss Grave and Mrs. Wright are well aware of that," Oliver said in a dry tone.

"Are we allowed to know your findings?" Helena asked. "Since they were discovered in *our* mortuary."

"Only upon Mr. Clarke's insistence, Mrs. Wright," Dr. Myers said. "I could have examined her at the hospital just as easily."

"Not without it getting all over town." Helena eyed him.

The doctor was silent for a moment as he finished off the last of the gingerbread. "Mrs. Bishop's cookies are always top quality, Miss Grave."

"I'll tell her you said so," Eve said. "I think my sister asked a reasonable question, Doctor. Don't you?"

"Well, Doctor?" Oliver looked hard at him.

Dr. Myers snapped shut one of the black bags. "I cannot deny that, for such delicate work, an examination room such as Mrs. Wright has created for herself is certainly more than adequate."

Helena sniffed but said nothing.

"I'd like Miss Grave and Mrs. Wright to hear what you have to say." Oliver leaned back.

"I should think that would be confidential."

"As confidential as the information in the newspaper," Helena snapped.

This made Dr. Myers shrink back a little. "I must concede again to Mrs. Wright's analysis. The girl died from drowning and not from a broken neck."

"I believe Helena said the broken neck was a result of the person holding her head down in the water," Eve said.

"Was it?" Oliver looked at the doctor.

The man nodded. "I can't say for sure, of course. But there were deep bruises on the back of her neck as if someone had been pushing with some vigor to make her head stay down in the water."

"I would think 'with some violence' would be more accurate, considering her neck is broken," Helena said.

"There's no doubt whoever did it didn't intend to be gentle," Oliver said dryly.

"Is murder ever gentle?" Eve echoed. Her hands suddenly felt cold. She poured another cup of coffee and held the cup for warmth. Oliver leaned forward and pressed her arm.

"What about the time of death?" Helena asked.

"Just as I said last night, Mrs. Wright," he said. "Twenty-four hours or thereabouts."

"That would make it around nine or ten o'clock on Friday night," Oliver calculated.

"About that." The doctor nodded. "Of course, I can't be completely accurate in these cases."

"Perhaps it was a late-night *rendezvous* with a beau, just as you said, dear." Eve glanced at her sister.

Her sister grimaced. "I didn't say it, remember? The papers did."

"Yes, they did, didn't they?" Oliver's dark eyes grew stormy. "I've already sent the sheriff to the office of the *Bee* to have a long chat with those boys."

"Won't get you anywhere," Dr. Myers said. "The Shane brothers can quote you the First Amendment word for word. Especially Jack."

"They wouldn't be printing that sort of nonsense if someone wasn't feeding it to them." Helena's violet-blue eyes shone crisp in the morning sun. "That wouldn't happen to have been you, would it, Dr. Myers?"

The doctor jumped up. "I resent that accusation, Mrs. Wright. And I won't stay here to be insulted."

Oliver grabbed his hand and pulled him back down on the couch. "Sit down, Doctor. What makes you think it was Dr. Myers, Mrs. Wright?"

"The detail about the broken neck," said Helena.

"The photograph in the paper showed the poor girl on her

back," Eve said. "No one could tell from that position that her neck was broken. It was something only a handful of us knew."

"And suppose it was *you* who told them?" Dr. Myers barked. "Or Sheriff Warner or one of his men?"

"None of his men were around when we turned the body over," Oliver said, now looking at him with sharp eyes. "And the sheriff knows his job."

"We would hardly have a word to say to the Shanes," Helena snapped. "They don't approve of Eve and me running a mortuary business."

"Well, my dear, it's not exactly women's work," said the doctor in a sly tone.

"I think we know your opinion of us too." Eve glared at him. "It's never bothered us and it never will."

"Bravo!" Oliver applauded. "I'm sure you've heard, Dr. Myers, ladies now have the right to vote?"

"I wouldn't put it past them to ruin this whole country with it!" the doctor snarled as he picked up his two bags. "Now, if you don't mind, I have patients to see."

"Anything else you need to tell us?" Oliver regarded him with a critical gaze. "I saw the look on your face when you were examining her, Dr. Myers. There *is* something else, isn't there?"

"I don't think it's for ladies' ears," he mumbled.

"Oh, for pity's sake," Helena said, "We probably know more about what's under her skirts than you do." She gave her sister a knowing look and Eve knew she was thinking about her own examination the night before.

"I would appreciate it if you would speak, Doctor." Oliver's tone was endearing. "We're all after the same thing. We all want to catch the killer who did this to the poor young woman."

Dr. Myers put down his bags and studied the district attorney. "I wonder if you'll think she's such a poor young woman when you hear what I have to say, Mr. Clarke."

"What do you mean?" Helena stared at him.

The little man sneered. "I mean, Mrs. Wright, that for all your medical training, you failed to see the obvious. The girl was with child."

"So *that's* why —" Eve put her hand over her mouth. She also couldn't help but think of Violet's mocking remark: *Maybe she was going to have a baby.*

"You're sure of that?" Helena gave him a hard look.

"I know my profession, Mrs. Wright," he said.

"Any idea how long?" Oliver asked.

The doctor shook his head. "That I really can't say, Mr. Clarke. The girl would have to be alive for me to determine that."

"Poor thing," Eve murmured.

"That alters your investigation, doesn't it, Mr. Clarke?" Dr. Myers asked.

"It certainly throws a wrench into the works," Oliver admitted. He rose, ambling over to the unlit fireplace, his hands in his pockets.

"That's all I have to say," said the doctor.

"Pass by the kitchen on your way out, and Agnes will give you a plate of gingerbread cookies to take with you," Eve said in a distracted tone.

The doctor put on his hat. "Mighty kind of you, Miss Grave. Sorry you and your sister had to hear all these sordid details. Ain't fitting for decent women."

"There's nothing indecent about a woman having a baby," Helena snapped. "Though I'm not surprised you would think so."

Dr. Myers did not answer as he made his way to the kitchen.

When he had gone, Helena turned to Oliver. "I suppose you agree the girl was indecent?"

"I'm no preacher, Helena," said the district attorney. "My job is to bring criminals to justice."

"Still, you don't approve, do you?" Eve asked.

His voice softened. "I don't blame the girl, if that's what you mean. But it certainly puts a different spin on the case."

"How so?" Helena asked.

"It might be she was meeting her sweetheart yesterday night after all," said Oliver. "Or some fellow that — well, got her into trouble. If she told him she was going to have his child, he might not have taken it very well."

"You mean he might have killed her to keep from marrying her?" Eve glanced at him.

"That, or to keep her quiet." When Eve didn't answer, he said, "We don't know what sort of person she was."

"In other words," Eve's voice was harsh, "you think she was trying to get him to do something he wouldn't do."

Helena nodded. "Which is it, Oliver? Marriage or blackmail?"

"Now, don't be like that." He looked from one to the other.

"I should think you've been here long enough to know we don't have girls like that in Gyver." Eve's tone was a little icy.

"Oh, come on, Eve," Helena said. "Girls these days are capable of doing anything. Even in a nice small town."

"It doesn't happen here." Eve was stubborn.

Oliver's deep and pleasant laugh filled the room. "Well, you're loyal to your birthplace, Eve. I'll say that for you."

"So far you've no evidence that it was blackmail," Helena pointed out.

"That's what we've got to find out," Oliver said. "Police work is a lot like those experiments of yours, Helena. We come up with theories, and it's up to us to prove or disprove them." He sighed. "I just wish we knew more about the girl."

"Perhaps we can give you some help," Eve said as she poured another cup of coffee and held it out to him. "Vi saw the girl last night."

"And what did little sister Vi have to say to big sister Eve?" A gleam appeared in his eyes.

Eve steadied her hands. "She thinks she's seen the girl before."

His tone became serious. "Where?"

"At the Brookline School," Helena answered.

He frowned. "I don't think I know it."

"You wouldn't," said Helena. "It's the elementary school across the street from the high school on the hill.

"It matches what Mrs. Whitman told us," Eve pointed out. "She also said she thinks she saw the young woman with children."

"Well, that gives us something," he said. "Of course, school teachers have a sort of look to them that make people see them everywhere."

"Vi also predicted the girl might have been pregnant," said Helena. "When we —" She stopped.

"When you examined the body in your examining room last night," Oliver finished. "Is that what you were about to say?"

"Helena meant no harm, Oliver," Eve said. "She's just as good at that sort of thing as Dr. Myers."

"His clients are mostly from the higher social circles," Helena insisted. "Women with reducing problems, men with high blood pressure, and children with stomach problems from overindulging in rich food."

"So I've heard." He patted Helena's shoulder. "I expected it, of course. Anything you have to tell me that the doctor didn't?"

"He found the bruises on the back of her neck," Helena said.. "We found hair torn at the roots in some places."

"Whoever killed her held her head and neck down," Eve said with an involuntary shiver.

"The girl must have put up quite a fight, then," he said. "Whoever this killer was, she didn't like him. And she probably knew him."

"I would hate to think there was some maniac killer on the loose," Eve said.

"Anything else you'd like to tell me?" He looked from one sister to the other.

Helena gave Eve a meaningful look, and Eve knew what she was thinking, as she had been thinking the same thing all night.

She put the silver tube of lipstick on the table. "I found this near the girl when we were looking at her clothes last night."

"You mean by the river?" Oliver bent down to examine it. "What is it?"

"I should think with those big city morals, you would know all about painted ladies," her sister said with a sly smile.

"Helena, really!" Eve snarled.

He grinned. "I prefer young ladies with as little paint as possible."

"Then you *do* know what it is?" Helena eyed him.

He shrugged. "I suppose I was ashamed to admit it. The Grave sisters are, as Dr. Myers pointed out, decent women."

"Perhaps not all of us," Eve said with a little embarrassment. "Vi knew all about it."

"That doesn't mean she isn't a decent woman," her sister defended.

"She's not a woman!" Eve insisted. "She's a girl of eighteen."

Oliver eyed both of them in turn. "I believe you would fight tooth and nail for each other, wouldn't you?"

"Why not?" Helena asked. "We've been taking care of one another for a long time."

"A long time," Eve echoed in a soft tone.

He pressed her arm again. "So the girl wore lipstick? I don't recall seeing anything like that on her last night."

Helena grinned. "According to Vi, it isn't waterproof."

"Oh." His mouth formed the letter as his face reddened slightly.

"She knows the shop where the young lady bought it," Eve said. "We can't be absolutely sure it was hers, of course, but Vi also insisted the dark circles under the girl's eyes came from makeup that could have only come from such a shop."

"What shop?" asked Oliver.

"Some French name." Helena shrugged. "Pretentious, if you ask me."

"La Belle Fille," Eve said.

"Mighty interesting," Oliver said. "Your sister certainly has a watchful eye."

"We all do," Helena said. "Out of necessity."

"I'm much obliged to all three pairs of your watchful eyes." He bowed.

Eve rose. "I'll see you to the door."

"I've some things to attend to," Helena said. "You'll forgive me, Oliver."

He bowed again and she disappeared down the basement steps to the mortuary.

Eve found his coat in the closet, but held on to it for a moment. "Oliver, may I make a suggestion?"

He smiled. "As you've just given me two more clues, I wouldn't dream of stopping you."

"If you or the sheriff walk into La Belle Fille, it might look — well, awkward." She played with the collar on his coat.

"You mean a woman might do better?" He grinned.

"Ladies' establishments are funny that way," she said. "Very cagey about their clientele. If another woman strikes up a conversation, however —"

He took the coat from her hands. "You don't have to draw me a picture, Eve."

"It's none of my business, of course." She suddenly felt ashamed.

"I'm making it your business," he said.

"What do you want me to do?"

"Find out all you can," he said. "If we could get the name of the girl who bought this thing —" he held up the lipstick, "— all the better. Though they probably sell dozens of these every day."

"Not this shop," said Eve. "Vi says they cost a pretty penny."

He laughed. "Here, you'd better take this with you." He pressed the lipstick in her hand. Eve felt the imprint of his strong fingers.

CHAPTER 7

$\mathcal{A}$fter Oliver left, Eve took the only car they owned. It was an ancient Ford Model T she had bought when Helena returned from her studies to take her place at the mortuary. Its boxy shape and practical black chrome made Violet turn her nose up, but Eve refused to get one of the flashier models, as every penny they could spend on automobiles went into the hearse. She insisted the car, though a good five years old, suited them just fine.

The roaring motor, which Violet complained sounded like a pack of lions, echoed in the quiet streets of Gyver as she made her way to Malwood Bridge. The mile-long cross over the river made her feel more assured as the car shook and rattled across the uneven pavement. Just before she reached the other side, a sign hung above saying WELCOME TO NEVADA!

It had always been invigorating for her to simply walk across the bridge and be in an entirely different state. She would never deny she loved California whose past wasn't nearly as shady as Nevada's. But the no-nonsense feeling of the sister state put her at her ease and the dry winds soothed her skin.

She turned up Harrison Street, the main part of town that skirted the edge of the river much as Oak Street did in Gyver. Moody was a smaller town, so the mid-morning crowd was modest with mostly middle-aged women and young mothers with baby carriages doing their shopping. She passed by the clock tower that belonged to the Moody Bank, which showed the hour as twenty minutes past ten. She parked the car and walked down a ways, peering through the shop windows. As she passed the tobacco shop, a young man collided with her. He apologized profusely, giving her a good-natured grin.

"How do you do, Miss Grave?"

Eve searched her memory. "I don't think —"

"Daniel Frazer." He peered at her, his grin widening. "I don't suppose you'd remember me. It was three or four years ago."

"Oh!" Eve suddenly had a vision of the man wrapped in veils of steam from a train that had just pulled into the Gyver station. "Of course! You knew my sister Helena in Pasadena."

"You've a good memory, miss." He tipped his hat.

"You were so kind to her." Eve smiled. "It wasn't an easy time for us."

"I remember," he said in a grave tone. "Mr. Eaton going off to the war like that left you in a bit of a pickle."

Eve sighed, remembering the man who had helped her father in the mortuary with his rosy cheeks and pear-shaped figure inside the stiff uniform as the train pulled out of Gyver toward San Francisco. "He never came back."

"Yes, I know," said the young man in a soft tone.

"His son works for us now," said Eve. "His mother died soon after the war, and he had nothing —"

"Very kind of you," he said. "Helena always said you would fill the house with strays if she wasn't there to keep you from doing it. And how is your sister? A fine woman, and so intelligent. She used to help me with my studies, you know."

"I didn't know." Eve smiled. "She's made good use of her college training at the mortuary."

His tone dropped. "I heard she got married a few months after she came back from Southern California."

"She did indeed." Eve peered at him. "Helena said you were studying to be a lawyer."

"That's so, miss."

"So you're a lawyer now?"

"Well, no, miss." He shifted the box of cigars from one arm to the other. "They elected me Moody County district attorney last year."

"Why, of course!" Eve recalled the argument Oliver had with the sheriff about calling in Dan Frazer for the poor dead woman. "Now I understand!"

"I beg your pardon?"

"Oh, nothing." She brushed away a fly that had just come between them. "I'm sure you're a fine district attorney over here."

"I haven't had much of a chance to prove it," he said in a rueful tone. "We don't get the sort of excitement you seem to on the other side of the river." When she looked confused, he laughed and said, "We read the *Gyver Bee* too."

Eve pressed her lips together. "You mean that poor dead girl they found."

"The papers don't make it sound like a very pretty story," he said.

"It wasn't pretty in the least." Eve swallowed as she thought about the bruised skin. "We saw her."

"'We,' miss?"

"Helena and I," she said. "Oliver wanted us to — he thought we might know who she was since we know everyone in Gyver."

"I'm sorry you had to see that." He bowed.

"It wasn't anything for us, Mr. Frazer," she insisted. "It's our work, remember."

"Yes, of course," he said. "I forgot that was why Helena came home from Pasadena. I suppose the girl is with you now? Funeral arrangements and all that."

"We still don't know who she is," said Eve. "It's really quite horrible when you think about it. An unknown girl left in the river."

"Only she didn't sink," he reminded her.

"The killer was rather brutal too," Eve went on. "He held her head down in the water so she would drown. Awful!"

He eyed her. "I don't remember the paper saying anything about that."

"Helena found fingerprints on the back of her neck."

"How very clever of her," he said. "But she was always clever."

Eve lowered her voice. "I know you don't gossip, Mr. Frazer, and you were Helena's friend. That's why I told you all of this."

"I hope I'm still her friend," he said with a shy smile. "I hope I'm yours too." He straightened his hat. "May I drop you off anywhere? My car is just over there."

"That's kind of you, but I've an appointment here in town," she said. "You're welcome anytime at our house for dinner."

"Thank you, Miss Grave." He bowed and moved away with a whistle on his lips.

As she turned into the courtyard at the end of the street, she recalled Helena's letters about Daniel Frazer. Her sister had called him a "scarecrow-looking fellow from our part of the world but a damn good lawyer, knows how to argue his point." She didn't think Helena remembered his name the night before and wondered what she would think when she told her he now had a respectable position as the Moody district attorney.

La Belle Fille looked like a reigning queen in comparison to the other modest shops in the courtyard. It had an elaborately carved entrance complete with angels and lions and a faux marble staircase leading up to the front door. When Eve walked in, the whiff of two different perfumes brushed her face, and she felt her head ache.

A bird-like woman flittered up to her, too elaborately dressed and made up for a small town such as Moody. Her fingers were long and tapered. "May I help you, madame?" The voice was carefully crafted to sound throaty and French.

"Mrs. Arton?" Eve inquired.

"Yes?" The woman blinked her painted eyelashes.

"I'd like to ask you a few questions about this lipstick." She took out the silver pearled container.

The woman glanced at it. "Not a very suitable color for you, madame. Now, we have some coral shades that might —"

"Oh! Not for me." Eve realized the horror in her tone didn't sit well with Mrs. Arton when she saw the bones of her cheeks point at her like knives. "I mean," she corrected, "I'd like to know who bought it and when."

The woman looked at her squarely. "Why?"

The bold question threw Eve off for a moment. She realized the woman would probably never believe her if she said she was sent by the police. So she tried another approach. "Well, as a matter of fact, I'm concerned about my younger sister."

"Indeed?" The woman's voice was a little more cordial.

"Well, you see, she's only eighteen, and I found this in her room." She took out the lipstick from her purse.

"One of our best, madame." The woman studied her plain face.

"Oh, I'm sure it is," Eve said. "But, well, as I said, she's only eighteen."

"Yes?" Mrs. Arton stood waiting.

"I'm afraid she may have gotten in with a — well, a racy crowd." Eve felt her face turn crimson. "I've seen some of the girls she goes around with now, and they wear rouge and lipstick all the time. Lots of it."

"Well, madame," the woman laced her fingers, "young girls do these days."

"Oh, certainly," Eve said quickly. "I appreciate that's your business. Only nice girls just don't wear lipstick every day, even nowadays. Do they?" She peered at the woman.

Mrs. Arden gave her a half-smile. "Some do."

Eve was annoyed at the condescension of the woman's smile. "I'd rather my sister didn't. I confronted her about this, and she told me she borrowed it from a friend. But they all say that, don't they?"

"Perhaps yes, perhaps no," said the woman in a cautious tone.

"I've raised her from a baby, so naturally, I'm concerned," said Eve.

"I fail to see what all this has to do with me," the woman said.

"I wonder — do you keep records of such things?"

"Well, each item we sell, we record in our sales book," said the woman. "But we don't keep records of who buys what." She said in a more severe tone, "And we wouldn't give out such information if we did. I beg your pardon, madame, but your sister is eighteen, you said?"

"Just a baby, really —"

"But she isn't a baby." The woman looked at her with even eyes. "She's a woman."

"Yes, yes," Eve said quickly. "But she can still fall under the influence of a bad crowd, couldn't she?"

Mrs. Arton seemed to consider this a moment. "Yes, I suppose so."

"Then you understand my concern," finished Eve.

"It's not the first time I've had older ladies show such concern," said Mrs. Arton. "Though usually it's the mother rather than the sister. But you raised her from a baby, you say." Her tone softened a little.

Eve took the opportunity. "I was wondering — do you mind checking the sales book — just to ease my mind?"

"Our mark is here." The woman pointed to the one Violet showed them.

"Well, then, perhaps you remember who bought it?"

"I wouldn't know," said the woman.

"Does your record book show who sold the item?" Eve persisted.

"Naturally," she said. "Our salesgirls get extra commission on everything they sell."

"That's what I thought," she said. "Perhaps we can look and see who sold this lipstick, and the salesgirl might remember who it was." When Mrs. Arton didn't answer, Eve said in a more appeasing tone, "Please. It's very important to me."

The woman took her arm. "Well, I must admit, if I had bought such a lipstick in my youth, my older sister would have — well, never mind. Let's check it, shall we?"

With a more amiable smile, Mrs. Arton led took out a large book. She flipped through the pages. "Do you have any idea when it was bought?"

"I really don't know," Eve admitted. "Perhaps a week or so ago." She prayed she was right.

"Well," the woman remarked, "it looks as if you're wrong, madame. It was bought only yesterday."

"Yesterday!" Eve thought of the dead woman lying in the grass. "Are you sure?"

"Here's the number right here," said the woman. "I see Miss Erickson sold this. It looks as if she sold your sister — if it was indeed your sister — a few other items."

"Are you sure?" Eve stared at her.

"I see the numbers here with the same date and Miss Erickson's name." Mrs. Arton scanned the shop. "Miss Erickson is over there."

"Can you call her, please?" Eve asked. "I really must get to the bottom of this."

"Really, I don't think —"

"Please." Eve pressed her hand. "My sister doesn't have much money, and your merchandise is expensive. There may be a young man in the picture who has — well, less than noble intentions toward her."

The woman's countenance suddenly changed. The lines softened, and her eyes became hooded with sympathy. "Ah, why didn't you say so in the first place? A niece of mine almost fell into the same trap." Her face grew hard. "Believe me, madame, it's the young men who are at fault."

"I couldn't agree with you more," Eve said in an emphatic tone.

Mrs. Arton motioned toward the salesgirl, who was straightening a row of powders. The young woman had her hair pinned up but short in the front, a slim figure, and clearly made good use of the products she sold to others.

"Yes, madame?" The girl folded her hands behind her.

"Miss Erickson, this lady has a few questions for you about a sale you made yesterday."

"Yes, madame?" She now turned her attention to Eve.

"Can you tell me when you sold this lipstick?" Eve held up the tube.

"Sometime yesterday morning," she said. "I don't remember the exact time."

"And can you describe the girl who bought it from you?"

"Well, madame, we get so many in here —" She glanced at Mrs. Arton.

"Why don't I give you a description, and you tell me if it fits anyone you sold to yesterday?" Eve suggested.

Miss Erickson arched her eyebrows and her employer supplied, "Mrs. —" She glanced at Eve.

"Miss Grave," Eve said.

"*Miss* Grave," the woman emphasized, "believes her sister may have bought some things at our shop."

"The girl I'm looking for is about medium height with brown eyes and brown hair," Eve said.

"Modern or frumpy?" the girl asked.

"Miss Erickson, really!" Mrs. Arton growled.

Eve smiled. "I suppose you would call her frumpy." She pressed her hands together to keep from laughing at the thought of what Violet's reaction would have been if she had heard her sister refer to her as "frumpy." "People say she looks like a school-teacher."

"Oh, that woman." The girl seemed almost uninterested now that the mystery seemed solved.

"Then she did come in?" Eve grew excited.

"Well, I can't be sure, of course," said Miss Erickson. "A woman with that description came in and bought a lipstick. But she wasn't completely frumpy."

"Explain, Miss Erickson," said her employer in a severe tone.

The girl stood up straighter as if she had just been repri-manded by a strict mother. "Well, madame, I mean she was trying to look modern. Her dress was the right color but it was — well, it looked like it was hand-sewn and a little wooden, if you know what I mean."

"Like someone following a pattern for a modern dress without having much experience wearing modern dresses?" Eve guessed.

"Yes, that's it." The girl seemed relieved.

"Was this the color of lipstick you sold her?" Eve pulled the cap off the tube.

Miss Erickson barely glanced at it. "Yes, that's the shade. Coral Rose."

"Mrs. Arton says she bought a few more things," Eve said.

"Well, yes, I believe so." The young woman glanced at the book. "She bought the Maple Glaze powder, the Ruby Rose rouge and our new waterproof mascara. She was most particular about having those shades, though I told her they may not be so becoming against silk chiffon."

"Silk chiffon?" Eve asked.

"She said she wanted to look fetching on her wedding day." The girl grinned.

"Wedding day?" Mrs. Arton looked at Eve. "Oh, dear."

"Well, that's what she said, madame. She asked me also if we do makeup for brides before their weddings." She smiled with pride. "I told her we don't have that sort of service officially, but I'm sure we could accommodate her at a special rate."

"You did well, Miss Erickson." Her employer nodded with approval. "Never tell the customers 'no,' that's my motto."

"She needs it, if you ask me." Here, the girl dropped the professional demeanor. "A pretty girl like that shouldn't look like a clown on her wedding day."

"Miss Erickson," her employer hissed, "this might be the girl's sister, I will remind you."

"Oh!" Miss Erickson covered her mouth.

"That's all right, dear," Eve said. "You mean she would look like a clown if she tried to put the makeup on herself?"

"Well, yes, miss," said the girl. "I'm awful sorry about what I said."

Eve pressed her shoulder. "It's an interesting observation. You got the impression she didn't know what she was doing?"

"She kept fluttering and looking around," said Miss Erickson. "And when I suggested making her up so she could see what it would look like, I thought she was going to run away."

"Why do you think she was frightened?" Eve asked.

The girl shrugged. "She just said, 'Watts would have my hide.' I suppose that's her landlady or something. Some landladies treat their boarders like children." There was no denying the resentment in her voice.

The name *Miss Watts* echoed in Eve's mind. "Thank you both. You've been very helpful."

"You won't be too hard on the girl, will you?" Mrs. Arton asked with a small smile. "Especially if there's a young man who put her up to it."

"Girl?" Eve blinked. "Oh. No, of course not. Someone else was hard on her already. 'Till death do us part' perhaps, only it didn't reach that point, did it?"

She walked out of the shop with the two women staring after her.

CHAPTER 8

*W*hen she crossed the bridge back into Gyver, instead of turning right to head for home, she turned left and parked the car right next to the county courthouse.

Oliver's office was on the third floor of a heavy brick building with a clock tower that struck noon just as the elevator boy took her up. The young man wrinkled his nose at the bonging that seemed to etch a deep and grave sound in the elevator shaft.

"Imagine having to listen to *that* all day," he complained as he opened the doors for her.

"I think it's rather comforting," she said as she drew her collar up to her chin.

"Comforting!" the boy snorted. "I'd wear cotton in my ears if the sheriff wouldn't box 'em out of me!"

Eve smiled as she followed the marble hallway to the last door on the right. Inside there was a small entranceway with a single desk where Gladys Hunt, Oliver's secretary, sat squinting at the page in her typewriter as she clicked away. Her little desk was arranged neatly with papers on one side, ink and pens on the other, and the blotter in the middle.

"Hello, Gladys." Eve smiled. She and Helena had helped Gladys with the funeral arrangements for her uncle the year before.

"Hello, Eve." The woman smiled back. She spoke in the clipped way of a woman dedicated to efficiency. "Is Mr. Clarke expecting you?"

"No, but I think he'll see me," she said. "I have some things to tell him about the mysterious girl by the river."

"Wasn't it awful?" Gladys shuddered.

Raised voices came from behind the closed door to Oliver's office. Eve could make out his deep tone and the sharp-edged responses of the sheriff.

Gladys's eyes followed hers. "Sheriff Warner's been in there for thirty minutes. I think Mr. Clarke would welcome the interruption."

"I'm sure he would," Eve said.

"Go right in then." Gladys pressed a button.

Before Oliver could answer it, Eve had opened the door. The district attorney's office was the complete opposite of his secretary's. Papers lay all over the floor. Pens were scattered on the desk, and the ink well sat precariously at the edge. Though the city had paid for a leather office chair, Oliver seemed to prefer to sit on the desk or recline on the velvet couch in the corner of the office.

Oliver was pointing a finger at Sheriff Warner leaning against the wall. "Now, listen. I don't care if those jewelers do sue you. It's your own fault if they do."

"Look, Mr. Clarke, I was only doing what you told me to," the sheriff retorted in a grated tone. "How was I to know they would gang up on me like that?"

"They're not ganging up." Oliver shook the paper in his hand. "Didn't you read the letter? They're 'standing on their constitutional rights refusing to submit to police brutality.'"

"Brutality!" the sheriff spit out. "Why, that's a damn lie!"

"I prefer you watch your manners in front of a lady," Eve cut in as she shed her coat.

"She's perfectly right, Sheriff," Oliver said.

"Sometimes you have to be brash to get at the truth, Miss Grave," Sheriff Warner mumbled. "If that's what they call police brutality—"

"Todd Hilton says you practically broke the glass of his diamond display," Oliver continued.

"You don't know the fellow," the sheriff argued. "Zak thought he was doing something fishy with those diamonds last year."

"And proved nothing," Oliver insisted.

"Well, we had to do *something*, Mr. Clarke," he said. "Seems like there ain't nobody bought any jewelry anywhere near this town in the last year."

"There isn't anybody," Eve corrected.

Oliver grinned. "Maybe we ought to ask the county to send him to finishing school, eh, Eve?"

"I fear it wouldn't help," Eve said. "The sheriff would probably have them speaking his language before they had him speaking theirs."

"Maybe it wouldn't be such a bad idea," Sheriff Warner retorted.

Oliver laughed and shuffled her into the leather office chair. "Did you get anywhere with the lipstick?"

"What lipstick?" The sheriff stared at her.

"Eve found a tube of lipstick near the dead girl last night," said Oliver.

Sheriff Warner gave her a sharp look. "Maybe you don't know, but there is such a thing as withholding evidence!"

"I had no idea it was evidence when I withheld it," Eve snapped.

"Lay off, Sheriff," Oliver growled. "She told me about it so she wasn't withholding anything. I'm the one who sent Eve to the shop to inquire after it."

"What shop?"

"La Belle Fille," Eve said.

The lawman sniffed. "Never heard of it."

"You wouldn't," Eve said as she thought of the sheriff's wife, who was even dowdier than she was and whom Violet called "Bird Brain Betty" behind her back.

"Is it evidence?" Oliver was all attention.

"I think it is," she said.

"So is the jewelry," Sheriff Warner grumbled. "Once we find out what it was."

"If they all told you they never saw the girl in their shop, that's that." Oliver put his hands in his pockets. "I never thought it would amount to anything anyway."

"It's a sure bet it was ripped off her coat to keep us from identifying her," the sheriff argued. "That's something, isn't it?"

"What Eve found is something also," Oliver said.

"This lipstick place —"

"La Belle Fille," Eve corrected. "It's a beauty parlor."

"You mean a poodle shop," Sheriff Warner grumbled.

"They know who she is?" Oliver sat at the edge of his desk.

"They didn't know her name," Eve said. "But it was her all right." She proceeded to tell the lawmen what she had discovered.

"A wedding!" the sheriff exclaimed when she finished. "Well, if *that* doesn't settle it!"

"Settle what?" Eve asked.

"Well, isn't it obvious?" Sheriff Warner sat on the couch. "She was planning a wedding. Only the guy — whoever he was — wasn't."

"You mean he was planning a murder instead?" Oliver eyed him. "I don't think it's that cut and dried, Sheriff."

"Clear as crystal to me," the sheriff murmured.

Oliver gave him a lopsided grin. "Have you ever taken a look at crystal up close? It's got lots of angles on it."

"I don't think she was chasing rainbows, Sheriff." Eve leaned back in the chair. Something about its high, curved back warmed her. "I think she really was going to get married."

"Don't tell me it's your women's intuition," Sheriff Warner scoffed. "As Mr. Clarke will tell you, Miss Grave, you can't make a case stick with women's intuition."

"But you can with evidence of behavior," Eve said. "The way she was dressed should have told the story right away. Maybe you don't know, Sheriff, but the teachers in this town are under very strict rules from the county."

"I know it, but how do you know it?" he countered.

"Dot once wanted to be a teacher," Eve said. "I went with her to talk to Mrs. Ferguson. You remember Mrs. Ferguson?"

"'Course I do," he scoffed. "She taught me as well as you, didn't she?"

"As well as lots of us in town," Eve said. "She told us everything about teachers in Gyver county."

"I guess San Francisco's a little more liberal," Oliver mused.

"I know all about those rules," said the sheriff. "Ain't we got instructions to be on the lookout for those girls if they step out of line?"

"Step out of line?" Oliver asked.

"Go to the movies or the drugstore or the bowling alley," Sheriff Warner said. "Step out with a fellow that ain't related to them."

"You mean the schools actually want the police to keep watch on them?" Eve stared.

"Well, no, Miss Grave, but we got a responsibility to make sure our kids get a virtuous education, don't we?"

She sniffed but continued, "They have strict dress codes for the teachers. And those dress codes don't include high heels or skirts shorter than what our mothers wore."

"And they don't include makeup," Oliver guessed, waving the lipstick.

"Violet said La Belle Fille has some of the most expensive

beauty products in the county. I saw the prices. Far too high for a schoolteacher's salary."

"What's that prove?" the sheriff asked. "Nothing. So she got past us and stepped out in some clothes and makeup. Now we know for sure a fellow was involved."

"It goes deeper than that, Sheriff," Eve insisted. "Vi suggested she might have had plans for her future other than being a teacher and was 'letting loose.'" She flinched at the slang. "I think she was conflicted about it."

"How so?" asked Oliver.

"She went to La Belle Fille in modern clothes and shoes," Eve said. "Like the kind she was wearing when you found her. But she wouldn't allow herself to be made up."

"Is that right?" Oliver looked interested.

"She told Miss Erickson, 'Watts would have my hide.'"

"Watts?"

"She's the principal of Brookline Elementary School," Sheriff Warner supplied.

"She must have used her savings to buy that makeup," Eve pointed out. "Teachers have to save most of their earnings so they won't be a burden on society later in life since they can't marry."

"She must have had a bundle stashed away," Oliver remarked. "She wouldn't have dared to spend it unless she was sure she was leaving the profession."

The sheriff gave her a shrewd look. "Why'd you make up that story about your sister buying the lipstick?"

Eve glared at him. "I didn't think the woman would be very forthcoming if she knew I was sent by the district attorney to fish for information!"

"Oh, for Pete's sake!" the sheriff growled. "I told you she weren't no professional, Mr. Clark. You should've let my boys handle it."

"Your boys would have been distracted by all the fluff," Oliver growled. "Eve got us what we wanted to know."

"It seems extraordinary the mystery woman went to see them the very morning she was murdered," Eve lamented. "More than coincidence, perhaps."

"Of course it's more than coincidence," Sheriff Warner said. "She came at the man who got her with child the night before and threatened him into an engagement. That means he had a whole day to plan his escape."

"Really, Sheriff." Eve sniffed. "What would Betty say if she heard you describe marriage as something a man needed to escape?"

Oliver laughed at the sheriff's bewildered face. "Well, at least now we know she was a schoolteacher," he said. "And we can now find out who she is."

"I'm right on it, Mr. Clarke." Sheriff Warner plucked his hat from the stand near the door.

"You needn't bother, Sheriff," said Oliver. "I want you to question the jewelry shops across the state line. And try to be a little more polite this time."

The man stared at him. "But we've got a much more important lead!"

"Which Miss Grave and I will follow up with." Oliver looked at her. "You will come with me, won't you, Eve?"

"I don't get it." Sheriff Warner scratched his head.

"Very simple." Oliver slipped on the heavy coat that made his shoulders look even broader. "I'm going to Brookline to question the principal, and I'm taking Miss Grave with me."

"Why take her?" the sheriff growled.

"Because if I walk in there alone, the place will buzz like a hive of bees," Oliver said. "A lawman at a school is big news. And we don't want the boys at the *Gyver Bee* getting wind of it too soon, do we?"

"If you'll pardon me, Mr. Clarke, I consider it my job to interview suspects." The man's eyes slid toward Eve. "And as Miss

Grave is apt to play silly games when it comes to getting evidence, I don't think it's a good idea to take her along."

"Sheriff." Oliver's dark eyes began to storm. "May I remind you we wouldn't have this lead if Miss Grave hadn't found it for us?"

The sheriff played with the rim of his hat. "Well, heck, Mr. Clarke, I could've gotten that lady to talk just as well."

"I don't think you would have, Sheriff," Eve said. "She's a very refined woman and a very discreet one."

"Now, are you implying —" The sheriff's temper rose.

"I would appreciate it if you would keep your voice down!" Oliver growled. "As district attorney of this county, I have the right to conduct my own interviews, don't I?"

Sheriff Warner bent back the rim of his hat. "I never said you didn't."

"And I don't need to give anyone a reason, do I?" When the sheriff didn't answer, Oliver pressed, "Do I?"

"No, sir." The response came in a softer tone.

"And I don't need to justify who I take with me, do I?"

"I suppose not, Mr. Clarke." The sheriff put on his hat. "I meant no offense, Miss Grave."

"I know that, Sheriff." Eve clutched the edge of her coat. "And maybe you're right. I've no business being here except that Oliver wanted my help and I was happy to give it. But I don't know about this."

"Having you there will make things easier," Oliver said. "It's not a stretch to think the school principal isn't going to be pleased to see a lawman."

"You're not a lawman anymore." The words came out in a rasping tone.

"What was that?" Oliver eyed the sheriff.

"I said, with all due respect, Mr. Clarke, you're not a lawman anymore." Sheriff Warner's tone was even. "You're no longer on the San Francisco police force." He flung open the door. "Zak never forgot that. Might be a good idea for you to remember it too."

Eve watched as he stalked out of the office, making the floor boards rumble and Miss Hunt look up from her proficient typing.

"Amiable fellow," Oliver mumbled.

"I don't want to cause you trouble," Eve said.

"Now, how can anyone who's been as helpful as you have cause me trouble?" He smiled.

"He'll go to the coroner or, worse, the governor!"

Oliver laughed. "He's just blowing off steam, Eve. Todd and Frank Cray got together after he questioned them about that lapel and wrote an angry letter to me. He's miffed about that." His eyes twinkled. "Sheriff Warner prefers to think of himself as a cherished individual in this town."

"He's a boar!" Eve burst out. "Oh, I'm sorry. I shouldn't have said that."

Oliver put on his hat. "I don't deny his ways are a little crude, but he's as honest and efficient a sheriff as I've ever seen." In a softer tone, he added, "Maybe he has a point that I'm not a lawman anymore. But this is my county and my town. I don't like it when people are murdered in my county and my town. Well, shall we go?"

Eve was silent for a moment, then smiled.

CHAPTER 9

The rain had given way to a sun that took the edge off the February chill and Eve smiled up at the blue sky with the puffs of clouds as Oliver eased the car out of the space reserved for county officials.

"Maybe we'll get lucky and they'll have some kind of school picture of the dead woman," Oliver said.

"And if they don't?" Eve asked.

"We ask a lot of questions, rub a few school officials the wrong way, and we get our answers."

"I never knew what spidery business it was to investigate a crime," Eve remarked.

"Spidery?"

"One inch at time crawling toward the center to the web where all the threads connect," she said. "That's what it felt like when I was questioning that woman at La Belle Fille."

He smiled. "It's more like unraveling a web made up of lies and deceit."

"You sound like the moving pictures," Eve said and he laughed.

"Ellen is always accusing me of speaking like I'm in the melodramas," he agreed. "I suppose it's my Irish heritage."

Eve grew quiet for a moment as they turned onto the road that went past the college. "How is Ellen getting along?"

"Oh, fine, fine." But something about his tone was distracted.

"She must be inundated with social invitations now that she's the county district attorney's wife," Eve said.

"The Ladies Guild asked her to become a member only yesterday."

"That's a great honor," Eve said. "Mrs. Beaton is quite choosy about whom she allows in the guild."

"So I gathered." He took the downhill slowly.

"I suppose you and she attended a lot of social functions in San Francisco." Eve focused her eyes on the row of trees that skirted the college buildings.

Oliver didn't answer as he slowed to the stop to let a few boys cross the street. "She didn't want me to take this job, you know."

"I didn't know," Eve said softly.

"The San Francisco D.A.'s office offered me an Assistant D.A. position," he said. "She wanted me to take it."

"I suppose there is more prestige in being an assistant D.A. in the city," Eve murmured.

"It's not her fault," he said. "Her father was a senator and her grandfather was a governor back in Maryland. The ladies always gave grand parties and organized balls and all that sort of thing. She was groomed for that kind of life."

"But you weren't," Eve said gently.

"My grandfather was a cop," he said. "My father was a sheriff. That I got to be a detective and a lawyer was an enormous achievement."

"And now you're the district attorney." In a more rueful tone, she added, "For a small forgotten county on the California-Nevada border."

"I don't care about that," he said fiercely. "I may have only been here three years, but I meant what I said. It's my county and my town."

"And you care what happens to both," Eve said gently.

He gave a small laugh. "You're one of the few around here who doesn't think of me as an outsider."

Although it was late morning, a row of school buses lined the curb, half loaded with children. Teachers already looked overwhelmed organizing rows and counting heads. As Oliver pulled up in his Dodge, the children's Monday morning lethargy gave way to curiosity and excitement. Many of them knew the district attorney's car by sight and knocked on the windows, waving.

Oliver got out, patting heads as he made his way around to the other side to open the door for Eve. In spite of teachers' shrill calls and whistles, children followed them across the schoolyard, asking a million questions. A ball flew over their heads and Oliver caught it. With a laugh, he threw it at a group of boys. They saluted him before they were herded onto the playground by a stern teacher.

The hostile greeting Eve and Oliver received from the school staff contradicted the children's eagerness. People glared at them from desks lining on either side of the hallway. Most looked to be in their late thirties or early forties and wore dark blue suits and dresses. The women's long hair was wrapped in tight buns, and most wore spectacles or lorgnettes. Eve shuddered, thinking of the fate Dot had narrowly missed, and, even more, the pretty dead girl was trying to escape.

They were finally allowed to see Principal Watts a good half hour after they arrived even after Oliver made a point of showing them his credentials. Miss Watts looked the perfect specimen of a schoolteacher who had slowly made her way up the ranks. It was clear she ran the school on the last century's harsh set of values. Eve could see why the dead woman had so violently rejected Miss Erickson's offer.

"To what do I owe this intrusion?" she asked in a chilly tone.

"To murder, ma'am," Oliver said. Eve saw a little of his temper had gathered during their long wait, and he was prepared to take no nonsense from anyone.

"Murder!" The woman looked dismayed.

Oliver took out the photograph George Parks had taken of the dead girl in the most flattering light and handed it to the woman. "We've had word, ma'am, that this woman was a teacher at your school."

There was hardly a shift in Principal Watts' wax features as she studied the photograph. "Is this woman no longer alive?"

"She's dead, if that's what you mean," Oliver said. "Did she work here?"

She studied the photograph for a few more minutes and handed it back to Oliver. "Please sit down." Her tone was lower now, though no less cold.

Oliver pulled back one of the chairs for Eve but remained standing. "Can you identify the young woman, Miss Watts?"

"Principal Watts," the woman corrected.

"Principal Watts," Oliver said carefully. "We must know who she is."

Principal Watts' eyes rested on the photograph. "Yes, I think I can."

"Well?" Eve saw Oliver was losing his patience and lapsing into the brassier side of his personality.

"It looks like Elizabeth Cinder," she said. "Of course, I can't be sure."

"Do you have a picture of her?" Oliver asked.

Eve could tell from the woman's tight lip that she was hardly appreciating the district attorney's direct ways, so she intervened. "Perhaps there was some picture taken at the school with the teachers that you could show us."

Principal Watts, clearly more receptive to Eve's ladylike ways, opened a file drawer and, searching in a folder, came up with a yellowed photograph. "This was taken on picture day earlier this year. Miss Cinder is seated in the second row."

"Yes," Eve said softly. "I see her." The young woman with the pretty features was unmistakable in the photograph, especially among her more average-looking peers. She did not fail to notice Miss Cinder was dressed in completely different attire than what she was wearing when they found her by the river. The dark blue dress looked made of heavy cotton with an unflattering shape.

She handed the picture to Oliver. She saw by the look in his eyes that he noticed the contrast in her appearance as well.

"We've found our mystery woman at least," he murmured.

"Cinder. Cinder," Eve pondered. "No wonder we didn't know her!"

"Eh?" Oliver glanced at her.

"Libby — that's what we called her — left Gyver when she was a child. She went to live with her great-aunt in Nevada, I believe." She glanced at Principal Watts for confirmation.

The woman shifted her stiff shoulders. "I wouldn't know about that. I don't pry into the private lives of my teachers."

"You just have the sheriff watch them so they don't go into the drugstore or the movie theater," Eve mumbled.

"A teacher must maintain an outstanding reputation, Miss Grave," said Principal Watts.

Eve turned to Oliver again. "We heard she was back in town last Easter. I suggested to Helena that we pay them a visit, but well — you know how things are." She glanced at the photograph again, feeling the shame rise in her throat. "We ought to have visited her."

"You could hardly know she would get herself killed," Oliver said in a kind tone.

"May I ask what this is all about?" Principal Watts looked from one to the other. "I know you, of course, Miss Grave. But I can't imagine what you're doing here."

"We're much obliged to you for telling us the name of our victim." Oliver slipped the picture back into his coat pocket. "You've read the paper, I'm sure."

"I don't read papers, Mr. Clarke. It is Mr. Clarke, isn't it?"

"It is," he said grimly.

"Naturally, I know a young lady was found by the river under unfortunate circumstances," the woman continued in the same cold and cautious tone. "One of the teachers told me this morning. I've given strict orders to all the teachers not to discuss the matter in front of the children. Children's minds are far too tender for such talk."

"Indeed," Oliver said with a grimace. "But we're not children, Principal Watt."

"I don't know what I can tell you." The woman folded her hands in her lap.

"For a start, you can tell us who Miss Cinder was," he said. "As you've probably read in the paper — oh, I'm sorry. You haven't read the paper." He gave Eve a side look. "The girl was found without any identification on her. We really know nothing about her."

"She was a teacher at this school," the woman said.

"That we gathered," he said dryly.

"What grade did she teach?" Eve asked.

"The third," said the woman.

"Was she a good teacher?"

"Quite good." Principal Watt relaxed a little. "Some of her students received the highest marks in the school. And Edna Coste won first prize for the children's poetry contest at the county fair last year."

"How long had she been teaching here?" Oliver asked.

"As Miss Grave already said, she's been back in Gyver since Easter of last year," said the woman. "She had an excellent record at her last school in Reno."

"So she came from the big city?" Eve asked. Principal Watt nodded.

"Weren't you afraid she would bring big city morals into the classroom?" Oliver eyed her.

"I told you, Mr. Clarke, her record was impeccable," she said icily.

Eve pressed Oliver's wrist to warn him against a retort. "Principal Watts, is there anything at all about Libby that might help the police find out who killed her?"

The woman glanced at the window. "Well, there was one odd thing."

"Yes?" Oliver looked eager.

"Miss State — the teacher who told me about this dreadful event — said it happened on Friday."

"That's right," Oliver said.

"Well, I don't know if this is useful to you, but Miss Cinder didn't come to classes that day." An irritated look crossed her face. "We had to call in a substitute teacher."

"Did she telephone or send a message?" Eve asked.

"Not a word," the woman said. "It was most unlike her. I would have thought so, at least."

"You mean she was a good girl?" Oliver asked.

The woman stiffened. "Mr. Clarke, Miss Cinder was twenty-three years old. Hardly a *girl*."

Eve hid a smile.

"I'm sorry," he said. "Do you know if she might have been meeting a young man that day?"

Something about the way Principal Watts looked suddenly jerked Eve's memory to a bit of gossip she had heard before Thanksgiving when the community ladies had come to bury poor Mrs. Knell: *Some schoolteacher from the big city got herself involved with a Falcon Hill boy!*

"I should say not!" Principal Watts snapped. "Such behavior is strictly forbidden, Mr. Clarke."

"A pity," Oliver said. "She was a pretty girl — lady. She had her whole life ahead of her."

"A life as a fine teacher!" A strained muscle appeared near the woman's eyebrow. "She had every intention of remaining in the profession. We spoke about her moving to administration one day."

"I thought you didn't pry into your teachers' lives," Oliver said.

"Their *private* lives, Mr. Clarke," she said. "Their professional lives are my responsibility."

Oliver seemed content to let it go at that. "Did Miss Cinder have a friend among the teachers, anyone she was close to?"

"Well, I suppose you could speak with Miss Horne," she said in a doubtful tone.

"Miss Florence Horne?" Eve asked.

Principal Watts nodded. "She teaches our fourth-grade class."

"If you tell us what classroom Miss Horne is in, we'll just mosey along," Oliver said.

"You mean you intend to visit her in her classroom?" The woman looked horrified. "With the children there?"

Oliver's gaze was sharp. "You don't seem to realize, Principal Watts, this is a murder investigation."

"And *you* don't seem to realize, Mr. Clarke, that *this* is a school," she snarled. "I realize you're the district attorney, but Mr. Walton would *never* have suggested bringing in such sordid goings-on to a school!"

"Zak would have done whatever was necessary to bring a murderer to justice, ma'am." Oliver's temper was clearly getting the best of him. "Including bringing in the militia to patrol the halls!"

"Well!"

Eve asked in a calm tone, "Oliver, perhaps Florence could come here? When she finishes her class, that is."

"If you wish it, Eve," he said gently.

Principal Watts hedged a little. "It's most irregular."

"This is an irregular circumstance." Oliver's voice was calm now. "I'm sure you're as anxious to find the one responsible for this terrible crime as we are, Principal Watts. She was your teacher, after all."

"Naturally, I want to do all I can," the woman said. "I shall go to Miss Horne's classroom myself and ask her to come to my office when she's through. That should be in about —" she looked at the old-fashioned watch around her neck "— twelve minutes from now."

"We would greatly appreciate it, ma'am." Oliver bowed.

"I prefer you stay here in the meantime," said the woman. "The children have already seen you, and we don't want more of a flurry than we've already experienced."

"I'm sure," Oliver mumbled.

"I'll ask Miss Niles to bring you some coffee in the meantime." Principal Watts opened the door. "I must ask you, Mr. Clarke, not to upset Miss Horne too much with your questions. Teachers must be always at their best in the classroom, and if you upset her, the children —"

"I promise I'll ask only what is necessary for our investigation." Oliver's eyebrows drew together, revealing he was not at all happy with this condition.

"I know Miss Grave understands what I mean." Principal Watts looked at her. "We both deal with sensitive issues."

"Yes, we do," Eve said, though she hardly considered teaching a "sensitive issue."

Before she closed the door, the school principal's cold exterior broke as she hissed at them, "And for heaven's sake, don't show Miss Horne that photograph!"

"Well, of all the —" Oliver exploded after the woman closed the door. "How the — how does she expect us to get along with our investigation if we don't ask Miss Horne to verify the identity of the dead girl?"

"Dead woman," Eve said softly.

He looked at her a little bewildered for a moment, then gave a short laugh. "I'm sorry. To me, every woman younger than forty is a girl. Thanks for saving me."

"Saving you?"

"Saving her, really, from my temper," he said. "I don't lose it often, but when I do —"

She laughed. "I don't blame you for being infuriated with her."

He propped his leg up on the bar under her chair and leaned forward. "You see now why I wanted you to come. People warm up to you more easily than they do me."

Eve felt a small flutter in her chest. "I'm glad to help."

Oliver surveyed the room. "I can see now why Miss Cinder was so keen to get away from here."

"Principal Watts clearly saw her as ripe for a school career," Eve agreed. "But maybe Libby wasn't so sure."

"You're getting a taste of the part of police work no one knows about," he said. "Getting to know the character of the victim."

"Oliver," she said. "I remembered something. The ladies were gossiping last year about a teacher who may have been seeing someone on Falcon Hill."

"Falcon Hill!" He let out a whistle.

"I see you know the place."

"Zak was always getting phone calls from 'the pillars of Gyver society,'" he said. "They seemed to think he was their own private judge and jury."

"I shouldn't wonder," Eve said. "Do you suppose the teacher could have been Libby Cinder?"

"What makes you think it was?" he asked.

"The ladies mentioned a teacher 'from the big city,'" she said. "I assumed at the time they meant San Francisco or Sacramento. I never considered it might refer to a city across the state line."

"Reno is hardly a big city," he pointed out.

"Maybe not compared to San Francisco or Sacramento," she argued. "But compared to Gyver, it's enormous."

He laughed. "Forever loyal to your birthplace, eh?"

She was relieved when the door opened and Miss Niles entered with the coffee.

CHAPTER 10

It was considerably more than twelve minutes later when the door opened again and Principal Watts came in followed by a young woman. Even though the heavy and long blue dress draped her figure, Eve could tell Florence Horne was quite curvaceous underneath. Her face was bare and her blond hair set in a tight bun like the others.

"Miss Horne?" Oliver leapt forward.

"Yes." The woman stood with her hands behind her back. "Principal Watts said you wish to speak to me, Mr. Clarke."

Oliver's dark eyes slid from Miss Horne to the stoic principal and assessed the situation immediately. "Principal Watts, I wonder if you could leave us alone for a few minutes."

"I don't think that's wise, Mr. Clarke." The woman's brows knitted together.

"I do." His tone was firm as he took her arm. "I assure you we won't do her any harm."

"As the school administrator, I'm responsible for —"

"Please, Principal Watts." Eve made her voice as appealing as she could. "It's very important to us."

The woman blinked at her. "Well, as Miss Grave is here, I suppose it's alright."

The moment the door closed behind the woman, Miss Horne's poker-faced expression eased and she collapsed in a chair. "Call me Florence, won't you?" Her tone was light and amiable.

"Then you call me Oliver." He smiled. "Coffee?"

"In the middle of the school day? I shouldn't." But she was eyeing the cup Oliver had put on the desk with hunger.

He poured the last of the coffee from the pot and pushed it toward her.

"I heard you're a very nice man." Florence smiled. "And of course, everybody knows the Grave sisters." She smiled at Eve. "I hope I can help you."

"I'm sure you can," Oliver said kindly. "I'll ask Miss Niles for more coffee."

Principal Watts came into the room when Miss Niles brought in the coffee. When she saw the cup in Miss Horne's hands, a deep frown appeared on her face. "I don't think you should be indulging when you still have classes to teach today, Miss Horne."

The words brought the blank stare back into Florence's eyes as she set the cup and saucer down carefully on the desk.

Oliver took immediate control. "Police interviews are private affairs, ma'am. That's why I asked you to leave."

"But I —"

"I'm already accommodating you by using this office." He took her arm. "This should really be done at the police station."

"Police station!" The woman's face turned pale. "Oh, if the board should hear of it —"

"They won't if you leave us in peace," he said. "If you insist on staying, I'll ask Sheriff Warner to send a police car down to take Miss Horne to the station."

"No need for that," she said, pushing Miss Niles out the door with the empty tray.

With a big grin on his face, he closed the door with a resolute snap.

Florence burst out laughing and crossed her legs, balancing the cup and saucer on her knee. "That was marvelous! She's really a dragon, isn't she, Eve?"

"She can be a little harsh," Eve said quietly.

"Now that she's out of the way, we can get down to business." Oliver produced the photograph. "She didn't want us to show you this, but I must have confirmation, Florence. We understood from the principal this woman we found by the river is named Elizabeth Cinder. Can you verify this?"

The young woman's fingers shook as she reached for the photograph. She let out a sob, covering her mouth.

Oliver patted her shoulder. "I'm sorry I had to put you through that. It *is* Miss Cinder, isn't it?"

The young woman nodded. Eve admired how Oliver slipped her his handkerchief and waited silently for her to dry her tears.

Florence's voice was calm as she handed him back the handkerchief. "Yes, the woman in the photograph is Libby."

"You and she were good friends." Eve pressed her hand.

"Since we were five years old," said Florence. "Even when Libby went to live with her aunt, we wrote to one another often. I visited her in Reno sometimes in the summer."

"So she really was a city girl?" Oliver asked.

"I suppose you could call her that," she said. "But not in the way you think. Coming from San Francisco, that is."

Oliver gave a small smile. "Not all San Francisco girls are flappers, Florence."

"Neither was Libby." Her voice was shrill. "I know that's what everyone thinks, but —"

"By 'everyone,' do you mean the teachers?" Eve asked.

"And Principal Watts." Florence sniffed.

"She told us Miss Cinder —"

"Libby," said Florence. "She would want you to call her Libby, Mr. Clarke."

"She told us Libby had excellent credentials," Oliver continued.

"It's just like the dragon to talk about that," the young woman snarled. "She always makes people think she doesn't care what teachers do outside of school as long as they follow the rules, but we all knew what she thought of Libby."

"That she was loose?" Eve asked softly, thinking of the dress and make up.

Florence shifted. "Well, not exactly. But Libby could have some fun once in a while when she was in Reno. They aren't so strict with teachers there."

"Why did she come back here?" Oliver asked.

"Because of her father," Eve answered before Florence could speak. "Mr. Cinder had a stroke six months ago, poor man."

Oliver eyed her. "I'm surprised you know that, Eve."

"Oh, we all know everything about everyone around here," said Florence.

He laughed. "I suppose that's one thing I should have learned in three years with the district attorney's office."

"You were sheltered by your official status, Oliver," Eve said with a smile.

"The rest of us can't help but know even if we don't want to know," Florence mused. "You go to the grocery store or the butcher or the hardware store, and people will tell you whether you're interested or not."

"But you are interested," Oliver said. "Everyone is interested. That's what makes this town different."

"We do look out for one another," Eve agreed.

"Is that the only reason Libby came back to Gyver?" Oliver leaned against his knee.

Florence's eyes rose to the window, polished to perfection,

which showed the bright blue sky and deep green grass. "What other reason could there be?"

Oliver glanced at Eve. "A suitor, maybe?"

"Libby knew the rules for teachers in this town," Florence said.

Eve thought her tone was a little too insistent, but Oliver seemed prepared to let it go.

"What sort of young woman was Libby?" the district attorney asked. "I don't mean you need to tell us any of her secrets, but —"

"As I said, Libby wasn't all innocence. She liked to go out sometimes. Oh, just to the drugstore or a picnic or boating, things like that, like most modern women." She winked at Eve.

"But she had no beau?"

"She wasn't a nun, Oliver." Florence's face was amused. "She did have some men friends."

"Nothing more?'

"Not that I know of." Again, the tone sounded a little too insistent.

"It must have been tough giving up all that freedom to come here," Oliver observed.

"She did feel a little trapped," Florence admitted.

"Do you think if it weren't for her parents, she would have chucked the job and gone back to Reno?" Eve asked.

"Maybe not Reno," Florence said. "But somewhere."

"She didn't like teaching, then," Oliver said.

"She loved children." Some tears returning to her eyes. "She was patient with them."

"But she had other plans for her future?" Eve guessed.

Florence smiled. "When we were kids, she always loved playing house. I was the tomboy who ran and jumped and got myself into all kinds of scrapes."

"She wanted a husband and children," Eve said quietly.

"More than most women?" Oliver asked.

"More than some women," Eve said, her voice more stinging than she intended. She felt Oliver's gaze on her.

"Eve's right," said Florence. "Husband and children are all right, but these days, many of us want more out of life. That's why we wanted to win the vote."

"I see what you mean when you say Libby wasn't a loose woman," Oliver said kindly. "Still, it's strange she didn't have a fiancé, or at least a sweetheart."

Eve noticed for the first time the intensity of Oliver's dark, snapping eyes under the dark brows. Their gaze filled the room, making her catch her breath.

Florence said in a careful tone, "What makes you think she had a fiancé?"

"The proprietress of La Belle Fille," he said.

"The beauty salon?" Florence looked stunned. "What would Libby be doing there?"

"What indeed?" Oliver grimaced. "Suppose you tell us."

"I haven't the faintest idea." Florence sat very still.

"She told Eve that Libby came in to buy cosmetics for a wedding."

"Libby had lots of friends back in Reno," Florence insisted. "If one of them were getting married, she might have wanted to buy her a wedding present."

"Makeup is a rather personal thing, don't you think?" Eve asked.

"I wouldn't know." The tone of bitterness returned.

"Neither would I," said Eve. "But my sister does." She tried not to let her embarrassment show. "She would never choose lipstick or rouge as a present for her friend Kitty, and I expect Kitty would never choose such a present for her."

"Do you really believe that's what she was doing, Florence?" Oliver said. "Buying a present for a friend?"

It was clear his dark searing eyes had begun to make an

impression on the young teacher, as she answered meekly, "It's possible."

"I didn't ask you if it was possible," he said. "I asked you if you believed it."

Florence played with her watch, twisting the chain around her thin wrist. "As a matter of fact, Libby called me the night she came back."

"Came back?" Eve asked. "You mean when she started work at Brookline?"

"No," said Florence. "When she came back from visiting her aunt."

"When did she go visit her aunt?" Oliver asked.

"After the new year."

"How long was she there?"

"About a month," said the young woman.

"What day did she come back?"

Florence blinked. "Is that important?"

"It might be," Oliver said.

"Thursday," she said.

Eve glanced at the district attorney, and his expression showed what he was thinking. "The day before she was murdered," she said softly.

"Oh! I see now why you said it might be important." Florence held her hand to her eyes, and Oliver offered her his handkerchief again.

"Go on," said Oliver as he took a stool from the corner and sat down.

"She called very late," Florence said. "Pa made an awful ruckus about it." She gave a rueful smile. "He still thinks I'm twelve."

"How late?" Oliver asked.

"Oh, close to midnight," said Florence. "But, really, Oliver, that wasn't unusual. We often called one another late at night if we had something important to say to one another."

"And she had something important to say," Eve guessed.

Florence nodded slowly. "She told me she was engaged to be married."

"So you were lying to us before?" Oliver eyed her.

"I wasn't lying, Oliver," she insisted. "I didn't know for sure until she called me."

"And she told you herself that she was engaged?"

"Yes."

Eve watched the woman carefully. The air had changed from discomfort to alarm. Florence tipped the coffee cup to her lips, but as if remembering she had already finished it, set it down with a thump.

"You didn't expect it, did you?" Eve asked quietly.

"No," Florence said. "Frankly, I didn't."

"You didn't think they were well-suited," Oliver suggested.

"Oh, no, that had nothing to do with it," she said. "It was just — Libby left for her aunt's so abruptly —"

"And you think it was because she and her fiancé had a fight," Oliver finished.

"I got that impression," she said. "I came with her when she told Principal Watts she was taking a month to be with her sick aunt."

"A shame Principal Watts didn't tell us that." Oliver threw Eve a glance.

"She wouldn't," said Florence with a grimace. "She wants people to think her teachers would never do anything as awful as take a leave of absence for a month."

"I imagine the principal wasn't exactly happy about it." Eve nodded.

"I think Watts knew she was lying about the sick part." Here, the young woman's eyes flashed. "But Libby was firm when she said she had to be with her aunt."

"She was devoted to her aunt?" Eve suggested.

"She was grateful to her for all she'd done," Florence said. "If

Miss Gilbert — Libby's aunt — were really sick, she would have gone to her."

"Would she have told Miss Gilbert she was engaged?" Eve asked.

Florence shrank in the wide chair. "I don't think they were that close."

"But she told you," said Oliver. "And you were close enough to her to know who he was." The district attorney took both her hands with a tender look on his face. "We must know who he is, Florence. You understand that, don't you?"

"Do you think he killed her like the papers say?" Florence's voice was barely above a whisper.

"I don't think anything," Oliver assured her. "But I need to question him, Florence."

"Well," Florence murmured. "It can't hurt her now, can it?"

"On the contrary," Eve said. "If he knows anything, it can only help her."

The young woman gave Eve a meaningful look. "It's just that he's from Falcon Hill."

Oliver threw Eve a look. "His name?"

"August Winters."

Oliver gave a rueful smile. "So Libby, the girl from the wrong side of the tracks, was engaged to the future leader of Gyver society."

"She didn't care about that!" Florence glared at him. "She loved him."

"And she wanted to leave teaching," Oliver said. "Being Mrs. August Winters would certainly have given her that opportunity."

"I told you, she wanted a family."

"She must have," Eve said kindly. "She was spending money she had saved on makeup."

Florence nodded. "She saved every penny she could. That's why she lived with her parents instead of a boarding house."

"That's why she sewed her own clothes," Eve said.

"She never intended to use that money for her old age," Florence admitted. "It was always for her wedding."

"She wanted a family that much." Eve couldn't help but feel a sense of regret, thinking of the small nest egg her father had put in her name. But that had been spent on taking care of Helena and Violet.

"And she was getting one, wasn't she, Florence?" Oliver bent his head a little so his dark eyes became even more intense. "She told you that too when you spoke with her that night, didn't she?"

Florence gave a cry and buried her face in Oliver's handkerchief. "Yes! Oh, you mustn't think —"

"We don't think anything," Eve said gently as she put her arm around her shoulders.

Florence's head flew up. "But how did you know she was —"

"How did *you* know she was?" Oliver inquired back.

Florence pressed her hands together. "She told me, of course."

"That same night?"

"That same night." She gave a small rueful laugh. "I suppose I should have seen it."

"Because she was letting her clothes out?" Eve asked.

The young teacher nodded distractedly. "How did you know that?"

"We saw her clothes," she said. "My sister Helena and I, that is."

"Oh, there were so many things I ought to have seen!" Florence burst into tears again, sobbing into Oliver's handkerchief.

"It's not always easy to see things with people you love," Eve said gently.

"How did she feel about the baby, Florence?" Oliver asked.

"She was ecstatic," said the young woman. "She was jumping out of her skin with joy."

Oliver made a half circle in the small office, his hands shoved deep into his pockets. "Florence, there's no easy way for me to

ask this. I'm not one to dance around things, as Eve will tell you."
Eve nodded "So I'm going to ask this straight out and apologize
in advance for the offense. Was Libby sure the child belonged to
this fiancé of hers?"

It took a moment for Florence to realize what he was asking.
The bones of her face seemed to protrude with agitation. "It
could only belong to August, Oliver."

"You did say she liked to have fun —"

"I also said she wasn't one of those flappers!"

Eve looked down at her hands, thinking of Violet and what
people in town said about her under their breath. Her hands
suddenly looked old and worn, misshapen from years of burying
the dead.

Florence pressed Eve's wrist. "Oh, I didn't mean anything,
Eve."

"I'm sorry I had to ask that question." Oliver's tone was a
little rough. "That's why I warned you I don't pussyfoot
around."

Florence smiled a little. "I suppose under the circumstances,
you had a right to ask that question."

"Did she tell you if August knew?" Eve asked.

The young woman shook her head. "She didn't talk about
August at all, except to say she was engaged to him."

"Do you think he does?" Oliver peered at her.

"I really can't say," said the teacher. "I never saw them
together."

"Never?"

"They didn't exactly share their relationship with others."
Libby glanced at him.

"Because of Libby's job?" asked Oliver.

"That, and, well, I don't think his mother would have
approved."

"I imagine she wouldn't," Oliver said ruefully. "If you never
saw them together, how do you know Libby loved him?"

"The way she spoke of him," said Florence. "A friend can tell when love is serious."

"They can indeed," Eve agreed.

"That's the truth, Oliver." She glanced at the clock on the wall. "I'm sorry, I really must get ready for my class."

"Of course." He took back his handkerchief, burying it in his coat pocket. "We're sorry to have caused you so much distress."

"I'm glad I could help." She opened the door a crack, then leaned against it. "Oliver, I've a favor to ask."

"Anything I can do," he said kindly.

"Do Libby's parents know anything yet?"

He shook his head. "We only just found out who the girl in the picture is."

"May I ask who's going to tell them?"

He smiled a little. "I imagine you don't want it to be Sheriff Warner."

"You picked up on his reputation very quickly." She smiled.

"I've had the pleasure of observing his rather bulldog ways more often than I care to," said Oliver. "You needn't worry." He took her hand in both of his. "I'll go right now and tell them, if you'll just give me the address."

"Certainly," Florence said. She took a piece of paper from the spotless pad on the principal's desk and a fountain pen and wrote it down. "I know Libby would want it this way."

"I'll even take Eve with me," he added. Eve started a little at the mention of her name.

"I'm much obliged." Florence smiled at Eve. "Eve will know how to comfort them, won't you Eve?"

"I'll do my best," she murmured.

CHAPTER 11

$\mathcal{I}$t was lunchtime when they came out of the administrative building, and they were immediately accosted by a barrage of children coming out of the building with their lunchboxes and lunch pails, flinging questions at them about "the lady by the river" in their high-pitched voices. Their bald openness shocked Eve.

Oliver, however, seemed unaffected as he playfully gave them humorous answers, chucking some of the little girls under the chin in a paternal way that made them giggle and rubbing some of the boys on the back of their necks. The children were clearly disappointed they weren't getting a word out of him, and their fallen faces lingered through the windows as Oliver drove off down the hill.

"How can their parents allow them to know about a thing like this?" Eve lashed out.

"I don't think the parents had anything to do with it," Oliver said. "Children are sensitive to trouble, and when there's a crime in town, the whole town is troubled."

"But to ask such questions!"

Oliver's eyebrows arched with amusement. "And how many

questions did little Evie ask about the stiffs brought in to her father's mortuary?"

She glared at him but suddenly burst out laughing. "I suppose that's what they call in the detective novels 'caught red-handed.'" She listened with pleasure to his deep and long laugh.

"I don't judge you, Eve," he said, turning a corner. "I used to ask my father all kinds of questions about being a policeman. Sometimes I think he'd have liked to paddle me for it, but he never did." In a softer tone, he added, "He was a peace-loving man at heart."

"I don't suppose you can become a police officer unless you are peace-loving," she said.

"You'd be surprised," he murmured.

They stopped at the hand of one of Warner's men directing traffic, who waved at them. They were silent for a moment. "Well, what do you think, Eve?"

"About what?" She blinked.

"About Mr. August Winters," he said. "If it's true he was going to be a father, he got himself in an awful mess."

"It's also true he was going to be a husband," Eve reminded him. "That's just what I would expect from August."

The officer motioned for them to proceed, and Oliver lurched the car forward. "I'm assuming, then, that he has a high recommendation from you?"

"He's not one of those idle young men who takes advantage of innocent young women and abandons them, if that's what you mean," Eve said. "At least, I don't think so."

"We'll have to find out, won't we?" he asked.

"You'll have to interview him, I suppose." Eve was quiet for a moment. "You may have a time getting past Rosalia."

"I've handled gatekeeping mothers before," he said gruffly. Then, without looking away from the road, he said, "I know I shouldn't have presumed you would come with me to the Cinders. It's not going to be pleasant."

"No, it isn't," Eve agreed. "Mr. Cinders had two strokes six months apart, and he's not very strong. He'll be broken up about losing his daughter."

She thought she saw Oliver flinch.

"You can still back out if you like," he said.

A moment of hurt turned to anger. "You forget, Oliver, I'm very equipped for dealing with bereavement. Besides, I would need to see them anyway about the funeral arrangement."

She felt a coldness wash over her. It was the sort of thing Helena would say in her measured, still tone, with a medical journal in her lap. She caught the storminess of Oliver's dark eyes, and his large hands gripped the steering wheel.

"I don't think it's the time to talk business, Eve," he said in a piercing tone.

She covered her face with her hands to keep from showing her tears. "I don't know why I said that."

He pulled the car over to the curb. "None of that now." His tone was soft. "We both deal with the practical side of tragedy, don't we? Sometimes it helps to let the practical side take over the emotional side."

"Yes, yes, that must be it!" She leaned back on the leather seat. "Papa's way of seeing it was uniting the soul and body once buried underneath the earth. He was a very sensitive man, really, even if he did what he did."

Oliver smiled. "There's no shame in what he did, Eve."

"I'm not ashamed of it." She slipped her hands out of his. "And I won't talk business with the Cinders, Oliver."

"I didn't think for a minute you would." He patted her arm and started the car.

The Cinder house was a modest two-story with dusty windows and a shabby front yard. The steps were so rickety that Eve had to hold on to Oliver's arm. She saw his displeasure as he glanced around the front porch.

"I always thought people in small towns take care of their homes," he snapped.

"We do," said Eve. "When we have the money for it."

The door opened and a woman in her forties blinked in the sunlight. Her skin had a wrinkled quality, and her face sagged but there were remnants of a pretty woman still there. As she shielded her eyes from the glare, something in her expression gave Eve a pang. She saw the face of the dead girl mirrored in that worn countenance.

"Mrs. Cinder?" Oliver held out his card. "I'm Oliver Clarke, the county district attorney."

"Yes, Mr. Clarke, we know who you are." The woman's voice was thin and soft.

"Who is it, Gert?" a voice called from within.

"Mr. Clarke, the new district attorney," she called back.

"We voted for him, didn't we?"

"Yes, we did."

"Nice fellow."

Oliver couldn't hide a grin as he called back, "Thank you, Mr. Cinder." Then, lowering his tone, he said, "I'm afraid I've come with rather bad news." Eve could see by the pinched look on his face that he was dreading their ordeal.

Mrs. Cinder was quiet for a moment, as if she were barely breathing. It occurred to Eve she had seen the morning paper even though the story hadn't mentioned the dead girl's name.

"Won't you both come in?" Mrs. Cinder looked at Eve. "One of the Grave sisters, isn't it?"

"I'm Eve, Mrs. Cinder." She tried to smile. "We met at the county fair last year."

The woman's eyes lit up. "You were the one who helped Lydia Bowen when she had to bury her husband two years ago."

"That's right, ma'am." Eve could see Oliver was a little relieved at the friendliness in the woman's voice as they hung up their coats in the hallway.

"She was ever so grateful." Mrs. Cinder's eyes were kind. "She's a friend of mine, you see. It was an accident, very sudden, and she was just — poor woman!" She sighed.

Eve felt a lump rise in her throat, thinking of how Lydia Bowen would no doubt be saying the same thing about Mrs. Cinder soon. "Poor woman," she echoed.

"Gert, ain't you going to invite them in?" the crackling call came again.

"That's just what I did, dear," she called back, motioning for them to follow.

A man whose figure looked shrunken in the large chair sat with both hands on his cane. Mr. Cinder looked frail, but he had an open, cordial way about him.

"We got some coffee left, don't we, Gert?" Mr. Cinder asked. "Coffee, Mr. Clarke?"

"No thank you, sir." Oliver leaned with his elbows on his knees, rubbing his hands together. Eve could see he was having a hard time looking at either of them. "The truth is, we've come about the girl in the paper."

"You mean the dead girl?" Mrs. Cinder's hand flew to her lips.

Oliver cocked his head, his dark eyes intense. "Yes."

"I knew it!" The last came as a small cry while the woman glanced at her husband. "The paper —"

"You saw the newspaper?" Eve asked.

"They said about the clothes — I knew it! Libby!"

"What about Libby?" The man was immediately alert. "She's at the school, ain't she?"

"She's not at the school, Mr. Cinder," Eve said quietly. Without realizing it, her hand reached for Oliver's.

"Not at the school?" The man blinked.

"I'm afraid, sir, the girl we found by the river was your daughter." Eve admired how Oliver said the last with a direct look at Mrs. Cinder, not shying away from her steady gaze.

Eve saw what Florence had meant about the Cinders. Mrs.

Cinder stumbled about, grabbing the dining room table with both hands as if to steady herself. Mr. Cinder looked as if he had been crushed by a boulder. His entire figure deflated inside the chair and he let out a cry. "No! No!" Then he burst into tears and the screech let out of the small man's lips was the most distraught Eve had ever heard.

Oliver eased him out of the chair and, with a gesture toward Eve, helped Mr. Cinder up the stairs, taking each step carefully while the man sobbed. Eve went to Mrs. Cinder whose head lolled forward.

Eve had comforted the grieving many times, and she knew the best thing she could do was to be within range of the woman, in case she wanted to take her arm or her hand, but remain silent and unobtrusive. Looking at Mrs. Cinder still gripping the table, she thought of what her father always told her: *Sometimes the best comfort is silence.*

This seemed exactly what Mrs. Cinder needed. Her eyes were still on the stairs as Oliver disappeared with her husband. Sounds of his deep, soothing voice and a door opening and closing came from the second floor.

Mrs. Cinder said in a broken tone, "Women are so much stronger than men, aren't they?"

Eve, who had observed the same thing in her work, agreed.

"I'm all right now," she said. And the woman indeed looked more composed, though her face was still pale. As Eve sat her down on the chair, she noticed the unsteadiness of her arms. "Are you sure it isn't a mistake?"

Eve shuddered at the thought that Oliver would probably show her the photograph. "We don't think so, Mrs. Cinder."

"But you don't know," she challenged. "Maybe Libby gave her clothes to another girl, and she was the one who got killed. Libby was always doing things like that."

Eve hesitated. "There was a picture —"

"Picture?"

She swallowed. "George Parks took it."

"He's the one who took all those photographs at the bazaar last year, isn't he?"

Eve nodded. "Oliver called him in to take some photos of the crime scene."

"I didn't know the police did things like that," the woman said softly.

"They do now," Eve said.

Oliver returned to the living room, looking wholly miserable. Eve's heart went out to him.

The woman's empty eyes filled with tears. "Eve was just telling me you called George in when they found the dead girl — when they found Libby."

"Yes, ma'am."

"And he took a picture of her." The woman's tone was almost a whisper, but she looked a little more alive. "I want to see it, Mr. Clarke."

"That isn't necessary, Mrs. Cinder," he said. "Florence Horne has already identified it for us."

"That's all well and good, but she was *my* daughter." Her voice was indignant. "I want to see. I have to *know*."

"I think you ought to honor Mrs. Cinder's request, Oliver," she said quietly.

Oliver put the photograph on the coffee table. The woman picked it up, holding the edge with both hands as if she were afraid it would fly away from her.

"She looks peaceful, doesn't she?" She gave Eve a wild look. "You know about these things, Miss Grave. She's at peace now, isn't she?"

"She's at peace," Eve assured her, fighting the tears coming to her eyes.

"May I keep this?" the woman implored Oliver.

"Of course," he said.

"This isn't Libby, you know." Mrs. Cinder gave a little laugh.

"She was livelier, I suppose you would say. She liked to laugh. Even as a child, she was always laughing at something."

She suddenly darted out of the chair and came back with a photo album, handing it to Eve. Pictures of Libby Cinder, from a baby to adulthood graced the pages. Eve's heart pinched as she saw the woman was right. The girl in the photographs was always smiling and laughing.

"She was a lovely young woman," Oliver said.

"She used to write us every week," said Mrs. Cinder. She added in a ragged tone, "Mr. Clarke, you must find out who did this. You must!"

"The police will do just that, ma'am. That I promise you."

Eve felt warmed by his assurance. Mrs. Cinder smiled for the first time since they had entered the house.

CHAPTER 12

"**Y**ou can help us a great deal by answering some questions," Oliver said after a few moments of silence. "But we can come back —"

"No, no," the woman insisted. "I'm sorry for the way I acted before. It's just such a shock to have your suspicions confirmed." She held her hand to her face. "I didn't want to tell Thomas about the newspaper. He's not been well, you see. So I didn't show him the paper."

Oliver took a place on the couch. "We understand Libby recently came back to town."

Mrs. Cinder nodded. "She's been living with my husband's sister since she was eight years old. She wanted to be a teacher ever since she could speak." She smiled faintly. "We didn't have the money to send her to school, so Teresa offered to take her in. She's alone, and her husband left her a comfortable income, so she was happy to pay for Libby's schooling and teacher's seminary."

"It gave her the opportunity to fulfill her dream," Eve said quietly.

"We did what we had to do. I won't deny we missed her terribly, of course. Especially Thomas." Her eyes lifted toward the stairway. "I can't think what this is going to do to him now. He was devoted to Libby."

"And yet, we understand Libby felt trapped in her work," Oliver said.

"I wouldn't say that, Mr. Clarke," said Mrs. Cinder. "I think girls have certain notions of what they'd like to be when they grow up and the reality is often much harsher than their dream."

"That's true," Eve admitted. She thought of Helena, who had always spoken of becoming a doctor and of the way Fieldstone College had made her, the only woman in the class, feel like an intruder.

"So she intended to escape the harsh reality by marrying," Oliver said.

The woman stared at him. "How did you know that?"

"Florence told us," Eve said.

"Did you know, Mrs. Cinder?" Oliver asked.

"Yes." She smiled a little. "She told me on Friday morning."

"The Friday she was killed," Eve said.

"Of course she had to put most of her salary aside, like the state required her to," said Mrs. Cinder. "But she always intended it for something else."

"Her trousseau," Eve guessed.

"So she knew she was going to marry August long before he asked her," Oliver said slowly.

The woman eyed him. "I see Florence has informed you well, Mr. Clarke. Yes, I think she did."

"Florence told us they'd had some kind of quarrel a month or so ago."

Mrs. Cinder twisted the damp handkerchief in her wrinkled hands. She tied it into a knot and then untied it. "I don't think it was a quarrel exactly. It was more of a serious discussion."

"Did your daughter tell you that?" Oliver leaned forward, his face grave.

"Not in so many words," she admitted. "But, well, we had planned on visiting my sister-in-law in the summer but Libby came home one night and insisted we go right away."

"You weren't concerned about that?" he persisted.

"Why should I be?" She glared at him. "Libby could take care of herself."

"Yes, of course," he said softly. "I'm sorry."

The woman gave a meaningful look. "Schoolteachers aren't all sugar water, Mr. Clarke."

"So we've been made to understand," he said dryly. "Do you have any idea what the serious discussion was about?"

"Their future, I suppose," she said.

"You mean their engagement?" Eve asked.

"That and his future," said Mrs. Cinder.

"Why his future?" asked Oliver.

"Well, she told me on the train to Reno she had made a new man out of August."

"A new man," Eve echoed.

"What did she mean by that?" Oliver asked.

"She never explained and I didn't ask." There was another silence as she tied the handkerchief in a knot again. "I suppose it had something to do with August's past. He was engaged to another young lady two years ago but broke off the engagement and ran away to sea. You remember, don't you, Eve?"

"He was engaged to Cecilia Feather." Eve nodded.

"Not very admirable behavior," Oliver remarked.

"He came back rather more grown up than he left," said Mrs. Cinder.

"That was your impression of him?" the district attorney asked.

"I never met him formally," she said. "I see him in town now and then, of course."

"A rather clandestine romance," Oliver muttered.

"You don't understand, Mr. Clarke," the woman insisted. "If

there would have been a breath of their engagement, it would have ruined both of them."

"Schoolteachers aren't supposed to get married," Eve agreed.

"And there was August's mother to contend with," Mrs. Cinder said.

"A formidable woman, so I'm told," Oliver said with a side grin.

"Not really formidable," Eve said. "Just socially ambitious."

He nodded. "And you believed he was sincere in his love for your daughter?"

"I had no reason not to." Her tone was a little defensive. "August has always been a good boy. A good man, I should say."

"Did your husband know Libby and August were engaged?" Oliver asked.

Mrs. Cinder shook her head. "Libby asked me not to tell him until it was announced."

"And she expected that to be soon?" Eve inquired.

"Oh, very soon." The woman untied the knot in the handkerchief.

Eve felt Oliver was studying Mrs. Cinder, his eyes half closed. She wondered if he was going to bring up the fact that Libby was with child, but instead, he asked, "Do you know what your daughter was doing by the river that night?"

"She was asked to meet August there," said the woman.

Oliver looked surprised. "That's a strange way of putting it."

"She received a phone call asking her to go down to the river to the place where she and August used to meet," said the woman.

"But the phone call wasn't from August?" Eve guessed.

Mrs. Cinder shook her head. "Libby said it was Cecilia who called."

"You mean she was doing her former fiancé a favor by calling his current fiancé to meet him down by the river?" Oliver stared. "An odd proposition, I must say."

"I thought it was odd at the time too," Mrs. Cinder confessed.

"They remain friends in spite of what happened," Eve supplied.

"Cecilia is a very sweet-natured girl," Mrs. Cinder said. "We all like her."

"But to the point where August would ask her to call his fiancée?" Oliver lamented. "That's taking agreeableness a little too far, don't you think?"

"It wasn't the first time, Mr. Clarke," said Mrs. Cinder. "As I said before, they had to be discreet. Cecilia sometimes called to let Libby know August would be waiting for her at a certain place at a certain time."

"So you think he might have asked Cecilia to make the call for him on Friday to ask Libby to meet him by the river?" asked Oliver.

"That's what Libby thought," said the woman.

"And what did you think?" Eve eyed her.

She hesitated. "I was the one who answered the phone when it rang. I'm certain it was Cecilia."

Eve leaned forward. "Mrs. Cinder, when did the phone call come in?"

"Around nine o'clock, I should say. The clock in the hallway had just struck."

"Isn't that rather late for a meeting?" Oliver asked.

She gave a small smile. "As I said, Mr. Clarke, they had to be very careful."

"Did they often meet by the river?" Oliver asked. "I wouldn't imagine the river a comfortable place to be at that time of night."

"August goes night fishing," said the woman. "Libby would join him sometimes." She gave a small laugh, though it sounded like a croak. "She would be so proud when she caught a trout. She would always insist on making a grand dish of it, you know, with butter and cream and all that. She'd present it to her father like a feast." The voice turned choking as she buried her face in her handkerchief again.

Oliver patted her arm. "Your daughter had no other reason for going down to the river?"

"None," the woman insisted.

"Mrs. Cinder, you understand we have to bring certain things up when we're investigating such a crime." He looked down at his hands. "We try to keep whatever we can out of the newspapers. Certain private matters, for example."

"Private matters?" Mrs. Cinder blinked. "You mean Libby's engagement?"

"No, ma'am, not the engagement." He was still looking down at his hands.

Eve realized he was looking for a way to break the news of Libby's pregnancy. She said in a kind tone as she took the woman's hand, "What Oliver is trying to say, Mrs. Cinder, is that Libby was with child." Oliver shot her a look of gratitude.

Mrs. Cinder sank back into the cushions as if she had been thrown from a train. The hollows of her cheeks revealed the skeletal bone structure underneath. "You mean she was going to have a baby?"

Oliver nodded slowly. "There's no doubt. The doctor confirmed it."

"Doctor?"

"Dr. Myers." Oliver coughed. "The county medical examiner."

"Her clothes had been let out," Eve added. "My sister and I examined them at Oliver's request."

Mrs. Cinder said nothing for a time as a pair of birds fought outside the window, their bickering calls echoing in the room. For a crazy moment, Eve felt like jumping up and shutting the window with a loud bang. But she remained sitting, her hands between her knees.

"I'm sorry we had to be the ones to tell you," Oliver said.

"So that's why she insisted on seeing Dr. Martin," Mrs. Cinder murmured.

"Dr. Martin?" He leaned forward, his eyes keen.

"When we were in Reno," Mrs. Cinder said. "She hadn't been feeling well and she refused to go to the doctor here. She said she wanted to see her old doctor in Reno. I thought it odd at the time."

"So you think she may have suspected she was going to have a child?" Oliver asked.

The woman collected herself. "Libby was a very practical woman and, as I said, she was very good to us. If she had gone to her doctor here, it would have gotten around town and she didn't want to disgrace us."

"But she was getting married," Eve offered.

"You know how people in this town can be about things like that, Eve."

Oliver nodded. "If there's one thing I learned about small towns, it's that they revel in the latest gossip and then verify the truth later."

"I should have known Libby was pregnant." Mrs. Cinder rubbed her eyes with the handkerchief. "For God's sake, I should have known!"

"Mothers can't know everything," Oliver said. "She was a grown woman, Mrs. Cinder."

Her eyes suddenly turned hard like marbles. "That means whoever did this didn't just kill one person. They killed two."

Eve let out a small breath, as she hadn't thought of it that way. She could see Oliver was affected also, as his features set with resolve.

He took out a pad and pencil from the inside pocket of his coat. "Will you please write down Dr. Martin's address for us, Mrs. Cinder? There are some things we need to confirm that he might know."

Eve's heart went out to the woman as she watched the shaking hand write down the information. "Florence told us Libby always wanted a family. She was getting what she wanted at last."

"Do you think she told August about the baby?" Oliver asked.

Mrs. Cinder dabbed at her eyes. "I really don't know, Mr. Clarke. She might have told him that night, I suppose."

"You said Libby claimed to make a new man out of August," the district attorney said. "Do you think this is what she meant?"

The woman looked at him. "What do you mean?"

"Men change their plans when they get that sort of news," he said.

"I don't know what you mean by 'changing plans.'" The woman stiffened. "Since Libby was already engaged, I don't think it would matter to him if she was already with child."

"We don't have real proof she was engaged," Oliver pointed out. "She told you and Florence she was, but —"

Mrs. Cinder stiffened. "My daughter was not a fanciful woman, Mr. Clarke. You don't think she would have told me she was engaged without having a ring, do you?"

"She had a ring?" Oliver glanced at Eve.

Mrs. Cinder nodded. "She was so happy on Friday because she said she could wear it openly, as there was no need to hide it anymore."

"She had no rings when the police found her," Eve said quietly.

The woman stared at her. "Oh, but she must have. You said you and Helena inspected her clothes, so you must have seen her jewelry too."

"We found no rings," Eve repeated.

"Well, perhaps she left it in her room," Oliver suggested. "I'd like to send the sheriff over to look for it later, if you don't mind."

"If she was meeting August at nine o'clock on Friday, wouldn't she have been wearing it?" Eve lamented. "It was dark, and they were meeting in a private place. No one would have seen it except the man who had given it to her."

"Well, she had a ring," the woman insisted.

"You saw it, then," Oliver said.

The woman looked uncomfortable. "Well, no. Libby didn't show it to me. But she told me about it."

"And you didn't see it at any time?"

Mrs. Cinder glanced at him. "I didn't go prying into my daughter's things, Mr. Clarke." In a steadier tone, she said, "She had a ring. I know she did. Otherwise, she wouldn't have told me about it."

"She may have had one," Oliver said slowly, "but that doesn't mean it would have been used."

"What do you mean?" Mrs. Cinder stared at him.

"Sometimes men give women things they don't intend for them to keep."

The woman's face turned pale. "I see what you're getting at. You think August proposed to her, gave her a ring to keep her silent, and then — I don't believe it!" Her voice turned shrill, and there was a small knocking sound from the second floor.

"Be careful, Mrs. Cinder." Oliver lowered his voice. "You don't want your husband to hear, do you?"

She let out a sigh. "No, I suppose not. But what you say isn't true, Mr. Clarke."

"I hope it isn't, ma'am," he said. "But sometimes young men do desperate things when they feel trapped."

Mrs. Cinder turned to Eve. "You don't believe August would have done such a horrible thing, do you?"

Torn between the two, Eve's hands grew damp. "I don't know the young man very well," she said with caution. "But I wouldn't have thought so."

"I'm sure August intended to keep his promise." Her tone was unyielding. "He wanted her to leave her teaching position as soon as possible so they could announce it."

"Is that what Libby told you?" Oliver glanced at her.

"Well, not in so many words, but that's the impression I got."

"Then why didn't she leave her job?" he asked.

She gave a wry smile. "I told you, Mr. Clarke, Libby was a

very practical person. She didn't think it wise to leave before the end of the school year. The money would have helped them as a young couple."

"Mrs. Cinder, are you willing to take a look at that photograph again?" Oliver asked.

"Certainly." The woman picked it up from the edge of the coffee table where she had placed it.

"Will you please take a look at your daughter's coat again?"

The woman scrutinized the photograph. "Oh, God! It's completely torn!" She covered her mouth with her hand.

Oliver said in a smooth voice, "Nothing like that. The doctor is sure of it."

"She wasn't attacked in that way, Mrs. Cinder," Eve added.

The woman's face calmed. "Then why —"

"We think she might have been wearing some sort of brooch," said Oliver. "Do you remember if she was wearing anything like that when she went out on Friday night?"

The woman glanced at the window as if it were a mirror reflecting the scene. "Why, yes, now that you mention it. She was wearing a pin August had given her."

"It must have been a rather large pin," Eve reflected.

"It was," said Mrs. Cinder. "He had it made especially for her."

"What was it?" Oliver asked.

"A redbud tree."

"Redbud Manor," Eve murmured. "The Winters' home." She looked at Oliver. "It was built by August's great-grandfather."

"You see now August wouldn't have done what you think he did," Mrs. Cinder said. "He had that pin made for her because he saw her as the future mistress of Redbud Manor. He told her that."

"Do you have any idea why it might have been taken, Mrs. Cinder?" Oliver asked.

She looked startled. "Well, isn't that obvious?"

"Obvious, ma'am?"

"It had diamonds in it," she said. "Pink diamonds, really. One on each branch of the tree. Twelve in all." A small smile appeared on her face. "Libby counted them once."

Oliver glanced at Eve. "You think the pin was stolen because it had value."

"Why else would it have been taken?"

Oliver closed the leather notepad. "Thank you, ma'am. I'll send the police over to look for the ring. Shall I send Dr. Myers to examine Mr. Cinder? Make sure he's all right?"

"He's — well, he's rather expensive." Mrs. Cinder said this with a great deal of embarrassment.

"Don't you worry about that, Mrs. Cinder," Oliver assured her.

"You're very kind, Mr. Clarke." The woman's lips relaxed into a genuine smile for the first time. She shook Eve's hand "I expect I'll be seeing you again, Miss Grave."

"Under more cheerful circumstances, I hope," Eve said kindly.

"I meant for the funeral arrangements." She paused as if trying to regain her dignity.

"I'll send word to you and Eve when I release the — when I release Libby for burial." Oliver pulled his hat a little over his right eye.

The woman said softly, "I didn't think of that. Dr. Myers didn't —"

"We had to do an autopsy," said Oliver gently. "We always do in these cases, Mrs. Cinder."

"But he didn't — well, cut her up, did he?" Before the answer came, she turned away and closed the door.

As they headed for Oliver's car, loud sobs erupted from the other side of the door.

CHAPTER 13

"Such a sad little pair," Eve sighed as they sped down the street.

"One of those couples who put everything into their daughter's future," Oliver agreed. "The old man was like a child when I put him to bed."

"Mrs. Cinder took it well, though." Eve waved to Dot, who was stepping outside the library as they passed.

"Took what well?" Oliver asked. "The news that her daughter was dead, or that she was going to have a child?"

"Both, I guess." Eve shrugged. "It was so much to take in."

"It's always worse when the victim keeps things from the family," he agreed.

"Maybe Libby just didn't have a chance to tell her mother."

"More likely she wanted to make sure August would do the right thing," Oliver said. "Having a child out of wedlock is a difficult thing for a young woman."

They were both quiet for a moment as they passed the Gyver Bank and Trust. "Oliver," Eve hedged, "do you really think a young man would give a woman an engagement ring and

126

encourage her to leave her job without carrying through his intentions?"

"I've seen it happen before."

"You don't know August," she said.

"Neither do you," he countered. "I don't suppose you tend to many Falcon Hill society funerals." He lowered his voice. "I'm sorry. That was a cruel thing to say."

"Not at all," Eve said. "It's true. The Falcon Hill set are very exclusive."

"As exclusive as small-town society can get," he said ruefully. "They don't hold a candle to Nob Hill."

"He wasn't the type of young man you're probably used to seeing in Nob Hill, Oliver," Eve protested. "He loved the sea since he was a child. Why, when a friend of Mr. Friske's who had been a fishing boat captain came to visit, August plied him with questions to no end."

"How would you know that?" He looked amused as he turned the corner.

"Vi, of course," she said. "Don't forget, Mr. Friske is Sudie's companion."

He laughed. "And you think a love of the sea makes August Winters a useful member of society?"

"More useful than his father was," Eve said in a harsh tone. "Mr. Winters wouldn't do anything for anyone unless it gave him more clout."

"One of those." Oliver rolled his eyes.

"He died well before you came to Gyver, of course," said Eve.

"And Rosalia Winters?" he asked. "I got the impression she was the clinging mama type."

"No, not really," Eve said, glancing out the window. "But she's very determined August should follow in his father's footsteps."

"In other words, she wants him to be a pillar of society," Oliver said. "And what does *he* want?"

"I don't think he knows," Eve said softly.

"A schoolteacher with no social background and expecting a child wouldn't exactly win the admiration of Falcon Hill or anyone else."

"So you think he set out to get rid of both!"

"I only say it's possible, Eve."

"Sheriff Warner will think it more probable than you do," Eve said softly. "Especially when he discovers Libby had an engagement ring she wasn't wearing."

Oliver pulled the car into a parking space outside the county offices. "We won't know until we question the young man." He got out of the car and opened the door for her.

"Strange about the jewelry, isn't it?" she mused as she took his arm. "First, there's no engagement ring, and then, her pin is stolen."

"Maybe the ring was taken too," he said as they entered the building. "We'll get a description of it from August when we question him, as well as where he bought it so we can start a search for it."

"But why would the killer have stolen the pin — and possibly the ring — and leave the bracelet and necklace?" Eve questioned.

"Perhaps when we find that out, we'll find out who did it," Oliver said with a chuckle.

"You think there was a reason, then?" The elevator operator opened the doors for them, bowing at Oliver.

"A man — or woman — who commits a brutal murder rarely stops to steal unless there's a reason," he said. "In my experience, anyway."

"Your experience is good enough for me," Eve said with a smile. "It ought to be good enough for the county too."

They were greeted by the sound of pounding keys as Miss Hunt sat typing furiously at the Remington. Lee Lambert, a clerk and researcher, glanced at her, his young face twisted with distaste.

"Mr. Clarke, I wish you hadn't sprung for that thing." He

pointed at the busy secretary. "Sounds like a bunch of wood-peckers are eating up the place."

Oliver's hearty laugh made Miss Hunt look up inquiringly. "Deputy Sheriff Elwood is waiting for you in your office, sir."

"Thank you, Gladys." He leaned a little over her desk. "And would you please spare Lee's eardrums with that thing for a little while?"

"It won't do him any harm to see someone doing an honest day's work," she snapped. "He's been looking at the racing form in the paper all day."

"I swear, Mr. Clarke —" The boy's hand flew to his heart.

"Don't go spending your money on long shots when your mother and sisters need bread and milk, Lee," Eve scolded. She knew the young man, a playmate of Violet's as a child, sometimes got reckless ideas.

"No, ma'am — I mean miss." His hand remained on his heart. "Say, is Violet going to the boat race on Sunday?"

"You won't be bothering Miss Grave about the races, son." Oliver hung up his coat and hat. "You'll be working here finishing up the Simmons' case file."

"Aw, gee, Mr. Clarke, Sunday!"

"Aw, gee, Sunday," Oliver said with a grin.

"You keep harping on making something of yourself," Miss Hunt said without looking up from her typing. "So far all you've done is make a nuisance of yourself!"

Eve and Oliver both laughed as they went into the inner office, closing the door to echoes of the young people's bickering.

The deputy sheriff shook Oliver's hand and greeted Eve with a smile. "I got the information you asked for, Mr. Clarke."

Eve glanced at Oliver.

"I asked the deputy to update me on a few things." The district attorney pulled out a chair for Eve and sat down behind his desk.

"Good thing you did," said Deputy Elwood. "The sheriff's still hopping mad you didn't let him do the school interviews."

"He'll just have to adjust to my way of doing things, won't he?" Oliver said sharply.

"That's the truth, Mr. Clarke," Deputy Elwood said. "I don't mean any disrespect to Zak, but he wasn't the most organized fellow in the world."

"Did Principal Watts and Florence come down to make their statements?"

"Yes, sir," said the young man. "That's why he's mad. It was a big break, and he wanted to be in on it."

"Eyeing my job already, eh?" Oliver raised an eyebrow. "No surprise there. He's always bragging how he and Jim Long have been playing golf together since he was in long pants."

"Not quite that long, sir." Deputy Elwood chuckled. Then, in a more serious tone, he added, "But if you don't mind my saying so, maybe you'd better watch out."

Oliver gave him a hard look. "I'll remember that, Deputy. By the way, did the sheriff get any word about the brooch?"

"We couldn't find any jeweler in the area that sold a brooch that size within the last year," the deputy said. "Might have been bought way before that, or somebody bought it in one of the cities, the sheriff reckons."

"The sheriff probably reckons right." Oliver played with a paperweight shaped like a terrier on his desk. "Anything else?"

Deputy Elwood glanced down at his notes. "Mrs. Woods told us the young lady had been in her store Friday morning to discuss the possibility of a trousseau."

Oliver looked at Eve. "I suppose that's no surprise now."

Eve nodded. "She probably went straight from La Belle Fille to the clothing emporium."

"New clothes and makeup," Deputy Elwood mused. "Guess she didn't plan on being a teacher for much longer."

"Go on, Deputy." Oliver leaned back in his chair, resting his feet on the desk.

"Well, sir, I went to Reno to see Dr. Martin," he reported. "He was positive Miss Cinder was twelve to fourteen weeks — with child." He glanced at Eve.

"It's alright, Deputy," Eve said with a small smile. "We knew about it well before you did."

"I see," Oliver said slowly.

"He said Miss Cinder didn't act like most young ladies in her position."

The district attorney lurched forward. "How do you mean?"

"Well, sir, he said most young girls who come to him in such a state — unmarried and with child, I mean — are very distraught. He said Libby practically floated out of the office."

"She was elated?" Eve asked.

"Something like that, Miss Grave," he said. "She even thanked him and said, 'This will change everything.'"

"Did she say what she meant?" Oliver asked.

Deputy Elwood shrugged. "No, but since we know she was engaged, wouldn't that be the reason?"

"Is that your guess or the sheriff's?" Oliver eyed him.

"Sheriff Warner's, sir."

"That remains to be seen." Oliver rose. "The sheriff in his office now?"

The deputy glanced at his watch. "He should be back from lunch, sir."

"Then we can have a nice long chat," Oliver said with a grimace. "Maybe I can get him to calm down."

"If you please, Mr. Clarke, there's more."

"Oh?" Oliver sat down again.

"I took the liberty of seeing Miss Gilbert."

"Miss Cinder's aunt?"

The deputy nodded. "I thought since I was already in town —"

"Good thinking." Oliver smiled.

"She told me Libby didn't go out very often, but she did sometimes meet up with friends for a picnic or a dance and such," he said. "They're not so strict with schoolteachers there."

"Just what Florence told us," Eve murmured.

"She wasn't wild, though," he said quickly. "She wasn't that kind. Just liked to get out for a breath of fresh air once in a while is how her aunt put it."

"As any young woman her age would," Eve said firmly.

"Her friends say the same thing," he said.

"Friends?"

"Yes, sir." He looked down at his notes. "I also took the liberty of getting a few names from Miss Gilbert — both women and men. All good people from good families, steady jobs, that sort of thing."

"Then you think they're trustworthy," Oliver surmised.

"If you want my opinion, sir, I think they are." Deputy Elwood closed his notebook. "I've only been deputy sheriff for a few years but Sheriff Warner's sent me on lots of interviews, and I think I can tell a good seed from a bad one."

"I don't doubt it, Deputy," Oliver said kindly as he rose and helped Eve into her coat. "Thanks for coming with me, Eve. You helped a lot. I don't think I would have gotten much out of Mrs. Cinder if you hadn't been there to comfort her."

Eve gave a shy smile. "I didn't do much, really."

"I'll ask Dr. Myers to get the autopsy report to Mr. Peterson to release the body," he said.

She sighed. "It's awful to have to bury your own child. You don't expect to have to do that."

"I'm sure you've seen it in your work, Miss Grave," Deputy Elwood offered.

"That doesn't make it any easier, Deputy," she said.

CHAPTER 14

$\mathcal{A}$ few days later, Agnes brought the morning paper to the breakfast table, laying it on Felix's empty chair with a grunt.

"I wonder what's in the paper that's upset her so much." Helena spread just the right amount of honey on her buttered toast.

"She gets huffy when they talk about the price of chicken going up," Violet said, languishing in a thin robe that barely concealed her chemise.

"I do wish you would come down to the table fully dressed, Vi," Eve said as she unfolded the paper. "These mornings are chilly."

"We're in California, aren't we?" her sister protested. "Where the sun always shines?"

"We're closer to Nevada, where it gets cold in the winter," Helena said.

"Are you going to quote us the exact temperature differences down to the last millidegree?"

"There is no such thing as a millidegree," Helena snorted. But she was looking at her older sister, whose face had grown a little pale.

Eve handed her the paper. "The police released the identity of the dead girl."

"So now everyone knows it was Libby Cinder," Helena said quietly.

"Libby Cinder!" Violet almost dropped her cup. "You mean she really was a schoolteacher?"

"She taught at Brookline, just like you said." Eve petted her head. "Oliver is grateful you gave him the lead."

"I didn't give him anything," Violet snorted. "You did."

Eve felt a wave of warmth in her gut as she ate the last of the bacon on her plate.

"They didn't print the young man's name at least," Helena observed as she scanned the paper.

"What young man?" Violet asked.

"'Miss Cinder was perhaps not the kindly schoolmarm Gyver County would have wished,'" Helena read. "'Rumors were going around last spring about her wild times in Reno, and there was speculation she may have been involved with one of the town's finest young men.'"

"What nonsense!" Eve exploded.

"I think it's fascinating." Violet showed some attention at last, leaning with her elbows on the table and her chin in both her hands. "Schoolteacher leads a double life as a vamp and gets killed by a local yokel."

"You sound like a window card," Helena said dryly.

"It's better than the moving pictures because it's real," Violet said.

"Miss Violet Grave, I'd be obliged if you would get your dirty elbows off my table!" This thundering reprimand came from Agnes, who entered with the mail.

"It's not *your* table, and my elbows aren't dirty!" Violet

growled, though she obeyed, just as she always did when Agnes gave a command.

"Oh, no? You're always putting some goo on 'em before you go to bed, aren't you?"

"It's not goo," Violet protested. "It's moisturizing cream so they don't look old and ugly before their time."

"You're eighteen," Helena said. "What fear could you possibly have about dry skin at your age?"

"Well, you just never know," Violet said with a pout. But the pout didn't last long as, when Agnes departed, her eyes sparkled again. "I wonder who the 'fine young man' is."

"They probably don't know." Eve guessed Oliver kept back August's name when he updated the Shane boys on the case.

"They're fishing," Helena agreed.

"They probably think he'll just show up at the newspaper office one day and reveal himself." Violet looked amused as she scooped out more blackberry jam. "They think everybody wants to be in the papers."

"Don't go finishing the pot now." Agnes sniffed as she removed the jam. "You ain't too young to put some weight on you."

"Weight!" Violet shrieked and Agnes toddled back to the kitchen, laughing in her folksy way. "Say, Eve, how old was Libby?"

"I'm not sure," Eve said.

"You've been prancing around town with Oliver asking questions, haven't you?" Violet asked. "You must have an idea."

"Twenty-four, twenty-five," Helena guessed. "I think she was a few years behind me."

"Then it probably wouldn't be Tim Hill or Bill Close." Violet put her chin in her hand. "They're younger."

Helena peered at her. "I thought it was fashionable these days for older women to go about with younger men."

"You can hardly talk about what's fashionable," Violet snorted.

"It wouldn't be either of the Beaton boys either. Old Clem would beat them to a pulp with her riding crop if she found out either of them were mixed up with a schoolteacher."

"Really, Vi." Eve shuddered. "The way you talk!" She went through the mail, handing her sisters those addressed to them. At the bottom of the tray was a folded sheet of paper with the Gyver County Courthouse address.

"You being arrested, Eve?" Violet asked with lazy amusement as she pressed a cigarette inside a holder Kitty had given her for her last birthday.

"You shouldn't smoke those things," Helena chided. "They're bad for your health."

"Who says?" her sister snapped.

"The *Medical World Review*," her older sister shot back.

"Oh, bunk!" Violet said. "I suppose it could have been Pedro Loy. The whole Falcon Hill social set never sat well with him, and he's just the kind to show them up by getting mixed up with a teacher."

"He's a nice kid," Helena insisted.

"Oh, I'm not holding it against him," Violet insisted. "I think he's the bee's knees. We see him sometimes at Sudie's. He's got plenty to say against all of those snoots but most of it is in Spanish!" She giggled. "Personally, my bet's on Mike Hill."

"His mother's practically a slave to Mrs. Beaton's social prompts," Helena remarked.

"True, but deep down, I think Edith Hill is dying to shock Old Clem down to her petticoats."

Eve was staring out the window, though she saw nothing but the line of blue and green from the sky and lawn outside. "It's not Pedro or Mike."

"Oh?" Helena glanced at her.

"You know who he is?" Violet leaned forward with eager eyes. "Oh, do tell, Eve!"

"If she does, it's not for you to repeat to anyone," Helena

snapped. "This isn't a joke, Vi. If the papers didn't say anything, that means the police didn't, and if the police are keeping it quiet, they're doing it for a reason."

"I know that," Violet snapped. "I'm no Telling Tillie."

"Florence and Mrs. Cinder told us Libby was engaged to August Winters."

"Applesauce!" Even Violet seemed taken aback as she leaned against the chair. "Well, she caught herself the ripest plum on the tree, didn't she?"

"Don't be vulgar, Vi," Eve snapped. "You can't breathe a word of this to anyone, not even Kitty."

Violet patted her hand. "Don't worry, Eve. I won't say one word. I promise. And I always keep my promises to you, don't I?"

Eve pressed her cheek to her sister's. "Of course you do, darling."

"I'll even spring for bail when they haul you into jail," her sister joked, nodding at the note.

"I hate to disappoint you, Vi, but this isn't an arrest notice," she said dryly, looking at Helena. "It's from Oliver. They've released Libby's body for burial."

"It's what the Cinders have been waiting for, isn't it?" Helena asked.

"Still, it's a terrible thing!" Eve sighed.

"Well, darling, when your time is up, it's up." Violet took another puff from the cigarette, filling the dining room with smoke. Agnes, who had just come in to take away the platters, wrinkled her nose.

"Vi, will you please put that filthy thing out?" Eve shoved an ashtray at her.

Violet made a face but stubbed out the cigarette. "Looks like you two have a call to make, then."

"And what about you?" Helena poured another cup of coffee. "What about this job you told us about yesterday?"

"What about it?" Violet asked. "They hired three other girls."

"I thought you said the factory was looking for ten girls," Eve said.

"That was just a ruse." Violet waved her away. "They put in an ad for ten when they have three positions open and get thirty girls coming. Then they have the pick of the lot."

"Oh, well, don't worry, honey, you'll get something." Eve finished the last of the toast.

"If she steps out the door once in a while and stops getting in my hair, she will," Agnes declared.

"Oh, you old hen, I'm not doing anything of the kind!" Violet snapped.

"Don't call Agnes an old hen," Helena chided. "She's saved your hide more than once."

"Stop acting like a petulant child, Vi," Eve said.

Her sister pondered this for a moment. She changed her tone, putting the packet of cigarettes in her robe pocket. "I'm sorry, Agnes. I didn't mean what I said."

Agnes chucked her under the chin. "Wouldn't give you two cents for a girl who can't give a little lip now and then." She turned to Eve. "Mrs. Cinder just phoned. She asked you to come to her house this morning."

Eve nodded and rose. "Oliver must have sent her word too. I can't help but feel like it's — I don't know, disrespectful."

"Why, because her daughter was murdered instead of dying a natural death?" Violet cocked her head. "Aren't you the one who's always saying it's better to help the bereaved sooner rather than later to ease their confusion and grief?"

"Vi's right, Eve," said Helena. "How Libby died doesn't change the duty we have to see to it that her daughter gets a decent burial with as little fuss to her and her husband as possible."

"No, I suppose it doesn't." Eve felt better at once and pressed her younger sister's shoulder. "You've always been the voice of reason, Helena dear."

"Like a well-oiled motor," Violet said with a grin.

"You know far too much about motors," her sister teased.

"Vi, I do wish you'd come with us," Eve said. "The business is one-third yours, remember."

"And listen to the wailing and heaving while you discuss coffins and graves?" Her younger sister shuddered. "No, thank you."

"I suppose you'd rather wait tables at the Buckeye Steakhouse and dodge George Griffin's pinching fingers," Helena remarked.

"Darling, that's what hatpins are for," said her sister.

"What have hatpins to do with it?"

"So you can poke a man if he tries anything fresh." Violet dug into her robe pocket and produced a long hatpin with a pearl tip. "Never without it."

Both her sisters burst out laughing.

~~~~~

The atmosphere at the Cinder house struck Eve as morose. There was a grayness to the curtains and the dust on the furniture. Mrs. Cinder admitted them with a wan smile. "Thank you for coming so soon."

"We're terribly sorry about all this, Mrs. Cinder," Eve said with remorse.

"We'll try to make it as painless as possible," Helena said.

"I know you will," said the woman.

"We'll need your signature on these papers to make the arrangements." Helena took some sheets of paper out of her leather case.

Mrs. Cinder led them into the living room. "This is Libby's aunt, Teresa Gilbert."

At first, Eve saw nothing, but then there was a stir near the window where the curtains were three-quarters of the way drawn, and a woman with prickly features came toward them.

"How d'you do?" Miss Gilbert's soft voice contrasted with her rather stern countenance. Eve's heart pinched as she realized this woman was the aunt Libby had lived with in Reno.
~~~~~

"Miss Grave and Mrs. Wright own the funeral home in town," Mrs. Cinder supplied. "Miss Grave is helping with the investigation."

"Oh, no, not really," Eve said quickly, feeling her sister's sharp eyes on her. "Since Helena and I know everyone in town, Oliver asked for our help when they found Libby —" She bit her lip.

"They didn't know who she was," Mrs. Cinder said to her sister-in-law.

"Didn't know?" the woman echoed.

"Remember Libby was away for so many years," said Mrs. Cinder. "She just came back six months ago."

"From a child to a woman," Libby's aunt murmured. "A lady, I should say."

"We were planning on paying a visit," Helena supplied. "We'd heard she was back in town."

"I'm glad you're both here," Mrs. Cinder said kindly. "I know you'll do right by Libby." Her eyes filled with tears, and she reached for her handkerchief. Miss Gilbert bit her lip and turned away.

"It will be easier once we get things in order," Helena assured her. "There's a lot to decide, you know." Her manner became business-like.

"Yes, I expect so," said Mrs. Cinder.

"And your husband?"

"He won't be joining us," she said in a firm tone. "He's indisposed."

"I see." Helena glanced at her sister. They had both seen it happen often enough — one family member always seemed the most practical while the others had varying degrees of confusion and denial.

"He's better, I hope?" Eve asked.

"He's calm," said Mrs. Cinder. "That's about the best we can hope for. He'll be at the funeral, of course."

"I don't know as that's a good idea, Gertrude," her sister-in-law said. "The doctor said —"

"It would be better if he could attend," Eve said gently. "So many fathers with their daughters — but the moment they see all is well, and their souls are at peace, they're at peace as well."

"It's not fair to deprive him of his daughter's burial," Helena added.

"I suppose you know these things," said Miss Gilbert, though she hardly sounded convinced. "Oh, can't we get on with it?"

They went through their usual pattern of discussing coffins, headstones, and memorial service arrangements.

"Have you a chosen a gravesite already?" Helena asked.

"Well, I don't know." Mrs. Cinder pressed her hands together. "Thomas's parents and brother are buried at Gyver Cemetery."

"Why would we think about such a thing?" Miss Gilbert interrupted, her face sour. "Who expects a twenty-three-year-old child to die so suddenly?"

"She wasn't a child, Miss Gilbert," Helena reminded her. "She was a woman. A lady, as you said."

She buried her face in her handkerchief. "And now they're going to blame that poor young man, just as you say, Gertrude."

"Poor young man?" Eve stopped shuffling photographs of coffins they had gotten from Jack Garfield, the casket maker in Gyver.

"August Winters," said Mrs. Cinder. "They think he killed Libby!"

"Who says so?" Helena asked.

"Sheriff Warner," said the woman. "He and Deputy Elwood were here this morning."

"They told you they thought August was the killer?" Eve stared at her.

"Well, not in so many words," Mrs. Cinder admitted.

"But they asked an awful lot of questions," Miss Gilbert said. "Mean questions."

"Sheriff Warner isn't exactly a delicate man," Eve said gently.

"He's downright boorish sometimes," Helena agreed.

"What did they want to know, Mrs. Cinder?" Eve put the coffin photographs on the table. Miss Gilbert flinched.

"They asked me a lot of questions about Libby and August," said the woman. "Where they met, how often they met, what they did, did he ever come to the house, things like that."

"The whole idea is ridiculous," scoffed her sister-in-law.

"How *did* they meet?" Eve asked, her chin in her hand.

Mrs. Cinder almost smiled. "You mean how did a poor schoolteacher meet one of the most eligible young bachelors in Gyver?"

"I didn't mean that." Eve blushed.

"It is puzzling," Helena said in her sister's defense.

Mrs. Cinder leaned back. "It is a strange story, really. Libby told me they had a lot in common."

"Indeed?" Even her sister-in-law looked surprised.

"You know how she felt about the teaching profession, dear," said Mrs. Cinder. "And she told me August felt the same way about — well, his mother's plans for him."

"I imagine Rosalia wanted him to pick up where he left off before he went to sea," Helena said.

"That's about right," said the woman. "He even went to the picnic with Cecilia."

"Picnic?" Eve questioned.

"The Valentine's Day picnic last year," Mrs. Cinder said.

"I thought that was only for —" Eve stopped, blushing again.

"You thought it was only for people like Cathy Beaton and her friends." Mrs. Cinder smiled again. "Libby wasn't there to have fun. She was there to work."

"Oh?" Helena questioned.

"She did things like that sometimes when she wanted a little extra money," said the dead woman's mother.

"She used to help with the neighborhood Halloween party and Christmas party in Reno every year," Miss Gilbert echoed.

"Miss Beaton needed a few maids to help serve," said Mrs. Cinder. "She was going all crazy trying to find them. Then she got the idea of going down to the school and seeing if any of the teachers needed a few extra dollars for the weekend."

"How very enterprising of Cathy," Helena said dryly.

"Libby wanted to do it, and she convinced another teacher to join her," said Mrs. Cinder.

"Florence?" Eve asked.

The woman shook her head. "No, someone else. As I said when you came with Mr. Clarke, Eve, Libby was always looking to help other teachers."

"August and Cecilia attended the picnic," Helena guessed.

"She said they made such a fuss over August when he came," the woman mused. "He hadn't been back for more than a week, and I suppose their mothers encouraged them to make him feel welcome."

"Just the sort of thing Mrs. Beaton would do," said Helena.

"August wasn't having any of it, though," said Mrs. Cinder. "He looked — what was it Libby said — like a monkey that had been taken out of the wild and away from its mother." She sighed.

"Not a very flattering picture, I must say." Miss Gilbert sniffed.

"She felt sorry for him," Eve guessed.

"And he felt sorry for her," said Mrs. Cinder. "Those young people with all the money treated her and the other teacher awfully. The other one walked out in the middle of it, saying she didn't care if she didn't get a penny. But Libby stayed."

"Perhaps it would have been better if she hadn't," Helena murmured.

"Why?" Miss Gilbert was indignant. "Because you think he killed her?"

"I wouldn't propose to say that, ma'am," Helena said. Eve

could hear the rationale creep into her tone. "But he did get her pregnant."

"It takes two to make a baby," said the woman in a stoic tone.

Helena smiled. "I'm quite aware of that, Miss Gilbert."

"If anything, the child was a good thing," the woman went on.

"Teresa, really!" Mrs. Cinder blushed.

"It probably gave the young man the push he needed to propose," she said. "Some young men are shy and need a little push."

"That was more like a shove off a cliff," said Helena.

"He's like that, though," said Mrs. Cinder. "He isn't like the rest of those young men on Falcon Hill."

"How do you mean?" asked Eve.

"Libby said they were all waiting for their fathers to turn over their inheritance to them," she said. "They think doing something for your living is for poor people and not worthy of them. But August was different."

"He wants to do something with his life." Helena nodded with approval.

"Both trapped, both lonely, and both with aspirations," Eve lamented. "I can see now why they fell in love."

"And you can see now why he wouldn't have touched a hair on her head," Miss Gilbert said firmly.

"If that's really true, the police will soon see it," Helena promised.

"We're just about through." Eve did a quick sketch of the tombstone and handed it to Mrs. Cinder. "Is this all right?"

"Libby liked Robert Barrett Browning, Gertrude," her sister-in-law reminded her. "Maybe a little something —"

"For the memorial, Teresa," the woman said firmly. "I don't like the idea of something like that on the tomb. Poems are — well, for a life long lived. And Libby was so young!" She buried her face in her handkerchief.

"Don't worry, Mrs. Cinder," Eve said softly. "We'll see her soul to heaven."

"We'll make all the arrangements so you needn't worry about a thing," Helena added in a reassuring tone.

"Thank you," said the woman, rising. "Come upstairs and I'll give you some clothes and things we want to go with her." She glanced at the stairs with a worried look.

"We'll be very quiet," Helena assured her as if she could read the woman's mind. "We won't disturb Mr. Cinder."

They went upstairs, taking slow steps. As Mrs. Cinder went through her daughter's meager closet, handing things to Helena, Eve peeked down the short hallway at the closed door. Something about its chipped wood read finality. She winced at the thought of it.

"There might be other things I think of before tomorrow," Mrs. Cinder said as she came out of the room, her voice a whisper. "If I send them before the funeral, will that be all right?"

"Whenever you're ready," Eve said with a smile.

The woman's face darkened. "The police couldn't find Libby's engagement ring. They were very thorough this morning."

"It will turn up, dear, I'm sure." Miss Gilbert pressed her shoulders.

Both women saw them to the door. Miss Gilbert patted Helena's back. "I'm sorry if I sounded a little crotchety just now, Mrs. Wright. But I knew my niece, and if she believed in August's sincerity, so do I."

"I didn't wish to imply he wasn't sincere," Helena said gently.

But when they started the car and drove toward the funeral home, Helena snorted, "A little push indeed!"

"The sheriff shouldn't have come today," Eve said with a sigh.

"They have their job to do, Eve," said her sister. "I noticed you had a few insinuating questions of your own."

"I was curious," Eve admitted. "I wonder if Oliver knows about the Valentine's Day picnic."

Her sister shrugged. "Why would that matter?"

"It might." Eve was silent for a moment. "If they arrest August, it might."

"No one is arresting him," Helena said.

"All the same, I might drop in to see him when I go down to the coroner's office to pick up the death certificate."

Helena nodded. "Then go to Wesley to order the headstone."

"And to Jack," her sister added. "They've got to have the specifications as soon as possible if they're going to be ready by tomorrow."

As they pulled into the garage, Charlie Eaton came out. In his stiff white coat and round-rimmed glasses, he looked more like a scientist than Helena.

"I just heard about Elizabeth Cinder," he said.

"From the papers, no doubt," Eve said with a grimace.

"Agnes said Mr. Clarke sent word the body was ready for release." He followed them into the house. "How soon can we expect it?"

"It's on the cooling board table," said Helena.

"Already?" He glanced at her, adjusting his glasses.

"Eve and I have been playing detective," she said with a snort.

"Nonsense!" Eve protested. "We were asked to identify the body when the police found it, and then Dr. Myers wanted to examine it in our morgue."

"Better equipment in ours than anywhere else," Charlie said. "Thanks to you, Mrs. Wright." He cast an admiring glance at Helena.

"It's our business, Charles," she said briskly. "We haven't the luxury of making our living on the tummy aches and fussy colds of the wealthy."

Charlie chuckled, knowing full well she was referring to Dr. Myers and his private practice.

They headed upstairs and met Violet just coming down. She

was now dressed and hatted, carrying a beaded handbag. "Everything settled?" There was a note of anxiety in her voice.

"And no wailing and weeping." Helena gave her chin a soft push.

"How d'you do, Miss Grave?" Charlie's shoulders hunched as if he were trying to hide his face between them.

"Just fine, Owl Eyes," she said.

"Isn't it time you gave up that childish nickname?" Helena eyed her.

"Isn't it time he got a new pair of glasses?" her sister shot back.

"You ought to help dress Libby, Vi," Eve said. "You used to love putting the clothes and makeup on them."

"You do it better than anyone else," Helena added.

"That was before I realized they were dead." Her younger sister shivered. "No, thanks. I've got an interview anyway."

"Don't forget your hatpin," Helena said with a wink.

Violet made a face.

"I'll take you downtown," Eve offered.

"Now the grind, eh?" Violet raised her arm. "'So shall the bereaved be unburdened by the weight of headstone and tomb —'"

"And embalming," Helena said. "Come, Charles, we've work to do." She headed toward the basement morgue with Charlie at her heels.

CHAPTER 15

$\mathcal{E}$ve dropped her sister off at the drugstore, as she insisted she was meeting Kitty who was going with her to the interview. She drove to the county coroner's office, a small gray building that had none of the fine etchings of the courthouse. Miss Duke, the coroner's secretary, had her lunch spread out on her desk and she nearly choked on her soup as Eve came into the room.

"Afternoon, Miss Grave," said the woman. "Gee, I never expected to see you in here."

"I've come for the death certificate for Elizabeth Cinder," said Eve.

"Oh, that poor girl." The young woman wiped her lips. "Mr. Peterson just put it away. I'll get it." She went off and returned in a moment, holding it out to her. "I expect this is the first time you've been asked to bury a murder victim."

Eve blinked. "How do you know?"

"Well, you haven't been here before, have you?" The woman eyed her. "I expect you get what you need from the doctor. It's only the suspicious ones that come to us."

"Yes, that's true." Eve felt a sinking in her stomach.

She was glad to walk to the county courthouse, where the clock tower greeted her with the tinkling bells of the noon hour.

Oliver was just closing his office door, his coat and hat in hand, when she came in. "Just in time, Eve." He grinned. "I was just going to lunch at Browly's." He tapped Gladys's desk. "Push that appointment with Mr. Frazer to one-thirty. I might be a little late."

"Already done, Mr. Clarke," said the young woman in a spritely tone.

"Now you know why I keep Gladys around," said the district attorney with a twinkle in his eye. "Not only efficient but a good cook." He nodded toward the plate of cookies near the coffee pot. "I haven't been this well-fed since I was living at home with my ma." He patted his gut. "Maybe too well-fed."

"You appreciate it, at least," grumbled the secretary. "All Mr. Wayne and Mr. Lambert do is complain I don't bring more."

He laughed and patted her on the shoulder.

Browly's Diner was crowded, but Mrs. Browly, an enthusiastic woman with a sharp tongue, herded a few of the younger crowd to the counter to make room for Eve and Oliver at a small table. Eve felt the sanctimonious look of Mr. Browly as his slitted eyes followed her.

Oliver noticed her discomfort. "We can go somewhere else if you'd rather."

"No, no," she insisted. "It's about time you tried their steak and eggs. And Mrs. Browly makes the finest homemade bread this side of the river." She tried to smile.

"And Mr. Browly?" He glanced at her.

"He considers himself one of the most God-fearing men in the county," she said shortly.

"So I noticed." Oliver nodded.

"He also doesn't approve of Vi." Her muscles stiffened. "He never lets me leave here without some quote about youth and sin." She gave a small laugh. "I suppose he doesn't think much of how I raised her."

"It wasn't your responsibility to raise her," Oliver pointed out. "You're her sister, not her mother."

"But when Papa and Mama died, there was no one else," Eve said. "She was so young — so confused by it all."

"Youth will have its fling," he assured her. "She'll settle down."

"I hope so," Eve said in a soft tone.

Mrs. Browly came, her pad and pencil poised. "What'll it be?"

"I'm told your steak and eggs can't be beat," said Oliver.

"No one's complained about 'em yet," said the woman with a smile.

"For two, then," Oliver said. "And coffee." As the woman started to leave, he took hold of her arm. "And tell your husband if I hear about him spurting out Bible phrases to people, I'll have the sheriff arrest him for unlawful preaching."

The woman gave him a knowing look. "Don't take to such doings myself, so don't you worry, Mr. Clarke. God has His place, I always say, but Merton gets a bee in his bonnet about things." She gave Eve a sympathetic look. "Not the young people's fault if the moving pictures and magazines give them ideas."

"Thank you," Eve said quietly.

"I take it you're downtown to get the death certificate," Oliver said when she had gone.

Eve pulled it out of her briefcase bag and waved it at him. "So odd to be getting this from the coroner and not the doctor."

"Dr. Myers signed it, so that's getting it from a doctor." He chuckled.

"I mean the circumstances," Eve said. "I can't even look at the cause of death. It just makes my stomach turn."

He patted her hand. "The world isn't a soft and gentle place anymore."

"I realize that, Oliver, but Gyver — well, we've always been shielded, I guess." She looked down at the plate Mrs. Browly put in front of her.

"Talking 'bout that poor lamb that was found by the side of the river, eh?" The woman raised an eyebrow. "Must've been one of those gangsters."

"How do you mean, ma'am?" Oliver asked.

She leaned forward, putting her hands on the table. "Well, I'll tell you, Mr. Clarke. Our place gets a lot of strangers coming in from out of town. Men in dark suits with their hats cocked over one eye. Them sort of people."

"Indeed?" Eve could tell he was more amused than serious. "And your theory is that these are gangsters?"

"Well, I don't have to tell *you*, Mr. Clarke," she said knowingly. "You been to the city and all that. They got to get rid of somebody, they take 'em into the fields and kill 'em. Then they come in for breakfast, smooth as you please, like nothing happened."

"But Miss Cinder wasn't found in the fields," Eve said. "She was found by the river."

"Oh, I don't mean she was his gun moll or nothing like that." The woman looked shocked. "Why, I remember Libby when she used to go to Gohl's Bakery and get a raisin hot-cross bun for her daddy on a Sunday morning. She was a good girl."

"I'm glad you think so, Mrs. Browly." Oliver rolled his eyes at Eve.

"But them gangsters, they don't spare nobody. The paper said she was out strolling on Friday night. Maybe she seen 'em do it — the gangsters, I mean — and they bumped her off to keep her quiet."

"And hid the first person they bumped off so well the police haven't found it yet?" Oliver gave her a doubtful look. "But kept Miss Cinder's body out in the open where the police would easily find it?"

"A distraction!" the woman insisted. "Get you chasing after some dumb young man who don't know any better than to look at a girl with cow eyes instead of the big boss." The woman tore the check off her pad and put it down on the table. "Well, that's my theory anyway."

"Marie!" Mr. Browly's voice came out like a loud growl. "We have customers here!"

"Don't hit the roof," she mumbled as she shuffled back toward the counter.

Eve looked at Oliver, and they both laughed.

"You must have heard a lot of 'theories' like that when you were working with the San Francisco police," Eve remarked, taking the honey pot from the table behind her, which a group of businessmen had just vacated.

"I don't know how many people I've heard blame a killing on a mobster," he agreed. "They happen more in the moving pictures than in real life."

"She had one point," Eve ventured.

He glanced at her. "About the dumb young man who doesn't know any better than to make cow eyes at a lady?"

"You knew who she was referring to, then."

"I'm surprised you do," he said. "I'm surprised she did."

"Mrs. Cinder told us the sheriff had been there this morning asking a lot of questions about August Winters," she said. "I expect the gossip is already going around about it."

He sighed, pouring more coffee from the pot Mrs. Browly had left on the table. "I was hoping the word wouldn't get out about that."

"You think he's going to be on his guard?" she asked.

"They usually are," he said. "When they hear they might be suspected."

She folded her hands under her chin. "Oliver, I understand you have to pursue every possibility —"

"Yes, we do, Eve," he said. "Not that I approve of Sheriff Warner taking it upon himself to ask questions, as I only sent him there to look for the ring. But you know how he is — like a bloodhound when he gets a scent."

"I consider him more like a bulldog chasing after a rotten piece of meat," Eve remarked, and he let out a deep laugh. "He upset Mrs. Cinder and Miss Gilbert terribly."

"I'm sorry to hear that," he said.

"Neither of them believes August had anything to do with the murder," Eve said.

He eyed her. "And what do you believe?"

Eve played around with the eggs on her plate. "Mrs. Cinder told us about how Libby and August met."

"Oh, I see." He leaned back. "I hope you're not letting sentiment cloud your judgment."

"I have no judgment!" Eve insisted. "I've nothing to do with any of this except to bury the body."

"If there's one thing I learned in my three years here, it's that Gyver protects its own. Like Mrs. Browly just now. I'll bet if I polled everyone in town, the majority of you would say he was innocent."

"We're just law-abiding citizens, Oliver," she protested. "We believe in the words 'innocent until proven guilty.'"

He drank the last of the coffee. "Well, so do I. I told Sheriff Warner not to make a move until we speak with August. I have a date to collect him tomorrow morning and head over to the Winters' place. What is it you call it?"

"Redbud Manor," Eve said. "Like the redbud tree."

"Oh, yes, that pin." He took his hat from the table. "I'd like you to come with us, Eve."

She started at him. "Me?"

"You obviously sympathize with him," he said. "That might work to our advantage."

"But I hardly know him!"

"The sheriff won't be such a bulldog in the presence of a lady."

He appealed to her with boyish eyes. "Won't you do it in the name of justice?"

She fiddled with her gloves. "I have to see some people."

"Today, not tomorrow," he reminded her.

She smiled as he opened the door for her. "You're persistent, aren't you?"

"Like a crocodile," he said, grinning. "Once I bite into an idea, I don't let go."

"I'm not so sure that's a compliment," she remarked as he laughed.

CHAPTER 16

Eve was nervous about what Sheriff Warner would say when he saw her the next morning. And, indeed, it was clear he was less than thrilled when he saw her walk into the police station with Oliver.

"I suppose I shouldn't be surprised to see you here, Miss Grave." He motioned toward Deputy Elwood to get his hat.

"I've asked Eve to come with us to Redbud Manor."

"But, Mr. Clarke, this is police business," the sheriff protested. "This ain't grave business."

"I want Miss Grave there." The stubborn tone came into the district attorney's voice.

"But we might have to — things might get a little personal."

"I can keep a secret as well as you can, Sheriff," Eve said, stiffening.

"Eve is no gossip, and you know it," Oliver snapped.

He put on the hat his deputy gave him. "Well, Judge Long won't like it. That's all I got to say."

Oliver eyed him. "And what has Judge Long to do with it?"

"I played golf with him yesterday," said Sheriff Warner. "Told him about some of the things you been getting up to with this case."

Oliver's face grew stormy. "If you have something to say, Sheriff, say it."

"I ain't saying nothing, Mr. Clarke. Only the judge ain't happy about things."

"Perhaps the judge would like to take over this case?" Oliver snapped.

Eve felt almost dizzy as she grabbed his arm. "Oliver, if the sheriff thinks I shouldn't go, I'll leave."

"The sheriff doesn't make those decisions. I do." He looked squarely at Sheriff Warner. "Not you and not Judge Long. Until I leave this position, I decide who interviews people and who doesn't. Is that clear?"

"Crystal clear," the sheriff mumbled. "I'm just saying he's not going to like it when he hears a woman's been tagging along to a suspect interview."

"No one is saying August Winters is a suspect yet, Sheriff," Oliver reminded him as he opened the car door for Eve.

As they drove up the hill where the Winters' mansion stood, its magnificent gray and blue panels shimmering in the sunshine, Eve caught sight of Rosalia Winters near the hedges, looking fashionable in work clothes with garden shears in her hand. The angularity of her face stood out as she seemed to be attacking a part of the hedge that looked like hair standing on end. Her usual composed countenance was racked with tightness, her jaw set as if it were tied with wire. They eased into the driveway and suddenly, the look was gone.

"Good morning, Mr. Clarke, Sheriff." Eve couldn't help but hide a smile at the dismissive way she nodded at the lawman. "I haven't seen you since the New Year's Eve party, Eve."

"Hello, Rosalia." For some reason, Eve's tone always lowered when she spoke with Rosalia or anyone on Falcon Hill, though her work put her in contact with people from all social classes.

As Helena reminded her once, "Even the rich have to bury their dead."

"What can I do for you?" she went on.

"We'd like to speak to your son, ma'am," Oliver said. "Is he home?"

"Why, yes, he's just finishing breakfast," she said. "I can't imagine what he might have done."

"Routine, Mrs. Winters," Sheriff Warner said in a brusque tone.

She lifted her chin a little. "Routine what, Sheriff?"

"You've probably read about the investigation we're doing," Oliver began.

"Investigation? Oh, yes, that poor, unfortunate girl," she said. "A schoolteacher, wasn't she?"

"Yes, ma'am." Oliver grasped his hat in his hand.

"What could she possibly have to do with August?" She blinked.

"The police only want to ask some questions, Rosalia," Eve said. "They're asking everyone who knew Libby."

"Knew who?"

"Libby Cinder," said Sheriff Warner with a trace of exasperation. "You know, the dead girl."

"I would appreciate it if you would keep your tone civil, Sheriff." A sharp edge entered her well-mannered voice. "I believe my husband told you that more than once."

"Yes, ma'am," he said quietly.

"We won't take up much of his time," said Oliver. "You're not denying August knew Libby?"

"They were acquainted, yes," she said.

"Acquainted!" Sheriff Warner let out a guffaw. "That's not how we heard it."

"I can't help what you heard, Sheriff," said the woman.

"You'd better let us in, ma'am." He stepped toward the house.

"I never said I wouldn't," she said. "I just don't like your forceful methods, that's all."

"I apologize for that, ma'am," Oliver said. "I asked Eve to join us, as I thought it would make things easier."

"Easier?" She eyed him. "You sound as if you're about to make an arrest."

"If it comes to that," the sheriff mumbled.

Eve was sure Rosalia had heard him, but she chose to ignore it as she opened the door, stepping aside to let them pass. "You won't keep August too long, will you? They're all going down to Palm Springs for the week, and he hasn't finished packing yet."

As they followed her through the high-ceiling corridor, Eve heard the sheriff whisper to Oliver, "Going slumming in Palm Springs while his fiancé's dead body lies in the morgue. Cool customer, Mr. Clarke."

Eve's heart sank.

August was in the dining room, an elaborate place Eve guessed was as big as the entire first floor of the funeral home. The panels on the walls made the place seem hollow, and the long windows framed August's slim figure with an illuminating light through the delicate closed curtains. Breakfast was laid out like a feast on the table.

August's blond hair looked almost white and his skin as pale as Libby's was under the harsh light of the mortuary, making Eve gasp. The newspaper was thrown open on a chair beside him, and his figure hunched a little, though he straightened out when they came in. His plate was filled with eggs, bacon, and ham, the bread plate beside it stacked with toast. But it looked to Eve as if it had been filled by someone else and placed there. He hadn't touched any of it.

"Nice hearty appetite, eh?" Sheriff Warner remarked.

Oliver gave him a warning look and removed the newspaper, folding it discreetly to hide the large photo of Libby. "You know who I am, don't you, August?"

"Certainly," said the young man in a strained tone. "Congratulations on your appointment, Mr. Clarke. Mother and I voted for you."

Oliver looked a little sheepish. "That's very gratifying, son. You've read the paper, I see."

"Yes. I read the paper." His eyes glazed over as they wandered toward the folded newspaper.

"Then you know your fiancée is dead." Sheriff Warner leaned against the edge of the table. "She was your fiancée, wasn't she?"

August whirled around, staring into the harsh light coming from the windows.

"What nonsense you talk, Sheriff!" Rosalia said. "August isn't engaged to anyone."

"I really think you ought to leave us, ma'am," said the sheriff. "We need to talk to your son alone."

"I most certainly will not leave." She sat down in a chair opposite her son. "I think I ought to call Hugh Adkins, August."

He blinked. "Whatever for?"

"These men aren't here for play, my sweet," she said. "They have ideas in their heads. Even if they did bring Eve to soften the blow." She glanced at her.

"Don't, Mother."

Eve's heart went out to him as she heard tears in his voice.

Oliver took the young man by the shoulders. "August, we need your help."

"Help?" The young man's voice was muffled.

"Help in finding out who did this."

"Did what?"

"Killed her, boy!" Sheriff Warner snarled. "What d'you think we've been talking about?"

"Ease up, Sheriff," Oliver barked. "The boy is upset."

Eve could see the sheriff was about to protest but thought better of it, and began turning the hat in his hands around like a wheel.

"As I said before, Mr. Clarke, neither of us can help you," Rosalia said. "We don't know anything about this."

Oliver sat down beside August. "Your mother told us you and Miss Cinder were acquainted with one another."

A snort escaped from the sheriff.

"Acquainted?" August asked in a vague tone.

"The Valentine's Day picnic Catharine Beaton gave in your honor, dear," said Rosalia. "She was one of the maids there. You told me about her."

"Oh, yes." The young man's face turned toward the window, though Eve thought it was an odd turn, since the window he was looking at was aligned with the corner panel. "We had so much in common." His lips quivered for a moment. Then he jerked his head away, and his eyes happened to rest on Eve. "We'd both just come back to town after being away for a long time."

"Not so long, dear," Rosalia said softly. "You were gone only a year."

"It was like a lifetime, Mother," he said.

"It's hard coming back home when you've been away for a while," Oliver said in a kind tone.

"It's hard when you have commitments." The young man let his hands slide into his lap.

"As I said, Mr. Clarke —"

"With all due respect, ma'am, we didn't come here to hear what you have to say," Sheriff Warner said. "It's August we're here to talk to. Let him answer."

"Yes, Mother, let me answer." August looked more composed. "It's time you let me speak for myself."

"Why, I don't know what you mean, dear," she said.

August opened his mouth to speak but then turned to Oliver. "I want to help, Mr. Clarke. Ask me anything you like."

"The truth is, August, we heard you and Miss Cinder were more than 'acquainted,'" he said.

His eyes moved to Eve, their lost look pulling at her heartstrings. "I loved her."

"And she loved you?" the sheriff sounded almost contemptuous.

"Of course she did," he said.

From the corner of her eye, Eve caught Rosalia's lips drawing a tight line. "Why, dear, you barely knew her." His mother gave a short laugh. "My son can get very attached to people."

"Well, August?" Oliver was looking at him, his dark eyes intense.

Finally, the young man was able to speak. "How did you find out?"

"Find what out?" Rosalia asked.

"Libby's friend told us," Eve supplied.

"Find what out?" the woman repeated.

"We were going to be married, Mother." The words came out with more force than Eve thought him capable of.

"What are you talking about?" Mrs. Winters asked.

"I told you, Mother," he said. "Isn't that why you invited Libby to come to San Diego with us last summer?"

"I invited her because I wanted to get to know her better," his mother admitted. "I want to know all your friends."

"We were engaged."

"Engaged!" Rosalia stared at her son. "But how is that possible?"

"I'll tell you how it's possible," said Sheriff Warner. "He gave her a ring, or so she said."

"I did give her a ring." August looked indignant. "I know how to ask a girl to marry me!"

"Darling, don't you think that was — well, just a little impetuous?"

Oliver glanced at her with a raised eyebrow. "When a young man loves a woman, Mrs. Winters, he generally proposes."

"But you didn't know her," said Rosalia. "One picnic isn't a reason to propose to a girl." Her tone turned dismissive. "I really must have a conversation with you one day about discretion, August."

"I know about discretion." The young man was furious. "Libby and I started seeing each other from the day we met."

"Seeing each other?" Eve asked.

He turned to her. "Oh, not in public. We couldn't do that. Libby didn't want the school to know."

"And you didn't want your mother to know," Sheriff Warner prompted.

To Eve's surprise, the young man looked sheepish. "I suppose I should have been honest with you from the beginning, Mother. I'm sorry."

"You really were reckless, darling," said Rosalia with another small laugh. Eve noticed how hollow it sounded. "And not very considerate of Cecilia."

"Cecilia Feather?" Oliver asked.

"She and August were engaged once, Mr. Clarke," she said.

"Until he broke his promise," the sheriff scoffed.

Oliver gave him a vicious look, and the sheriff began playing with his hat again. To August, he said in a more businesslike tone, "Is that true, August?"

"I suppose so," he mumbled.

Eve leaned forward. "But Cecilia forgave you, didn't she, August?"

"She's been swell," he said. "I don't know where I would have been without her."

"You were quick to replace her with someone else, weren't you?" Sheriff Warner eyed him.

The sheriff's words clearly shook the young man. "I want you to find out who did this, Mr. Clarke. Who killed my Libby. We'll pay anything to help you, won't we, Mother?" He looked wild-eyed at her.

Rosalia pressed his shoulder. "Of course we'll help all we can, dear."

"Didn't Libby mind your friendship with Cecilia?" Oliver asked.

"I didn't see much of Cecilia after I met Libby," he admitted. "It was as if no one else existed."

The sheriff looked slightly amused at this passionate confession. "And I suppose you conveniently forgot to tell her you were once engaged to this childhood friend of yours," he growled. "Of all the —"

"Sheriff!" Rosalia gave him a severe look.

"Libby knew all about Cecilia and me," August defended. "Cecilia came with us a few times when we went to the moving pictures in Pilead."

The sheriff whistled. "That's quite a distance, son."

"Was it really necessary to be so clandestine, August?" Rosalia asked softly.

"We had Libby's job to think about, Mother," he said.

"Why would that matter if she was going to get out of it by marrying you?" Sheriff Warner asked. "Or so you say."

"We weren't thinking of that at the time," August said. "We were just friends then."

"Friends!" the sheriff snorted.

"When did you last see Libby?" Oliver asked.

"The day she came back," he said.

"You mean from visiting her aunt in Reno?"

The young man looked surprised.

"We spoke with Mrs. Cinder," Oliver explained.

"Yes, of course," he said. "You had to tell her, didn't you?" He looked at the corner window again. "I never met her, of course, but it must have been awful."

"It was," Eve said softly.

"Mrs. Cinder mentioned she thought you and Libby had some kind of quarrel before she left," Oliver said.

"What could it matter now?" The young man hid his face in his hands.

"Everything matters in an investigation, son," Sheriff Warner said.

The young man gazed out the corner window in silence for what seemed like a long time. Eve could see just a hint of the river in the distance, though it looked hardly more than a gray finger with the cloudiness that had entered the sky. It suddenly struck her that was the attraction of that strange gaze — the water.

"I think you'd better answer the sheriff's question, August." Oliver's tone was firmer now.

"It was about her job."

"What about her job?" the sheriff asked.

"We'd been talking about getting married the week before." A small gasp escape from his mother's lips. "Just throwing around the idea. You know."

"Quite a big idea to throw around," Oliver remarked.

"We were both serious, Mr. Clarke," August said. "That's why I wanted her to quit Brookline."

"And she didn't want to?" Oliver guessed.

"She said it wouldn't make sense to quit until we were officially engaged at the end of the school year," he said. "She thought we would need the money to start over."

"I thought you had a mint." Sheriff Warner grimaced.

"My father left me something." He took a piece of toast and began to crumble it, scattering the bits all over the table.

"I wish you wouldn't do that, dear," said his mother. "It makes an awful mess for the maid."

Eve glanced at her.

"She wanted her own money too." He pushed the toast away. "Girls want that these days."

"Yes, they do," Eve said.

Oliver eyed August. "Are you sure that's what the quarrel was about?"

"Of course he's sure," Rosalia said.

"Did you give her the ring then?" Oliver asked.

"No, not then." August looked at him with knitted brows. "I hadn't gone with Cecilia to buy it yet."

Sheriff Warner let out a whistle. "Taking your former fiancée to buy a ring for your current fiancée. You got more guts than I figured, son."

"One more vulgar insinuation like that, Sheriff, and I'm calling Hugh Adkins," Rosalia barked.

"All that was over and done with," August insisted. "Cecilia's like a sister to me now."

"When was this?" Oliver asked.

"A month or so ago," he said.

"Before or after Libby left for her trip to Reno?"

"A little after, I guess."

"You guess?" Sheriff Warner glared at him.

"A few days after she left!" August said with exasperation.

"August, darling, she didn't pressure you, did she?" Rosalia ventured.

"Please, Mrs. Winters." Oliver held up his hand. "Let your son speak."

"Of course not." His face shone red. "I told you, we'd been talking about it for some time."

"Where did you buy the ring?" Sheriff Warner asked. "Not around here, eh?"

"No, sir," he said. "I didn't want it to get around."

Eve noticed he was trying to avoid looking at his mother.

"Where, then?" Oliver asked.

"San Francisco," he said. "I know a jeweler there. Nice fellow."

"So you and Cecilia drove down to San Francisco," said the district attorney.

"Cecilia helped me pick it out." He smiled a bit. "She even wore it for the whole day."

"That's rather strange," Eve murmured.

"I thought if I could see it on a woman's hand, it might give me the courage to ask Libby," he said.

"Courage!" Sheriff Warner snorted. "Not like it would have been the first time."

"That's enough, Sheriff!" Rosalia's calm tone went up a notch.

"Can you describe the ring, August?" Oliver asked.

"Well, sir, it's silver with a square setting and a raised diamond." He then looked confused. "But wasn't she wearing it on a chain around her neck? She promised me she would."

"I thought you said you were keeping your affair a secret," Sheriff Warner said.

"It wasn't an affair!" August said. "I told you, we were engaged."

"She didn't have no ring when we found her," Sheriff Warner said.

"But that's impossible!"

"It's true, son," Oliver said. "We couldn't find it among Libby's things either."

Very quietly, Rosalia turned on her heels and walked out of the room. The sheriff gave a grunt of satisfaction.

"Now, why wouldn't a young woman wear her engagement ring if she promised to?" Eve heard the nasty undertone of the sheriff's words. "Maybe because she never got the ring?" He eyed August.

This seemed to bring the young man to life. "Of course she got the ring! Cecilia will tell you." He grasped Eve's arm. "Make sure she's buried with it, Miss Grave, won't you?"

"That's up to her mother," Eve said.

"No, it isn't, Miss Grave," Sheriff Warner said. "When we find it, it will be evidence."

Rosalia came back into the room with a redheaded maid

carrying a large tray with coffee cups and a coffee pot. August immediately rose to help her.

"Very kind of you, Mrs. Winters, but you didn't have to do that," Oliver said.

"Don't be too grateful, Mr. Clarke," she said. "I didn't leave the room just to ask Missy to bring you coffee. I called Hugh Adkins. He's coming over right away."

Oliver glanced at the sheriff. "That wasn't necessary, ma'am."

"I think it is," she said. "I don't like the way this is going."

"They just want help finding out what happened to Libby, Mother," her son protested.

"Mr. Adkins advised us not to say another word until he arrives," she said in a stuffy tone.

"Is that what you want to do, August?" Oliver asked.

"I'm willing to go on if you are, sir," said the young man.

"Good lad." Oliver patted him on the back.

His mother looked less than pleased as she folded her arms. "Perhaps you should ask yourself this, Mr. Clarke. If August was engaged to Miss Cinder, why would he have anything to do with her death?"

The sheriff looked grim. "Well, ma'am, sometimes there are circumstances that might push a man to extremes."

"What circumstances?" Rosalia's gaze fell on him, the angles sharp. "What circumstances, Sheriff?"

"I think your son should answer that," he said quietly.

CHAPTER 17

It was then Eve realized what Sheriff Warner was implying. She felt sick inside at the thought of what he was about to reveal.

Oliver saw it too, as he suddenly sprang up. "Sheriff, I'd like to see you outside for a moment."

The two men left the dining room, closing the double doors behind them.

There was a pained silence in the room for a moment, though the raised tones could be heard just outside. Rosalia reached for the velvet cord on the wall. "I may as well have Missy clear the dishes."

"I can do it," Eve offered.

"You're a guest in my house, Miss Grave," said the woman with a faint smile. "Perhaps you're the only one who's wanted here. I see now why Mr. Clarke brought you. You're a comforting presence."

"Thank you," Eve said softly. She covered August's hand with hers. "I'm sorry for your loss, August."

"Loss?" Rosalia echoed.

"Libby," she said softly.

"Thank you." His voice came out in a squeaking tone. He looked at her, the boyish features of his handsome face hanging with the bewildered look of a child. "Eve, they don't think — they couldn't!"

"Think you killed Miss Cinder?" Rosalia echoed. "Why, of course they do."

"Nobody said that," Eve insisted. "They're just trying to find out the truth."

"I suppose I'm the most likely suspect," August admitted. "I see that now. I didn't before, but I do now."

"Nonsense!" his mother snapped. "You don't even kill spiders when they get into the plants. Don't worry, darling, Mr. Adkins will come and put a stop to all this." She paused. "August, dear, I urge you once again to say nothing until he gets here."

"It's all right, Mother," he said. "They didn't know how it really was with Libby and me before. I expect they heard a lot of gossip about us."

"There was some talk about a year ago of someone on Falcon Hill and a schoolteacher," Eve admitted.

"Fools!" Rosalia hissed. "Clementine always did have a mouth too big for her face."

Eve tried to hide a smile. Mrs. Beaton's lips and teeth were known to be just a little out of proportion with the rest of her face.

The doors opened and Oliver returned alone. "I must apologize, Mrs. Winters, for the sheriff's behavior."

"My husband tried to dissuade the board of supervisors from allowing him to run for sheriff, but they wouldn't listen to him," Rosalia said.

"He's a good lawman, ma'am," Oliver said with some pride. "Nevertheless, I asked him to cool off for a while." He turned to August. "I only have a few more questions for you, son. Where were you on Friday night?"

"Friday?" the young man echoed. "I don't know if I can remember."

"August and I had dinner with some friends in Brenas," Rosalia intervened.

August's wide eyes told Eve this wasn't true and she saw Oliver noticed this too.

"I see," he said. "I'll need the name of these friends."

"Why?"

"We need to verify your son's alibi, of course," said Oliver.

She sighed. "All right. *I* was there. August was here when I came back at around ten o'clock."

"And the name of these people?" he inquired. "For reference only, Mrs. Winters."

"Combs. Edward and Ella Combs," she said. "482 Prospect Street in Brenas."

Oliver closed the notebook where he had written down the address. He then looked at August, the ferocity making his eyes heavy. "Now that we know where your mother was, where were you until ten o'clock?"

"August was at home, naturally," Rosalia answered. "He wasn't feeling well. That's why I went to the Combses' without him."

Oliver turned to the young man. "Were you at home?"

"Yes," he said quickly. "Mother's right. I didn't feel well."

"All evening?" Eve fidgeted, as it was clear from Oliver's tone he was starting to doubt the young man.

"Yes. No! I— I needed some air. I took a walk downtown."

"You didn't feel well so you took a walk," Oliver repeated. "I suppose you don't keep time either, so you don't know when that was."

"No." Now August showed defiance. "What difference does it make?"

"The difference, son, is that your fiancé was killed by the river between nine and ten o'clock Friday night and you were taking a walk downtown."

The blow from Oliver's brash words made the young man jerk back as if he had been hit. "My God!"

"August was home well before ten," Rosalia insisted. "I think we're through answering your questions, Mr. Clarke. I'm going to call Mr. Adkins' office again."

"Please wait, ma'am." Oliver put his hand on the young man's arm. "Did anyone see you downtown?"

"I saw him," his mother insisted. "When I came home, he was here."

"But you yourself admit you don't know what time that was," Eve pointed out.

The woman glared at her. "I thought you were here to help us, Miss Grave."

"Josh might have seen me," August said. "I was down near his shack. I tried knocking on the door but there was no answer." He bit his lip. "Maybe he was home and just didn't answer the door. He does that often."

"I understand he's a boyhood friend of yours," said Oliver.

"He's like a father to me," August said. Eve did not miss the distressed look that crossed Rosalia's face.

"Is there a way for Josh to see who's at the door?" Oliver asked.

August blinked. "Well, yes. There's a panel that pulls back where he can look through a hole to see who's there."

"And he always uses it?"

"Yes."

"Then is it likely he wouldn't open the door for you if he was home?" Oliver looked at him.

August seemed caught in confusion, but then he said in a defeated tone, "No. He always opens the door for me."

Eve's eyes wandered to the corner window, stirred by the gray line of the river. She suddenly turned to him and asked, "Where were you walking?"

"I walked down to Josh's shack," he said.

"And then you walked back home when he didn't answer your knock?"

"Well, no." His eyes were hollow. "I went to our place and sat for a while."

"Our place?" Oliver asked.

"Libby's and mine." There was silence for a moment. "Where we used to meet all the time so no one would see us."

"Is it far from Josh's shack?" asked Eve.

"Not very far," he said. "But it's beyond the spot where the river spills into the creek."

"And you sat for a while?" Oliver asked.

"Yes, sir," he said. "I needed to think."

"Just stared out at the black river and thought, eh?" Oliver asked.

The young man glared at him. "It's the truth, Mr. Clarke, even if you don't believe me."

"I didn't say I didn't believe you," Oliver said quietly.

Eve touched August's arm. "If Josh were out, say, night fishing or hunting, and he saw you there, would he have talked to you?"

August blinked. "Well, no, probably not," he said. "He knew Libby and I were meeting there. He might have thought we had a meeting and he always said he didn't get himself mixed up with lovers." He covered his face with his hands. "Oh, God!"

Eve looked at the district attorney. "Josh is always wandering about up and down the river at night, Oliver."

"Yes, yes!" Rosalia grasped her son's shoulders, as if trying to keep them from shaking with sobs. "He saw August, I'm sure of it." She gave Oliver a majestic look. "Ask him, Mr. Clarke."

"I'll certainly do that, ma'am," he said.

The doorbell rang, echoing throughout the house. "At last!" Rosalia strode out the door, shooing Missy away, and came back with Hugh Adkins, the sheriff at his heels.

The man whose reputation as one of California's best criminal lawyers, in the ranks with Clarence Darrow, took up less bulk than the latter but was no less impressive with his tall, slim figure and upturned blue eyes, which, it was said, could reduce anyone in the witness box to a pulp.

"Well, now, what's all this about?" His voice sounded heartier than his figure would admit.

"The police think August was involved with the death of this poor young woman in the newspapers, Hugh," said Rosalia.

"We're only asking questions, Mrs. Winters," Sheriff Warner said. His tone was almost congenial.

"I see." The lawyer looked at August like a bear examining an ant. "I assume you've told Mr. Clarke you don't wish to speak without a lawyer present?"

"Why would I tell him that?" August asked. "I'm not under arrest, am I, Mr. Clarke?"

"As the sheriff said, Mr. Adkins, we're just asking questions," Oliver said.

"I told August not to speak, as you advised me," Rosalia said. "August is just too honest."

"So you *have* talked, have you?" Mr. Adkins continued to look down at August. "That wasn't wise, son."

"I didn't do anything," August mumbled.

The man gave Oliver a sweeping gaze. "Naturally, Mr. Clarke, August won't be answering any more of your questions."

Oliver looked at the young man. "Is that how you feel, August?"

"I'll answer any questions you ask," August said firmly. "I want to get to the bottom of this."

"Your cooperation is much appreciated," mumbled the sheriff.

"Darling, Hugh said —"

"I don't care what he said!" The young man's voice was shrill. "I don't need a lawyer!"

"Yet," Mr. Adkins mumbled as he closed his briefcase.

"I'd like you to stay, Hugh," said Rosalia. "If August persists in answering questions, I would feel better if he had a professional advising him."

"I think that's wise, ma'am," said the lawyer. His bug-like eyes rested on Eve. "And who is this? Your secretary?"

"This is Eve Grave, Hugh," said Rosalia. "Her family owns the funeral home in town."

"Grave, eh? An appropriate name, I must say." He chuckled. "May I ask what you're doing here?"

"I brought Eve here," Oliver said with a glare. "Any objections?"

"Certainly I object," said the man. "There's no cause for anyone outside of this case to be present while my client is being questioned."

Eve did not miss the satisfied look on Sheriff Warner's face. She guessed he still resented Oliver sending him out while letting her stay.

"I am not your client!" August snarled. "I want Eve to stay."

"Eve has been very helpful, Hugh," said Rosalia. "She knows August had nothing to do with this gruesome event."

"I assume as district attorney of this county, I still have a right to choose who is present when I question a witness?" Oliver asked in an arch tone.

"Is that why I found the sheriff here twiddling his thumbs in the police car when I came in?" asked Mr. Adkins with a snort. "I believe it's the usual procedure to have the police question a suspect."

"August is not a suspect," said Oliver firmly. "Now, are you going to let us do our job or aren't you?"

"There's still a lot we need to know." Sheriff Warner looked squarely at August.

Mr. Adkins accepted the coffee Missy handed him and settled himself on the chair at the head of the table. "You know my job is to make it as difficult for you to convict my client as possible, Mr. Clarke." August glared at him. "You may continue with your questioning and I shall advise the young man as I see fit."

Oliver gave an exaggerated bow. "Much obliged for your consent, Mr. Adkins." He turned back to August. "What were you thinking about when you were sitting down by the river?"

"Oh, lots of things," said the young man.

"Are you trying to be a mind reader now, Mr. Clarke?" Mr. Adkins eyed him.

"I'm trying to get at the truth!" Oliver snapped. Eve could see he was on the edge of losing his temper.

To her surprise, it was the sheriff who came to the rescue. "We're not in the courtroom, Mr. Adkins," he said. "You might keep your snide remarks to yourself."

"Please, Hugh," Rosalia said softly. "We want to get this over with."

The lawyer buried his nose in his coffee cup.

"You were saying you were thinking about a lot of things," Oliver continued.

"Your upcoming marriage to Miss Cinder, for instance?" the sheriff added.

"Yes, sir," he said. "That, and —" He pressed his hands together.

"I really don't see where this line of questioning —" Mr. Adkins began.

"Shut up!" August jumped out of his seat. "Mother, please tell this man to shut up!"

"Easy, son," said Mr. Adkins. "I'm only trying to help you."

"And what else?" Oliver persisted.

"Maybe you were thinking about what she told you when she came back from Reno?" Sheriff Warner hedged.

August's face turned pale. "I didn't know you knew about that."

"We know everything, son," said the sheriff. "So you may as well come clean."

"Yes," he said softly.

Eve leaned forward. "Perhaps it would be better, August, if you told us exactly what Libby said."

"That's good advice, Miss Grave." Mr. Adkins nodded with approval. "I glad to see you seem to have more sense than most women."

Eve glared at him.

"She said she'd been to see her doctor in Reno while she was away and he confirmed her suspicions."

"Suspicions?" Rosalia's asked.

"She was going to have my child, Mother." The words echoed in the quiet room.

The isolation of Falcon Hill suddenly struck Eve, as no sound from the outside penetrated the room. She felt like she was in a metal cage. It was the same feeling she had as a child sometimes when she went down to the morgue to see her father. She looked wildly at the windows but they seemed tall and imposing.

"It's hot in here," she whispered.

Her words broke the silence, and Rosalia softly screeched, "No!"

August looked at his mother. "Now do you see why I have to help the police find out who did this awful thing? Don't you see, Mother? He killed two people."

"Two people," Rosalia whispered. "Two people."

"Whoever did this killed Libby and my unborn child." August's voice strengthened. "I'll answer any questions you have, Mr. Clarke. I'll do anything."

Rosalia stumbled out of the room. Eve followed her. She found the woman leaning against the wall, her arms clutching at her stomach. "Are you all right, Rosalia?" She motioned to Missy, who was hovering nearby.

"Of course I'm all right," the woman said with clouded huskiness.

"Perhaps some Veronal?" Eve suggested. "I could send for my sister —"

"I said I'm all right!" The voice was now composed. Even though her features still looked ashen, she patted Eve's hand. "Thank you for your kindness. I just felt ill for a moment."

"It is shocking, I know," she said kindly.

The woman pressed her lips together and said nothing.

As they returned to the dining room, August said, "She called me the night she came back from her aunt's and said she wanted to speak to me."

"In that place where the river spills into the creek?"

"The creek, eh?" Sheriff Warner glanced at him. Oliver gave him a look that said he would fill him in later on.

"No, sir," he said. "She came here."

"Here!" Rosalia interjected.

August looked embarrassed. "After you went to the Hatton Farm."

"Had she ever been here before?" asked Oliver.

"Mother invited her to tea once," he said.

"Where did you meet?" he asked.

"Really, Mr. Clarke, I can't see any of this is relevant," Mr. Adkins murmured.

"I'm asking the questions, sir," Oliver said with the brutal firmness Eve had come to admire.

"In the garden," August said.

"Is that why you proposed to her?" the sheriff asked. "'Cause she was going to have your kid?"

"Oh, no," he said. "I was going to call her the next day and do that. But when she asked to meet me the night she came back, I asked her. I was so anxious to know." He looked around the room. Then, he burst out laughing and put his hands on his knees and rocked with laughter. "It's absurd! Absurd!"

"I won't have you upsetting my son," Rosalia said sharply.

"What does it matter now?" August asked. "What does any of it matter now? She's dead. Our child is dead. Nothing matters."

"Did you tell anyone about this meeting?" Oliver asked.

"Who would I tell?" the young man asked.

"Josh know?" August shook his head at Sheriff Warner's question. "Cecilia?"

"And just who is Cecilia?" Mr. Adkins glanced at him.

"The young lady August was going to marry before he went to sea," said Rosalia. "You remember, Hugh."

"I can't see what connection she might have to this," said the lawyer. "You're wasting everybody's time, Mr. Clarke."

"I haven't seen Cecilia since we went to the jewelry store," said August.

"Mr. Clarke," Rosalia spoke in a clear tone, "I don't like to suggest this, but you do realize there's no proof the child was August's."

"Mother!" Her son stared at her.

"That's correct," Mr. Adkins said. "The young lady was in Reno for a while, I gather. The child could have easily been someone else's."

"You mean that sort of woman and that sort of town." Eve felt her anger rise. "Two and two don't always make four, Mr. Adkins."

"Libby wouldn't lie to me!" August insisted. "Anything else you want to know?"

"Miss Cinder's coat was torn," Oliver said.

August's face turned pale. "You mean the fiend —"

"She wasn't attacked," the district attorney assured him. "The medical examiner ascertained that."

"Then why mention it?" Mr. Adkins asked.

"Because we think Libby was wearing some kind of pin," Sheriff Warner said.

"That's hardly relevant," the lawyer insisted. "Those river currents can be brutal."

"If the current ripped her clothes, it would have shredded the whole coat, not just that one place," the sheriff argued.

"Do you know of anything she might have worn that night if she thought she was going to be meeting you?" Oliver asked.

"Libby didn't have much jewelry." August seemed a little confused.

"Mrs. Cinder told us you gave her a brooch," Eve said. With a small smile, she added, "Libby was very proud of it."

August smiled too. "I did give her a brooch of a redbud tree."

"The family emblem," Rosalia said softly.

"It was my promise to her that she would be part of the family," the young man mused.

"So you gave it to her before you gave her the ring," said Oliver.

August nodded. "I went to Shreve and had it made especially for her."

Sheriff Warner glanced at Oliver. "No wonder we couldn't locate it around here." Eve could see he was annoyed at having wasted so much time. "Did you take Cecilia with you when you bought that too?"

Ignoring this, August turned to Oliver. "You're asking about it because you think the killer might have taken it?"

"It's obvious, isn't it?" Rosalia jumped in. "Robbery! That's why she was killed. Don't you think so, Hugh?"

"That depends." The lawyer looked expectedly at Oliver. "Was anything else stolen?"

The district attorney shook his head. "She had other jewelry on her and a purse."

"He took only that, then," August murmured.

"Maybe he had a grudge against the family," Eve offered. "Everyone around here knows about Redbud Manor. These are the only redbud trees in town."

"Have you any enemies who might do such a thing, Mrs. Winters?" Oliver asked.

She shrugged. "I'm sure my husband had enemies. He had a lot of influence in this county."

"But you don't know who they could be?" He eyed her.

"We never talked about such things, Mr. Clarke," she said with dignity. "We had other, more important things to discuss."

"Why would they go after Libby?" August asked. "And why now when Father's been dead all this time?"

Oliver held out his pen and pad to the young man. "Will you draw a picture of the brooch? We might be able to trace it if the killer pawned it."

"Is that really necessary, Mr. Clarke?" Rosalia asked.

"I would allow it, Rosalia," said Mr. Adkins. "If it was pawned, the owner of the pawn shop might identify it and that would help clear your son."

Rosalia drew in a breath. "I hadn't thought of that."

"Earning your fee, aren't you?" the sheriff remarked.

"I always earn my fee, Sheriff," the man shot back.

August drew carefully. He stopped once, his hand shaking a little as he looked at Eve. "Libby said it was the finest gift anyone had ever given her."

"No commentary, son, just the picture," Mr. Adkins said in a stern tone.

Eve glared at him. "A young man is allowed to reminisce about his lost love, isn't he, Mr. Adkins?" She saw the sheriff roll his eyes.

August finished and handed it to Oliver, who put it in his coat pocket.

Mr. Adkins rose. "I think you've kept my client long enough, Mr. Clarke."

"I'm not your client," August growled.

"Anything else you have to ask should take place in a courtroom," said the man. "If you get that far. Frankly, I don't think you will. You've nothing concrete against the boy."

"We'll get it," Sheriff Warner barked.

CHAPTER 18

The sheriff's words left a dent in the air. August stared at him, and Rosalia grasped the back of her son's chair. Even Mr. Adkins looked uncomfortable.

"Mr. Clarke, I'd like to ask the young man something, if I may," Sheriff Warner said. "Outside of a courtroom." He looked meaningfully at the lawyer.

Oliver studied him for a moment. "All right."

Mr. Adkins reluctantly sat down again.

The sheriff reached into his pocket and took out a piece of rope. "Recognize this, son?"

August examined it. "I've seen ropes like this before, yes."

"Where?" Oliver asked.

"During my seafaring experience." He said this a little dryly.

"Bet you learned to tie some sailors' knots too," the sheriff continued.

The young man gave a sheepish grin. "It was the only thing I was really good at."

"Why don't you show us some of your skills?" asked Sheriff Warner.

Mr. Adkins stiffened. "I really don't see where this is going, Sheriff."

"I'm curious." The sheriff looked at him sideways. "The boy says he's good at it and I'd like to see how good. Kepler showed me a couple of his. Clove hitch, reef knot, rolling hitch, round turn with half hitch —"

"You mean round turn with two half hitches," August corrected.

"See, I knew you knew them better than me." Sheriff Warner nodded with approval.

August's voice became more confident. "Josh says I'm even better than he is."

"I had a yearning to be a fisherman once myself," he said with a half-smile.

"Your boyhood dreams don't concern us, Sheriff," Mr. Adkins snapped. "August, I advise you to let your mother show these men out."

"Why?" The young man looked at him. "What harm could there be in tying a knot?"

"You should do as Hugh says, darling," Rosalia said. "He knows what he's talking about."

"I'll show you, if you like, Sheriff," August said.

"August, don't!" His mother was more alarmed now. "It's a trap of some kind. Isn't it, Hugh?"

Mr. Adkins looked sharply at Oliver. "Is it?"

"We're not trying to trap anybody, Mr. Adkins," Oliver promised.

"How can tying a few knots be a trap?" August asked with a smile. "I showed you, didn't I, Mother?" He took the rope from the sheriff's hands. "Which one would you like to see?"

"Well, how about that last one with the long name?" Sheriff Warner asked.

"The round turn with two half hitches?" August asked. "What do I tie it to?"

"Eh?" the sheriff looked at him.

"A round turn knot has to be tied to something." The young man gave a sly smile. "Didn't Josh show you?"

Sheriff Warner seemed put out, but Oliver moved an empty chair closer to August. "Tie it to this."

It seemed only seconds and the slick piece of white rope hung on the arm of the chair in two loops with two elegant knots folded over.

"Very nice," Sheriff Warner said. A steady grin appeared on his face.

A spark of horror ran through Eve as she suddenly realized what the demonstration had really been about.

"Now that the sheriff's curiosity has been satisfied, Mr. Clarke, I think it's time you left this young man alone." Mr. Adkins rose for the third time, clearly having no intention of sitting down again.

Oliver nodded. "August, Mrs. Cinder told us someone called the house that night and said you wanted Libby to meet you at this special place you and she used to go to on Friday night."

"What do you mean, 'someone?'" Rosalia stared at him.

"She couldn't say who it was, ma'am," said Oliver. "She only said it was a woman's voice."

"I never met Libby there or anywhere that night," August said. "I told you, I went down to the river alone."

"Did you ask anyone to call her for you?" Sheriff Warner asked.

He looked from one lawman to the other. "Who would I ask?"

"Cecilia, maybe?" the sheriff persisted. "She's been rather obliging to you since you got back, hasn't she?"

"And she's done it before," Oliver added. "Mrs. Cinder told us that."

"Well, yes, but not for a long time." August pressed his hand to his temples. "What are you getting at?"

"Steady, darling," his mother said in a soft tone as she grasped his shoulders.

"I don't understand any of this!"

"August," Eve said gently, "Mrs. Cinder told Oliver and me she thought the woman's voice sounded like Cecilia."

"She was wrong, then!" His voice rose. "It's all wrong!"

"Of course it's all wrong," Mr. Adkins said. "This entire questioning has been wrong. But you persisted in allowing it and now you have to take the consequences."

"Hugh, please," Rosalia hissed.

"We'd like you to show us the exact place where you went on Friday night to sit and think," Oliver said. "And we'd like to see the place where you and Libby used to meet. The one she was told to go to that night."

The young man's face paled. "Do you think they're one and the same?"

"We won't know until we see." The district attorney straightened out his hat before he put it on.

August rose. "I'll get my coat, Mr. Clarke."

"I wouldn't advise you to do that, August," said Mr. Adkins. "The district attorney wants to put you at the scene of the crime."

"We haven't said anything about the crime scene," Oliver insisted. "We're not sure where Libby was found was the crime scene anyway."

"You give me permission to see the file on the case?" Mr. Adkins eyed him.

"I can't very well refuse if you're representing the boy." Oliver eyed him back.

"Darling, I think you ought to let Hugh come with you," said Rosalia. "Just in case."

"In case of what?" August glanced at her. "You almost sound as if you believe I'm guilty, Mother."

The color drained from her face. "How can you say that?" The tone was almost a whisper.

August was clearly touched by this, as he put his hands on his mother's shoulders and said in a tender voice, "I'm sorry, Mother. Of course Hugh can come with us if you prefer."

"That's the first sensible thing you've said all afternoon, son," Mr. Adkins murmured.

"Mr. Clarke." Rosalia looked at the district attorney with large eyes. "Must all of this get into the papers?"

"I told you, Mrs. Winters, we're not arresting your son," he said. "People know we're asking questions around town."

"I didn't mean that," said Rosalia. "I meant about — you know — Libby and her being in a family way."

"You mean you're not proud your son was going to be a father?" Sheriff Warner gave a sly grin.

"Don't be vulgar, Sheriff," Eve snapped.

"You don't know what those Shane boys are like." The woman pressed her hands together. "They want nothing more than to make the *Gyver Bee* as sensational as the *San Francisco Examiner*."

"They do seem mighty ambitious," Oliver admitted.

"They'll make a sordid story of it," Rosalia continued.

"But it's all true, Mother," August said.

"It's not true!" Just for a moment, the self-possessed tone broke into rapturous anger. Then, as if getting hold of herself, she said, "That is, we don't know for sure." She then turned to the district attorney. "August hasn't been home long and he's trying to get his feet back on the ground. We're all trying to help him as much as we can. You want to help him too, don't you, Mr. Clarke?" Her eyes were like chestnuts. "I'm sure you do."

"I see no reason for Miss Cinder's condition to come out in public, ma'am," said Oliver. "Not at this stage of the investigation anyway."

The woman looked relieved. "There are certain people in this community who wouldn't understand. You see that, don't you, Mr. Clarke?"

"Yes," he said quietly. "I see that."

Rosalia grasped Eve's arm to hold her back as the men proceeded to the door. She asked in a soft voice, "You'll help us too, won't you, Eve?"

"I'll do all I can." Eve suddenly felt uncomfortable by the woman's grasp.

"You know everyone in town," she said. "You have more communication with the ladies than I do."

"I should think you would," Eve mumbled, "since most of them live on Falcon Hill."

"Yes, but I can't speak to them the way you can."

"You mean because they volunteer to help us prepare the bodies for burial?" Eve asked.

"Exactly," said the woman. "You have a more liberal relationship with them than I do."

"Neither Helena nor I are their friends, Rosalia," Eve said.

Rosalia's tone grew more hissing. "I can just imagine what talk there will be about Miss Cinder. You are taking care of the funeral, aren't you?"

Eve didn't answer, wishing she could get away from the woman.

"You'll be sure our name doesn't come up, won't you?" Rosalia's gaze sat on her like a buzzard on a dying rabbit. "Won't you?"

"I'll do what I can," Eve mumbled again.

"I know you will." The woman finally let go of her arm.

~~~~~

August first showed them the place he and Libby used to meet. Eve's breath grew a little labored when she realized he directed the sheriff to park the police car almost exactly where the police car had been parked when she and Helena had arrived the night they found Libby.

August stopped at the small curve where the trees began to grow thick on both sides. "We usually met here, Mr. Clarke."
~~~~~

"Just a few feet away," Oliver murmured. Eve knew he was also thinking of where Libby's body was found.

They then walked through the brush with Eve feeling her shoes get muddy from the ground still damp from the morning dew. August led them past Josh's shack with the door closed and barred. She recognized the curve that fed into the creek with the little wooden bridge that led to nowhere. The spot was a pleasant one with very green grass and wildflowers.

"We would meet at the place I showed you and then come here," August said. "We'd sit and have picnics and sometimes fish in the river. She would bring a book and read to me." His lips curved into a small smile.

"That's fine, son, that's fine," Mr. Adkins said in a hurried tone. "We ought to get back to your mother."

"I don't see how it could have been Cecilia who called," August suddenly said. "She didn't know anything about this place."

"Did she know about the other place?" Sheriff Warner questioned. "The one where you and Miss Cinder used to meet?"

"Well, yes," he said. "She and I used to meet there when we were kids."

"So she might guess that's the place you would go," Eve said softly.

The young man looked at her, startled. "I never thought of that!"

"Seems you didn't think of a lot of things, son," Sheriff Warner said under his breath.

"Thank you for showing us." Oliver grasped his hand. "You and Mr. Adkins can go now, but I'm afraid your Palm Springs trip will have to wait."

"In other words, don't leave town?" August echoed.

"That's right," Sheriff Warner said. "We may need to ask more questions."

"Not without me you won't," the lawyer said in a brutal tone. "Come on, August."

"I think I'll visit with Josh if you don't mind," said the young man. "All this has gotten me so nervous —" He gave the district attorney a fierce look. "I hope you find the man who did it soon, Mr. Clarke."

"We intend to, son," Oliver said.

"Nervous!" Sheriff Warner spit out as they began to walk back to the police car. "He's pretty cold-hearted as far as I can see!"

"You didn't have to be so barbaric," Eve snapped. "Investigation or no investigation, he's grieving."

"I think I know a little more about questioning suspects than you do, Miss Grave," said the lawman in an even tone.

"And I know more about grief than you do!"

"Sometimes those direct tactics get more answers than tiptoeing around, Eve," Oliver said in a firm tone. "I do think you went too far at times, Sheriff, but you did what you had to do."

"Certainly I did," Sheriff Warner said in a self-satisfied tone.

Oliver opened the car door for Eve, but she shook her head. "I have a few errands to do in town and I'd rather walk. The air will do me good."

"I'll walk with you, if you don't mind," said Oliver.

Sheriff Warner snorted and drove off. She and Oliver followed the path near the river. From up close, the water was cleaner, with a tint of green and blue.

"It doesn't look so dirty from here," Eve lamented.

"Eh?" Oliver took out his pipe.

"The river," she said. "You could see it from the window of Redbud Manor. But it looked so gray and dark."

He smiled. "Water can be deceiving."

"So can a lot of things," she murmured.

"Such as?" He glanced at her.

"I don't know," she said. "The way Rosalia spoke to me when we left —"

"I noticed she held you back," said Oliver. "What was that about?"

"She wants me to crush the gossip about August and Libby," she said.

"Why you?"

She smiled ruefully. "Apparently, I have a 'more liberal' relationship with them than she does."

He laughed. "Well, I can't disagree with her, Eve. Those rich folks will eat their young and anyone else who doesn't see them as top dog."

"It's bound to get out," Eve said. "You can't keep people from talking."

"It will all come out sooner or later," Oliver agreed. "I never understood this sort of hush-hushing that goes on in these small towns."

"It's what happens before the official word gets out that's the problem," Eve insisted. "Oliver, you realize what the sheriff was getting at with that rope?"

Oliver nodded. "He told me what he was going to do when I sent him back to the car."

"Wasn't that dangerous?" she asked. "Couldn't Mr. Adkins make a case for police coercion?"

"That's why he did it the way he did it," said Oliver. "He never coerced anyone. He asked August to show him a sailor's knot and August willingly submitted. You and I were witnesses to that."

"Where did he get that rope?" Eve asked. "No rope was found on Libby."

"I suspect the sheriff asked for it after we talked to Josh," said the district attorney. "He probably went back to the shack later on and asked him to show him some knots and give him the rope." He looked annoyed.

"And he didn't tell you," Eve guessed.

"I don't ask the police to report their every move," Oliver said. "But I did hope he would keep me informed."

"You think the sheriff has some ideas about that rope?" Eve asked.

"If he thinks he can make a case against August with it, he's going to have to do better than that." His tone was vicious. "I told him I won't prosecute unless I have concrete evidence that won't be thrown out of court."

They got to the end of the river walk and onto the main street, passing by a small gazebo where Kate Talbot, who sometimes helped Agnes with the laundry, waved at her. Her five children, all under the age of six, were running around the gazebo, screaming with laughter.

Eve absently took Oliver's arm. "Oliver, do you really think August is guilty?"

"The evidence is beginning to point that way," Oliver said. "I'm sorry, Eve. I know you like the boy."

"Why are you so apologetic about it?" Eve stiffened. "I thought lawmen are anxious to get a conviction as quickly as possible. It would be a feather in your cap, wouldn't it? A quick conviction for your first murder case as district attorney in Gyver County."

There was silence for a few moments. "I thought you of all people would know I'm not that kind of district attorney, Eve."

She looked at the softened profile. "I didn't mean to offend you, Oliver. I suppose the evidence does look damning from your point of view."

"I don't say it's conclusive," he said. "But meeting the boy has put a different light on things."

"What do you mean?"

"The sheriff talks about the evidence," he said. "But if there's one thing I learned as a police detective in the city, it's that there has to be that little push over the edge for someone to commit a crime. That little moment when something becomes one thing too many."

"What sort of push could August have had?" she asked.

He stopped. "I didn't think I had to explain it to you, Eve."

"You mean the child?" she asked. "But he was happy about that."

"I didn't notice he was particularly happy," Oliver argued. "He seemed more resigned than happy."

"Oh, but that's just because of the circumstances," she said. "You saw how he reacted when he realized the murderer killed two people."

"That could have been the power of suggestion," he said quietly.

"Did you notice Rosalia's reaction?" she asked.

"No, I didn't." He glanced at her. "Should I have?"

"She looked as if someone had punched her in the stomach when I found her in the hallway," Eve said.

"I don't blame her," he said. "I imagine it was the last thing in the world she expected."

"I didn't think of it that way." They reached the entrance of the courthouse.

"I'll tell you one thing, Eve," he said. "I'm not entirely satisfied with this whole interview."

"It was difficult with the lawyer there," Eve agreed.

"Not to mention the mother," he said. "Mothers never help matters."

"You'll be interviewing him again?" Eve guessed.

"If we need to," he said. "It's not for you to worry about. Your worry now is to get the poor girl to her resting place."

Eve nodded. "We can at least do that for Mrs. Cinder."

"And Mr. Cinder," Oliver said with a sigh. "I feel sorry for the old man. He won't live long after this."

"I expect not," she murmured.

"I appreciate you coming with us today," he said. "It couldn't have been easy for you."

"It was a little sordid," she admitted. "But I'm used to sordid things." She played with the strap of her purse. "Oliver, why don't you and Ellen come to dinner tonight?"

He looked touched. "That's mighty kind of you. I'm afraid Ellen has a previous engagement."

"Then you come," she said.

He lingered for a moment, still holding her hand. "You're sure it won't be too much trouble?"

"Not at all," she said. "If you can stand Vi asking you a million questions. You know what young people are like with their taste for sensationalism."

He laughed. "I'll spare her the gruesome details, I promise. I'll be glad to come."

She watched him take the courthouse steps two at a time.

CHAPTER 19

Eve didn't get home until late afternoon. The minute she walked into the house, Agnes accosted her. "Seen this?" She shoved a newspaper in her hand.

Eve forced herself to read the item with the soaring headline "Falcon Hill Prodigal Son Involved in Sordid Affair with Dead Woman!" The paper felt like lead in her hands as she read August's name "connected with the latest tragedy" and how "Sheriff Warner put two and two together" with the gossip that had been going around town about "a certain schoolteacher" getting "too cozy" with "a certain Falcon Hill swell." She was relieved to see the Shane brothers stopped short of accusing August of killing Libby but was horrified they had guessed "the pretty schoolmarm may have decided to end her career earlier than expected due to being in the family way."

"How did they —" She began but bit her tongue, remembering Agnes standing over her with an expectant look.

"Did Helena see this?" she asked.

Agnes nodded. "So did those busybodies."

"You mean Mrs. Beaton and the others? How do you know?"

"They're all downstairs," she said, adding with a sniff, "They're the ones who brought the paper."

"Oh, Lord!" Eve sucked in her breath. "But Libby won't be buried until tomorrow."

"Garfield brought the coffin early," said Agnes.

Eve sighed as she put away her hat and coat. "I suppose Helena was on the phone with them."

"She could convince a farmer to give up his prize chicken for Sunday roast once she sets her mind to it," Agnes agreed.

"I should have been here to help," Eve lamented. "Helena doesn't have the patience for them."

"Well, if you weren't gallivanting all over town with the district attorney, you might have been." The housekeeper sniffed.

"Oh, Agnes, please!" She pressed her temples.

"That ain't your business, Eve, if you'll allow me to say so."

"Have I ever discouraged you from saying anything in this house?" Eve asked warily. "Oliver wanted me to be there when he spoke with August."

"Waste of time, if you ask me," the housekeeper said. "Madge once told me he's got the wits of a goat. That ain't the kind to murder anybody."

"Madge Bradford?" Eve stopped arranging her hair in the hall mirror and looked at her. "How would she know?"

"Used to work in a couple of places around town, including Rosebud Manor for a time," said the woman.

"I suppose I'd better go down there." Eve looked at the stairway leading down to the morgue with apprehension. "I shouldn't leave Helena alone to supervise them."

Agnes grinned. "You always did look out for one another, didn't you, Eve?"

"Had to, Agnes," she said quietly. "She is down there, isn't she?"

The woman nodded. "Said to tell you she's settling the paperwork. Poor Charlie's pushed in the corner like a puppy done wrong. We should treat that boy better, his papa getting killed in the war and all."

"Yes, we should," Eve agreed. "But he's Helena's assistant and you know Helena."

"When she runs the show, ain't nobody can get a word in," Agnes agreed.

Eve made her way down the narrow stairway. She could already hear the women's high-pitched voices. It sometimes grated on her nerves the way Mrs. Beaton and some of the others treated such important work as getting the body ready for burial like a morning tea.

"Well, Maisy Shelton heard Mrs. Parks say — oh, hello, Eve." Mrs. Beaton threw her thick chin at Eve, a typical greeting for those whom she considered indispensable yet still beneath her. "Back from helping the police?"

"I wasn't helping them. I was running some errands in town." Eve approached the long table they used to sort the clothes and belongings of the deceased. Helena was already there in her lab coat, looking through some papers. Charlie was leaning against the wall with his hands behind his back, a sour look on his face.

"Mrs. Parks said how the young man has looked positively flushed and pale the last few months," Mrs. Beaton continued. "Make of *that* what you will."

"Yes, make of *that*," said her echo, Mrs. Hill.

"It's physically impossible for someone to be pale and flushed at the same time," Helena said without looking up from her papers. "Unless someone has certain rare medical conditions."

"Mrs. Parks isn't a doctor, is she?" Mrs. Loy picked up a silver-gilded brush. "My, but Libby had such pretty things."

"How a schoolteacher could afford shoes with silver buckles, I'll never know," Mrs. Close remarked.

"How do you think, Ida?" Mrs. Beaton winked. "Big city girls like her know just how to get all they can out of a man."

"Those poor boys never have a chance," sighed Mrs. Dayton.

She was an older woman whose mother had pushed her into the social circle of Gyver.

"Well, Pearl, I wouldn't quite say *that*," Mrs. Beaton said. "Men of that sort know what they're getting in a girl like that."

"Libby wasn't a city girl," Eve protested, her face growing tight.

"Reno isn't San Francisco," Helena agreed.

"Nevertheless, she knew what she was doing," Mrs. Beaton said with her eyelids half lowered, a sign that she held exclusive rights to a piece of gossip and was about to reveal. All the women leaned toward her eagerly. "Cathy told me just how she operated at the picnic."

"What picnic?" asked Mrs. Loy.

"The one Cathy gave on Valentine's Day, of course," said the woman, a little miffed. "Libby came down with another teacher to help serve. Poor Cathy couldn't get a maid at the last minute, so she went down to the school to ask the teachers. Their salaries are so paltry, you know."

"Oh, how clever of her!" Mrs. Hill clapped her hands.

"Those city girls know what to do when they come upon a man with money," said the woman. "I'm sure her aunt taught her some tricks."

Eve and Helena exchanged a look. Eve thought about the woman they had met at the Cinder house with her practical reasoning and plain clothes.

"Not that I don't think August could have shown more restraint," Mrs. Beaton continued. "But you know how those Falcon Hill boys are."

"Sowing their wild oats." Mrs. Close fanned herself.

"August is a fine fellow!" Charlie leapt forward. "You won't find a better man."

"Charles Eaton, you oughtn't to be here!" Mrs. Beaton shot out. "Mrs. Wright, I *do* wish you would send him out. We have to dress her, you know, and well, it just isn't fitting for a young man to see a young woman undressed."

"Charles's interest is purely clinical, I assure you," said Helena.

"Well, it isn't fitting!"

"I'll thank you to remember this is my establishment," Helena snapped.

Charlie threw a triumphant grin at the society lady.

"And I'll thank *you* to remember we're doing a community service," Mrs. Loy, who had Mexican blood and never hesitated to speak her mind, snapped back.

Mrs. Beaton gave her a sign to be quiet. Then, in a friendlier tone, she asked, "Well, you can ask him to turn around, can't you?"

Helena glanced at the young man. "You'd better do as they say, Charles."

Charlie grumbled but turned around.

"It's just as the paper said," Mrs. Hill ventured. "That poor boy lost his head."

"Helena and I met Libby's aunt and she's a lovely person." Eve carefully went through the jewelry box Mrs. Cinder had sent over. In a low voice, she said to her sister, "Maybe we ought to give this to the police."

"They've been through it already." Helena's attention went back to her papers. "Mrs. Cinder said so when she brought it over this morning."

"Well, then. Libby must have learned from her fellow schoolteachers." The society woman glanced once more at Charlie as he stood in the corner, his arms crossed, staring at the wall, before she arranged Libby's hair.

"I doubt that very much," Helena mumbled.

"Oh, but you don't know those city schoolteachers, Mrs. Wright," said Mrs. Hill. "Why, I had a cousin who taught at a high school in Los Angeles. She wore her skirts short and bobbed her hair and no one said a word!"

"They stay out until all hours even on school nights," Mrs. Loy added. "I heard some of them can dance the Shimmy better than any flapper."

"I wouldn't be surprised if Libby Cinder was meeting a beau the night she was killed," declared Mrs. Close. "And he did her in with an ax."

"There are no ax marks on the body," Helena said.

"Yes, I can see that," mumbled the woman.

Eve's hands were cold as she grasped the table. "There's no evidence she was meeting anyone, Mrs. Beaton."

"What, you think she was just going for a stroll by the river late at night?" The woman eyed her. "You know more than you're telling, don't you, Eve?"

"It wasn't August!" Charlie's voice was muffed from facing the wall. "He wouldn't do a thing like that."

"Nobody is saying it was, Charles," Mrs. Beaton insisted. "I suppose she trapped some man and he killed her. That's the only explanation."

"Maybe she was killed by a gangster, just like Mrs. Browly told me," said Mrs. Hill, her eyes wide.

"Don't be ridiculous, Edith," her leader snorted. "What would a gangster be doing in Gyver?"

"At least you admit *that*," Helena said.

"I wouldn't be surprised if she did want to trap him," Mrs. Loy said with a wink. "After all, girls like that —"

"Money or with child," Mrs. Close agreed.

Eve's gut tightened. "Aren't you letting your imagination run away with you, Mrs. Close?"

"Dr. Myers didn't think so," said the woman. "He was talking about young girls getting themselves in situations they didn't know how to get out of the other day."

Eve saw the fire in Helena's eyes as she snarled, "Dr. Myers needs to learn to keep his non-medical theories to himself!"

"I didn't say it was *true*," said Mrs. Close. But she openly stared down at the deceased's stomach.

"Must you be so vulgar, Ida?" Mrs. Dayton flinched. "Really, I don't think it's proper to talk about a young woman like that when she's going to be buried tomorrow. What's done is done."

"When it concerns one of the oldest families in town, Pearl, I think we have a right to know the truth." Mrs. Beaton suddenly planted a firm eye on Helena. "You're the only one who has had intimate contact with the body, Mrs. Wright."

"What a way of putting it," Helena mumbled.

"Nonetheless, for the good of the community, I ask you straight out — is there something about Libby Cinder that might come out and tarnish our reputation?"

"Don't you mean *her* reputation?" Eve asked.

"I mean *ours*, Eve. What concerns one concerns all." She continued to study Helena. "Well, Mrs. Wright?"

Eve gritted her teeth. She and Helena both knew Mrs. Beaton was apt to beat the same drum to death until she got her answer.

Her sister turned over the page in front of her and said nothing.

"Mrs. Beaton, has it ever occurred to you if Libby did stray — and I don't say she did, but *if* — she may have had cause to?" Eve played with a beaded necklace still lying at the bottom of the jewelry box.

"Why, Eve, you surprise me." The woman stared at her.

"You of all people," mumbled Mrs. Hill.

"Now who's been losing her head?" Mrs. Close asked with a sly look. "Don't tell us Violet's been convincing you —"

Eve was about to speak but Charlie came to her defense. "You hold your tongue about Violet! She just likes to have fun."

The woman shrugged and went back to smoothing down the pockets of the jacket they had slipped over Libby's shoulders.

"There is no justification for loose behavior, Eve," Mrs. Beaton said in a sharp tone. "Especially in women."

"Why especially women?" Helena eyed her. "A man could lose his reputation as much as a woman if he goes too far."

"It's not easy being young and living a life destined for spinsterhood," Eve said. "Everything is dictated to those teachers, including who they can be seen with in public and what they can do. They can never marry."

"How would you know that?" Mrs. Loy asked.

"Eve's friend Dot was once contemplating the life," said Mrs. Close.

"You make it sound like she was going to become a nun," Helena said dryly.

"Well, it nearly amounted to that, didn't it?" the woman challenged.

"And you think that's an excuse to ensnare a man?" The leader of Gyver society studied her.

"Libby didn't ensnare anyone," said Eve. "She and August were in love."

"That's what *he* said," said Mrs. Beaton. "Poor boy, he probably was. Whether Libby was, I imagine, is a different story."

Mrs. Dalton looked down at the young lady. "Maybe Eve has a point, Clementine. I do hate to see young people on this table. Do you think we ought to put some powder and rouge on her, dear?"

"Well, we don't know much about *that*, do we?" asked Mrs. Beaton. "I imagine Violet will be down soon? She seems to have a knack for painting faces." She gave Eve a pointed look.

Eve's blood boiled at the insinuation but Helena grabbed her wrist.

In a calm tone, Eve asked, "Did Mrs. Cinder leave word regarding any special clothes or jewelry she wanted to go with Libby?"

"She said something about a butterfly ring she used to wear as a girl," Mrs. Beaton said. "I seem to recall my Cathy having one just like it when she was a child."

Eve looked through the jewelry box again, noting there was

no sign of the engagement ring August had described. She found the butterfly ring and handed it to Mrs. Beaton.

The woman examined it before putting it beside the waxy hand as Eve handed her a light pink scarf. "Oh, that's lovely, Eve. You do have the utmost taste when it comes to laying out the dead."

"We *have* been doing this for a while, Mrs. Beaton," said Helena. Though she didn't look up from her papers, Eve saw a half smile on her face.

"It will make her look so innocent," sighed Mrs. Loy. "I think that's the proper tone for a young lady about to be buried regardless of her life on earth, don't you, Clementine?"

"The Lord does like angels entering His gates," the woman agreed.

"One can be an angel in heaven even if one is not on earth," Mrs. Hill added.

"Libby was a good person," Eve insisted.

Mrs. Beaton cast the fly gaze on her. "And just how do you know that, Eve?"

"From people I've spoken with who knew her."

"You mean from people the police have spoken to," Mrs. Loy said.

She felt Helena's warning eye on her, but she continued, "Mrs. Cinder, Miss Gilbert —"

"Who's Miss Gilbert?" Mrs. Dalton asked.

"Libby's aunt," Helena supplied.

"Florence Horne, a good friend of Libby's," Eve continued. She felt as if a whip were flying on the back of a stone horse as her words flung out without effect.

Mrs. Beaton patted her hand. "You're a nice person, Eve. You're just the sort to believe in what family and friends say about someone."

"Eve knows people better than you do, Mrs. Beaton," Helena lashed out.

"Libby was a good teacher," Eve continued. "Even Principal Watts said that. She cared about the children she taught. She loved children."

"No doubt," said Mrs. Beaton. "She couldn't wait to have some of her own, could she?" Her insistent eyes bore on Helena, who again said nothing.

"Mrs. Earle said she always struck her husband as fast," Mrs. Close said. "He's the janitor of the school where she taught, you know."

"We know better than you do," Helena said dryly.

"He once saw her come out of the ladies room with her hair out of pins," Mrs. Close continued. "And once he overheard her telling one of the teachers about a piece of silk she'd bought for a song she was going to make into an afternoon dress. As if Betty Cain's shop weren't good enough for her!" She received sniffs of approval, as the community ladies had a very low opinion of anyone who didn't contribute to the local economy.

"I shouldn't think you would take the word of a school janitor," Eve remarked.

Mrs. Close glared at her. "Mrs. Earle is the best cook I've ever had and I trust what she says!"

Helena's smile was condescending. "My, but you do have the most interesting sources of information among the working class."

Mrs. Beaton gave her a stern look. "We care deeply about everyone in this community, Mrs. Wright."

"We must look out for the young people or this town will become another San Francisco," Mrs. Loy declared.

"All the girls will have loose morals and all the boys will develop criminal minds like the gangsters in the moving pictures," Mrs. Beaton agreed and Mrs. Hill shuddered.

"One dead woman does not mean the town has run amok, Mrs. Beaton," Eve said.

"Not statistically, anyway," Helena added.

"August didn't do it!" Charlie declared to the wall.

"Of course he didn't do it, Charles." Mrs. Beaton clasped a bracelet on Libby's limp wrist. "You keep your head turned now."

"We're just putting on her shoes," Mrs. Hill pointed out.

"A young man should not be looking at a woman's ankles," Mrs. Dalton declared, who had somewhat of a prim nature. Charlie giggled in the corner.

"Not that I would blame him if he did," Mrs. Loy said. "If she were with child, well, what's a young man to do?"

"You've always been rather broad-minded when it comes to that sort of thing, Rosa,."Mrs. Close said. A vicious look appeared in Mrs. Loy's dark eyes.

"Eve said he was in love with her," Mrs. Hill said in a meek voice.

"Even if he were, Edith, he wouldn't have married her," Mrs. Beaton declared.

Eve paused as she contemplated whether to use the new pair of stockings Mrs. Cinder had dropped off, then decided they would be too complicated to put on the lifeless body. "August was engaged to Libby."

"Is that what *he* said?" Mrs. Beaton asked.

"That's what *he* said," Eve snapped.

Charlie peered over his shoulder and, seeing Libby was now fully dressed, turned around. "That's exactly the sort of thing August would do."

"Impossible," the woman declared as she buttoned up Libby's jacket. "Rosalia wouldn't hear of such a thing."

"Mothers don't know everything about their sons," Helena said and was rewarded with a flash of concern on the women's faces, all of whom had at least one son.

"Everyone knows he's going to marry Cecilia." Mrs. Loy lay a pearl necklace against Libby's white throat. "I don't know, Clementine, I rather think this makes the girl look a little old."

"Not old, dear, mature," said her friend. "Just because a lady is young doesn't mean she has to look it in death. Death requires dignity, after all."

"There's been no announcement of an engagement." Helena opened a file cabinet already overflowing as she tried to slip the folder with the papers in it.

"You mean not yet," Mrs. Dalton corrected. "He's still trying to get his bearings, poor boy."

"If August didn't marry Cecilia two years ago, what makes you think he'll marry her now?"

"They were destined to be a match ever since they were children," said Mrs. Beaton. "That other time — well, that was unfortunate."

"There was nothing unfortunate about it, Mrs. Beaton," Helena said, closing the file drawer a little too neatly. "He broke off the engagement to go to sea."

"When a young man of our sort gets an idea into his head, it's impossible to stop him," Mrs. Close insisted. "Rosalia always said he would come back and he did."

"Back into the fold where he belongs," Mrs. Loy said in a stoic tone.

"They'll marry before the year is out," Mrs. Beaton said. "Mark my words."

"Clementine is always right about these things," Mrs. Hill said with a look of admiration.

"Perhaps you're right, Mrs. Beaton," Eve said. "After all, she did forgive him for breaking off the engagement."

"Exactly my point," the woman insisted. "Cecilia may not have much spirit, but she has more brains than people give her credit for."

"And more brains than her mother," Mrs. Close added. "The way Eleanor treats the boy you'd think he had leprosy."

"Cecilia won't let that stop her," Mrs. Beaton said. "I've always said of that girl that still waters run deep."

"Still waters run deep," Eve murmured.

"I rather thought her to be like a sugar bride," Mrs. Hill lamented. "Sweet but — well, dissolving."

"Why, Edith, what a thing to say!" Mrs. Beaton clearly disapproved. "She is sweet-natured, to be sure, but it's as I said."

"It's not fair to blame the girl for her mother's eccentricities," Mrs. Loy added.

"Nonsense, Rosa," said the leader of Falcon Hill society. "We ought to praise her for all she's done for the communities here with her charity auctions and balls."

"I rather thought accolades were the point for her," Helena murmured, and Charlie, now sitting opposite her at the desk helping to go over the last of the forms, chuckled.

"Isn't there a pair of gloves somewhere in that box, Eve?" asked Mrs. Close.

"Help yourself." Eve pushed the box toward her. "Mrs. Beaton, what do you mean by still waters run deep?"

"The way Cecilia acted toward Libby at the picnic for one," Mrs. Beaton said in the clear way of wanting to lead into a piece of gossip.

"How did she act, Clementine?" asked Mrs. Dalton. Again, all the ladies leaned toward her. Eve found her own ears perked.

"Cathy told me all about it," she said. "Spilled her punch all over the front of Libby's uniform. Cathy *insisted* she wear a uniform." She leaned back with a satisfied smile.

"It may have been an accident," Helena pointed out, the glasses she used for paperwork slipping down her nose.

"Cathy didn't think so," Mrs. Beaton said in a knowing tone.

"Is Cathy an expert on maid behavior?" Helena sniffed.

The woman stiffened. "You clearly know very little about hosting a party, Mrs. Wright."

"Indeed," Helena murmured and went back to her papers.

"A good hostess is constantly watching her servants, ready to intervene when the least unpleasantness arises," Mrs. Beaton continued. "Cathy knew from the first glance at August and

Libby talking in the corner that something was going to happen so she concealed herself behind a tree nearby."

"Clever Cathy," Mrs. Hill sighed.

"Naturally, dear, she has my intelligence." Mrs. Beaton smoothed out her hair. "She said the look in Cecilia's eye — well, it alarmed her, that's all."

"Do hostesses also have to be mind readers?" Helena asked.

"I always thought Cecilia could put a knife through someone's heart clean as butter," Mrs. Hill shivered.

"Don't talk like the fan magazines, Edith," her friend snapped. "It's vulgar."

Helena finally put the cap on the fountain pen. "Charles, I think we're done here."

"I thought she'd sue August for breach of promise for sure," Mrs. Loy said.

"Rosalia talked her out of it," said Mrs. Dalton. "Rosalia's a crafty one."

"Can't a man change his mind without some woman trying to get money out of him?" Charlie growled.

"Mind your own business, Charles," Helena said. "Here, come help me find an envelope so you can take these down to the courthouse." She waved the packet of papers in her hand.

"That's just not true, Pearl," Mrs. Beaton insisted. "Rosalia has always been like a mother to her. Heaven knows, she hasn't had much maternal love from her own."

"Why, Mrs. Beaton, I didn't think you thought much about such sentimental things," Helena said.

The woman's mouth set in an annoyed pout but she said nothing.

Helena at last found the envelope she was looking for. "You're going to have to hurry if you want to catch Bill Peterson before he leaves, Charles."

"With pleasure, Mrs. Wright." The young man glared at the

ladies who were now helping Eve gather what they hadn't used on Libby to give back to Mrs. Cinder and went out the door.

Mrs. Hill put the last of the clothes in the leather suitcase. "I can take these back to her if you like, Eve."

"Thank you, Mrs. Hill." Eve smiled.

"If it weren't for Rosalia, I'm sure Cecilia wouldn't have given August a second glance when he came back," Mrs. Beaton said.

"They were certainly heading in the right direction," Mrs. Dalton agreed.

Eve leaned against the desk. "How do you mean, Mrs. Dalton?"

"Why, they're always about town together," said the woman.

"Why wouldn't they be?" Helena asked. "They've been friends since childhood."

"Pearl means they go about arm in arm, my dear," Mrs. Close said. "Looking cow-eyed at one another."

"She's looking cow-eyed at him," Mrs. Loy corrected. "And he's not exactly turning away."

"What do you mean by always?" Helena put her hand on her hip.

"Oh, everywhere in town," said Mrs. Beaton. "The drugstore, the movie theater, Browly's, the post office."

"He told us he was lonely when he first came back," Eve said absently.

"Us?" Mrs. Beaton eyed her.

"Eve went with Oliver to see August," said Helena.

The woman looked at Eve. "Do you think that's wise, dear? Considering you're handling the body?"

"You said no one was accusing him, Clementine," Mrs. Loy pointed out. "It's not his body."

"I'm not talking about when he first came back," Mrs. Close insisted. "I'm talking about this past month. They were together nearly every day. Billy's been trailing Sam Hewitt — he's studying civil engineering, you know — and he said he saw them together walking by the river, laughing and throwing pebbles in the water."

Eve made a silent note to tell Oliver about this, recalling August had been clear he hadn't seen Cecilia since she went with him to buy the engagement ring a month ago.

Mrs. Beaton frowned at herself in the small gilded mirror hung on the wall. "Really, Eve, you ought to get this cleaned."

"I will," Eve promised. She couldn't help but think how Libby was restored to her non-schoolteacher prettiness as she and Helena closed the coffin lid.

CHAPTER 20

That evening, Oliver arrived promptly at seven. The comfort of fried chicken and mashed potatoes enveloped the house.

"It's nice to have an old-fashioned housekeeper like Mrs. Bishop," he remarked as Felix handed him a highball. "Our cook prefers to try all the latest culinary fads. Sunday roast for us has become chicken à la king and pork chops in wine sauce."

Felix's lips twisted into a mocking smile. "I think I'd rather have rice and beans."

"Maybe we ought to have rice and beans once in a while," Helena remarked as she accepted the cocktail he gave her.

"Would that be one of your experiments, my love?" Her husband looked at her with uneven eyes as he always did when he was in one of his sarcastic moods. "Perhaps you could go down to the Mold District and get some recipes."

"That wasn't what I meant," she said quietly.

"I'm glad to hear it." He crossed his long legs. "It wouldn't be a lark, I assure you."

"Where's my cocktail?" Violet asked, her mouth curved with displeasure.

Felix glanced at Eve, the cocktail shaker poised over a glass. "That's for Big Sister to decide."

"It is not!" Violet flared. "I'm old enough."

"Not until you're a few years older," Eve declared.

"Who says?" her youngest sister demanded.

"Eve and I say," Helena retorted.

Felix chuckled. "Sorry, my pet, grape juice for you."

"I'll join you, Violet." Oliver set his cocktail aside and reached for the glass Felix handed him. Eve shot him a look of gratitude for helping keep the peace.

Violet looked smug. "You ought to bring that shaker to the service tomorrow, Felix. That would liven things up."

"Vi, don't be disrespectful!" Eve snapped.

"That might be a new venture for me," Felix chuckled. "What do you think, my love? Selling cocktails, fifty cents apiece, at the cemetery."

"Now *you're* being disrespectful," Helena growled.

"Not at all," he insisted. "Everyone needs a good stiff drink at a funeral."

"I don't think you should tease your wife and sister-in-law about their business," Oliver said in a steel tone.

Felix downed the cocktail. "I've tried telling them they should raise their prices. They're charging the same as what their father did twenty years ago." In a more distant tone, he added, "Got to save for tomorrow, for tomorrow you never know what will come."

Eve felt a pang of sympathy as his slick good-looking face suddenly filled with deep lines at the memory of the poverty that had ruined his family when he was barely fifteen. "We don't work that way, Felix."

"We're the only place for miles around so it wouldn't be fair to take advantage of that," Helena agreed.

"You mean it wouldn't be right." Felix studied her.

"It wouldn't be right," she said softly.

"Papa always said everyone deserves their place in the earth," Violet defended.

Felix's eyes grew like a crab's. "I'm surprised to hear you say that, my pet."

"Well, they do," she sulked.

"The soul must be united with the body in proper burial," Eve said with a sigh.

"It's not a question of reuniting the soul and the body," Helena argued. "It's pure sanitation. If those who couldn't pay for a funeral didn't come to us, what do you think they would do? They would bury their dead themselves and improperly too."

Felix shuddered. "Maybe you're right, my love. I don't fancy having my air stinking to high heaven from rotted corpses."

"They might even throw them in the river," Violet offered. "Or put them in whiskey barrels like the grave robbers did a hundred years ago."

"Don't be fanciful, Vi." Eve felt her face redden.

Oliver, who had been silent during this family exchange, burst out laughing.

"I don't know how we got onto this rather morbid conversation," Eve said. "And in the presence of our guest too."

Agnes appeared, looking a little ridiculous in the maid's uniform she insisted wearing when the family had guests for dinner. "Dinner is served," she said in an almost haughty voice.

"You look like a dressed lamb in that hat, Agnes," Violet teased. The housekeeper gave her a dirty look.

"My, but this is a celebration," Felix remarked, eyeing the dusty wine bottle on the table. "Don't tell me you dug it out of the cellar, Agnes."

"Where else am I going to get it?" She sniffed. "Ain't like I can go to Arkins General Store and get a bottle nowadays."

"I thought you approved of Prohibition," Violet said.

"Don't see nothing wrong with having wine on a special occasion," the woman insisted.

"Maybe Oliver would rather not." Eve cast an eye in his direction.

"Prohibition is against making and selling liquor, Eve, not drinking it," Helena pointed out.

"I've no objection to it," Oliver said, "but if you've a limited supply —"

"Then you'll pour us all a glass, won't you?" Violet held hers up.

"Not for you," Helena said firmly.

"Oh, let her have a glass," Felix said. "This is an occasion, after all. It isn't every day we have the distinguished district attorney at our house for dinner."

"That's so, Jake," Violet declared. Felix growled at her flapper slang.

"Half a glass, then." Helena sat her sister down. "That's all you'll get."

"It's a shame Ellen couldn't join us," Eve said as Oliver poured wine all around, filling Violet's glass halfway.

"She sends her deepest regrets," he said.

"I'll bet she does," Violet said under her breath, then, out loud, in a bubbly tone, "Now that we're all fortified, let's talk about livelier subjects, like this investigation."

"I consider murder as morbid as death," Eve said.

"That's because they're one and the same," Felix said.

"Well, I don't!" her youngest sister said.

"We're making slow progress." Oliver took the ladle from Agnes and served himself soup.

"I heard all the old hens were out here this afternoon, my love." Felix shook out his napkin before spreading it neatly on his lap. Even though the Grave household was informal at mealtimes, even with guests, Felix still insisted on the manners of his upbringing.

"Don't call them that, Felix." Helena leaned back a little to allow Agnes to serve her. "They save us a lot of time and effort."

"And money," Felix chimed in. "Don't forget that."

"*You* never forget it," Violet mumbled.

"When one has lost it, my pet, one never forgets," he said with a trace of bitterness.

"Oliver doesn't need to hear our family squabbles tonight, so stop it, both of you," Eve snapped.

"We don't squabble!" Violet insisted. "We're a very nice family, aren't we, Oliver?"

"Very nice," he said with a grin. "What's a family without a squabble or two?"

"Perhaps you're right, my love." Felix's tone was serious for the first time that evening. "They do save you and Eve from a gruesome task."

"There's nothing gruesome about it," Helena insisted.

"It's rather soothing, in fact," Eve added.

"Soothing to dress a dead person?" Felix shuddered.

"They don't look dead when you dress them," Violet said. "They look like they're in a peaceful sleep."

Eve paused with her spoon over the soup. "It's like you're preparing them for meeting the other world."

"I never thought about it that way," Oliver said. "You have a way of putting things, Eve."

Felix regarded her with his crab eyes. "Not everyone goes to that heavenly place in the sky, you know."

"Don't talk nonsense, Felix," his wife snapped.

"Even the sinners deserve to go out in style," Violet declared, taking a large portion of the mashed potatoes. In spite of her friends being so concerned about their figures, she refused to let go of her hearty appetite.

"Sinners," Eve lamented. "That's what they think."

"They?" Felix asked.

"The community women."

"That's what the town thinks after the Shane boys ripped the poor girl apart in the paper this morning," Violet said.

Eve glanced at her. "Kitty showed it to you, did she?"

"We were all reading about it this morning," Violet said. "Kitty and Jimmy and Ruth and all the rest."

"And what did your jazzy crowd think of Miss Cinder and her unfortunate demise?" Felix asked, amused.

Violet said in an almost child-like tone, "I don't think they were right at all. Libby was nice. She always seemed nice."

"Still waters run deep," Felix warned, shaking his fork with every word.

"Still waters run deep," Eve repeated, glancing at Helena.

"Is that what the community women think, Eve?" Oliver asked.

"Yes, but they didn't say it about Libby," she said. "They said it about Cecilia."

"You mean Mrs. Beaton said it," Helena said.

Violet snorted. "Cecilia is a chump!"

Felix laughed. "I'm with you, my pet. If Cecilia were a well, it would be dry down to the bottom."

"That's a terrible thing to say about a woman," Helena said sharply.

"Obviously, Mrs. Beaton doesn't agree with you," Oliver remarked. "I wonder why."

"It had to do with August and Libby's first meeting," Eve said. "I told you about that, remember?"

"You didn't tell *me*." Violet took two more rolls.

"Maybe they were afraid you would gag at the sentimental story," Felix teased. "I'm assuming it is a sentimental story?"

"As I recall, Cecilia spilled punch all over Libby's uniform," Oliver said, putting more green beans in his plate. "There's some question as to whether it was deliberate or not."

"Oh, do tell!" Violet's eyes sparkled as she leaned forward.

"Elbows off the table, missy," Agnes growled. "Or you don't get no dessert."

"I'm not five anymore, Agnes," she snarled.

"Frankly, I was surprised to hear it," Oliver admitted. "She seems a courteous young woman."

"Never underestimate a girl who's about to lose her man." Felix poured himself another glass of wine.

"He's not her man," Helena reminded him. "He hasn't been for a few years."

"I don't believe it was deliberate," Eve insisted. "Cecilia may have been hurt, but she would never do a thing like that."

"Her kind would stomp around in the privacy of her own room," Violet agreed.

"Hence the still waters, my pet," Felix said.

"I didn't say I believed Cathy's colorful imagination," Helena said dryly. "I'm just relating what was said."

"I wish she'd show some backbone," Violet said. "If a man threw me over, the only attention he would get from me is a spit in his eye."

"Females are rather cold-blooded animals." Felix winked at Oliver.

"Don't forget Cecilia and August have known one another for a long time," Eve said.

Violet waved her hand away. "If that were the only criteria for forgiving a cad, I'd be engaged ten times over."

"In a pig's eye you would," Agnes barked.

"Heaven help the man when you do get engaged." Felix rolled his eyes. Violet snapped her napkin at him.

"There's something you ought to know, Oliver," Eve said as Agnes put a fresh plate of rolls in front of her. "The ladies said they saw a lot of August and Cecilia together."

Oliver put his fork down. "He told us he hadn't seen her in over a month."

"Ooohhh, liar, liar!" Violet playfully shook her finger. "They've been going around together like two cooing doves for several weeks."

"Cooing doves?" Helena eyed her.

"All right, maybe not cooing, but they've been together," Violet insisted.

"Your set is expert at petting and cooing, isn't it?" Felix asked.

Eve looked away.

"I don't do any of that," Violet said. "It's silly sap stuff."

"We're glad to hear it," Helena mumbled.

"Are you saying you saw them?" Oliver asked.

"Sure I did," she said.

"Where?"

"At the drugstore, of course. The bakery too. Oh, everywhere."

"Nice of you to tell me now," Oliver said dryly. He handed the half-full bottle of wine to Agnes and made a gesture. She promptly took it back to the kitchen.

"Well, I didn't know it was important, did I?" asked Violet with indignation. "I'm not a lady detective like my sisters."

"We're not lady detectives," Eve protested.

"Your sisters have been a great help to me," Oliver said in a sharp tone.

Violet leaned back. "Well, now I can be a great help. What would you say if I told you I saw them drive off together?"

"Is it too much to hope you knew where they were going?"

"They passed Kitty and me on the way to the drugstore in an old clunky Chevy toward the main road out of town," she said.

"One of Rapp's cars," Felix supplied. "He's got two, both practically horse-drawn and both overpriced."

"I wonder how you know that," Helena said without looking up from her plate.

A tense curtain hung in the air for a moment but it was gone in a flash as Felix laughed. "Don't you remember when my brother wanted to come out here for a visit last year? I made enquiries."

"Yes, you did," Helena said. A breath of air entered the dining room. "I forgot about that."

"I thought all those well-to-do young men have cars of their own," Oliver remarked.

"Rosalia doesn't approve of automobiles," Helena said. "They still have a carriage in their garage, though no horses to pull it."

"So he has to rent a car if he wants to go anywhere," Oliver said. "Well, we'll have to ask him about his sojourns out of town." He looked at Violet. "You wouldn't happen to remember when you saw this, would you?"

"January sixth," she said. "Do you want the hour too?"

"No, that will do," he said with a grin. "I see all three Grave sisters are observant. Much obliged."

"Better than Eve, I'll bet," she mumbled as the grandfather clock in the hall struck. "Lord, Kitty's outside!"

"How on earth could you know that?" Helena asked. "You can't see the door from here."

Just then, a loud honk came from outside It sounded three times, then twice, and then once.

Violet jumped up from the table. "May I be excused?"

"Would you stop if I said no?" Eve asked warily.

"Not in the least, darling." Her sister kissed her cheek. "But as we have company, I thought it prudent to ask."

"Don't go tearing up the town now," Oliver warned in an amused tone.

"Since we know just where the district attorney is tonight, we'd be safe from prosecution, wouldn't we?" Violet winked as she rushed into the hall for her coat and hat.

"Don't be home late," Eve warned. "We're up early for the funeral tomorrow."

"Funeral?"

"Libby's funeral."

Her sister appeared in the hall. "You don't expect me to go to *that*, do you?"

"We should all be there," Helena said. "For the service, at least."

"But it's so damn ghoulish!" her sister protested.

"You mind your tongue, missy," Agnes scolded.

"Please, darling." Eve used the soft reasoning that sometimes worked on Violet.

"No, Eve," her sister said firmly. "I'm old enough to make my own decisions."

"You will be when you make the right ones," Helena said.

Violet glared at her older sister. "I suppose you think you know what the right ones are?"

Helena smiled sweetly as her sister stomped out of the room, the door slamming after her.

Felix burst out laughing. "My love, you do have spirit sometimes."

"You mean when I'm not buried in my experiments?" Helena asked without smiling.

He rose, kissing her cheek. "I'm sorry I can't stay, Oliver. Duty calls, you know."

"I know," said the district attorney.

"May I go on record to say that I think you're on the wrong track?"

"Eh?" Oliver stared at him.

"I mean with this August Winters business. The boy's a sissy, you know. Wouldn't even kill a fly. I'll bet he stayed below deck the whole time he was on that ship sick to his stomach." Felix chuckled as he went up the stairs.

"We'll have coffee in the living room, Agnes," Eve instructed. "You'll join us, Helena, dear?"

Her sister shook her head. "Bring mine to the laboratory, please, Agnes." The housekeeper made a sour face and retreated.

"Laboratory?" Oliver questioned as they settled in the living room.

Eve smiled. "Helena calls it that. It's really the garden shed behind the house." She nodded toward the window behind her.

Oliver peered out. "Funny I never noticed it."

"It's the shrubbery," Eve said. "Papa built it for her when she was only nine. A pet frog of hers died and she wanted to know why it died so he gave her a place where she could dissect it."

"Sounds rather gruesome for a nine-year-old," Oliver said.

Eve laughed. "Helena never shrank from the guts of any animal. Remember how she would help you clean the turkey for Christmas, Agnes?"

The elderly woman shuddered as she set the tray down carefully on the coffee table. "Wanted to inspect all the innards. Clean as a whistle, that bird was."

Oliver laughed.

"I'll pour the coffee, Agnes," Eve said. "You go to bed."

"With that one out?" She looked toward the front door where Violet had left her mark in a whiff of perfume.

"I'll see she gets in early, Mrs. Bishop," Oliver promised. "I'll make a phone call right now to the police station so they'll keep an eye on her."

"Better tell 'em not to let her see 'em," Agnes said. "She'd outrun 'em for sure." The woman gave Oliver a knowing look as she retreated.

He went to the phone and came back in a few moments, accepting the cup Eve handed him with a sigh. "Maybe I shouldn't have gotten you involved in this case, Eve."

"We would have been involved anyway," she said. "We're burying her, remember?"

"I suppose it's as difficult to deal with the grief as it is to deal with the crime."

"You can't separate one from the other," Eve said softly.

They sat quietly next to each other in silence for a moment.

Eve was the first to speak. "Oliver, maybe it's true August saw a lot of Cecilia when Libby was away, but that doesn't mean he didn't propose to Libby when she came back from Reno like he said."

"No, but it does rather point to a callousness on his part," said Oliver. "He's been callous toward Cecilia from the beginning."

"Not callous, surely," Eve said. "Thoughtless, maybe."

He grimaced. "Ah, the way you ladies make amends for a young man with a baby face."

"You don't believe he intended to marry Libby?" Eve looked at him.

"I've seen dozens of young men make promises of marriage and never follow through."

"Do they also go as far as to buy a ring?" Eve challenged.

"If they have plenty of money so the expense of a diamond ring would hardly put a dent in their monthly allowance, they might." He began pacing in front of the fireplace. "It's not just the callousness, Eve. He's been lying to us this whole time."

She stared at him. "What do you mean?"

"The argument he had with Libby, for one," said the district attorney. "Do you believe it was about her work?"

"No," Eve admitted. "It sounded a little too trite for an argument that led Libby to insist on going away."

"Exactly!" Oliver pointed.

"I assume you have another theory about the quarrel?" Eve asked.

"The sheriff does."

Eve's throat tightened. "And what does the hasty Sheriff Warner think?"

"August wanted to go back to sea and Libby tried to stop him," said Oliver.

Eve stared. "But his seafaring experience wasn't exactly a success."

"That doesn't mean he's given up the idea, Eve."

"No, I guess it doesn't." Eve remembered the wistful way the young man had stared out the window at the river. "But kill a woman for that? It seems a little far-fetched."

"She wasn't just a woman," Oliver argued. "She was the mother of his child. An illegitimate child, I should add."

"Do you seriously think August is the type to shirk that kind of responsibility?"

"I don't think anything," he said. "I've only lived here three years and have had little contact with the Falcon Hill people."

"Well, I've lived here all my life," she insisted. "August has never struck me as that kind of young man."

"That boy was lying about the argument," Oliver said. "If he was lying, it means there's something he's trying to hide."

"With you and Sheriff Warner acting like Baskerville hounds, I'm sure you'll find out what it is," Eve snapped.

Oliver leaned against the mantel, looking at her. Then he threw back his head and laughed. "You certainly don't back down from a fight, do you?"

She felt her face grow warm. "That argument can't matter now Libby is dead."

"It's not about the argument," Oliver said. "Once a suspect lies —"

"You said he wasn't a suspect!"

"I said he wasn't being arrested," Oliver corrected. "He was a suspect from the beginning and still is, Eve."

Agnes came in. "Just found some coffee cake in the icebox," she grunted as she laid the plate on the tray. With a warning glare, she said, "Now don't you go filling her head with all this crime nonsense before bedtime. Enough to give a person bad dreams." She retreated to the other side of the house.

"I thought you told her to go to bed," Oliver said.

"Agnes is rarely in bed before we are," Eve said. "I suppose it's her privilege to worry about us even though we can take care of ourselves now."

"She doesn't approve of me much, does she?" he asked ruefully.

Eve smiled. "It's your talking about police business she doesn't approve of."

Oliver sat down. "Perhaps I ought to talk about the weather, then."

"What you're trying to say is once a suspect tells one lie, he can't be trusted to tell the truth."

"It's not just one lie," Oliver said. "There were other lies too."

"You mean like where he was the night of the murder?"

Oliver smiled. "So you noticed that."

"His story did seem a little flimsy," Eve admitted. "This may be a small town but there's always someone about even at night, and people greet each other here."

"We checked with Josh," said Oliver. "Unlike Rosalia, he told us straight out he didn't see August as he was fishing up the river most of the night."

"You mean he didn't lie like his mother did," Eve murmured.

"Not that I blame her." The district attorney took a pipe out of his pocket and gave Eve a questionable look, making sure she nodded her approval before he lit it.

"It was a foolish thing to do," Eve agreed. "Rosalia isn't a foolish woman, Oliver."

He chuckled. "I don't know how many times I've caught mothers lying, even in the face of their sons bragging to high heaven about their crime."

"Just because he may not have taken a walk downtown doesn't mean he was out killing his fiancée and unborn child," Eve insisted.

"I'm having the sheriff and his men check all over town," said Oliver. "Just as you said, there's always somebody about. Even if they didn't wave hello, someone still may have seen him, and his alibi might check out after all."

"And if it doesn't?"

Oliver shrugged, looking into the fire.

She took a slice of coffee cake and held it out to him but he shook his head. As she set it down, she said, "There is another possibility, you know."

"In a murder case, there are endless possibilities," he said. "Police work is more about eliminating the possibilities that don't make sense than it is about stabbing in the dark to find the right one."

"Maybe the papers were right about Libby," Eve ventured. "Maybe she was — a little spirited."

He eyed her. "Weren't you the one telling the ladies what a virtuous woman she was?"

"Well, maybe she really did veer away from virtue over the years!" Eve insisted. "Maybe the restricted life of a schoolteacher got to her and she became one of those flirts one reads about in the magazines."

Oliver chuckled. "That sounds like something Violet would say."

Eve blushed. "Maybe she was seeing other men, and one of them was the father of her child."

He strolled over to the mantlepiece again. "So she expected, and got, a proposal from one young man and told him she was having his child while she was running around with other men, one of whom was the real father of her child? All under our very noses without anyone, including her mother and her best friend, knowing about it?"

"All right, so maybe it doesn't make sense!" Eve collected the dishes in an agitated way. "Agnes! Come take the coffee, for heaven's sake. The smell is making me sick!"

Agnes appeared, her brows knitted. "What'd I tell you? All this talk about blood and guts and now you've upset Eve." She shook a thick finger at him. "You ain't got no business disturbing the peace of a good-hearted woman who's only been kind to you."

"Agnes, please!" All at once, Eve felt ashamed. "Go to bed. I'm sorry I called you. I'll take the tray to the kitchen, and I'll wash the dishes."

"*I'll* take the tray," Agnes said emphatically as she carefully scooped it up. "You'd likely break things in the mood you're in."

The breath went out of Eve. "I'm sorry, Agnes."

"Don't let this man upset you, honey," said the housekeeper. "You want me to toss him out, you just say so."

Oliver looked a little sheepish.

Eve glared at her. "Oliver is a guest here, Agnes."

"Guest!" The woman sniffed as she retreated to the kitchen.

Oliver laughed in his hearty way but then became serious. "I'm sorry if I upset you."

"Of course you didn't," she insisted. "I feel ashamed, throwing out a silly idea like that. I don't believe any of it."

"There's no evidence Libby had other beaus, Eve," he said. "We checked that thoroughly the first thing."

"Of course not." Eve sat back. "It was as silly of me to mention it as it was for Mrs. Browly to talk about the gangsters."

"Yours was a much more plausible theory than hers," Oliver assured her. "It just happens to be a theory we rejected."

Eve looked into the jumping flames of the fire. "I just can't fathom August would even think of doing such a thing."

"Maybe he changed after he came back from sea," Oliver offered. "Those sailors can be rough. If they badgered him for being mollycoddled because he was rich —"

"That wouldn't explain murder!" she insisted.

"Perhaps not, but it might explain his thoughtless behavior, as you prefer to call it," said Oliver. "Remember, he *was* seeing a lot of Cecilia while Libby was away. And he lied about it."

"Maybe he didn't," Eve defended. "Maybe it was all just gossip."

"Including your sister?" He eyed her.

"Vi likes to embellish when she's bored," Eve said. "She and Kitty were probably roaming town bored to tears that day so they saw something and made up a story about it to amuse themselves."

"Not a very nice thing to say about your own sister," he murmured.

"Vi would never lie," she said passionately. "But storytelling has always been her way of — well, making things seem not so bad."

He sighed. "I suppose I'll have to ask Cecilia about it when we see her, then."

Eve stared. "You're going to talk to Cecilia?"

"Naturally," he said. "She may be involved in all this. Mrs. Cinder said it was her voice she heard on the phone that night."

"She could have been wrong," Eve pointed out.

"She could have been," he agreed. "But we want to ask Cecilia about that engagement ring anyway."

"And if she confirms August did buy a ring?" Eve looked at him squarely.

"Maybe he did," Oliver said. "And maybe he gave Libby the ring but got scared later when he had time to think about it."

"That's only if he proposed to her *before* she told him she was going to have a child," Eve pointed out.

"Suppose he proposed to her well before she told him?" Oliver questioned. "We only have his word for it he proposed to her the night she came back from Nevada."

"But she told Florence." Eve blinked.

"She told her she was engaged," Oliver said. "She didn't tell her when she became engaged."

"And La Belle Fille?" Eve asked. "She went the day of the murder, remember."

"She still could have been engaged before that," he argued. "She might have been afraid August would break the engagement once he found out about the baby. Men have been known to do that."

"This is all conjecture, Oliver," Eve said. "Even the sheriff's rope trick is conjecture. Just because August knows how to tie the knot that matches the bruises on Libby's ankles doesn't mean he killed her."

"You caught on to that too." Oliver grinned. "There isn't anything you miss, is there, Eve?"

"It's all speculation," she insisted. "All — what is it — circumstantial evidence? You're not going to prosecute based on that, are you?"

"I don't know yet."

"Oliver!"

"I might not have a choice, Eve." He looked uncomfortable. "In a case like this, where no one saw anything, it's sometimes better to go to trial and let the jury decide whether the evidence is circumstantial or not."

They were quiet for a moment as her mind swirled. "And the jury could decide one way or another."

"If I decide to bring this to trial," he said firmly, "it's my duty to see they think one way over another."

She sighed. "I'm sure you'll do what you feel is best, Oliver."

"What I feel is best," he mumbled, staring into the fire.

"The sheriff wants to arrest August, doesn't he?" Eve felt a cold shiver.

"I can't deny it," he said. "I had to keep him from doing it this evening."

"This evening!"

"After we interviewed Josh and he admitted he didn't see August that night," he said. "He was already jingling the handcuffs."

Eve sank into the couch. "What did you say?"

"I said we didn't have enough conclusive evidence and I wouldn't consider making an arrest without it," Oliver said.

She studied him as he held the pipe to his lips, an intent look on his face. She realized the pipe was no longer letting off curls of smoke.

"Your pipe's out," she said.

"Just as well." He rose. "Ellen doesn't like me smelling of smoke and she'll be home by now."

Eve saw the heavy lines around his forehead. "You're worried, aren't you? What is it, Oliver?"

He put the pipe back in his pocket. "I think the sheriff has some ideas about how he can get conclusive proof. He hinted that by tomorrow we might have an arrest."

"Not at the funeral!" She was alarmed.

"No, of course not," he promised. "Zak used to say you had to let the lawmen work on their hunches without interfering, but I don't like it."

"He ought to tell you," she insisted. "You're the district attorney. He works for you."

Oliver chuckled. "Both of us work for the county, Eve."

"What do you think it is?" Eve asked. "You must have some idea what's on his mind."

"I imagine he thinks August and Cecilia were in it together."

"Good Lord!" Eve gasped.

"He'll be even more convinced when he hears she and August have been inseparable ever since he got back," Oliver said.

The clock struck eleven. "It was a lovely dinner, Eve. Thank you for keeping me from spending an evening alone in that big house."

She led him to the door. "You can invite yourself over any time Ellen is out."

He smiled at her. "Perhaps you'll do me another kindness."

"Anything."

Oliver slipped on his coat. "Will you come with me after the funeral to talk to Cecilia? I've a feeling the girl is going to be tough to get at so I need all the help I can get."

"Of course I'll come if you want me to." She smiled.

A pleasant buzz from his grateful smile stayed with her after she closed the door. She stood there for a moment, then slowly climbed the stairs to her room. Just as she slipped into her nightgown, there was a firm knock on the door.

Helena was holding the white coat she used when she worked

in her laboratory over her arm. "I met Oliver on my way in," she said. "He said he asked Deputy Elwood to send one of the assistants out to make sure Vi and her friends aren't up to any mischief."

"He's so kind," Eve said with a sigh.

"He promised she would be home within the hour." She watched as Eve unpinned her hair, letting it fall into tresses around her shoulders. "Eve, do you really think it's your place to be talking to him about the case?"

"I didn't talk to him," Eve stiffened. "He talked to me."

"I don't doubt a lawman unwinds by discussing such things with people not involved with the law." Her sister was silent a moment with uncharacteristic hesitation. "But shouldn't he be doing that with his wife?"

"I fancy Ellen takes as much of an interest in his work as Felix does in yours," Eve snapped.

A dark shadow passed across her sister's face. "We're not talking about me now," Helena said. "We're talking about you."

"Are we?" Eve challenged.

"Yes," said her sister. "We are. When a man chooses another woman to talk to about his troubles, she starts to think — well, I just don't want you to get hurt, that's all."

"Oh, honey, I didn't mean that." Eve took her by the shoulders. "I won't talk to him at all, if that's what you want."

Helena smiled. "You could hardly do that without him thinking you were a bad egg."

"Heaven forbid!" Eve rolled her eyes at this echo of Violet's loose words and they both laughed.

CHAPTER 21

The sun came out early the next morning. The sky was a crisp blue, and there were no clouds. All the colors outside looked brilliant, from the deep green of the leaves to the lavender color of the wild violets growing between the rocks in the backyard.

"It looks almost as if someone is welcoming Libby into a brighter afterlife," Eve remarked at breakfast.

"Someone?" Helena raised her eyebrow.

"All right, God, then," Eve said.

Her sister took another slice of toast. "There's never been the least bit of evidence such a thing even exists."

"Helena, that's blasphemous!" Eve shrank back.

Agnes grunted. "You talk as if you've never opened a Bible."

"The Bible, dear Agnes, is a document written by people," Helena pointed out.

"Please, dear," Eve begged. "None of your scientific arguments today."

Helena's face softened as she covered her sister's hand. "I'm sorry, Eve."

Violet came in, dressed in the high-collared dark gray blouse and skirt she rarely wore and her face with only a little powder. They all stared as she demurely settled herself and straightened the place setting. Even Agnes seemed frozen in her place, a covered plate in her hands.

When the effect of her appearance had sunk in, Violet said, "I've decided to go to the funeral after all."

"So it appears," Helena said dryly.

"I thought it over," her younger sister continued. "Not because of what you said."

"We know you don't make decisions without thinking them through, darling," Eve said.

Violet's large eyes grew somber. "Libby was older than me, but she still had her whole life ahead of her."

"She was twenty-three," Eve said softly. "That's what it said on the death certificate."

"She was stuck in an old-maid's place." Violet took a generous portion of bacon. "She wanted to get out. And someone might have killed her for that."

"Might have," Helena emphasized.

"It isn't fair!" Violet's lips pursed forward. "She shouldn't have died like that, even if she was running around town with August and other men."

Agnes placed a small plate of donuts in front of her. "Karl sent these over with the bread this morning."

"What a love!" Violet's eyes lit up.

"You got no business letting him waste his parents' merchandise on you," Agnes grumbled.

"He's not wasting it," she insisted. "He told me his mother always makes extra so if there's anything left, she can sell it to the people on the East Side for a penny."

"Then we'll give them five pennies when we go in next time," Eve said.

"Why interfere with a man's generosity?" Violet asked.

"You ought to be ashamed of yourself!" Agnes spat out.

"You are leading him on, Vi," Helena said. "He probably wants to ask you to the dance next week and we all know you have no intention of going with him."

"With that old man?" Her younger sister looked at her as if she were crazy.

"He just turned twenty-eight," Helena argued.

"Well, he looks like an old man," Violet pouted. "Joe's already asked me anyway."

"I thought Joe was Kitty's sweetheart," Eve said.

"That's why he's going with me," said Violet. "They had a blow up, and she's going with Tom so I offered Joe a date so he could make her jealous."

Helena rolled her eyes at Eve.

"You could at least share them with your sisters, you selfish thing," Agnes snarled as she left the dining room.

Violet, in spite of her flamboyant youth, was always generous. She dropped a donut in each of her sisters' plates. The simple gesture made Eve's heart ache as she thought about the four-year-old girl with the big eyes and solemn face who had been left in her charge, along with the level-headed sixteen-year-old Helena when the authorities broke the news to her that their parents had died.

"I'm glad you're coming, Vi," she said.

"I just didn't like it when you talked about it yesterday, as if it were a given," Violet grumbled. "I have nothing to do with the business, after all."

"It's a third yours, Vi," Helena said. "Papa and Mama wanted it that way."

"How would you know what they wanted?" her sister challenged. "They didn't even have a chance to — to make a will." Her voice dropped.

"Papa told me," Eve said. "He told me exactly what he wanted even though he didn't have time write it down."

"He ought to have left a will," Violet said softly. Then, with a sudden vicious gesture, she threw the last of her donut on the plate. "I think it was stinking of him!"

"Vi!" Eve's voice was sharp.

Helena was surprisingly tender. "How was he to know, honey?"

Eve's heart went out to her youngest sister as the tears gathered in her eyes. "The funeral made you think of them, didn't it?"

"That's why I didn't want to go." Violet turned away from them and Eve saw she was dabbing her eyes with her napkin. "I'm not going into the business, Eve. Ever."

"No one expects you to," Eve promised.

"Don't be surprised if you find yourself changing your mind one day." Helena pushed her empty plate away.

"You mean death has a way of growing on you?" Her sister gave her a wary look.

"I mean you'll lose the battle between your compassionate heart and your devil-may-care persona," Helena said. "They're at odds, you know."

"What baloney you talk, Helena," Violet snorted as she took the last of the donuts.

~~~~~

Since the Cinders had never been consistent churchgoers, Mrs. Cinder had asked them to arrange for the memorial service in their chapel. "I know Reverend Miles wouldn't mind if we had the service at his church, but I don't feel right about it," the woman had said. Eve and Helena had reassured her, though they suspected the woman's reticence had more to do with the cost the good reverend imposed upon his followers than anything else.

So they had set up the memorial service in the chapel the night before, making sure the place was spotless and the prayer books complete. That morning, just as they unlocked the door to the chapel, Mrs. Chaney came in with the flowers.

"A sad, sad business," said the woman, her chest heaving. "She
~~~~~

always used to buy a carnation from me on Sundays and put it in her father's lapel so he would look 'dashing' in church. Such a decent girl." She fanned herself with her handkerchief. "And to think someone in our midst murdered her!"

Maybe he isn't in our midst," Violet said in a bored tone. "Maybe he was just one of those dippy ex-soldiers passing through."

"Really, Violet." The woman shuddered. "I do think your fondness for moving pictures has warped your mind."

"Well, isn't it better to think a stranger did it than someone in town?"

"If there was some unsavory individual roaming the county, we would have heard of it by now." Helena pushed her sister toward the door. "Go help Charles with the flowers, Vi."

Violet made a face, then, in a sweet voice, added, "I've heard those dippy ex-soldiers have a fondness for carnations in their buttonholes too, Mrs. Chaney. Better watch out!" She waved a finger at her, her eyes sparking as she slammed the door of the chapel behind her.

"Well!" The woman stared after her.

"She's only playing, Mrs. Chaney." Eve felt a little embarrassed. "It's how she deals with the sadness of the situation."

"I hope she'll show more respect when the Cinders get here," Mrs. Chaney said. "I saw them in town yesterday. Poor Thomas. I don't think his nerves can take much more."

Eve felt the weight of her words when, a half hour later, the Cinders arrived. Thomas looked half his size, his face so wrinkled with grief that his eyes looked only half open. His wife and Miss Gilbert held on to each arm as he took one step in front of the other. Oliver immediately went to him, taking the poor man's frail figure off their hands, motioning for Deputy Elwood to take the other arm. They guided the grieving father to the front pew. Oliver took off his coat for the old man could to sit on, and Eve made a mental note to order cushions for the front pews at the first opportunity.

She was surprised to see the chapel full to capacity. She recognized some faces, such as Alice Watts and Florence Horne, the latter sniffing into a handkerchief beneath her veil. A group of studious young women sat with them and Eve reasoned they were fellow teachers and school staff. Others she did not recognize.

Just before the service began, she glanced at the door to make sure Charlie had closed it and saw August and his mother siting in the last pew. August, in a dark suit too big for him, looked undone, his blond hair ragged and his eyes dark with circles. He leaned forward with both elbows on his knees. Rosalia wore black, the style of her dress at least a decade old, the hat and mourning veil long and heavy. Eve realized with some horror that the outfit was probably the same one she had worn at her husband's funeral.

Reverend Herbert adjusted his collar and cleared his throat several times.

"Why does he always have to look like he's preaching in a brothel when he comes here?" Violet hissed.

"Vi!" Eve tried to hush her.

"It's not far from the truth," Helena said. "You would think he's never been here before every time he comes."

"I suppose pastors feel ill at ease when they're not in their own church," Eve said.

"It's *our* chapel." Violet sniffed. "It's just as good as that church of his with the monstrous arches and that marble staircase. So he'd better treat it with respect." The determined pout on her face made Eve almost smile.

Eve knew that in spite of the reverend's opinions about delivering his service in an inferior chapel without grand arches and marble staircases, he had respect for his congregation. He also was considerate of Thomas Cinder's delicate health. He omitted the sort of grandstanding he sometimes indulged in at the Gyver First Congregational church. He kept his tone soft and reassuring, praising Libby for coming home to take care of her parents and also her work at the church daycare. He delivered a surprising caveat that, while one could not deny each of God's children were taken to their place in Heaven as His will, those in charge would benefit from His guidance to find the beast of prey in the case of Libby Cinder's death.

"We pray only that those in charge will listen to the voice of God to discover who did this terrible thing." His eyes shifted toward Eve and her sisters and she was alarmed at first. Then she realized Oliver and Deputy Elwood had taken a position against the wall right behind them. She glanced at the district attorney and saw the resolute look in his eye.

"Oliver looks like he just swallowed a live fish," Violet whispered with a giggle.

"Hush, you rude thing," Helena hissed.

The service ended with a passage from Browning's "Evelyn Hope." Reverend Herbert pulled back the black curtain. The coffin with Libby's still body lay inside. People went up to the podium to pay their last respects with quiet murmurs.

Oliver joined them. "Something tells me the sheriff isn't going to be too happy about the notion of a guiding hand in his investigation." Violet giggled.

"Where is he, by the way?" Helena surveyed the chapel.

"He'll meet us at the cemetery," said Deputy Elwood.

"Why isn't he here now?" Helena persisted.

"Does it matter?" Violet rose and stretched.

"He had something to take care of first, Mrs. Wright," the deputy supplied.

Eve did not miss the lines drawn across Oliver's forehead.

"Shall we go and view the body?" Oliver asked.

"Do we have to?" Violet turned a little pale.

"Of course not, honey." Eve pressed her hand. "It's enough that one of us goes."

"You don't want me to come?" Helena asked.

Eve shook her head with a smile.

As they made their way in the line, Eve explained in a whisper, "Papa never forced either of them to view the bodies. They were both so young, he didn't think it was fair."

"I suppose it is jarring to a child," Oliver agreed. He glanced in front of them. "You were right about Cecilia, Eve."

"I didn't think she would come," she said. "Most people won't attend a funeral unless they're afraid others will talk if they don't."

"I can't imagine August or his mother concerned about that, given people have been talking about them for days," Oliver remarked as he watched the two pillars of Falcon Hill society approach the casket.

August held his mother's arm tightly. The young man's eyes gazed down at the still face. His features contorted with a heavy sob. Rosalia led him away, her head bending toward him. In the silence of the chapel, her soothing but firm tone could be heard.

"She looks almost like the grieving mother-in-law," Eve observed.

"Hugh Adkins probably suggested it," said Oliver. "He's a smart lawyer. He knows when this goes to trial, regardless of who we prosecute, the engagement will come out. Better to act like the grieving mother-in-law-to-be now than to have people talk."

"You don't believe she's genuinely sorry the girl is dead?" Eve glanced at him.

"Do you?"

"People around here have scruples, Oliver," she insisted. "We may not like someone, but they belong to this town and we're sorry when they're gone." She lowered her head. "I suppose that sounds naive to you."

"Maybe we're both naive children, eh?" he said in a rueful tone.

"I like to think we're hopeful," Eve said.

They were the last to reach the coffin, other than the Cinders, who had remained seated until everyone else had taken their turn. She gazed at Libby's peaceful face. There was even a small smile on her lips. Oliver heaved a deep sigh.

"Take as much time as you need." Eve laid her hand on Mrs. Cinder's arm.

"Thank you for arranging everything," Mrs. Cinder whispered as Helena and Violet joined them.

Oliver and Deputy Elwood helped Thomas up the podium stairs. He shuffled his feet like a man approaching the gallows. But seeing his daughter, even with her tranquil, resting face proved too much for him. He let out a wail and nearly collapsed in Deputy Elwood's arms. With a sign from Oliver, the deputy carried the frail man to the couch in the waiting room.

"It was the newspapers," said Miss Gilbert tearfully. "They're to blame for this."

"Those nasty Shane brothers," Violet grumbled.

"We knew it would get in the papers about August and Libby," said Mrs. Cinder. "We tried to hide them from Thomas. But when he read what they said about Libby — about Libby —" She hid her face in her handkerchief.

"About Libby being a hussy," Miss Gilbert declared. "You ought to sue them, Gertrude."

"They never said that word, Teresa," Mrs. Cinder protested.

"They implied it!"

"They can imply whatever they want," Helena said. "No one in town believes it. We all knew Libby from childhood."

"My sister's right, Mrs. Cinder," Eve said. "The town may talk, but it's just conversation over their morning coffee. The gap between talk and belief in this town is wide."

"Yes, that's true," said the woman in a faint tone.

A howling sob came from the waiting room. Eve started toward it, but she felt a hand on her arm. It was her younger sister Violet.

"Let me go, Eve," she said. "The poor man!"

She watched as her sister sat beside Thomas, taking his hand. She heard her sweet, fluted voice speaking though she didn't hear the words. The despair left Thomas's face, replaced with peace.

Oliver watched her with his hands in his pockets. "Looks like the kid is as tender-hearted as her big sister."

"She used to get angry at me for dissecting frogs," Helena said in a rueful tone. "When I'd catch rabbits or mice for the laboratory, she'd sneak in at night and let them go." She gave a small laugh. "She ruined a lot of experiments for me."

"She's always had a sense for people's feelings," Eve agreed. "Papa used to say out of all of us, she would be the one who would make the best heavenly guide."

"Is that what he called you?" Oliver smiled. "Heavenly guides?"

"This is a profession just like any other," Helena insisted.

Thomas calmed enough for them to get him into the hired car. Charlie and Helena drove the hearse while Eve and Violet rode with Oliver and Deputy Elwood in Oliver's Dodge to Gyver Cemetery. It was on the hill and spanned a vast ground with pine trees. There was everything there from grand crypts with carved stone angels and crosses to small plots near the outskirts of the cemetery.

Charlie and three other men who always helped with funerals were pallbearers who carried the coffin delicately to the burial place. Eve scanned the headstone, satisfied Westley Burgess had done his usual careful and precise work.

"Looks like your concerns last night about Sheriff Warner were unfounded, Eve," Oliver whispered as Reverend Herbert began the last words. "He's not here either."

"You're still worried, aren't you?" Eve observed.

"He's got something up his sleeve and I don't like it," Oliver said.

"You don't think he would arrest August here, do you?" Violet asked.

"Don't be silly, Vi," Helena growled. "It's highly unlikely the sheriff would do that unless he thought August was going to flee."

"We know it's not illegal," said Eve. "But highly unwise."

"Not to mention unfeeling," Violet grumbled. "Adding more to all that suffering."

The group of well-dressed young people glanced at them, though not unkindly.

"I wonder who they are," Eve murmured.

"Friends of Libby's from Reno, I expect," Oliver said.

"How do you know?" Helena asked.

He chuckled. "Do they dress and behave like small-town people?"

"They're city people," Violet agreed. "Libby must have had a lot of friends."

"She did spend most of her childhood there," Eve pointed out. "And she was a likable girl."

One by one, the cars drove to the Cinder house where Agnes and a few of the domestics she knew had set up the funeral reception. Eve noted with some satisfaction they had also taken it upon themselves to tidy up the living room and kitchen a bit so the house didn't look as dark and dreary.

Oliver and Deputy Elwood helped Thomas up the stairs and safely tucked him into his room with the door firmly shut. Eve and Helena tried to help Mrs. Cinder and Miss Gilbert with the mourners but they both shooed them away.

"Where's Vi?" Eve surveyed the crowded room.

"I told her she could go." Helena held a cup of tea with both hands. "Mr. Cinder breaking down like that did her in, Eve."

"I suppose I shouldn't have assumed she would come yesterday," Eve lamented. "She's right about being old enough to make her own decisions."

"You heard her this morning," Helena said. "She wanted to come. She knew what to expect."

They both stood in the corner in silence as the quiet chatter filled the small room.

"Libby had a lot of friends," Eve remarked. "I suppose no one realized it."

"You don't think of a schoolteacher as having any friends," Helena agreed. "But we know Libby had other plans."

"Maybe she went about fulfilling them too fast," Eve murmured.

"It's not our job to find out why she was killed," Helena insisted. "That's what the police are for."

Oliver and the deputy joined them. "The old man's resting comfortably," Oliver reported. "Dr. Lloyd's just given him something to make him sleep."

"Lucky thing the doctor was here," Deputy Elwood said.

"I wish your superior was here," Oliver said in a sharp voice. "It doesn't look right when the sheriff isn't present at the funeral of a murder victim."

The deputy looked uncomfortable. "I could call the station, sir."

"Do that," Oliver said.

"It's not his fault, you know," Helena said as they watched the young man approach Mrs. Cinder, who pointed to the hallway.

"I know." Oliver shook his head. "I guess I just need to take it out on someone."

August and his mother came through the crowded room. Eve's heart went out to the young man, who looked barely able to stand.

"Thank you for all you've done, Miss Grave," he said, grasping her hand. "And you too, Mrs. Wright."

Rosalia had lifted her veil, and the face underneath was the usual self-possessed countenance. "I'm sure the Cinders appreciate it."

"Murder or not, the dead need their resting place," Eve observed.

August looked at her with wide eyes. "When someone — well, doesn't die a natural death — does the soul really rest? Or does it wander until the murderer is brought to justice?"

Eve was taken aback. She glanced at Helena. "Maybe Oliver is in a better position to answer that question than I am," she mumbled.

"I'm no priest, Eve," said Oliver. "I only know I intend to catch the person who killed Miss Cinder. What happens with the girl's soul after that is out of my hands."

"There's no soul involved," Helena protested. "It's a matter of taking care of the body in a proper way."

"How very practical of you, Mrs. Wright," Rosalia said with admiration. "One must be as practical about death as one is practical about life."

"How do you mean, Mrs. Winters?" Oliver asked.

"My uncle owned a farm in Kentucky," she began. "He raised chickens and sold them around the county."

"I never knew that, Mother," August mumbled.

She almost smiled. "I don't like to talk about my humble beginnings, but your father understood." She looked at Oliver. "He used to catch wild dogs and tame them. Those dogs sometimes used to go after the chickens. Dogs can do that, you know."

"Indeed they do," Deputy Elwood agreed and Eve remembered he also had relatives who owned a farm near Sacramento.

"One night, one of the dogs got out and went into the henhouse. I went with my cousin to chase him out, but the dog wouldn't go. I shot him." She said the last as if it were the most natural thing in the world. "He was a nice dog."

"Then why did you shoot him?" Eve asked, shuddering.

The woman gave her a strange look. "I had to. He might have killed one of the chickens."

"He might not have," Oliver said. "You said your uncle was taming them."

"That's what my cousin said," she said. "I wasn't willing to take that chance."

"So you were practical about the death of that dog," Helena said.

"I think it's awful!" August burst out. "Death isn't practical. Death is — is —"

"Terrible," Eve said softly.

"Yes, but something else too," he said. "You can't keep your distance from it." He looked at Eve. "You and your sisters, for instance. I saw you at the service. All of you were just as sad as everyone else."

"Naturally, we're sad," Helena said.

"Even you, Mrs. Wright," he lamented. "You're always so — clinical. But you were sad too."

"Yes, I was sad," Helena said in a soft tone. Eve took her arm.

Mrs. Winters pressed her son's hand. "I only meant death isn't always personal, August, dear. People can feel sad without it personally affecting them."

"You forget, Mrs. Winters, we're not talking about death here," Oliver said. "We're talking about murder."

She looked at him steadily. "And is murder always personal?"

"Always." His tone was sharp. "I've never met a murderer who didn't have a personal stake in the victim."

At that moment, a fresh breeze shot through the room as if someone had thrown open the front door. Sheriff Warner appeared, his figure large and imposing, with Deputy Elwood scurrying behind him.

"It's about time you showed up, Sheriff." Oliver did not hide his anger.

"I'm sorry, Mr. Clarke," he said in a hurried tone. "I need to speak to you for a moment. In private." He didn't even glance at the people around him.

Oliver's expression grew into a hard shell as the sheriff led him outside with the deputy at their heels.

August's face suddenly gained a little color as he watched them. "Maybe he's discovered who the murderer is!"

"He certainly looked excitable," Helena observed.

Eve wandered to the front door where she could see Oliver and Sheriff Warner talking some distance away through the screen door. She couldn't hear their words, but she could see from their expressions they were arguing. The sheriff's hands were flying around and Oliver's remained on his hips as if taking a defensive stand. Deputy Elwood stood between them, an anxious look on his face.

As they came back into the house, Eve whispered to Oliver. "What's wrong?"

He gave her a bothered look but said nothing. He motioned toward August and the young man followed him outside with Rosalia, a steely look on her face. Eve allowed herself to linger on the porch. Helena joined her.

"August," he said in a grave tone, "I'd like you to go with Sheriff Warner."

"Why?" Rosalia immediately pounced.

"There are some questions we'd like to ask you," said the district attorney, ignoring her. Eve could see the sheriff was impatient with this delicate approach.

"Is my son under arrest, Mr. Clarke?"

"Not exactly, ma'am," the sheriff intervened. "We're taking him in for questioning."

"Taking him in?" Rosalia turned pale. "You mean to jail?"

"If it comes to that," he mumbled.

"This is absurd!" She grabbed her son's arm. "August isn't going anywhere until Hugh Adkins arrives."

"Mr. Adkins can come down to the station," Sheriff Warner said roughly. "He knows the law."

"August, don't say anything until Hugh gets there," Rosalia commanded. "Don't say a word."

The young man, who had been standing in silence, now said slowly, "I want to speak to them, Mother."

"Want to speak to them!" Her poise shattered as she snarled, "Can't you see they're trying to corner you?"

Oliver said stiffly. "I told August before we might want to speak with him again."

"Please, Mother, don't make a scene." August lowered his voice. "Not now, not today."

This calmed her. "Do I ever make a scene, darling?"

"No," he said softly. "You never do." He looked at the sheriff. "Please don't handcuff me. It would upset the Cinders."

"I wasn't planning to, son," said Sheriff Warner in a mild tone. "Not if you come quietly."

Rosalia yanked open the police car door. "I assume I can call Hugh Adkins from the police station, Sheriff?"

"You'll have to stay in the waiting room, ma'am," the sheriff said.

"As long as I can get to a phone," she snapped and climbed into the back seat.

"Get what you can out of him before the lawyer gets there," Oliver said in a low tone.

The man looked almost triumphant. "Even Hugh Adkins can't help him now."

Eve felt her stomach turn as the car drove off. "Oliver, what is this all about? What did he mean?"

"He means to arrest August for murder, doesn't he?" Helena asked.

"Not arrest him, Helena," said Oliver. "At least, not yet."

CHAPTER 22

By this time, Mrs. Cinder and Miss Gilbert had joined them. The morning breeze had now given away to an oppressive chill and even the sun hid between some misty clouds.

"We saw the sheriff come in," said Mrs. Cinder. "What's wrong, Mr. Clarke?"

"Ma'am, I couldn't be sorrier this happened." Oliver looked genuinely distressed and even miserable as he placed his hand on her arm.

"Sorry what happened?" Miss Gilbert's crow-like features became even sharper. "Make sense, man!"

"August Winters has just been taken in," he said.

"You said he wasn't arrested." Eve's voice shook.

"He's being held on suspicion of murder," said the district attorney. His usual warm and gracious tone was hard and unyielding. Eve was taken aback.

"Why?" Mrs. Cinder asked.

"Oliver doesn't owe anyone an explanation if he was acting within the confines of the law," Helena insisted.

"What do you mean, doesn't owe us an explanation?" Miss

Gilbert demanded. "The boy is being held for murdering *our* family!"

"Helena speaks the truth, ma'am," said Oliver. "The police aren't obliged to disclose anything about the case to outsiders."

"We are not outsiders!" Miss Gilbert was clearly losing her temper. "We're the murdered girl's mother and aunt!"

"Please, Teresa." Mrs. Cinder glanced toward the house. "Go back inside, dear. One of us ought to be there before people start asking questions."

The woman looked at her for a moment, and the crow features softened. "I'm sorry, Gertrude. I suppose I don't understand the ways of country lawmen." With a glare at Oliver, she turned on her heels and went back inside.

"I'm sorry I had to be harsh with her, Mrs. Cinder," said Oliver. "I have the law to uphold, you understand."

"It sounds more like you're afraid of a mob of hysterical women on your hands," Eve said in an even tone.

He did not smile. "I suppose you do have a right to know some things, given you're the victim's mother."

"I appreciate that, Mr. Clarke," said Mrs. Cinder. "This is very trying for all of us."

This made his face less abrasive. "We're not arresting him yet, but we do have to hold him on suspicion for now."

"With what evidence?" Helena asked. "You wouldn't hold him unless you had some pretty conclusive evidence."

Oliver leaned against the banister. "When we discovered the empty purse we suspected belonged to Libby, I requested the sheriff and his men search the river for any of her belongings. We didn't know who the girl was at that time, you understand. We thought if we found something, it might help us identify her."

Mrs. Cinder nodded. "Go on, Mr. Clarke."

"I called off that search once we discovered who Libby was," he continued. "I only now found out the sheriff, however, decided to pursue the search on his own."

"Pursue it on his own?" Eve asked. "He went against your wishes?"

"Not exactly," he said. "Sometimes lawmen decide to follow up on a piece of evidence on their own time and using their own resources. When they have a hunch, that is."

"And he had a hunch?" Helena guessed.

Oliver nodded. "That hunch paid off."

"And just what was that hunch?" Mrs. Cinder asked.

"We know there was a rope that held Libby's ankles to some heavy object," said Oliver. "Someone was trying to make the body sink to the bottom of the river."

Mrs. Cinder looked ill for a moment, but with admirable fortitude, collected herself and nodded. "I remember reading about that in the paper."

"We thought at first the rope floated downstream somewhere when we realized it broke free from the body," he said. "But the sheriff had a hunch it was still tied to the heavy object."

"And he was right," Eve said.

"They found a piece of rope lodged underneath a piece of bark at the bottom of the river."

"Good God!" Mrs. Cinder pressed her hands to her face.

"How do they know it was the rope that was tied to her ankles?" Helena asked. "It might have been there for years."

"It wasn't a common type, Helena," said the district attorney. "We checked with Josh."

"Josh would never incriminate August," Eve said in a shaking tone. "He's like a father to him."

Here, Oliver's face gained back some of its police detachment. "We didn't tell him what it was about, naturally."

"Naturally," Mrs. Cinder echoed.

"We asked him his expert opinion."

"Expert opinion!" Eve's heart grew icy. "You were trying to trick him!"

The wounded look on Oliver's face was unmistaken. "We were only doing our job."

"Yes," said Mrs. Cinder softly. "I expect you were."

The screen door opened and Miss Gilbert appeared, waving at her sister-in-law. Mrs. Cinder spoke in a hushed tone for a few moments, then came back. "Thomas is awake. I must go inside." With an uneasy look at the district attorney, she said, "I hope you know what you're doing, Mr. Clarke."

"Oliver," Eve said when the woman had left, "*do* you know what you're doing?"

He put his hands in his pockets, his face grim. "Would it comfort you if I said I didn't?"

"Don't be silly, Eve," Helena said sharply. "Oliver is an experienced lawman. He wouldn't let the sheriff take August unless there was just cause."

"What just cause?" Eve asked.

"I'm not at liberty to say," he mumbled.

"Because you think we'll spread it around town?" Eve looked hard at him. "You know we wouldn't do that."

"You've involved us, Oliver," Helena said simply.

"Yes, I suppose I did," he admitted. "I asked for your help and you've helped a great deal. I suppose I owe it to you not to keep you in the dark."

"How do you know the rope you found in the river was used on Libby?" Helena began. "There are other fisherman along the river."

"Josh told us it's a rare silk rope he got from his days working off the coast of Japan," he said. "They only make it in one of the remote villages there." He eyed her. "You're a woman of numbers, Helena. What do you think is the probability of another fisherman in Gyver—in the state, for that matter—getting hold of the exact same type of rope?"

Helena glanced down. "I'd say it was slim to none."

"Did you also get Josh to confess he gave August that rope?" Eve snapped. "Is that how you're putting two and two together?"

"It was the sheriff's idea, Eve," said Oliver.

"Sanctioned by you!"

"Only after the fact," he shot out.

"You must have more than the rope," said Helena. "You wouldn't have taken August away if you didn't."

"We do," Oliver said. "The piece of rope was cut from one we found in August's closet."

"The sheriff broke into his house and searched it." Eve stared. "That's why he wasn't at the funeral!"

"The police don't break into houses, Eve," said Helena. "They get search warrants."

"That's right, Helena," Oliver said.

"And just how did he get one?" Helena inquired.

Here, Oliver's dark eyes turned as murky as the bottom of a swamp. "From his golfing buddy, Judge Jim Long."

"You mean without telling you?" Eve began to realize why she had seen both men so angry a little while earlier.

"He told me about it afterward."

"He searched the house and found rope that matched the one from the river," Helena concluded.

"Almost a hundred and ten feet of rope," said Oliver.

"Just because it was the same type —"

"The sheriff brought an expert with him," Oliver interrupted. "A man who knows as much about ropes as Josh does."

"Why didn't he take Josh?" Eve asked.

Oliver grimaced. "He didn't think Josh would oblige when he found out what it was all about."

"And this expert identified the cut piece of rope as being the same type as the rope in August's closet?" Helena guessed.

"It wasn't just the type, Helena," he said. "It was the cut."

Eve glanced at him. "What do you mean, the cut?"

"The piece we found was clearly cut from a larger one," he said. "The edges were frayed and wavy."

"Someone must have cut them with a pair of dull scissors," Helena remarked.

"Or a pair of sewing scissors," he said. "The sheriff found a broken pair hidden in the garden shed."

"Good Lord!" Eve sighed

"The edge of the rope they found in the house matched the frays of the cut piece," he said.

Eve sighed. "I see now why the sheriff took August away."

"It's still not indisputable," Helena argued. "Mr. Adkins might make a case that the rope may have belonged to a fisherman who used it to anchor his boat."

"Building a case is like building a puzzle, Helena," said Oliver. "It's only in the moving pictures you find one indisputable, conclusive piece that clinches the whole matter."

"In other words, you have more?" Eve looked at him.

"We know now August wasn't telling the whole truth about what he was doing the night of Libby's death," he said.

"What do you mean?" Eve stared.

"Horace Rapp came to see the sheriff this morning."

"And what did whiskey-jolly Horace have to say?" Helena asked.

"Whiskey-jolly Horace is on the wagon," Oliver insisted. "His wife confirms he's been on the wagon for the last few weeks."

"All right, former whiskey-jolly Horace," she snorted. "What did he have to say?"

"He told us August rented one of his cars on Friday night," he said. "He saw him drive off in the direction of the river. He returned it a few hours later."

"What time did he take the car and when did he return it?" Eve asked.

"That he couldn't say for sure," said Oliver.

"I shouldn't wonder," Helena remarked. "They don't keep records."

Oliver chuckled. "We told him that. He insists most of the people who rent from him are those he's known since they were in the baby carriage so he doesn't need to keep records." In a more serious tone, he added, "He gave us approximate times, though. They match those Dr. Myers gave us for Libby's death."

"He might have returned the car before Libby was killed," Eve said.

"He might have," Oliver admitted. "But, remember, nobody can vouch for his whereabouts that night."

"Except his mother," Eve said softly.

"Except his mother."

"It also works the other way around, Oliver," Helena pointed out. "Since no one saw him, no one can testify he was anywhere near the river when Libby was killed."

"We're well aware of that, Helena," he said. "I'm sure his lawyer will make a point of it."

Eve sighed. "You'll be going down to the police station now?"

"I think I'll let the sheriff handle August for a while," he said. "I've got something else in mind."

"Oh?" Helena eyed him.

"Cecilia might be able to shed some light on a few things." He glanced at Eve. "I've asked your sister to come with me."

"I think Helena should come too," said Eve. "I'd like her to come."

Oliver saluted them both.

~~~~~

They gave Mrs. Cinder and Miss Gilbert their condolences. After instructing Agnes on her duties while they were gone, Eve and Helena climbed into Oliver's car with Helena directing him to the Feather house.

"I suppose it's going to be as grand as Redbud Manor?" he guessed as they entered the road leading into Falcon Hill.
~~~~~

"Not quite," said Eve. "Mr. Feather was a miser, if ever there was one. They have more than they know what to do with."

"Mrs. Feather found plenty to do with it," Helena said dryly. "She was inconsolable — so they say — after her husband's death. So she became the town organizer."

"I don't follow you," Oliver said.

"You probably noticed Gyver county has a lot of charity functions," Eve said. "She organized or helped organize most of them."

Oliver nodded. "And where did that leave Cecilia?"

"With a mother engrossed in helping the community?" Helena asked. "Rather lonely, I should think."

"Now I see why everyone says Rosalia was like a mother to her," he said as he turned the corner.

Eve sighed. "She's never really had much of one."

"A shame August wasn't more a brother to her than a fiancé," Helena added.

"I wonder why," Oliver said.

"Cecilia was always trying to please others," said Eve. "I think she saw it would please Rosalia — and maybe August too — if she became his wife."

"Cecilia has never been the brightest lamp on the chandelier," Helena remarked.

"How is she set financially?" asked the district attorney.

"She has a separate inheritance," said Eve. "But if her mother told her to give it all to charity, she probably would."

"That girl's never had a life of her own," Helena said. "It might have been a good thing if she had married August. At least she would have had a chance."

"She may still marry August." Oliver parked the car in front of a large, partly run-down house.

"If he doesn't hang for murder, you mean."

"Helena, please." Eve shuddered.

"Let's go inside and see if Cecilia can give us a reason not to," Oliver said.

As they approached the house, he put his hand out to stop them, indicating a loose board on the stairs. He found a longer one, placing it on the step and after satisfying himself that it would hold, helped the ladies up. "They need to get that fixed," he snarled.

"I doubt they get many visitors." Eve glanced at the layer of dust in the corners of the front porch.

"That's no excuse for negligence," Helena said. "A child could get killed."

"I quite agree with you, Helena." The voice came from the open doorway where Mrs. Feather, tall and almost holy-like, stood in a white suit. "It is Helena Wright, isn't it?"

"It is," she said.

"And your sister, Miss Grave." She nodded at her. "I didn't expect either of you. I fully expected Mr. Clarke, though." She cast a glance in Oliver's direction.

"Does that mean you're going to do something about the steps?" Helena challenged.

"I've already contacted Mr. Landry to fix it," she said. "I've been so busy with the Elk Club raffle, I haven't had time to tend to it." She stepped away to allow them to enter. "You've seen the handbills in town?"

"We have." Eve nodded.

"It would indeed be a sin to allow anyone to break their leg or arm on the broken step," said Mrs. Feather in a severe tone, closing the door.

"I was thinking more about the danger to human life," said Helena.

The woman looked at her boldly. "So was I."

Oliver glanced around. "I assume you know what this is about, Mrs. Feather?"

The woman lifted her head a little as if she were looking at him through reading glasses. "I don't recall seeing you at any of our events, Mr. Clarke."

"Well, ma'am, I haven't much time for such things," he mumbled.

"I expected your wife to join us at the Red Cross by now," she said. "I sent her several invitations last year."

"If you don't mind, ma'am, we're here to talk about a very serious matter —"

"Helping the Red Cross *is* a serious matter, Mr. Clarke."

Eve was about to intervene, but Cecilia appeared in the hallway. She had a softer tone to her skin than her mother and none of the commanding presence. Violet had described her as a chipmunk with long lashes. "What's going on, Mother?"

Oliver took out his credentials. "I don't think we've met formally, Miss Feather. I'm Oliver Clarke."

"We know all about you, Mr. Clarke," said Mrs. Feather. "We do read the papers."

"Yes, I see that." He glanced behind her. Eve realized the morning paper was lying on the table with the screaming headline LIBBY CINDER FUNERAL TODAY!

"You'd better come in, then." But the sour look on Mrs. Feather's face was less than inviting.

As they settled into the living room, the woman continued, "I hope you're not here to upset my daughter. We have a meeting at the Salvation Army in an hour."

"Pity your charity didn't extend to the Cinders," Helena said. "You read about the funeral, didn't you?"

"I wanted to go," Cecilia ventured. "Mother didn't think it was a good idea."

"Maybe it's better you weren't there." Oliver glanced at Eve.

Cecilia sighed. "I suppose August is very upset. We'll go see him, won't we, Mother?"

"If you wish," her mother said shortly.

"I'll make a peach pie and we'll take it to him." Cecilia smiled at Eve. "Rosalia taught me to make it just as he likes it, with the peaches just a little sour."

Eve felt sorry for the young woman as she looked into the bright blue eyes.

CHAPTER 23

$\mathcal{E}$ ve could see Oliver felt sorry for the girl, as his tone lost a little of its lawman roughness. "August won't be at home, Cecilia."

"Won't be home?" She blinked.

"We're holding him at the police station for questioning," he said.

"You've arrested him?" The milky countenance suddenly disappeared. Cecilia looked ten years older. Eve noticed the almost self-satisfied look on her mother's face.

"When the police detain someone for questioning, it's not an arrest," Helena said in an authoritative tone. "Right, Oliver?"

"Correct, Helena," he said.

"But why?" Cecilia's asked. "August had nothing to do with this. Just because a man has a — a fling with a woman doesn't mean he's killed her!"

"Is that what August told you?" Oliver asked. "That we accused him of murdering Libby?"

"The papers made it clear your visit to Redbud Manor wasn't a social call," Mrs. Feather said. "You know, Mr. Clarke, I'm not at all sure that you're wrong."

"Mother!"

"Well, my dear, August has never been what one would call virtuous, has he?"

"You mean because he broke off an engagement with your daughter?" Oliver glanced at her.

"I hold no grudges about it," Cecilia said firmly.

"But apparently, you do, Mrs. Feather." He continued to glance at the mother with intense eyes.

"Wouldn't you if it were your daughter, Mr. Clarke?" Eve had to admire Mrs. Feather for not withering under his gaze.

He gave her a crooked smile. "I suppose I would, ma'am." He looked at Cecilia for a moment, then patted her hand. "Still, it must not have been easy for you to see him with another woman."

"I understood that."

"Did you?" He eyed her.

"Rosalia explained it to me," she said. "We've seen it often enough here too."

"Seen what?"

"Oh, the young men here," she said. "They have to stretch their wings before coming back to their duty."

"And what is their duty?" Eve murmured.

"Helping their fathers run their businesses, taking their place in society, marrying well," Cecilia lamented.

"And all that Rosalia explained to you?" Helena asked.

"You have your duty too, my dear," said Mrs. Feather. "Perhaps now that the poor girl is buried, you can return to it and stop moping around the house."

"She was your friend too, eh, Cecilia?" Oliver asked.

"Oh, no!" The words came out so violently that Eve jumped. "I mean," she said in a milder tone, "I knew her only slightly."

"Tell me, Cecilia, what did you think of Libby?" Oliver leaned forward.

"Think of her?"

"My daughter just told you she barely knew her," Mrs. Feather said. "Do I need to call a lawyer, Mr. Clarke?"

"That's up to you, ma'am." He turned back to Cecilia. "I realize you didn't know her well, but you must have formed some opinion."

"Oh, she was alright." Cecilia shrugged. "She worked hard and helped her parents as much as she could. August admired that."

"And you?"

"Everyone should lend a hand to those who need it most," Mrs. Feather said boldly.

"Yes, Mother," said her daughter in a meek tone.

"We've heard some things about you and Libby," Oliver said.

"Gossip, no doubt," Mrs. Feather snarled. "I should think you would know by now, Mr. Clarke, not to believe everything you hear in town."

"I suppose you mean the Valentine's Day picnic," Cecilia said.

"I don't blame you for reacting that way when the man you were with was paying more attention to a maid than to you," Oliver remarked.

"He felt sorry for her," Cecilia said. "Cathy was treating her terribly — she always treats maids that way. She wasn't used to it, being a teacher and all."

"Did you feel sorry for her?" Eve asked.

The girl was quiet for a few moments. "I offered to give her the money Cathy was paying her so she could leave."

"You mean leave him alone," Helena mumbled.

"But she didn't accept it?" the district attorney asked.

"She said she never took money unless she worked for it," said Cecilia. "August admired that too."

Oliver pulled a chair out in front of her. Eve noticed he was so close that their knees almost touched. She realized he was trying to divert her attention from her mother, who sat within her line of vision.

"He told us what good friends you were and how kind you

were to him when he returned, in spite of everything," Oliver said.

"In spite of everything?" she echoed.

"The broken engagement," Helena said. Eve could see her sister was beginning to grow impatient. "Surely you haven't forgotten."

"Of course we haven't forgotten!" Mrs. Feather snapped.

"That was a long time ago," Cecilia said.

"Not so long ago," Eve said. "You must have been very disappointed."

"I was for a time," she admitted. "I even went to San Francisco. Remember, Mother?"

"You should have listened to me," her mother said. "You should have sued him for breach of promise."

"And brought about all that publicity?" She eyed her. "Surely, you don't approve of *that*, Mother?"

The woman looked at the paintings on the wall.

"You went to San Francisco after him?" Oliver asked. "That was brave of you."

"Not so brave, Mr. Clarke," she said. "As Mother just said, I went after him to tell him I would sue him for breach of promise if he didn't come back and marry me." She looked mortified. "It was a terribly vengeful thing to do."

"But understandable," Helena said. Eve saw she admired the girl for the first time.

"What stopped you?" Eve asked.

"The boy had already boarded the ship," said Mrs. Feather. "Probably took the first one he could find. He knew what was coming!"

"That wasn't it at all, Mother," Cecilia insisted. "I suppose I have sort of a temper." She looked embarrassed. "I'm good at keeping it in check, but sometimes —"

"Sometimes it flares up," Oliver said with a small smile. "I know what you mean."

"I'm grateful I took the train instead of renting a car from Rapp's Garage," she said. "It gave me time to think."

"Think about your actions?" Eve asked.

"Think about August," she said. "I still loved him, you see, and I didn't want to hurt him."

Eve heard a snort escape her sister.

"I turned around and came right back," Cecilia said. "I didn't even leave the station."

"Did August know what you were going to do?" Oliver asked.

"Oh, no." She looked alarmed. "You mustn't tell him!"

"Why not?" Mrs. Feather challenged. "He ought to know you're not going to be pushed over again!"

"Nobody's being pushed over, Mother," Cecilia said. "I told you, Rosalia explained it to me."

"Did she?" Helena eyed her.

"All young men with money have their weak moments," Cecilia said. "They want to prove something to themselves. So they get ideas about going out into the world. We were lucky August wanted to do something useful." She chuckled. "Ivan Beaton went to Texas that one time to look for oil wells and almost got himself shot."

"An adventure he won't soon forget." Eve tried to keep from smiling at the way he had bragged about that incident, to Mrs. Beaton's utter horror.

"Is that what Rosalia told you?" Oliver asked. "August was just looking for an adventure?"

Cecilia nodded. "And she was right, wasn't she? He came back."

"Why didn't he marry you when he came back?" Helena asked.

"Helena!" Eve hissed.

"She's quite right, my dear," Mrs. Feather declared. "It would have been the decent thing to do. I don't care how important Rosalia is in this community. He acted shamefully toward you and there's no excuse for it."

"A man can't just take up where he left off after being away for so long," Cecilia insisted. "It takes time to get your feet on the ground."

"Is that why you forgave him?" Oliver asked.

"We're friends and we'll always be friends." Her voice trailed off as she added, "I ought to have remembered that."

"What do you mean?" Oliver's eyes were keen.

"Nothing," she said.

"You're talking about the engagement ring, aren't you?" He leaned forward. "August told us you went with him to buy it."

"What engagement ring?" Mrs. Feather stared. "What's all this about?"

"August asked me to come with him to Shreve's in San Francisco," she said. "He wanted me to help him choose the ring he planned to give Libby."

"That brazen boy!" Mrs. Feather's indignation was genuine. "Cecilia, I forbid you to see him ever again."

"Not very charitable of you, is it, Mrs. Feather?" Helena raised an eyebrow. "I thought you were all about charity."

"To those who deserve it!" she thundered. "To those who don't lie and cheat!"

"He wasn't lying or cheating!" Cecilia insisted. "It wasn't his fault."

The torn look on the girl's face and the way she curled her hands, her fingers like claws, made Eve's heart go out to her. "You thought the ring was for you."

"Beast!" Mrs. Feather screeched.

"August asked me to come with him to San Francisco one morning," Cecilia said. "He didn't tell me what it was about at first. He just said he needed to muster up the courage to do something." She smiled. "We always used to do that for one another as children. Take one another for company when we needed the courage to do something."

"It's nice to know you always have someone you can turn to when you're afraid," Oliver said kindly.

"He didn't tell me what he was doing," Cecilia said. "It was only when we started looking at the diamond rings that I realized what it was"

"Why make her suffer, Mr. Clarke?" Mrs. Feather asked. "What could this have to do with August or the murder?"

"We're trying to verify the story of the ring, Mrs. Feather," Oliver said.

"Why?"

"Libby wasn't wearing it when they found her," Eve supplied.

"The police think there was no ring," Helena added.

"Of course there was a ring!" Cecilia said. "I wore it for a day."

"You wore it!" Mrs. Feather's face turned pale.

"Why shouldn't she, if she thought it was for her?" Eve asked in a sharp tone. "Please, Mrs. Feather, you're not helping matters."

"Did you think it was for you?"

"Yes." The girl broke down and sobbed. "It was all my fault. He never said it was. I just took it for granted."

"Because he asked you to come with him and let you wear it," Helena said. "A logical conclusion."

"You say logical. I say beast!"

"Yes, we know what you think of him by now, Mrs. Feather," Oliver said dryly.

"I feel like such a fool now," said Cecilia.

His face softened with sympathy. "He's the one who was foolish and thoughtless."

"That's not true, Mr. Clarke," Cecilia insisted. "He never made any promises. We've never spoken of marriage since he got back."

"And yet you were sure he would propose to you again," Eve pointed out.

"Rosalia was sure he was going to," Cecilia said. "After he got his feet on the ground. And for a while, it seemed as if he would."

"You mean until he met Libby," Eve said.

"Not just that," she said. "After Libby went away, I was sure —
but, as I said, I was a fool." She dabbed her eyes.

"We were told you and August saw quite a lot of one another
when Libby went to see her aunt in Reno," Oliver said.

"Yes, we did," she said. "I thought he was finished with her."

"And then he takes you to buy her an engagement ring and
even asks you to wear it for a day." Helena's voice was harsh.
"That was very callous of him."

"Oh, no," Cecilia defended. "I think he wanted to see how it
would look on a woman's finger."

"You have a lot of patience, Cecilia," Oliver said. "Most
women wouldn't tolerate a man behaving that way."

"I've learned to tolerate a lot, Mr. Clarke." Though her gaze
remained steady, Eve felt as if the remark were meant for her
mother.

"And after the day in San Francisco was over, you gave the
ring back to him?"

"I thought he was still afraid to propose," she lamented. "I
thought, when he gets up the courage, it will come." She strug-
gled to speak, clutching the handkerchief. "Well, it came all right.
But not to me!" She covered her face with her hands.

The sight of her sobbing daughter clearly affected Mrs.
Feather, as the outrage gave way to despair. "You were too good
for him, my dear. He's getting his just desserts now."

"Don't say that!" Cecilia cried.

"I suppose the girl was with child?" The mother's eyes were
like pins on Oliver.

Eve held her breath as she waited to see what Oliver
would say.

"Why do you think that, ma'am?" he asked carefully.

"Mr. Clarke, I may be tucked away in this comfortable corner
of town, but I still know what goes on in the world," she said. "I
work with unfortunates all the time."

"You mean people who haven't much money," Helena corrected.

"I've seen many young women force a marriage on a man for getting them into trouble," the woman continued.

"Are you also implying you've seen the same young women killed because they tried to force a man into marriage?" Oliver asked.

"It's been done, hasn't it?" She looked squarely at him. "Is that what the police are thinking?"

"He didn't do it!" Cecilia shrieked.

"Right now, we're trying to gather information, Mrs. Feather," Oliver said firmly. Turning to Cecilia, he spoke in a softer tone. "I know this is hard for you, but if we're to find the ring, we need a clear description of it."

"I'll do better than that, Mr. Clarke." The young woman darted to a corner of the room and swung open a cabinet door. She came back with a photo album. "August took photographs of me that day."

"Photos!" Mrs. Feather looked ready to swoon. "How could he do such a ghastly thing to you?"

"I asked him to," Cecilia insisted. "And it was my camera."

Helena gazed at her. "You just happened to take a camera?"

"We went sightseeing in the city afterward," she said softly.

With Oliver and Helena glancing over her shoulder, Eve went through the album. The black-and-white photographs clearly showed Cecilia and August posing in front of various sights in the city, arms linked and smiling.

"It must have been a lovely day," Eve murmured.

She turned to the last page. There was only one photograph. Its white glare stood out against the black heavy paper. Cecilia, alone, beamed with radiance, thrusting her hand at the camera, her fingers extended like a spider's web. A ring sat on the left hand. Even through the faded gray, she could see it matched the description of the ring that August had given them.

Cecilia said in an almost triumphant voice, "I told you he bought a ring."

"Let me see that!" Mrs. Feather snatched the album from Eve's lap. Her face grew dark. "To think he made you wear it!"

"He didn't make me, Mother," Cecilia said. "I wanted to." In a sudden cold tone, she added, "I led myself into the trap."

"The trap of thinking he was going to propose to you?" Helena's voice was not without sympathy.

"The trap of thinking he still loved me," Cecilia said. "How could he when *she* had everything he admired?"

"By 'she,' you mean Libby?" Oliver eyed her.

"I was sick of hearing how wonderful she was with children, how she took care of her father, how she wanted August to be something in this world and how she believed in him." The icy tone that sounded so much like her mother suddenly faded away. "I'm sorry. I shouldn't speak of her like that now that she's dead."

"It sounds more like you were speaking of him," Eve said quietly.

Oliver looked at her with his dark eyes contemplating for a moment. He held out his hand to Mrs. Feather. "I'd like to keep that for a while, if you don't mind."

"Don't tell me it's evidence?" Mrs. Feather asked. "I don't want Cecilia involved in this, Mr. Clarke."

"I'll try to keep her out of it as much as possible," he promised. "But the ring is an important clue, and this is the only evidence that it existed."

"There's me!" Cecilia said. "I'm evidence. I'll testify he bought the ring fully intending to ask Libby to marry him and that he loved her and his intentions were honorable."

"Did he tell you all of that?" Oliver asked quietly.

"He didn't need to tell me," Cecilia insisted. "I know him."

Oliver took the chair opposite Cecilia again. "Have you any idea what could have happened to the ring?"

"You said he gave it to Libby," she said. "He must have proposed to her."

"We also said she had no ring when the police found her," he said. "And there was no ring among her things. The police checked."

"Could it have been stolen?" Mrs. Feather offered. "We get tramps by the river now and then. Poor men will steal for a loaf of bread." Her voice sounded regretful.

"It's unlikely," he said. "Libby was wearing other valuable jewelry that wasn't stolen."

"I haven't the faintest idea where the ring is," Cecilia said. "It's as Mother says, I'm sure. Someone stole it."

"Without stealing other jewelry Libby was wearing?" Helena eyed her.

"I'm sure I don't know what a thief would do," Cecilia said. "But if you think August never gave it to her, you're wrong. August isn't the kind to buy an engagement ring for a woman and then not give it to her."

"You thought he bought it for you and didn't have the courage to propose," Helena pointed out.

"That's different," she said softly. "He wanted to marry Libby."

"We're not interested so much in whether he gave it to her or not, but in what his motive might have been either way," Oliver said.

"What do you mean?" Mrs. Feather stared at him.

"Well, ma'am." He looked a little sheepish. "You guessed it before."

"Guessed it?" Her face suddenly became white. "You mean she was with child after all?"

Cecilia was silent for a moment. "I don't believe it."

"It's true," Helena said. "She was going into her third month."

"Who says so?" Cecilia shrieked.

"Her doctor in Reno," Helena shot back.

"Dr. Myers also confirmed she was going to have a baby," Oliver added.

The girl's eyes dropped. "I'm sorry. I'm sure you're right." But, in a more defiant tone, she added, "But you can't tell who the father is, can you?"

"August told us himself," Eve said.

"Because that's what Libby told him!" Cecilia was rigid. "Girls don't always tell the truth when they want a man to marry them, do they?"

It was as if the room decompressed and the light shining from the windows disappeared behind clouds. Eve glanced at Oliver. He looked as if he were contemplating his next move. He finally said in a low tone, "Do you really believe that, Cecilia?"

She looked wildly from one person to another and suddenly burst into tears. "I don't know what I believe! This is all a nightmare!"

Her mother moved swiftly to her side, putting her arms around her. "I asked you before not to upset my daughter, Mr. Clarke. She's told you all she knows."

"I'm sorry, ma'am," he said. "I only have a few more questions, and then we'll be on our way."

"Please, Eleanor," Eve said. "The police have to find out who did this and they need all the help they can get."

"Yes, yes." Cecilia dried her eyes quickly. "I'm sorry for my outburst. The sooner the police find out who did this, the sooner they'll let August go."

"You're a very sensible young woman, Cecilia," Oliver complimented. "This is a matter of routine, but what were you doing Friday night?"

"You mean the day Libby was killed?" she asked.

"We were helping with the dinner for the veterans," Mrs. Feather said.

"You mean the American Legion?" Eve asked.

The woman nodded. "We've been doing quite a lot of work

with them since the war ended." She shook her head. "Those poor, lost boys. You really ought to join us, Eve. Most of the businesses in Gyver have."

"Helena and I will certainly look into it," she said, glancing at her sister.

"You were there how long?" asked Oliver.

"We got there early — about four-thirty, I should think — and we were there helping with the cleaning up until almost midnight."

"Both of you?" He glanced from one to the other.

"I left early," Cecilia said. "I was tired from being on my feet for hours."

"How early?" He leaned forward.

"I didn't look at the time," she said. "It was dark when I came out of the American Legion."

"I see," he said. "That's just past the Malwood Bridge, isn't it?"

"Yes," said Mrs. Feather. "Does that matter?"

"No, no," he mumbled. Eve knew he was thinking the path that passed under Malwood Bridge led down to Josh's shack.

Mrs. Feather's sharp eyes caught his gaze and she said in a crushing tone, "I'll ask you again, Mr. Clarke. Do I need to call a lawyer?"

"No, ma'am," he said firmly. "We're almost through." He pressed Cecilia's hand. "I know this wasn't easy for you, but you've been a great help."

"I hope you see now August couldn't have done this awful thing," Cecilia said.

"We were told you sometimes called Libby on August's behalf," Oliver said. "Especially since they were trying to keep their relationship a secret."

"Who told you that?" Mrs. Feather shot out.

"Mrs. Cinder," Eve said.

"Cecilia, you wouldn't —"

"Yes, I did," she said boldly. "Why not? August would have done the same for me."

"Did you call her on Friday night to tell her August wanted to meet her by the river?"

Cecilia stared at him. "Of course I didn't!"

"Are you sure?" Helena asked. "Mrs. Cinder said it was your voice on the phone."

"Of course I'm sure." She looked alarmed. "When I got home on Friday night, I went straight to bed."

"That's true, Mr. Clarke," Mrs. Feather insisted. "When I came home, she was sound asleep."

Oliver rose, motioning toward the Grave sisters. "I'm sorry to have taken up so much of your time. But the picture of the ring will help us a lot." He smiled again at Cecilia, whose face relaxed a little.

"Mr. Clarke," she said anxiously. "I'd like to see August."

He looked a little embarrassed. "I'm afraid that wouldn't be possible right now."

"Has he a lawyer?" Cecilia jumped up.

"Rosalia called in Mr. Adkins," Eve assured her.

"Leave it to Rosalia to get the best for her boy," Mrs. Feather assured her daughter.

"Do you think he'll need him?" Cecilia looked at Eve with pleading eyes. "I mean — they'll charge him, won't they, Eve? Won't they?" The last was almost demanding.

"We're not the police, Cecilia." Helena came to her sister's defense.

She turned to Oliver and in the same demanding tone, repeated, "Won't they?"

Oliver was silent for a moment. "I think it's time we went. Thank you again for the photos." He tucked the album under his arm.

Cecilia suddenly collapsed. Mrs. Feather's authoritative presence melted with maternal soothing as she whispering kind words, leading her up the stairs.

ornings after funeral services were always filled with a heavy air for Eve. Even though the flower pattern on the china and the bright colors of the knick-knacks on the sideboard shone brightly with the sun flooding in, Eve still choked from the Cinder house grayness and dust. Violet's lively chatter did not lighten the mood. Felix, whose job rarely allowed him to appear at breakfast, had joined them. His mood was amiable enough to exchange some of his bitter sarcasm for the charm that had attracted his wife. But nothing could comfort Eve.

She knew Helena felt the same way as her sister looked far away, giving only vague answers to her husband's repartee. But Eve guessed Helena's mood was not because of the funeral but the events that had taken them away from it.

"You two look like the house just burned down," said Violet.

"I heard yesterday's occasion was irregular." Felix waved the paper Agnes has set down on the table. "A funeral and an arrest."

"August wasn't arrested," Helena said. "They have him down at the station only to ask questions."

"He may not be down there much longer," Eve said. "Oliver promised to come by this morning and give me an update."

"Why would he be giving you an update?" Violet asked.

"I asked him to," said Eve.

Helena glanced at her. "That wasn't very prudent."

"Why not?" her younger sister asked. "I think it's all so exciting."

"You would," Felix snorted.

"Our involvement in the case ended yesterday with the visit to the Feathers," Helena insisted. "You might have compromised his position, Eve."

"What do you mean?" Her older sister stared at her.

"Do you think the district attorney can talk about a case to anyone he pleases?" Helena's tone was firm. "He has to keep what he knows very close to the vest. It might ruin the case if he doesn't."

Eve's finger became so stiff that she dropped her fork. "I never thought of that!"

"If Oliver wants to tell her about it, why shouldn't he?" Violet plucked a cinnamon roll from the plate Agnes put on the table. "Another present from Karl?"

"They're my own," Agnes said with a tone of dignity.

Felix laughed. "You can't have them buzzing around you all the time, Vi."

"He's only waiting for lunchtime," Violet said. "He hinted yesterday he has a whole box of éclairs hidden in the bakery icebox just for me."

"I should have been more discreet," Eve lamented.

"I agree with Helena," said Felix. "It's not right to compromise the district attorney's — shall we say, affection? — for you." Eve blushed furiously. "Even if he's willing to compromise it."

"That wasn't quite what I meant, Felix," Helena said dryly.

He laughed and put his arm around his wife's shoulders. "Don't let it disturb you, my sweet. Oliver's got enough brains to know what to tell and what to hold back. There are still plenty of us with brains, though not scientific ones." His tone was gallant as he held up his arm. "We may be meek, but, as the good book says, we shall inherit the earth."

"Oh, applesauce," Vi mumbled as she selected another cinnamon roll.

Agnes came in followed by the district attorney.

"Good morning, Oliver." Eve greeted him with a smile, motioning for Agnes to put another place setting. "Breakfast?"

"I've had it, thank you." He sat down beside her.

"Look here, Oliver." Felix's glib tone suddenly grew serious. "I'm not sure I like how you've involved my wife and sister-in-law in this sordid murder business."

"And I'm not sure it's any of your business!" Helena snapped.

"My sisters do as they please," Violet said hotly. "They don't need any man to tell them what to do."

"And neither do you, I suppose?" he retorted.

"And neither do I!"

"Oliver asked for our help, remember?" Helena challenged.

"That's right, I did," said the district attorney.

"Well, if it's all the same to you, I'd rather they not join your sleuth hunt." His tone was commanding, grating on Eve's nerves.

"Crime detection has always interested me." Helena's tone was equally commanding. "From a scientific perspective."

"It's all the rage now," Violet chimed in.

Felix's voice rose. "And if I forbade you to —" He stopped mid-sentence. His face relaxed and his usual careless attitude returned. "But, of course, who am I to forbid you to do anything, my sweet? Dead bodies are, after all, what pay our bills." He kissed her cheek. "It's too early in the morning for me to hear about dead bodies. I shall go back to bed." He passed Agnes, who had just brought another plate of toast. "Don't wake me up until lunch, Agnes. I shall be deep in dreamland."

"Wasn't planning on waking you up anyway," she mumbled. "That's what alarm clocks are for."

He laughed and threw his head in Oliver's direction. "Forget everything I said, Oliver. I've been living among outspoken women for so long, I have to get up on my hind legs once in a while."

"Good Lord," Violet sniffed, "you would think he didn't know women can vote now."

"It hasn't been easy for him," Helena said softly. "He's right about all of us being outspoken."

"Does that mean he should have the last say on everything?" Violet glanced at her sister. "Even Papa never believed women should be seen and not heard."

"Papa treated women as equals," Eve agreed.

"I didn't mean to cause a tiff," Oliver said slowly.

Helena regained her composure. "You didn't cause anything, Oliver. We're both eager to help."

"Did you ask August about the ring?" Eve inquired.

Oliver nodded. "He confirmed everything Cecilia said. He looked pretty ashamed of himself."

"I hope so," Helena said.

"What ring?" Violet looked around the table.

"August gave Libby an engagement ring," said Helena.

"What has Cecilia to do with that?"

"She went with him to pick it out," her sister supplied. "She even wore it for the day."

"Golly!" Violet stared. "What a rotten egg."

"Vi, isn't it time for you to get going?" Eve motioned to Agnes, who promptly took the dishes away from under Violet's nose. "The car keys are in the usual place. If you need help hand-cranking, call me. Good luck with the interviews."

"I want to stay and hear what Oliver has to say," her sister pouted.

"You can't," Helena said. "Your first interview is at nine. It's eight-forty now."

"I will not be chased out like a kid!" Violet banged her fists on the table.

"Why not when you're acting like one?" Helena retorted.

"I have ten minutes before I have to leave," Violet said in a calmer tone. "Let me at least hear what August said."

"No," said Oliver promptly. "Your sister told you to go, and you'll go." He pulled her up from the chair, took the hat and coat Agnes brought to the table and put them on her. Amidst Violet's loud protests peppered with profanity, he herded her out the door.

He returned with a sheepish grin. "That's two members of the Grave family I've upset this morning."

"They'll get over it," Eve said. "By evening, they'll both be pumping us for details."

"What about the rope, Oliver?" Helena poured him another cup of coffee.

"He admitted the rope was his," he said. "And that it was a special kind of rope, just like Josh said."

"Did he admit he tied Libby's ankles with it too?" Eve snarled.

"Eve, don't," said her sister. "The police have to ask these questions."

"Are you going to arrest him because of the rope?" Eve looked squarely at Oliver.

"The police don't make an arrest based on one piece of evidence," he said.

"Then you finally believe him about the ring?"

"We know he bought it," said Oliver. "While we were talking with Cecilia, the sheriff verified it with Shreve. They said he bought a diamond engagement ring. Sheriff Warner sent one of his men with the photograph Cecilia gave us to verify."

Eve watched him carefully. "But you're not convinced he actually gave it to Libby."

Oliver was quiet for a moment. "I never said that."

"It's the sheriff who isn't convinced," Helena guessed.

He gave a lopsided smile. "The sheriff now has a new theory."

"Oh?"

"I talked him into allowing Cecilia to see August," he said.

"That was kind of you, Oliver." Eve smiled. "She was so worried about him."

"Kind nothing." Helena looked at him steadily. "The sheriff was listening in, wasn't he?"

"Don't be silly, dear," Eve said. "That's the kind of crazy idea Vi would come up with."

"Maybe not so crazy, Eve," her sister insisted. "They do have devices they can plant anywhere and record conversations. A professor of mine in college was trying to perfect such a device."

Oliver burst out laughing. "Those are the kinds of shenanigans the police do in the detective novels, Helena."

"Only because if you tried to present such evidence in court, the judge would throw it out," Helena said with a nod. "I should have thought about that."

"What has that to do with the sheriff's new theory?" Eve asked.

"They had a lot to talk about," Oliver said.

"And the sheriff formed a theory based on *that*?" Helena asked.

"He did indeed," said Oliver. "He's taking Mrs. Cinder's insistence that Cecilia phoned Libby very seriously."

"Surely, he can't believe Cecilia would be capable of such a crime." Eve stared.

"We have to explore every avenue." Oliver tapped the edge of the cup against the saucer. Agnes came in with a sour look on her face and took it away.

"Do you believe it, Oliver?" Helena asked.

"I don't believe or disbelieve anything until I see proof," he said. "But we may not have a choice."

"What do you mean?" Helena asked.

"When one thread of inquiry falls through, the police have to pursue another," he said. "Or drop the case. And no one is ready to do that yet."

"Falls through?" Eve sat up. "You mean you don't think August did it?"

"Remember what we talked about yesterday, Eve?"

"What did you talk about?" Helena looked from one to the other.

"We both knew August was lying about where he'd been the night Libby was killed," he said. "Well, we were right. He finally admitted it."

"He wasn't taking a walk that night." Eve swallowed.

"He took a walk all right," he said. "But after ten o'clock."

"After Libby was killed." Helena nodded. "Where was he before that?"

"Having dinner with a naval officer," said Oliver. "A friend of Josh's. Seems he was thinking of going into the Navy." He grimaced. "The sheriff was right about one thing. The boy hasn't given up the idea of going to sea."

"Why didn't he say anything before?" Eve asked.

"He didn't want his mother to know."

"I don't blame him," Helena said. "I'm sure Rosalia wouldn't take too kindly to him making his own plans for his life."

"We're checking with Lieutenant Commander Dale," Oliver said. "If the story checks out, there goes our suspect."

"And if it does?" Helena asked.

"There's the sheriff's new idea," he said ironically.

"Cecilia," Eve breathed.

"Well, you must admit, Eve, Mrs. Beaton may have been right about her," said Oliver. "She wasn't exactly sympathetic toward Libby when we spoke to her."

"Still waters run deep," Eve murmured.

"What does the sheriff intend to do?" Helena asked.

Oliver reached into his jacket pocket. "He consented to let me get the search warrant this time."

"A search warrant!" Eve stared. "What for?"

"To look for the ring, of course," Helena said.

"Have it right here." He waved the folded piece of paper. "I'm heading over to the Feather house now."

"I suppose he made it clear if you refused, he would go to Judge Long again," Eve said dryly.

"It's not just that, Eve," he said. "I've got to pursue every small detail in this case. It's like tracking down the cricket who's bothering people at night with his chirping."

"Murder is more than an annoying cricket," Helena said with a smile.

He rose. "It bothers me in the same way, Helena."

When Eve saw him to the door, he said, "Will you come with me to serve it, Eve? Sheriff Warner and his men are waiting near the Feather house."

"Our work is done, Oliver," she said quietly. "We've laid Libby to rest."

"Your work may be done, but mine isn't," he said. "You can help me with Mrs. Feather. I don't think she's going to take this well."

"Neither will Cecilia, for that matter," she said ruefully.

"She'll be glad at least to know August may have an alibi," he pointed out.

CHAPTER 25

Sheriff Warner and Deputy Elwood were outside near the house when they reached the Feathers. The sheriff was tossing the handcuffs from one hand to the other.

"You look as if you're expecting to arrest someone, Sheriff." Eve eyed him.

"You never can tell what will happen, Miss Grace," he said in a sly tone.

"You could have parked it in the alleyway," Oliver barked. "We can still respect they won't want the neighbors gossiping."

The sheriff grunted. "Let's get this thing over with." He glanced at Eve. "I suppose I don't have to ask what you're doing here, Miss Grace."

"Maybe if you behaved more like a churchgoer and less like a browbeater, I wouldn't need to be," Eve snapped.

"I do my duty, miss." Sheriff Warner looked at Oliver. "Let's go."

"You stay behind me," Oliver ordered. "Wait until I've served the warrant before you go barging in."

"I always follow the law, Mr. Clarke," said the sheriff with a smirk.

Mrs. Feather wore an apron dusted with flour when she answered the door. Eve could see Cecilia puttering around in the kitchen.

"I'm sorry to disturb you, ma'am," Oliver began.

"You caught us at a bad time, Mr. Clarke," said the woman. "We're making some cakes to take to the American Legion picnic."

"I'm sure the vets will appreciate it," Sheriff Warner mumbled.

She looked at the two lawmen, their badges shining. "I thought this whole business with my daughter was finished."

Cecilia came into the hallway, wiping her hands on her apron. "Mother, let them in."

"I'm not sure I should." Mrs. Feather eyed them. "Not without a lawyer."

"Mr. Clarke arranged for me to see August yesterday." The young woman was clearly calmer than the previous day and her bright eyes shown with enthusiasm. "Thank you for doing that, Mr. Clarke."

"You stayed a while, didn't you?" Sheriff Warner remarked.

"Yes, I did," she said with a smile. "I feel better now that he told me he asked to stay overnight."

Eve stepped into the hall. "The police think August has an alibi, Cecilia. He might be getting out very soon."

"We're still checking on that," Sheriff Warner insisted.

"Oh, I'm so glad!" She pressed Eve's hand.

"You realize if August gets out, that leaves the door wide open for someone else to have committed the crime," the sheriff said.

"What does this all mean, Mr. Clarke?" Mrs. Feather put her arm around her daughter's shoulders.

"I'm afraid, ma'am, some questions have come up about some of the evidence in this case," Oliver said.

"Evidence? What evidence?" Mrs. Feather glared at him. "If it's about that engagement ring —"

Sheriff Warner shoved his way beside Oliver. "As a matter of fact, it is."

"I've a search warrant, ma'am." Eve had to admire the firm and calm way Oliver spoke.

"Search warrant!"

The sheriff motioned toward his deputy and pushed past the woman into the house.

"That's right." Oliver unfolded the paper. "You can read it for yourself."

Mrs. Feather looked at it as if it were on fire.

Cecilia took the warrant and read it. "It looks legal, Mother."

"I don't care if it is!" the woman snapped. "You're not doing anything until I call my lawyer."

"Maybe you should call Hugh Adkins," Sheriff Warner said with a smirk. "I'm sure Mrs. Winters will give you the number."

"That's uncalled for, Sheriff!" Eve snarled.

"You have that right, Mrs. Feather," Oliver said. "But it won't stop us from searching."

"What is it you're looking for?" she asked.

"It says right here they're searching for items related to the Elizabeth Cinder murder case." Cecilia shivered.

"But what does that mean?" Mrs. Feather looked at Oliver. "My God, it's the engagement ring, isn't it?"

"I told you before I haven't seen it since I gave it back to August." Cecilia grew agitated. "Why don't you believe me?"

"We have a legal right to search." Oliver's tone was that of the stoic lawman. "Remember the Fourth Amendment, ma'am."

"The police just need to make sure, Cecilia," Eve intervened. She felt Oliver's grateful eyes on her.

The young woman sighed. "Oh, let them, Mother. They won't find anything."

"Appreciate your cooperation," Sheriff Warner mumbled as he started up the flight of stairs with Deputy Elwood following close behind.

"Go with them, Eve," begged Cecilia. "I don't like to think of those men going through my things." She looked genuinely ill.

"They're always careful," Oliver promised.

"All the same —"

"Of course, dear," Eve said quickly.

They found the lawmen in Cecilia's bedroom, a simply furnished room with a four-poster bed and bright-colored sheets.

"I think we should let Eve look through that," Oliver declared as the deputy opened the top drawer of a shabby bureau.

"This is not time for delicacies," snarled Sheriff Warner.

"If I find anything, I'll show you immediately," Eve promised. "I'm not completely feather-headed, Sheriff."

"No, but I gather you're more sympathetic to the girl than she deserves." The sheriff stared at her shrewdly.

"Eve is more willing to give people the benefit of the doubt than most of us, Sheriff," Oliver intervened. "But I trust her compassion won't interfere with the duty of the law."

"She ain't bound by the law, Mr. Clarke," Sheriff Warner said. "Remember that."

Oliver pressed Eve's hand. "Look in the drawers, Eve."

She found the task more difficult than she imagined. It wasn't the physical part of going through clothes and linens, which she did with the same care she showed toward her own. It was feeling like she was an intruder to another person's life. She had learned long ago how one's clothes and linens gave so much away. Cecilia's garments were surprisingly impractical and more modern than Eve would have thought. They looked as if they belonged to someone else.

She reached the bottom drawer. It was filled with patterned scarfs and shawls. The way they were stuffed in the drawer made Eve think Cecilia's mother knew nothing about them. She imagined Cecilia would take one in her purse when she left the house and put it on away from her mother's eye. She picked through the scattered silks and beaded fringes and was surprised to find one at the bottom that seemed quite tame. The wine-colored silk contrasted with the bright floral and seashells of the others. It was folded neatly so each corner met in the middle.

"What have you got there?" Oliver peeked over her shoulder. "Not bad."

"And unlike the rest of her things," Eve remarked.

"My sister has a lot of those things," Deputy Elwood offered. "She says there's no point in wasting money on clothes that will go out of style in a year when she can spend a few dollars on a scarf or a pin and keep them looking modern.

"That's very sensible of her." Eve smiled.

"Can we dispense with the fashion show?" Sheriff Warner growled as he yanked the frilly bedspread to look under the bed.

"Odd, though," Eve murmured as she touched the burgundy scarf.

"What is?" Oliver inquired.

"Everything is thrown in this drawer except for this," she said. "Why is this one so special?"

Sheriff Warner was suddenly alert. "Why? 'Cause she's hiding something in it, that's why!" He snatched it from her and shook it out. A flash of gold fell to the carpet.

Oliver was the first to grab it. There was no doubt it was the engagement ring.

Sheriff Warner grinned. "Thanks, Miss Grave. You've just solved our case."

"But she said —"

"Looks like your compassion was misplaced." Oliver's voice sounded hard as nails.

"Sure it was." The sheriff took out a paper envelope and sealed the ring inside it.

Eve fought back tears. "You'll arrest Cecilia now?"

"That's up to Mr. Clarke." The sheriff looked at Oliver.

Oliver's face looked grim and rough. "Let's go."

"Oliver, you can't believe —"

"I said before I don't believe or disbelieve anything until I see proof," he said quietly.

"Well, this is proof alright," Sheriff Warner insisted.

As they climbed down the stairs, Eve could hear Cecilia saying, "She was always talking down to me. Always looking at me as if I were useless because I didn't work for a living."

"You help people in need," Mrs. Feather said in a soothing tone. "That's more important."

"I'm glad I got to wear that engagement ring even if only for a little while," Cecilia said. "I'm glad it wasn't on Libby's finger when she died. Does that make me a bad person?"

"Of course not, dear."

"It wasn't on Miss Cinder's finger because you ripped it right off!" interrupted Sheriff Warner as they spilled into the living room.

"Don't be absurd!" Mrs. Feather snapped. "Now that you've done your search, you can leave us in peace to do our work."

"We have our work too, ma'am." Oliver nodded at Sheriff Warner, and the sheriff spilled the contents of the envelope on the coffee table.

Both women stared down at the ring, its small but tastefully cut diamonds adding a warm light to the room.

Cecilia's soft features gathered with bewilderment as she dropped into a chair. "Where did you —"

"I found it," Eve said meekly. "Wrapped in a scarf in your drawer."

"Good God!" Mrs. Feather squeaked like a mouse. "I'm calling a lawyer."

"Do that, ma'am," Sheriff Warner said. "Your daughter's going to need one."

"I don't understand." The young woman pressed at her temples. "I gave it back to August." She looked wildly at Oliver. "Didn't he tell you that?"

"He told us that," Oliver said, his voice like iron.

"But you took it back," Sheriff Warner said. "You took back what you thought was rightfully yours."

"Sheriff —" Oliver cautioned and Deputy Elwood looked alarmed.

"You knew August would be out," the sheriff continued. "You called Miss Cinder and told her he wanted to meet her by the river. But you showed up instead and held her head under the water until she was dead. Then you tied her ankles to a heavy piece of wood just lying by the river and pushed her in so she'd sink to the bottom. Only it didn't quite turn out that way."

"Be careful, Sheriff," Oliver snarled.

"I'm only telling the truth, Mr. Clarke," he insisted. "She did just what I said — ripped the ring off Miss Cinder's finger because she didn't think it belonged to her. And I'm willing to bet money she took the pin for the same reason."

"Don't say a word, Cecilia," her mother commanded, heading toward the hallway for the phone.

"Mr. Adkins said he'd be down at the jail this morning," Sheriff Warner remarked. "You might try calling him there."

Mrs. Feather glared at him. "Don't say anything, Cecilia."

The young woman's breath was coming out in gasps. Eve took her by the shoulders and she almost sagged in her grasp. "Cecilia," she asked softly. "Why was the scarf folded?"

The girl looked at her with vacant eyes.

"Only that scarf was folded," Eve said.

"I never fold things," Cecilia lamented.

"She had to fold it to hide the ring," the sheriff insisted. "We're wasting time, Mr. Clarke. Deputy, go and tell Mrs. Feather she and her lawyer can come down to the station."

"Wait, Sheriff." Eve saw a glimmer of sympathy in Oliver's eye as he bent down to the grieving young woman. "Cecilia, where is the pin?"

"Pin?"

"The pin Libby always wore," Eve said. "The redbud tree."

"I don't know about any pin." Cecilia looked at Eve. "I swear I don't know!"

"You took it for revenge, just like you took the ring," the sheriff snarled.

"I didn't!" Cecilia stared at him. "I liked Libby, I really did."

It didn't sound much like it from what you said just now." Oliver's tone hardened.

"I didn't mean it," Cecilia cried.

"Then how did the ring get into your drawer?"

"I don't know. I tell you, I don't know!" Cecilia's howling made Eve flinch.

"You told us you knew the ring wasn't for you when August asked for it back," Oliver said.

"Yes," she said slowly. "Yes, I knew then."

"You hated Libby."

"Yes, I hated her. I hated her!" The girl's voice lost its sweetness.

"So you lured her to the river," he continued.

"No, no!"

"Oliver, stop!" Eve shrieked.

"Don't worry, Mr. Clarke," said the sheriff. "We'll get it out of her, lawyer or no lawyer."

Mrs. Feather came back. "I called George Decker. He'll meet us at the police station." She glared at the sheriff. "I assume that's where you're taking her?"

"For now, yes." Oliver put the ring back in the envelope and gave it to Deputy Elwood.

"You're arresting her, then?" Mrs. Feather stared.

"No, ma'am," Oliver said. "But we need some explanations." His tone was softer. "No one is going to hurt you, Cecilia. We just want the truth."

Mrs. Feather turned to Eve with desperate eyes. "Eve, you have some influence with these men. You've got to stop them."

"I've nothing to do with the law, Mrs. Feather," Eve said. "But I'll go down to the station with Cecilia if you like." She smiled at the girl.

"I'm afraid that's impossible," Oliver said.

"It's all right, Eve." She rose, shaking a little. "Mother will come with me. It seems I'm the charity case now."

Mrs. Feather's lower lip trembled, and she covered her face.

"Now, none of that." Cecilia pressed her mother's shoulders. "This is all a big mistake, and Mr. Decker will make them see that."

"I'm sorry, dear." Her mother wiped her face with the handkerchief Deputy Elwood had given her. "I know this is all a mistake." Looking hard at Oliver, she added, "Mr. Clarke will see that very soon."

Cecilia glanced at the handcuffs swinging in the sheriff's hands. "Must I wear those?"

"I think we can dispense with them, Sheriff," Oliver said firmly.

"I won't run away," Cecilia promised. "I've been running away from life and from the truth, but no more."

"What do you mean?" Eve murmured.

"August never loved me," she said. "I only thought so because Rosalia was so nice to me."

"I'm sorry, Cecilia," she said.

"She taught me how to choose my own clothes, how to use the stove, how to sew, everything," Cecilia lamented. "She used to say even a society woman needed to know those things to make her husband proud."

"She promised August would be that husband," Eve suggested.

"No, no!" The young woman looked at her. "I made myself promises. It wasn't fair to August." Her eyes became blurry. "Poor August!"

"Poor August!" Mrs. Feather echoed with contempt.

"It's awful to lose the one person you truly love," Cecilia said.

"But you know that, Mother, don't you?" Her mother nodded sadly.

Eve and Oliver watched the sheriff carefully guide Cecilia and her mother into the police car. The young woman's face was covered in tears. Oliver took his handkerchief out of his pocket and gave it to her with kind murmurs. She managed a smile as he closed the door and Deputy Elwood, at the wheel, drove off.

Eve felt her anger rise. "I hope you and the sheriff are proud of yourselves!"

"Justice isn't about pride, Eve," he said. "It's about right and wrong."

"Apparently, it doesn't always matter which is which," she snapped.

"Just what do you mean by that?"

"That girl couldn't kill a fly!"

"The sheriff was right." His voice grew harsh. "You're no lawman. Lawmen don't let sentiment get in the way of their duty."

"Maybe not sentiment, but they do have compassion, don't they?" Eve asked. "They use their heads, don't they?"

His eyes narrowed. "Are you implying we weren't using our heads with the evidence staring us in the face?"

"The rope was evidence staring you in the face, wasn't it?" she challenged. "And then you found out August has an alibi."

"Maybe he has an alibi," Oliver reminded her. "We're still verifying it."

"He wouldn't have told you about meeting with that Navy officer if he didn't know it would clear him," Eve said.

There was silence for a moment as someone down the street got into their car and drove past them. Oliver's bear-like gaze melted into the boyishness she was used to, and he let out a chuckle. "Maybe you're more a policewoman than I thought."

"I'm sorry, Oliver." Regret washed over her. "I know you did what you had to do." She got into his car. "I'm glad you asked me to come. I think it helped, don't you?"

"I'm sure it did," he said. "You can help even further."

"I won't help you ferret out the pin, if that's what you want." Eve sniffed. "You'll have to find your own incriminating evidence from now on."

He gave her a lopsided grin. "Nothing like that. This is more of a pleasant task." In a more serious tone, he said, "I want you to see Rosalia."

"She'll be very upset her protégé has been arrested," Eve remarked. "If one could call Cecilia that."

"I wasn't thinking about Cecilia," he said. "I was thinking about her son. I promised her an update on August, remember?"

"Oh, yes," Eve recalled.

"Let her know we're checking on a few things but it's quite possible August will be home later today," he instructed. "You can tell her we think he may have an alibi, but don't tell her exactly what he said. Say only he was visiting a friend of Josh Kepler's that night."

"You're keeping August's confidence," she said with a smile.

"There's no reason she should know," he said. "A young man has a right to make his own decisions about his future." He started the car.

"Why isn't Adkins updating her?" asked Eve. "I thought he was August's lawyer."

"August dismissed him last night," he said. "He has no reason to keep him now."

"You can count on me, Oliver." She smiled. "I'll take Helena with me, if you don't mind. She's as interested in this case as I am."

"Then I'll have two policewomen working for me." He grinned.

"I'm not sure the sheriff would appreciate that," Eve said, and he laughed.

CHAPTER 26

She found Helena and Agnes cleaning up a few things in the chapel. She could hear her sister's voice from the lobby, its dragging quality weaving through the sweet tone they had all inherited from their mother.

"They extracted the insulin from a dog and were able to keep him alive for a few months," her sister said.

"If it had that stuff in the first place, how come they had to take it out?" Agnes placed a prayer book lying on the floor back in its place. "It don't make sense."

"The dog may have had the insulin in its system," Helena explained as she nodded to Eve. "But it couldn't use it properly. They took it out of the pancreas and injected it back into the blood so the dog's body could use it properly."

Agnes shrugged. "Don't make sense to me anyhow," she mumbled as she went to the other side of the chapel.

"I shouldn't even bother explaining the marvels of modern medicine to her," Helena grumbled. "She thinks you live forever with three square meals a day, church every Sunday, and a soft pillow."

Eve smiled. "Agnes, can you take care of the rest of this on your own?"

The older woman stiffened. "Been taking care of it and you three besides since you was babies."

Eve took her sister's arm and led her into the lobby.

"What's going on?" Helena asked.

"Oliver asked me to see Rosalia," said Eve. "I thought you would want to come."

"It may be our duty to visit the relatives of the bereaved, but Rosalia isn't a relative," her sister reminded her.

"He promised to tell her about what's happening with August," Eve said. "Now that we know he has an alibi, he wants us to bring her the good news."

"Well, it will be nice to bring someone good news for a change," Helena admitted.

They decided to walk. The gentle wind shook the higher limbs of trees, making leaves tumble to the ground. The despair Eve had felt at the Feather house began to lift.

Helena studied her. "Where did you go with Oliver?"

"Who said I went anywhere with him?"

"You left when he did and I saw his car driving up just now," said her sister. "You went with him to serve that search warrant, didn't you?"

Eve smiled, taking her sister's arm. "I forgot how good you are at deductive reasoning."

"I take it things didn't go well at the Feather house."

"They found what they were looking for," Eve murmured. "That is, I found it."

"You mean the engagement ring?" Helena stared.

Eve related the events of the morning. She found herself feeling dreary again when she got to the part about the sheriff and Oliver accusing Cecilia of murder.

Helena picked up a thin stick lying on the sidewalk, stripped it of its leaves, and swung it like a riding whip. "You feel sorry for that girl, don't you?"

"She's been in someone else's shadow all her life," Eve said. "Her mother's, August's, Rosalia's. She doesn't know who she is."

"That's no excuse for murder," her sister pointed out.

"Cecilia couldn't have murdered anyone," Eve insisted.

"She may have done it without realizing."

Eve stared at her. "Whatever do you mean?"

"You've heard of blind rage," Helena said. "It's not only a metaphor, Eve. I was reading a little about it this morning."

"There's no rage in Cecilia," Eve said sharply.

"She admitted she hated Libby," her sister said. "I suspect she also hated August though she would never admit it. Both have been festering for some time. Hate can be fatal, Eve."

She flinched. "You sound like you've convicted her already."

"I don't think she would get jail time if she is convicted," said Helena. "I'm sure a lawyer could argue for insanity. Like they did with Harry Thaw."

"But Cecilia isn't insane," Eve insisted.

"A judge probably wouldn't see it that way," Helena argued. "According to the law, someone deemed insane is unable to understand what he or she did was wrong at the time they were doing it. I'm sure a lawyer could make a case Cecilia was blinded by rage and jealousy when she killed Libby."

"Do you really think she could have done that?" Eve peered at her.

"I didn't say I thought so," Helena said. "I said a lawyer could make a case."

"What would they do with her then?"

"Put her away in an institution, of course," said her sister.

Eve shuddered. "A fate worse than jail."

"I'm not sure she hasn't been in jail already with her mother dictating her life," Helena said quietly.

"It's all so sad." Eve sighed.

"We didn't ask to become a part of this, Eve," said her sister. "Remember that."

A maid answered the door and after asking them to wait a few minutes, showed them into the front room. Rosalia was sitting in an overstuffed chair sewing. The large windows were open and the sun streamed through, casting spotlights around her. The brightness brought out the angular features of the woman's face. Eve noted while the woman looked reserved and calm, there was concern in the lines of her face.

"Hello, Eve, Helena." She smiled. "May I offer you some coffee or tea?"

"Coffee would be lovely," Eve said.

"Coffee, Missy," Rosalia instructed the maid. After Missy left, she leaned forward a little. "It was good of you to come with news of August."

"How did you know?" Eve blinked.

The woman smiled. "It's no secret you've been aiding Oliver during this horrible time. And quite right too," she added. "I'm sure he wants to assure everybody of his solid position as the D.A. and choosing your family to guide him was a wise decision."

"We're not guiding anyone," Helena said. Eve noticed her sister hadn't taken her eyes off Rosalia's face since they sat down.

"Well, you're helping," she said again. "Who better than the ladies who helped — well, take care of the body?"

"That's our work, Rosalia," Eve began to feel uncomfortable, as if she were wearing an itchy sweater.

"And we're all very grateful for it," Rosalia assured her. "Now, about August?"

"Oliver asked me to tell you it looks as if he'll be coming home very soon."

"Naturally." The voice was assured and elegant as the maid brought the coffee tray. "I'll serve, Missy. You may go now."

"Then you know?" Eve glanced at Helena.

"I knew my son had nothing to do with this unfortunate affair from the beginning," she said. "He may have had ideas about Libby when she was alive, but beyond that — sugar?" She held up the sugar bowl.

"August told the police he has an alibi for that night," Eve said.

"He already told them his alibi," the woman insisted. "They just didn't want to believe it."

"He wasn't just sitting by the river thinking, like he said," said Helena.

"Oh?"

"He went to see someone."

Rosalia stirred cream in her cup. "Really?"

"A friend of Josh Kepler's." Eve's throat was dry.

"In Moody," Helena added quickly.

"I wasn't aware Josh had any friends in this county," said the woman slowly. "Are you sure that's what he said?"

"Well, I didn't speak to him personally —" Eve admitted

"Then that's what Mr. Clarke said."

"Yes."

"How very interesting." The woman leaned back, her brown eyes studying her. Eve suddenly noticed Rosalia's eyes were her only round feature.

"You don't seem happy about it," Helena said.

"Of course I'm relieved," she said. "It just seems odd August wouldn't have said that in the first place."

"Well —" Eve felt helpless.

Her sister came to the rescue. "It's been a distressing time for both of you. People are apt to forget things when they're in distress."

"I suppose that's true." Rosalia seemed to accept this explanation. "Did Mr. Clarke tell you anything else, Eve?" Eve shook her head. "You know, it's not like August not to tell me something like that. He used to tell me everything when he was a boy."

"He's no longer a boy, Rosalia," Helena said. "He's a man."

The woman laughed. "When you have children of your own,

Helena, you'll find they always stay the child you remember in your mind."

"I don't think I will feel that way when I have children of my own," she mumbled.

"And what will the police do now that August is innocent?" Rosalia questioned, looking at Eve even as her hands were steadily sewing.

Eve smoothed down the velvet, which reminded her of the upholstery she had seen at La Belle Fille. "Are you speculating or asking me?"

"I thought you might know," said the woman with a smile. "You seem to have good connections with the law in this town."

"That sounds a little smug," Helena glanced at her.

"I didn't mean it that way." Rosalia put down the needle and laid her hand on Eve's arm. "I admire you for wanting to help the police find out who killed this girl."

"It wasn't as if we really had a choice," Helena said. "We did take care of the body."

"Who do the police suspect now?" the woman asked. "They suspect *someone*, don't they, Eve?"

"Just because Eve came with the police to question August doesn't mean she knows what they're thinking." Helena raised her eyebrow.

Rosalia pulled the thread out of the needle and chose another one from the pin cushion. "This is not idle curiosity, Helena. I care about what happens in this community just as much as anyone."

"Maybe you, more than anyone, have a right to know," Eve said. "Since you were like a mother to her."

She grasped the needle. "You mean they've arrested Cecilia?"

"Not quite," Helena said. "They took her down to the station for questioning just like August."

"They must have had a reason," said Rosalia. "You'll tell me what it is, won't you Eve? Maybe I can help the girl."

"They found Libby's engagement ring," Helena said.

"*I* found it," Eve said. "I wish I'd never gone!"

"Nonsense, dear," said the woman. "You're hardly responsible for Cecilia's foolishness."

"Do you believe she did it?" Eve looked at her.

"I can't say." Rosalia threaded the needle perfectly. "What did Cecilia have to say for herself?"

"She didn't know anything about it," Eve said.

"A very convenient denial," Rosalia remarked.

Eve stared at her. "I thought you liked her!"

"Oh, I do, I do," Rosalia insisted. "But that doesn't stop me from recognizing Cecilia as a very unbalanced girl."

"Then why did you want her to marry August?" Helena asked.

The woman was quiet for a moment as she concentrated on the edge of the tablecloth she was sewing. "Because I didn't know she was unstable until August came back."

"What made you change your mind about her?" Helena asked.

"Call it a feeling," said the woman.

"Nothing more concrete than that?"

Rosalia smiled. "I'm afraid I haven't your logical mind, Helena."

"They spent a lot of time together, didn't they?" Eve asked.

The woman nodded. "She was over here practically every day at the beginning."

"But that stopped when August started to step out with Libby?" Helena asked.

Rosalia shuddered. "I wish you wouldn't put it that way. It sounds so — definite."

"I'd say an engagement ring was definite," Helena said firmly. "He proposed to her, remember? As far as we know from Mrs. Cinder, Libby accepted."

"Yes, well, we don't have to think about that *now*," said the woman.

"Did Cecilia continue to come to this house after August met Libby?" Eve asked.

"Yes, of course," said Rosalia. "She would come even when August was away, helping me with the sewing and gardening." She smiled. "I always prefer to do my own gardening."

"I'm assuming she spilled the beans?" Helena asked. "That's what you're getting at, isn't it?"

"Well, yes, in a manner of speaking," said Rosalia. "She talked about Libby a lot."

"Talked in what way?" Eve asked.

"She didn't speak very kindly about her," said the woman. "Perhaps I should tell the police."

"I'd wait and see what happens," Helena advised.

"I beg your pardon?" Rosalia looked at her sharply.

"Helena thinks even if the police build a case against Cecilia, a lawyer can get her off on a plea of temporary insanity." Eve glanced at her sister. "Isn't that what it's called?" Helena nodded.

"I'm glad of that," said Rosalia. "It hasn't been easy for her, poor girl. I'm quite ashamed of the way August treated her. I plan on having some serious discussions with him about it when this whole mess is behind us."

"You mean because he misled her with the engagement ring?" Helena asked in a rough tone. "You know that's what she thought, don't you?"

Rosalia smoothed out the edge of the tablecloth. "Yes, I know. Poor girl. I was fooled for a moment myself when she told me he'd taken her to San Francisco."

Eve sat up. "You mean you knew about it?"

"Of course," she said. "Cecilia told me when they got back."

"Why didn't you tell Oliver and the sheriff when they interviewed you?"

"I didn't think it important," said Rosalia. "August told them all they needed to know. He's a very honest boy."

"Except he didn't tell them the truth about where he was on Friday night," Helena reminded her.

"He had his reasons." Rosalia glared at her. "Even if we don't know what they are."

Helena rolled her eyes at her sister and Eve knew what she was thinking: There was no logic in the mind of a devoted mother. Out loud, Helena said, "I suppose no woman is ever good enough for a mother's son."

"Well, in a way that's true," Rosalia admitted. "But in August's case, it's really justified."

"Justified enough to reject two fiancées?" Helena persisted. "That's what it amounts to."

"I didn't reject them, dear," said the woman with a smile." August did."

"He rejected one of them," Eve said. "The other one was killed."

"Yes, I realize that. More coffee?" She motioned toward Missy standing in a discreet corner.

"I wouldn't mind," Helena said.

"Missy, bring another pot, please." Rosalia looked at both of them. "Well, I must say, I don't think I've had lady friends here for coffee for a while."

"No coffee bashes on Falcon Hill?" Helena didn't bother to hide her smile.

The woman glared. "That sounds rather vulgar."

"Not in the least," she said. "My college mentor, Zadie Hummer, used to have them all the time. She called them coffee communes."

Rosalia laughed. "I heard Miss Hummer is quite eccentric."

"Money makes room for eccentricities," Helena said with a smirk.

"Perhaps we're not all as snobbish as you think, Helena," said the woman in a wry tone. "I don't want you to misunderstand me. I've never had anything but affection for Cecilia, and I had nothing against Libby. In fact, I admired her dedication to her profession."

"How did you know she was dedicated?" Eve asked.

"She spent a few weeks in San Diego with us, remember?" She eyed her. "You were with Mr. Clarke when we told him."

"Now I remember." Eve nodded.

"But one must be practical about these things," said Rosalia. "Neither of them would have been able to shoulder the responsibilities that come with being the wife of a leader."

"Is that what August is?" mumbled Helena.

"It's what August will be," said the woman firmly. "When this tragedy is behind us." She started to fold the tablecloth. "I'll admit I didn't want to push him when he got back. But it's time for him to take his place on Falcon Hill where he belongs. His father was already involved in local politics from the age of nineteen."

"A very enterprising man," Helena remarked.

"He was, as a matter of fact," said Rosalia.

"And how do you know neither of his fiancées would have been enterprising?" Eve lamented.

"What, dear?" Rosalia put a lump of sugar in her coffee.

"I asked, how do you know Cecilia or Libby wouldn't have been up to the task of being a society wife?"

"Well, dear." The woman's voice slowed as if speaking to a child, "Libby wasn't born on Falcon Hill, was she?"

"And that makes her ineligible to be a socialite?" Helena asked.

"You don't understand our community," said the woman. "We don't sit around at the spa or have those coffee things you mentioned —"

"Coffee bashes," Helena said.

"We serve our community in some way," she said. "People think all we do is hold large and expensive social events, but most of the time, those events are for a reason."

"Like Mrs. Feather," Eve said.

"Precisely," she said. "You need a certain charm, a certain

social grace and awareness to get people to do what you want them to do for the good of the community."

"I never thought of it that way," Eve admitted.

Rosalia folded her hands in her lap. "My husband believed helping the community was the duty of those with money."

"You sound like Mrs. Feather now," Helena remarked.

"I've no objection to what she's doing, only how she's doing it," said the woman. "One does not sacrifice one's child for the greater good."

"I'm glad to hear you think so," Eve said.

"There are so many unfortunates out there," sighed Rosalia. "Especially young women. They barely have room for them at the Hatton Farm."

"You mentioned going there, didn't you?" Eve murmured.

"I more than go there," said the woman. "I help teach the girls." Her tone rose a little with pride. "I've taught them some of the domestic arts and helped them get work as maids."

"Is Missy one of them?" Eve glanced at the maid still leaning against the wall at the far side of the room.

"Yes, as a matter of fact." Rosalia smiled. "She's only been with me about a month but she does her work very well." The pride in her voice made Eve think she was prouder of having trained her than of the work Missy actually did.

"I approve of people who practice what they preach," Helena said.

"I suppose you would expect any woman August marries to follow in your footsteps," Eve said.

"I can only hope she would." The woman began putting things away in the sewing box.

"You taught Cecilia those things too, didn't you?" Eve asked.

"I tried." Rosalia shrugged. "I'm afraid Cecilia doesn't have much talent for the domestic arts."

"Yes, I know," Eve said. When Rosalia gave her a questioning look, she added, "I saw her bureau drawers. They were very untidy."

"Oh, dear." The woman sighed. "And I worked with her on that."

"You must have worked with her for a long time," Helena remarked. "I like Cecilia, but I wouldn't call her the brightest star in the sky."

Rosalia laughed. "I prefer to think of her as a bird whose wings are a little crooked."

"A very apt description." Helena laughed.

Eve put her hand on the tablecloth, feeling the silky smoothness and the perfect circles of the pattern "I don't think I've ever seen a shade of blue bright and deep at the same time."

"Azure," Rosalia said. "That's one of my triumphs. I taught Betty Cain how to order fine linens from the wholesaler catalogues. Did you know she was going to the local markets to get them?" She shuddered.

"How very provincial of her," Helena said dryly.

"Cecilia had something like this, but it was more a reddish-pink," Eve said. "Sort of like the claret Papa used to drink after dinner."

Missy took the coffee tray away. The maid's shuffling feet scraped the carpet. The sound made Rosalia jump, even though it was softer than the birds tweeting outside the open window.

"She must have bought some of the same fabric but in a different color," said Rosalia. "Mrs. Cain doesn't seem to value variety in her merchandise."

"Violet is always complaining about that," Helena agreed.

"It's not very fashionable." Rosalia nodded.

Eve's hand was still on the silk, thinking how it felt like water. Water from the sea August was so crazy about. Water from the river when it was calm. Blue, smooth water…

"I'm sorry I have to leave, but I have a luncheon in Moody, and I don't want to be late." Rosalia rose.

"Eve and I have to get back to business as well." Helena accepted the hat Missy handed her.

"Yes," Eve said slowly. "Yes, we do."

"Thank you both for coming." The woman grasped Eve's hand. "And thank Mr. Clarke for being so kind throughout this whole business. He didn't think August was guilty for a moment, did he?"

Ignoring this, Eve suddenly said, "Is there any message you'd like us to give August?"

"Message?"

"I might go down to see Oliver," she said. "I could stop by the police station."

"That's very kind of you." Rosalia smiled. "If you do, tell him I'll have a pot roast waiting for him when he gets home. It's his favorite."

"Pot roast!" Helena growled as they went down the walk. "Do you think someday she'll realize he's twenty-three and not five?"

"Only when he forces her to," Eve murmured.

She felt her sister watching her as they crossed the small mound in the direction of their house. "You're not going to see Oliver, are you?"

"I thought I might," Eve said mildly.

"What for?" asked Helena. "Didn't you say he told you August would be released this afternoon?"

"I can still give him a message from his mother, can't I?" Eve snapped.

"And what's all this interest in tablecloths all of a sudden?" her sister inquired. "I remember when you ran a needle clear through the tip of your finger and vowed never to pick one up again."

"It reminded me of something," Eve said.

Helena picked up a branch in the middle of the sidewalk and gently laid it in the grass. "I guess the city hasn't sent the clean-up crew for the sidewalks yet. Reminded you of what?"

Eve pressed her hand. "I'm not sure yet."

They walked home in silence. Agnes was waiting for them at the door.

"You two taking a stroll while a customer's waiting," she grumbled. "Just ain't right. Your papa didn't leave things in your hands to have you go paying calls during business hours."

"Oliver asked us to," Helena defended.

Eve clasped the collar of her coat. "Helena, dear, you'll have to see the Mercers on your own."

"Why?"

"I have something to do in town."

"But you just said you weren't going to see Oliver."

"Not Oliver," she said. "August. I have a message to give him, remember?"

"A message about pot roast?" Helena snorted.

"Speaking of pot roast," Agnes said. "That imp snatched the pineapple upside-down cake from the ice box I was saving for today's dinner."

"Vi is feeding the neighborhood again," Helena said. "Her friends won't spend a dime more than they have to at the drugstore."

"Never mind, Agnes, dear," said Eve. "I'll stop off at Gohl's Bakery and get a pie on my way home."

"That should take at least one thing off your plate," Helena said with a grin. "No pun intended."

The housekeeper went back to the kitchen, mumbling, "Ain't as if my plate won't be filled up again just as fast!"

CHAPTER 27

Eve stopped at the bakery first where Mrs. Gohl chatted on about her son Karl and his intention to go to night classes at Warren College to study accounting, lamenting how he had been doing the accounts for the bakery for years but never really learned it formally.

"He'll be going out on his own and working for big people from Sacramento and even San Francisco before long," she boasted.

Eve agreed as she carefully took the box with the cherry pie in her hands. She had a feeling Mrs. Gohl was telling her all this about her son because she knew of his interest in Violet, though what the twenty-eight-year-old Karl would want with an eighteen-year-old girl was beyond her

She stored the pie carefully in the car and walked to the police station which was at the end of the main street. As she approached the steps, her heart pounded a little more but she squared her shoulders and pushed the door open.

Deputy Elwood was sitting at his desk, and a few assistant deputies were milling around, clearly relaxed. Their superior was nowhere in sight.

The deputy greeted her with a smile. "What can I do for you, Miss Grave?"

"Is August still here, Deputy?"

He was immediately alert. "How did you know we were releasing him?"

"Oliver told me." She paused. "And I'm no gossip, Deputy."

"Oh, I didn't mean that, miss," he said. "They probably already know anyway. You know how people poke their heads outside their door around here." He chuckled. "Some of them have probably already seen him and are spreading the word. My bet's on the Shelton sisters."

"They can hardly help it," Eve said with a smile, thinking of the two ladies who ran the Gyver switchboard and provided the local town news even before the Falcon Hill ladies or the Shane brothers had a chance to get to it.

"Mr. Clarke sent us the release form this morning," he said.

"Then he's out?" Eve felt her chest ease. "Thank goodness!"

"His alibi checks," said Deputy Elwood. "At least it does for Mr. Clarke."

"But not for the sheriff?" she asked.

"Well, miss, I'll tell you." He propped his elbows on the desk. "The sheriff's a suspicious person. And this Lieutenant Commander Dale, he's a friend of Josh Kepler's. And Kepler is a friend of August's."

"And friends back friends up even if it means lying," Eve concluded.

"That's how the sheriff figures it," he said. "But Mr. Clarke thinks a naval officer isn't about to wreck his reputation by lying, even if he and Josh are friends."

"And what do *you* think, Deputy?"

The young man ducked his head. "Well, no one asked me what I think."

"I'm asking you."

"I think August would rather shoot a horse than so much as flick a fly off a woman's nose," he declared.

Eve laughed. "I take it you thought he was innocent all along." She became quiet for a moment. "I suppose Cecilia is going to be the sheriff's new sacrificial lamb?"

He shifted a little. "Well, miss, that's not really information I can give you."

"Of course not," she said. "I would never ask you to betray your legal obligation as a lawman, Deputy."

"I know that, miss." He tipped his hat.

"Does August know Cecilia is now Sheriff Warner's new target?" Eve asked.

The deputy stiffened. "The sheriff knows what he's doing."

"Of course he does," she said kindly. "I admire your loyalty, Deputy."

"August saw us bring her in," said Deputy Elwood. Then, with a wary look, he added, "So did Jack Shane."

Eve sighed. "That means the story about the ring will be in the headline in this evening's *Gyver Bee*."

"Looks like it." The deputy nodded. "The sheriff always says it's no good keeping things from the public because they'll discover them anyway and blow them out of proportion. He prefers to spill it to the reporters in his way rather than have them find out about it."

"That's wise of him," Eve complimented and his smile told her she had redeemed herself. "I suppose I'd better tell August before he reads about it in the paper. Did he say where he was going?"

"He said something about thinking things over," said the deputy. "But I imagine he probably went home."

"Thinking things over." She took a breath. "Deputy, I wonder if you could do me a favor."

"Be glad to, miss," he said.

"I have a pie in the car but I need to run a few more errands. Could you ask one of the assistant deputies to run the pie down to Agnes for me? I'd hate to leave it in the car with all the dust blowing around."

"I'll run it down myself," he said as he opened the door for her.

As she handed him the box, he asked in a lower tone, "Mrs. Wright at home?"

"She had to meet with a customer, but she should be through now," said Eve. Then, as an afterthought, she said, "Tell her I said to give you some coffee and a slice of pie."

"That's very kind of you, miss." She watched as he headed down the street holding the box with both hands whistling a tune.

Eve drove to Gyver River, parking in a quiet place not far from Josh's shack. She found the young man near the circle of poppies, his blue eyes staring at the water.

"Hello, August," she said in a gentle tone.

He glanced up. She could see his face was worn with tears.

"They told me they let you go at the jail." She sat down beside him.

He grimaced. "It seems the sheriff has a new suspect."

"You mean Cecilia."

"I heard them in the next room as I was being led out," he said. "The interrogation room." His tone was grim. "Why did they bring her in, Eve?"

"They found the engagement ring in her room," she mumbled.

He stared at her. "But how could they?"

"I don't know, August."

"Well, then, I'll swear she gave it back to me," he insisted. "Otherwise, how could I have proposed to Libby?"

"They think Cecilia got it after you proposed."

"What do you mean?"

"Someone took the brooch from her," Eve said carefully. "They might have done the same with the ring."

"You mean they think Cecilia took the ring after —" His face turned white. "Impossible!"

"For the moment, the police think differently," she said. "Cecilia admitted she hated Libby, August."

"I suppose she did," he admitted. "She spilled a drink on her, you know."

"Yes, I know," said Eve.

"But is that any reason to kill someone?" he demanded. "Cecilia isn't the type — well, she just wouldn't."

"I agree," she said. "But I'm not the police."

He crumbled the dry leaves on the ground. "Does Mother know?"

"Helena and I told her this morning."

"I suppose she was happy."

Eve stared. "Happy?"

"Yes," he said. "Even if they let Cecilia go, no one will speak to her now. That means there's no possible way we could get married."

"Then you know she's changed her mind about that," Eve said.

"I've known for a while," he said. "Mother — well, she likes things her way. You know, she sort of runs things. Even when Father was alive, she was the one who told him who to see and where to go and all that."

"I didn't know that," Eve said.

"She has a program for everyone," he said. "Including me."

"But you changed the program," she pointed out. "You took that job on the whaling ship like you always wanted."

"I was never on a whaling ship."

It took her a moment to realize what he was saying as a far-off creature on the opposite side of the river shrieked.

He smiled. "River otters. Libby and I used to see them all the time when we went boating. They usually come out at night."

"August," she said slowly, "what do you mean you were never on a whaling ship?"

"Well, that's not exactly true," he admitted. "There was a ship docked in San Francisco and they let me stay on board for a few hours, but then I had to leave."

"But you never worked on one?

"You mean when I went away to sea?" He gave her a half-smile. "I worked on the *SS Scotia.*"

"I didn't know that," she said.

"Don't I look like a cabin boy?" he asked ruefully. "I wasn't really, of course. I was taken on as a steward."

"But they treated you like a cabin boy," Eve said softly. "I'm beginning to understand now."

"Oh, it wasn't their fault really," he said. "They all knew I came from money. They resented it. I suppose I would have too if I were in their shoes."

"That's why you came back after a year," she said.

"I couldn't take them riding me," he admitted. "I wasn't very thick-skinned then."

"Were they cruel?" She laid a hand on his shoulder.

"It wasn't pleasant," he said. "I did a lot of privy work."

Eve shuddered. "I hope they got arrested for that!"

He laughed. "It's expected, Eve. You either takes it like a man or —" his voice dropped, "— turn tail and go home like I did."

"No one should have to endure that kind of treatment!"

"I told you, I wasn't very thick-skinned," he insisted. "But I am now. Libby helped me see I'm tougher than everyone thinks." He covered his face with his hands and Eve allowed the silence to carry through the flow of the river for a time until he recovered. "I'm sorry."

"Don't be," she said kindly. "You're still grieving for her loss."

"In a way, Libby has helped me in death too," he said. "All this business with the police showed me I can take things better than even I thought I could. Better than Mother thinks for sure."

"Why do you say that?" she asked.

He chuckled. "You didn't see her when I came back. It was all I could do to escape her pampering and fawning. The trouble is, she convinced everyone else to do the same."

"It was a nice homecoming," Eve offered.

"For a boy who spent a year in boarding school," August insisted. "Not for a man who comes home a failure."

"You weren't a failure," Eve insisted.

"Oh, she was grand and so was Cecilia," he said. "But they both behaved as if that was it. They referred to it as 'this sea nonsense.'"

"But it wasn't nonsense to you," Eve said softly. "It still isn't."

"You understand," he said with gratitude in his eyes. "I think people who have to make something of themselves understand. You and Josh and Madge —"

"Madge Bradford?" Eve inquired, thinking of what Agnes had told her the day before the funeral.

"She worked for Mother, you know," he said. "I could talk to her about it and she understood."

"I wouldn't imagine your mother would be happy with you confiding in a servant," Eve said.

He laughed. "You do say things boldly sometimes, Eve."

She blushed. "I didn't mean to put her down."

"No, you're right," he said. "Mother can be strange about people. At first, she didn't mind my chatting with Madge as she did her work. She even said it was good for Madge to know some decent men." His tone lowered. "You know Madge has trouble with her husband."

"Yes, I know." Eve remembered the rumors in town about Curtis Bradford who was too free with his fists when the liquor was flowing, even during Prohibition.

"Mother felt sorry for her," he said. "That was all the more reason it was such a shock when she fired her."

"Fired her!"

He nodded. "I tried to find out why but Mother never told me. She just said her work was 'unsatisfactory.'" He suddenly looked at her. "You hear things around town, Eve. Do you know what became of her?"

"I'll find out," she said with finality.

"I'd like to help her if I can," he said. "I won't have much money now, but —"

"Because you'll be going into the Navy?"

He nodded. "It's a sort of — well, I guess you could call it a promise."

"To Libby," she said quietly. "Is that what you and she were talking about before she went to Reno?" He stared at her. "You still haven't told the police what that argument was about."

He stared across the river, tapping a long dandelion up and down. The feathery spokes went flying all around. "Was it that obvious?"

"I suppose it doesn't matter now," she said.

"I don't mind telling you," he said. "You always believed in my innocence, didn't you?" He smiled at her. "I'm grateful for that."

"Were you arguing about the Navy?" she asked. "Libby didn't want you to go?"

"It was more complicated than that," he said. "Libby gave me an ultimatum that night."

"Ultimatum?"

"She knew I loved her but I was tied to Mother." He looked down. "Libby wanted us to go away together."

"To Reno?" Eve sat up.

"No, to Houston or New York," he said. "They both have big ports with lots of ships sailing in and out."

"So you could go back to sea," she said.

"She was afraid of Mother," he admitted. "I didn't see it then, but I see it now."

"Why do you think she was afraid of her?"

"Mother would have, well, taken things over," he said.

"Yes, I suppose she would have." Her mind wandered for a moment.

"She means well," August defended. "She just gets ideas about people and when they do differently — well, she's not very understanding."

"Like Cecilia?" Eve asked.

"Cecilia and some of those girls she helps at the farm," he said.

The water blurred for a moment into a silky wave of blue and gray. "August," she gripped his hand, "do you think Libby knew she was going to have a baby before she went to Reno?"

It took him a few moments to respond. "I don't know, Eve. Do women know these things?"

"I think they do," she said. "She wanted you to go away with her and get married. What was the alternative?"

"She would go back to Reno and send her parents money from there."

"An ultimatum," she agreed.

"You see why I couldn't tell the police," he said. "Not the first time, anyway. Mother was right there and it would have hurt her terribly."

"Yes, I see," she said. "No, you couldn't tell Oliver the truth then."

"And later on, well, after telling them about Lieutenant Commander Dale, it didn't seem to matter anymore."

"No, of course not." She rose. "Can I drive you home, August?"

He smiled. "I'd like that very much."

Her hands were nervous at the wheel as the car made its way along the dirt path. The wind kicked up a fuss and tree limbs shook, letting go of dry leaves that splattered on the windshield like bits of brown paint.

She cleared her throat. "I think I might be able to convince the police Cecilia didn't kill Libby."

"How?"

"I'd rather not say," she said shortly. "I don't want to get your hopes up if all —" She suddenly slammed on the brakes, making them lurch forward.

"What happened?" He looked wildly around.

"I'm sorry I had to stop so suddenly," she said, her heart beating quickly. "A beaver scurried across the road."

He relaxed against the seat. "I'm glad you stopped." He chuckled. "Some people don't care to run over beavers or other animals." He closed his eyes. "I remember one time we were late to a rally. Father let Mother drive the carriage — we had horses then. A rabbit ran into the road and Mother —" He shuddered.

"She probably didn't see it in time," Eve said quietly.

"It wasn't that," he said. "Father told her she shouldn't have done that because it's bad luck to hit a rabbit. She just laughed and said, 'It was in the way.'"

"It wasn't a very nice thing to do," Eve said, starting the car.

"No, I suppose it wasn't." He shrugged. "Father laughed with her and said, 'Maybe you're right, dear. It's more bad luck for the rabbit!'"

"Bad luck all around," Eve murmured as she turned carefully onto the main road.

CHAPTER 28

After she dropped August off at the bottom of the hill, she turned the car toward town and went to the Rooty Toot Drugstore. The place was quiet, as it was mid-morning and well before the lunch crowd. The soda fountain and lunch counter with its glistening marble and metal-legged stools were on one side, and the drugstore merchandise with glass displays on the other. Six tables that Sudie had added only last year to "liven up the place" sat in the middle of the store. A vague scent of vanilla and antiseptic filled the place.

She frowned as she saw Kitty Markie behind the lunch counter leafing through a fashion magazine, the white coat her grandmother made her wear over a black sheath dress with eye-like peacock feather drawings. She glanced at Eve with heavily-shadowed eye and a sullen bowtie mouth, nodding in greeting, The ends of her bobbed hair brushed forward as she bent toward the magazine.

Eve went into the phone booth and leafed through the Gyver directory for Madge Bradford but found nothing. Her hopes plummeted as she placed it back on the shelf. Sliding open the door, Sudie Markie came out from the back with an armful of small bottles.

"Morning, Eve," she called cheerfully. "Here, try one of these." She handed her one reeking of rose and lilacs. She tried not to choke.

"Free samples." Sudie grinned. "And don't they make the place stink to high heaven!" She laughed heartily. "Kitty's been bothering me to get samples for a while. Ain't you, Kitty, dear?" She threw a glance at the young lady, who nodded without looking up from the magazine. "Thinks I should put them in a basket on the counter, all pretty-like."

"I suppose the young people in town like that sort of thing." Eve thought of how many perfume bottles Violet had sitting on her vanity. "I'll give this one to Vi."

"She's already got three," Kitty said without moving.

"Well, then, I'll give her one more," Eve said impatiently. Kitty's ever-ready petulant moods always got on her nerves.

"You keep it, honey," Sudie said.

"Sure," Kitty said. "Might get her a spooner."

"What is a spooner?" Eve asked, though she wasn't sure she wanted to know.

"A flirtation, of course," Kitty said.

"Don't you talk disrespectful to Eve, Kitty, dear," snapped her grandmother.

Kitty at last looked up. "Sorry," she mumbled, giving Eve a huge smile that showed all her glowing teeth. Even Violet said Kitty had a little too much pride in her mouth.

Eve leaned against the glass counter. "Sudie, you hear a lot of things around here, don't you?"

"Can't help it if I got ears and Kitty's friends talk over their cream sodas," Sudie said. "And then there's Paulie bringing in all his friends."

Eve tried not to flinch at the mention of Sudie's male

companion, twenty years her junior. "I was just thinking you might have heard about Madge Bradford."

"Madge?" She squinted. "Girl who used to do odd housework around here?"

"That's her," Eve said. "I'd like her to come around our place and help Agnes out."

Kitty smirked into her magazine. "Agnes will eat her alive."

Eve said in a haughty tone, "Agnes is a very generous and giving person, Kitty." The young woman shrugged. "I couldn't find her name in the phone book."

"Well, you wouldn't now, would you?" Sudie flattened out her sleeve over her thick wrist. "She ain't married to that Bradford boy no more."

"You mean she's divorced?" Eve asked.

Kitty's head shot up. "Why shouldn't a woman divorce a brute like that?"

"Well, finally something got your nose out of that trash," Sudie snarled.

"I'm glad she did." Eve made a mental note to tell August. "So her name is no longer Bradford?"

"She went back to live with her folks in Chester, or so I heard," said Sudie. "Probably went back to her maiden name too. What was it now? Neely? Neil?" The woman squinted again as the bell above the door shook and a girl and boy about Violet's age walked in.

"Norman," Kitty answered as she put the magazine under the counter, welcoming the newcomers.

"That's it, Norman," said Sudie. "Now I recall." She leaned against the counter with one arm. "Did I ever tell you about the Norman cousin who used to chase me around the Bohemian Club when Brett Hart was there and —"

"I'm sorry, I'm late for an appointment," Eve interrupted with a soft smile. When Sudie got into one of her stories about the Bohemian Club in San Francisco, she could go on for hours.

"Look for Norman in the Chester phone directory." Sudie jerked her head toward the phone booth. "You ought to find her for sure."

"Thank you, Sudie." Eve waved.

She went back to the phone booth and found the Chester phone book which was little more than a pamphlet. "Sudie," she called, "I can't find Madge here."

The woman leafed through the directory. "Can't understand it," she mumbled. "I see Pamela and Scott Norman here, but no Madge."

"Who are they?"

"Her parents." She closed the book. "Say, I'll bet they'd know where she is. You don't suppose she got married again, do you?"

"I'll find out," Eve said with a smile.

Chester was little more than a tiny town with only a post office and grocery store, usually empty, as many of the town folks preferred to drive the twenty miles to Gyver to get their provisions. She found the Norman house easily, and Madge's mother, a comely woman who remembered Eve's parents fondly, told her Madge was indeed married to a man named Hughes, who worked for the furniture factory a few miles away. They lived in one of the shacks the factory leased to its workers.

"He's a good man, Miss Grave," said Mrs. Norman. "He treats her right, praise the Lord."

"Praise the Lord," Eve repeated with genuine relief.

The home where Madge lived was rundown and creaked in the wind as if its foundations were about to collapse. But there was plenty of grass about and a small garden in front. Eve recognized Madge bent over a lettuce patch with a hoe.

"Madge Hughes?" Eve ventured as she opened the rickety wooden gate.

"Yes?" The woman moved some weeds out of the way before she looked up. After a moment, she asked, "I've seen you somewhere before, haven't I?"

"I'm Eve Grave."

"Oh, yes! The Grave sisters. We always thought it was funny that your name was Grave, I mean, considering the business your parents were in." She leaned against the hoe. "Don't tell me you have someone seeking your services in this place. We know everyone and I don't recall there being a death recently."

"I'm not here on professional business," Eve said. "Not mortuary business, that is Mrs. Hughes —"

"Call me Madge, won't you?" She set the hoe against the wall of the house. "I could make us some iced tea, if you like."

"I don't want to disturb you." Eve glanced at the garden.

"I was going to stop for a while anyway. Sun's so hot today, you'd think it was summer." She chuckled.

"It must be very peaceful here," Eve remarked as she held the back door open for the woman.

"It is." Madge was silent for a moment. "You don't mind sitting in the kitchen? It's nice and cool there."

"Of course not," Eve said. "I'll get the tea. You take a load off your feet."

Madge eased into a chair. "Thank you. I'm trying to get those peas in so they'll grow by spring."

Eve poured out the iced tea. "I'm sure you've heard about what happened in Gyver."

"That young woman found by the river?" Madge nodded. "I still read the *Gyver Bee*. Thank goodness August is no longer involved. I used to work for the Winters, you know."

"Yes, I know," said Eve. "But how did *you* know about his release?"

"Why, it was in the paper." She stepped into the living room and came back with the *Gyver Bee*. "Bill read it to me this morning."

Eve glanced at the headline RICH BOY RELEASED FROM JAIL, RICH GIRL IN HIS PLACE.

August Winters, a prime suspect for the Elizabeth Cinder murder case was released from jail this morning. Sheriff Arthur Warner of the Gyver Police ascertains the young man was "dining with a friend" on the night Miss Cinder was killed. But all is not lost, as the police have now turned their attention to Cecilia Feather, Mr. Winters' former fiancé. According to Sheriff Warner, certain incriminating evidence was found on the premises of Miss Feather's home, and she was known to have been an enemy of the deceased woman. Sheriff Warner indicated Miss Feather had the motive to kill Miss Cinder and the opportunity but hinted she "may have been encouraged by certain parties" to perform the dastardly deed. Miss Feather is being held for questioning.

Without thinking, Eve slammed the paper on the table. "Nonsense!" She immediately controlled herself. "I'm sorry. I hope I didn't upset you."

Madge smiled. "I don't have much cause to be upset these days. Thank God!" The last was said in a meaningful tone more to herself than to Eve.

"The sheriff shouldn't be flinging around theories," Eve snarled. "I know for a fact there is no proof Cecilia was 'encouraged' by August or anyone else to commit murder."

"It's absurd," Madge agreed.

"You knew her?" Eve sipped the tea.

"Only slightly," she said. "She used to come see Rosalia quite often while August was away."

"Is that when you started working for the Winters?"

Madge nodded. "It was only a few days a week, but it was what I needed at the time."

"Rosalia was rather close to Cecilia, wasn't she?" Eve asked.

"She treated her almost like a daughter," Madge said.

Eve leaned forward. "Why 'almost?'"

"Mothers ought to be warm and affectionate toward their children. That's what I think, at least."

"Rosalia certainly isn't the warm and affectionate type," Eve agreed.

Madge laughed. "I see you've met her." She stared down at the paper still lying on the table. "Rosalia has a way of maneuvering people."

"That's a strange way of putting it."

"I don't know if I can explain it," she said. "She taught Cecilia a lot, but it was like she was trying to win her over so she could know things."

"You mean know about her son?" Eve inquired.

"I think that was it," said Madge. "She did the same to me."

"Oh?"

"I won't say she didn't help me a lot," Madge defended. "I'd never say a word against her."

"Of course not," Eve said gently.

"She paid me more than I asked for and gave me clothes and shoes and even offered to pay for a lawyer so I could leave Curtis." She looked down.

Eve pressed her hand. "He was a brute, and you've nothing to be ashamed of, Madge."

She smiled. "Without Rosalia, I don't think I would have mustered up the courage to divorce him."

"But she expected something in return," Eve guessed.

"I think she wanted me to spy on August," said Madge. "When he came back, the poor boy was at loose ends. He didn't really fit in anywhere."

"You mean he didn't really fit into his society anymore," Eve murmured.

"He was restless too," said Madge. "He spent as much time away from the house as he could. Rosalia never questioned him but —"

"She questioned you," Eve guessed. "He told me how much of a comfort you were to him."

"The days I came, he would stay home," she said. "He'd walk around the house with me while I did my work and talk." She grinned. "He always offered to help me, but Rosalia was so fussy about the housework I didn't think it wise."

Eve nodded. "Rosalia would question you afterward."

"She wanted to know where August went, what he did and with whom," Madge said. "It made me very uncomfortable."

"And you think she did the same with Cecilia," Eve guessed.

"I'm sure she did," she said. "Only Cecilia was more willing to tell her. She was a nice girl but rather feeble, if you know what I mean." She stiffened. "I don't hold with mothers knowing every detail about a child's life when that child is grown."

"You have very definite views about motherhood," Eve remarked.

Madge laughed. "I suppose I do." She rubbed her stomach. "I'm going to have one of my own in the fall, you see."

"Congratulations." Eve smiled. "I'll tell August. He'll be delighted."

"I'm surprised she let him go on that whaling ship," Madge said. "The way she was always hovering over him."

"He didn't go on a whaling ship," Eve said. "He told me he spent the year on the *SS Scotia*." She saw Madge's confusion. "That's a luxury passenger ship."

"How odd." Madge blinked. "He was always talking about how Josh Kepler taught him all about whaling and told such exciting stories he couldn't wait to try his luck on one."

"Very odd," Eve agreed. "Madge, August told me you were fired."

The woman's face went gray. "It wasn't fair!"

"What happened?" Eve asked.

"Why do you want to know?"

"I won't tell the Gyver gossips about it, if that's what you're worried about," Eve said.

Madge patted her hand. "They wouldn't care anyway. It's not as if I were anyone special to them. I don't even live there anymore."

"August was very upset about it when he told me," Eve offered. "He tried asking his mother but she wouldn't tell him."

The woman's jaw set. "I'm not surprised she didn't tell him. She ought to be ashamed of herself!"

"What happened?"

"It was about four months or so after August came back," she said. "She had gone to some breakfast event but she left the key for me. I heard her come back around noon. I had finished my usual work and so I went upstairs to ask her what instructions she had for me." She paused. "I thought she was in August's room."

"Go on."

"She was in her own room," she said. "She never let me clean it. She always kept the door locked."

"But it wasn't locked this time?"

Madge shook her head. "I'll admit my manners could have been better. I should have knocked even though the door was open. But I just walked right in."

"That's not such a bad thing," Eve said with a small smile. "My sister Violet walks into my room all the time. Sometimes I'll come out of the shower, and she'll be reclining on the day bed, doing her nails and chatting away, even though I haven't heard a word she said."

"I used to do that with my mother." Madge sighed. "Rosalia goes by different rules."

"She didn't like you coming into her private space," Eve guessed.

"It was more than that," said Madge. "She was putting her jewelry away, and I think she didn't like that I saw. As if I would steal anything!" she snarled. "I'd been working for her for several months at that point, and she knew I would never do such a thing. Especially since she had it well hidden."

"What do you mean?"

"I saw her fiddling with some panels above the fireplace."

"Is that why she fired you?"

Madge rose and began to collect the tea things. "She didn't say a word about my coming in. She only stepped away from the fireplace with that eerie smile of hers."

Eve nodded, remembering the day they had interviewed August.

"But it was like she had something on me after that," Madge said. "The way she looked at me when I came in." She carefully put the sugar in the cupboard. "And she interrogated me about August every chance she got. I think he was seeing the poor girl who got killed then because he was home less often."

"Interrogated how?"

"It was like the third degree," Madge said. "I finally had to tell her August didn't really talk much with me anymore except for when he wanted something special done in his room."

"Was that when she fired you?" Eve sat up.

As I said, it was more complicated than that." Her face became stiff. "Only it came out very simply."

"What do you mean?"

"I came to work one day and she had a check ready for me," said Madge. "She was very pleasant when she told me my services were no longer needed."

"With no explanation?"

"Oh, she had an explanation all right," Madge said bitterly. "I demanded one, of course. She said a diamond necklace of hers was missing and that I must have seen her put it away the day I came into her room."

Eve stared. "She accused you of stealing?"

"Oh, she didn't say it in that way," Madge said. "She spoke all about how she understood how 'things stood' with me — I had left Curtis by then and I was living with my parents, trying to scramble for money to get a divorce — and she wasn't going to the police but, under the circumstances, she couldn't keep me on any longer." She suddenly grabbed Eve's shoulders. "I would never steal from anyone!"

"Of course you wouldn't," Eve said in a soothing tone. "I don't know what Rosalia was thinking."

"She wouldn't let me say goodbye to August or explain," Madge said. "I felt terrible about that." She added with a growl, "Rich people shouldn't be allowed to talk that way to people they employ."

"Not even when those people get in the way," Eve murmured, thinking about the story August had told her.

CHAPTER 29

By the time Eve got home, the car headlights glared against the canvas of black sky. Her sisters were already seated at the dinner table with the steam rising from their soup plates curling past their chins. She endured Agnes's disapproving look as she served her soup, mumbling about the roast chicken getting cold.

"Where's Felix?" Eve asked.

"Having dinner with some friends," said Helena. "He's going to work straight from there."

"Why are you so late?" Violet asked. "Agnes, the soup's too salty."

"You had no complaints about it last week," snapped the housekeeper.

"You shouldn't be serving the same soup within a week," Violet scolded. "What happened to that Hawaiian cookbook I gave you for Christmas?"

"You can't find nothing in those recipes at Arkins," sniffed Agnes.

"Well, then, you ask him to order it," Violet instructed. "He keeps bragging about how he can get hold of anything."

"Ain't good for digestion, raw fish and coconut pudding," the woman mumbled as she retreated to the kitchen.

"I had to see some people," Eve said.

"Ruth Mason said she saw you driving out of town," said Violet.

Eve felt Helena's gaze, but her sister was too discreet to ask questions.

"I was out of town, as a matter of fact." Eve finished the last of the soup. "I was in Chester."

"Chester!" Violet wrinkled her nose. "What on earth were you doing in that hellhole?"

"Watch your language, Vi," Helena warned. "If Eve was in Chester, she had a very good reason."

"I did." She looked at Helena. "We know August didn't kill Libby, and I don't think Cecilia did either. But I don't think the police should look very far for the culprit."

"Do you, Sherlocka?" Violet mocked.

"Sherlocka!" Agnes growled. "Land sakes!"

"Hush up, Vi," snapped Helena. "Deputy Elwood said you asked about August when he came with the pie."

"He sure is stuck on you, Helena!" Violet whistled. "He could barely keep from drooling."

"Oh, don't be a fool!" her sister growled. "It wasn't just about giving him Rosalia's message, was it?"

"No." Eve looked down at the food, which suddenly seemed colorless on her plate. "It wasn't."

"What was her message?" Violet held the plate of mashed potatoes with both hands.

"Here, missy, give that to me!" Agnes snatched it from her. "Gonna ruin my best china."

"August didn't know they found the engagement ring," she said.

"He'll know now," Violet remarked. "The Shanes have it all

down in black and white." She indicated behind her where the evening paper sat on the hall table.

"You shouldn't to be looking at that before dinner," Agnes said. "Spoils your appetite to read them things."

"Nothing could spoil my appetite, Agnes dear." She smiled sweetly.

"I'm guessing he didn't take it well," Helena said.

"It wasn't that," said Eve. "He told me some interesting things about his mother. Things we never would have imagined about her."

"I never imagined anything about her," Helena said.

As always, her sister's logical mind knocked her down like a blunt instrument and she answered with agitation, "You haven't any imagination at all, even when you're taking apart a dead animal!"

Violet's eyes opened wide, and Agnes grumbled, "Dead animals at the dinner table!"

Helena said quietly, "Maybe science and imagination are closer to one another than you think, Eve."

Eve sighed. "I'm sorry, dear. I didn't mean to snap."

"Something he said about Rosalia upset you." Helena put her hand on her sister's arm. "I wish you would tell me what it is." Her cerebral tone left her, and she became what she had been to Eve in their childhood — the younger sister eager to help lift the burdens off her shoulders.

"Tell *us*," Violet said firmly. "I'm part of this family too." She reached for Eve's other arm.

Their sweet and sincere faces brought tears to her eyes. "Oh, stop it, you two. I'm all right." Her tone was still muffled but steady. "Bring out the cherry pie, Agnes."

The housekeeper came out with the pie and a bowl of ice cream. "Next time you go giving away my upside-down cake to them deadbeat friends of yours, you'd better plan on staying home and making dessert!" She shook a finger at Violet.

"Maybe Kitty and I gave it away to some poor family in Marlestra." Violet stiffened. "Did you ever think of that?"

"No, I never thought of it!" Agnes declared as she retreated.

"It's not what he told me," said Eve. "It's what I deduced, I guess you might say."

"Now you really do sound like Sherlocka." Violet chuckled.

"Who is this Sherlocka you keep talking about?" Helena glared at her sister.

"Sherlock Holmes' sister," she said simply.

"Sherlock Holmes didn't have a sister," she argued.

"It's a pretend sister," said Violet. "Kitty and I used to makeup stories about her when we were kids."

"When you were kids?" Helena eyed her.

"All right, when we were still playing with dolls," her sister retorted.

"That's a little what I feel like," Eve admitted. "A Sherlock."

"Well, what did you find out, for Heaven's sake?" Violet put her chin in her hand.

"I know what he and Libby were arguing about before she left for Reno."

"It wasn't a lover's spat?" Helena asked.

"Lover's spat!" Violet shook her head. "So silly."

"No sillier than you and Kitty going around huffy all day over a dress," Helena said.

"She gave him an ultimatum — marry her and leave Gyver or she would go back to Reno on her own."

"I think that was very sensible of her." Helena nodded with approval. "She probably knew she was with child and what it would mean without marriage."

"People don't look at it like that anymore." Violet waved her hand. "That's old-fashioned."

"Old-fashioned or not, people here would see it as a disgrace," Helena argued. "That's why he didn't tell the truth in front of his mother, isn't it? Rosalia would hardly have taken it well if she had known he was going to run away with Libby."

"That's what doesn't sit well with me," Eve said. "I think she found out about the ultimatum."

"How could she?" Violet asked.

"Cecilia," Eve said. "She has the girl wrapped around her finger. Or did, at least."

"How would Cecilia know?" Helena questioned. "We know she knew about the engagement — or, rather, put two and two together — but the rest of it?"

"She wouldn't have to know," said Eve as she rose. "Cecilia would only have to report to Rosalia what August was doing, and Rosalia would know. Agnes, dear, bring coffee into the living room, will you?"

"Elopements, babies, killings." Agnes collected the rest of the plates. "Ain't fit for a child's ears."

"I'm not a child!" Violet hollered.

"Who says I was talking about you?" Agnes challenged.

Helena led her younger sister to the living room. "No one thinks you're a child anymore. Here, take my chair."

"Well, if you insist." Violet settled in with a grin.

"I suppose it could be true," Helena said. "Cecilia keeps saying Rosalia treated her like a daughter."

"Rosalia's attentions came at a price," Eve said. "Remember how she kept insisting she felt sorry for Cecilia?" Helena nodded. "It's entirely possible she was only doing it because she thought Cecilia would make August a good match."

"I concluded that a long time ago," Helena said with a wave.

"Imagine feeble Cecilia as a social butterfly," Violet said with a giggle.

"Take care you don't overdo it on the sugar, missy," Agnes ordered as she set the coffee tray down.

"All right, all right."

"Feeble," Eve murmured. "That's just the word Madge used to describe Cecilia."

"Who's Madge?"

"Madge Hughes," she said. "She used to be Madge Bradford."

"The girl who was married to that rotten egg Curtis?" Violet asked.

"You took her on a few times, didn't you, Agnes?" Helena glanced at the housekeeper who was piling up the leftovers on a platter in the dining room.

The woman nodded. "Needed some help with the spring cleaning last year. Nice girl, Madge."

"She's remarried and lives in Chester now," said Eve. "She's going to have a child in the fall."

"Well, praise the Lord, I'm glad of that," said the woman as she departed.

"So that's why you went to Chester," Helena said.

"What does Madge have to do with August?" asked Violet.

"She worked for Rosalia," said Eve. "Agnes told me that."

"Madge told you Cecilia was a spy for Rosalia?" Helena asked.

"She hinted at it," said Eve. "Rosalia wanted her to be a spy too."

"How maddening," Violet said. "Why can't mothers leave their children alone?"

Eve chuckled. "Madge said the same thing. She also said Rosalia fired her when she discovered her hiding place for her jewelry."

"That's not entirely unjustified," Helena pointed out. "A little excessive, maybe."

"Is it also excessive to accuse Madge of stealing a diamond necklace, when she knew she could trust her, just to have a reason to fire her?" Eve raised her eyebrow.

"How do you know Madge didn't steal it?"

Eve set down her cup and rang the bell. Agnes appeared,

wiping her hands on a towel hanging on her shoulder. "Agnes, you knew Madge pretty well?"

"Sure did," Agnes said.

"Do you believe her capable of stealing a diamond necklace?"

Agnes's face immediately darkened. "Who's been saying she's stealing?"

"Rosalia Winters," Violet said.

"Madge never even took the leftovers I offered her," Agnes declared. "Diamond necklace!"

"You could be wrong, you know, Agnes." Helena tried to hide her smile. "Maybe Madge was holding out for bigger game."

"Listen, dearie, I know women who work in what fine-toned people call 'domestic service,'" she retorted. "You can't tell me I don't know who'd steal the silver and who wouldn't. And I'm telling you, Madge wouldn't."

"Thank you, Agnes." Eve grinned at her younger sister as the housekeeper departed, mumbling to herself, "Steal a diamond necklace!"

"I believe Agnes," Violet weighed in. "She annoys me sometimes, but I'd take her word for anything."

"I didn't say I didn't take her word for it," Helena said mildly. "But what does it prove? Nothing."

"It proves Rosalia may be a more calculating woman than any of us thought," Eve insisted. Her eyes fell on the cover of one of Helena's magazines on the coffee table. A picture of hares with their wide eyes stared back at her. "She got rid of Madge just like she got rid of the rabbit."

"What rabbit?" Violet asked.

"August told me a story about a rabbit his mother ran over once because it was in the way." Her mind was cloudy.

"You're not making any sense, Eve," Helena said.

"Did you know August never worked on a whaling ship?"

"What do you mean?" Violet stared at her. "Of course he did."

"That's what we all thought," Eve said. "He told me he went away to join the crew of the *SS Scotia.*"

"Oooohhh, swank!" Her youngest sister whistled.

Eve glanced at Helena. "It seems odd Josh Kepler, with his roughshod seaman career would have connections to a luxury liner, don't you think?"

Helena's eyes narrowed a little as they always did when she engaged her analytical mind. "And you think Rosalia did."

"You mean his mother got him the job?" Violet put down her coffee cup.

"Why would she?" Helena asked. "She told us she was grooming her son to be a leader of society."

"Leader of society!" Violet snorted.

"Don't be cruel, Vi," Eve said. "That young man has been through a lot."

"I wasn't referring to August," said her sister in a haughty tone. "I think he's nice and he doesn't put on airs. It was his mother I was referring to."

"August told me his mother likes to take things over." Eve leaned forward. "What better way to ensure her son follows her plan for him than to take over his seafaring adventure?"

"What do you mean?" Helena stared at her. "That sounds like nonsense."

"I know what Eve means," Violet declared. "Rosalia knew he would have a miserable time on a cruise ship and would beat a retreat back home."

"Exactly!" Eve looked at her younger sisters with shining eyes.

"Now who's playing Sherlocka?" Helena asked dryly.

"I can be a policewoman too when I want to be," Violet insisted.

"Well, what if she did?" Helena asked. "It's not uncommon for mothers to do such things so their children will see the error of their ways."

"This wasn't about an error in judgment, Helena," Eve insisted. "She set him up to fail."

"He failed on his own," Helena argued. "This is all theory with no proof."

"I think we should get some proof, then," Violet said.

"How do you intend to go about getting it?" Helena asked. "Cross-examine Rosalia?"

"Why not?" Violet giggled. "It would be fun to see her squirm."

"And end up with a lawsuit on our hands," Helena remarked.

"Lawsuits!" Agnes took the coffee away. "Cross-examinations! This ain't no courtroom."

"Well, how else are we going to know?" Violet challenged.

"It's not for us to know," Helena argued. "It's for the police. And right now, all we have is a wild theory."

"There might be someone who can tell us," Eve said. "I was thinking about it all the way home from Chester."

"Who?" Violet asked.

"Josh Kepler."

"What would Josh know?" Helena asked. "August is his friend, not Rosalia."

"He could tell us if we're wrong and he got August the job on the *SS Scotia* after all," Violet pointed out.

"That still wouldn't prove Rosalia arranged it," Helena said.

"But it might give us something to take to Oliver. He has the authority to question her," Eve said.

Helena finished her coffee and set the cup down on her magazine. "What if she did arrange it?"

"Don't you see, Helena?" Eve asked. "If she's capable of spoiling her son's dream of going to sea, she's capable of anything."

"Even murder?" Helena studied her. "That's what you're thinking, isn't it?"

"Golly!" Violet was open-mouthed. "Rosalia Winters, a cold-blooded killer."

"The police have no leads," Eve said quietly. "They're stuck."

"They already spoke to Josh," said Helena. "I don't see what you could find out that they couldn't."

"We all know Josh has no love for the law."

"He got into a lot of trouble in San Francisco when he was my age," Violet said.

Eve stared. "How in the world do you know that?"

"He used to tell me stories, remember?" said Violet. "He told me some whoppers about his arrests."

"He shouldn't have told an impressionable young girl those kinds of stories," Eve mumbled.

"I was twelve," Violet growled. "Hardly a kid, Eve. Just like I'm not a kid now."

Eve smiled. "I know, darling. I'm sorry."

"You really think Josh will tell us more than he's told the police?" Helena asked.

"We won't know until we see him, will we?" Violet jumped up.

"We?" her older sister asked.

"I'm going with you, of course," she said.

"Of course *not*," Eve said as she rose. "You stay here. Helena and I will go."

"I want to go too." Violet smoothed down her chiffon skirt.

"Vi, this is sordid business and I don't want you involved," Eve said.

"You're involved," Violet pointed out. "Helena's involved."

"That's different, dear," she said. "We were asked to help."

"No one's asking us now," Helena said. "Oliver wanted us to identify the body. We've done that. We even buried it."

"That makes it our duty to see the soul is completely put to rest." Eve's anger rose. "That's the part of our business you never understood, Helena. You've got to reconcile the body with the soul, and a restless soul is never at peace."

"If we all go, it's a family affair," Violet insisted. "Josh never had a family and he likes to see everyone together. He told me."

"We don't know what we'll find out," Eve said. "It might be rather nasty."

"If you're determined to do this, I think we should all go," Helena said. "Josh isn't likely to say anything nasty in front of Vi. He liked spinning stories for her as a child."

Eve was silent as she put out the fire. "I suppose you'll have to call Kitty and tell her you're not going out tonight."

Violet kissed her sister's cheek, then rushed into the hallway to use the phone.

"Well, she'll be home early for one night, at any rate," Helena said dryly.

CHAPTER 30

*H*elena drove and parked the car near the place where Eve parked it when she went to see August. They walked the path, Violet taking Helena's hand and swinging it back and forth with a little skip. Eve was touched by how innocent she sounded as she chattered on about things she remembered about the river when she was a child.

"Remember when Dad took you and Helena fishing near Lear Bridge and I cried because Mother wouldn't let me go?"

"You didn't cry," Helena said. "You threw a tantrum."

"I did not," Violet said. "I was more dignified than that."

Eve laughed. "You were three years old, honey. The fish would have swallowed you whole."

"I remember that day," Helena said in a vague tone. "We both pulled in that huge sturgeon and Mother fried it in butter for dinner. She wouldn't let Agnes touch it."

"Agnes was grumbling all night about that," Violet agreed. She was quiet for a moment and then in a solemn tone, added, "I miss them!" She ran ahead a little. Eve knew she was trying to keep from crying.

But when they reached Josh's shack, her youngest sister was in a cheerful mood again.

He greeted them with warmth. He was in his seventies but still had energy and a voice that boomed with enthusiasm. His gray hair and beard were messy and long and his clothes shabby, but he made a point of boiling the kettle for tea and serving it to them in delicate china cups.

"Got that from my ma," he said. "She left it to me when she died as a — what do you call them things?" His eyes zoomed immediately to Helena, as if he expected her to know everything.

"Heirloom," Helena answered, pulling her coat around her shoulders, as it was chilly in the shack.

"Yeah, that thing," he said.

"You should hide it, Josh," Violet said. "Somebody's going to see it and steal it from you someday."

His laughter sounded almost like a bird's cawing. "Hell, girl, I ain't got no safe in this place. Guess I could bury it out back, but won't be very clean when I gotta use it." He grinned, showing several missing teeth.

"Can you still make a rope doll?" Violet questioned. "You used to make me one in two minutes."

"Well, my hands ain't so good anymore, but I reckon if I can find some rope around here, I could try." His face became grim. "The police took about all I had, the blockheads!"

"They're doing their job, Josh," Eve defended. "They're not out to catch anyone who isn't guilty."

"Neither were the San Berdoo police," he flashed. "But I still got the scars from the beating I took for doing nothing."

Eve shivered and Violet's eyes showed sympathy.

"August told me about all you done for him," the elderly man continued. "He's mighty grateful and I reckon I am too."

"We didn't do anything." Eve felt suddenly shy.

"You made them blockheads see he didn't do it," Josh insisted. "As if he'd ever touch a hair on Libby's head!"

"They loved each other." In spite of her youthful cynicism, Violet sighed.

"'Course they did," he scoffed. "They used to use my fishing boat all the time. You never seen such lovebirds."

The word "lovebirds" brought Violet back to life, and she said in a wry tone, "That's the name for it all right. Love is for the birds."

He burst out laughing. "You'll change your tune one day, youngster."

"The police suspect Cecilia now," Helena said. "Did August tell you that?"

"The sheriff never did have no sense." Josh poured the tea with a rather unsteady hand. Violet quickly relieved him of the heavy kettle. "Thanks, darlin'. You always were a good kid." He pinched her cheek. "Never believed this talk about you being like them flappers in the city."

Violet looked down.

"That new district attorney ain't no better than the rest of them," Josh flared. "He just wants an open and shut case."

"That's not true!" Eve said. "Oliver is decent and fair."

"Never trust the word of a woman who's sweet on a man," he mumbled.

"That's ludicrous and you know it!" Eve's face reddened.

He chuckled. "All right, girlie, all right."

"I take it you don't think Cecilia was responsible for Libby's death either," Helena concluded.

"That's even crazier than their thinking August did it," he snorted. "Why, she's been coming around with him since they were kids. She wouldn't even touch the fish for fear of hurting 'em."

Violet perked up. "She was pretty nasty to Libby last year at the Valentine's Day picnic."

"Oh, she's got a temper, but that ain't nothing." He waved his hand. "Like one of them matches Browly gives people to light their cigarettes. It puffs up, all big and important-like, and then a couple of seconds later, it's gone."

"Did you ever teach Cecilia how to tie sailors' knots?" Helena asked.

"That's a strange question." He eyed her. "What're you up to?"

"We're trying to get the police to see things your way," she said.

"I heard you all are working for the police."

"We're not," Violet protested. "We're trying to get Cecilia off."

"Is that right, darlin'?" The elderly man looked doubtful.

"We think someone else —" But a sharp glance from her sisters stopped Violet. "We think the whole rope idea is a lot of nonsense."

"The police said you told them you gave August some rope and taught him how to tie sailors' knots," Eve said. "You must have taught Cecilia too, since she was with August before he met Libby."

"That's true enough," he admitted. "Tied 'em good, she did. Not like a girl at all!"

"Are you inferring a *woman* can't do the things a sailor can do?" Eve asked dryly.

The man laughed. "Don't get all huffy, dearie. Ain't good for your digestion."

"How come you never taught me?" Violet pouted. "I wouldn't tie them like a girl."

He roared. "No, darlin', I believe you wouldn't. Teach you now, if you like." He disappeared into the closet. After some knocking around, he emerged with a piece of rope. "Had this one hidden that I didn't give the police."

"Is it the same kind you gave August?" Helena asked.

"Sure is."

"May I see it?" Helena held out her hand. "It's rather sturdy, isn't it?"

"China silk's the best," said Josh. "You tie something down

with it, it ain't going nowhere. Provided you tie it down well, that is."

"That's my point," said Helena.

He squinted. "I don't know what you mean, girlie."

"She's not a girl, Josh," Violet said. "She's a woman."

"Is it difficult to tie a double turn with half hitches?" Eve asked.

"Well, land sakes!" He stared at her.

"That's what the sheriff asked August to do," Eve said. "I want to see what they look like."

The man pulled out his chair and tied the knot. Violet watched with fascinated eyes and even Eve was impressed by the perfect knots and loops.

When he finished, he sat on the chair and grinned. "That what you wanted?"

"That's exactly what we wanted," Helena said. "And you say both August and Cecilia tied this knot perfectly?"

"Well, nothing is perfect, but damn good."

"So for that knot to come untied, it had to be highly imperfect." Helena looked at her sisters.

"I don't get your meaning." He blinked.

"That's a pretty secure knot," she remarked as she pulled the rope so hard it started to tip him over. He growled, and she let go, letting the chair fly back into place. "I can't imagine once someone knows how to tie it properly, that they would suddenly tie it badly. Especially if they were using it for a purpose."

"Never in a million years," the man declared.

"Not even accidentally?" Violet asked.

"Not accidentally, darlin'," he said. "Now, you want to tell me what this is all about, Helen?"

"Helena," she corrected.

"Never liked me calling you by your short name, did you?" His eyes sparkled. "All right, *Helena*, what's this all about?"

"The police found rope burns on Libby but no rope," Helena

explained. "That rope was tied around her ankles by someone who didn't know how to tie it securely."

"I see what you're getting at." Eve sat up straight. "And if they did know, they wouldn't know how not to tie it securely."

"Not if they wanted to be sure Libby's body would sink to the bottom of the river," said Helena. "They would have made sure. Someone may have been shown how to tie that knot, but they never did it themselves, so they wouldn't know how to make it secure."

"Isn't that very unscientific?" Violet questioned. "You're always jabbering about science and facts."

"I'll admit it can't be proven," said her sister. "But when most of us know how to do something, we do it the exact same way without thinking about it."

Eve leaned forward. "Josh, do all sailors learn how to tie those knots?"

"Sure do," he said.

"Even those working on the *SS Scotia*?"

"What's that?" He frowned.

"The boat that sails between San Francisco and Canada," Violet supplied. "I thought you knew all about the sea."

He wrinkled his nose. "That ain't sea, darlin'. That's a mansion with fins!"

Violet giggled.

"Then you didn't get August the job on the *SS Scotia*?" Helena asked.

"No, ma'am," he said with an emphatic nod. "Job I got him was on a tried-and-true whaling ship."

"So he intended to go on a whaling ship!" Eve stared. "But he changed his mind."

"More like his ma changed it for him," he grumbled.

"What happened?" Helena asked.

"He came to me one night little more'n a year ago and said he couldn't do it," Josh explained.

"Couldn't do what?" Eve asked.

"Get married." He glanced at her. "You remember that time when he was gonna marry Cecilia?" The sisters nodded. "He was feeling cornered, I reckon. I offered to get him a spot on a whaling ship, and he jumped at it."

"And then he didn't," Helena guessed.

"When I told him it was all set, he said his ma got him a place somewhere else," he grumbled. "Come to think of it now, he did say it was a fancy ship. Didn't say nothing about no mansion with fins, though."

"He specifically said Rosalia got him the position?" Eve asked. "This could be important, Josh."

"Why, sure," he said. "He told me, 'Mother's taken care of it.'"

"Why would he agree to have his mother arrange things instead of you?" Eve asked. "You're like a father to him."

"Well, darlin', I'll tell you." The man propped his leg up on a chair. "He was a regular weakling then."

"That's a horrible thing to say about a young man you've been mentoring all his life," Violet scolded.

"Well, maybe you're right, girlie." He was clearly ashamed of himself. "But he weren't much of a man then, always letting her decide things for him. It wasn't all his fault. She's got a way with him, his ma."

"What do you mean?" Helena asked.

"That silky kind of way some women have of making people do anything," he said with a sniff. "Met a couple of 'em myself. 'Course I was never taken by 'em."

"I'm sure you weren't," Eve said dryly. "Rosalia is like that, isn't she?"

"I tried telling him not to go," said Josh. "They'd make mincemeat out of him."

"Who would?" Violet asked.

"The sailors, naturally," he said. "They may work on a mansion with fins, but they still got dirt under their fingernails."

"August said they gave him a hard time," Eve murmured.

"I ain't surprised," said Josh. "His ma shouldn't've interfered. But then, I ain't surprised at *that* either." He took out a pipe. "Mind if I smoke?"

"Got any cigarettes?" Violet asked. Both Eve and Helena glared at her.

He pinched her cheek. "Not for you, darlin'."

"August admitted he was weak before he left for sea," Eve said. "He said he knows his own mind now. I suppose his experience with the *SS Scotia* wasn't such a waste after all."

"That wasn't what did it," Josh insisted. "It was that girl of his."

"You mean the ultimatum?" asked Helena. "We know about that."

"A man's gotta take responsibility when he gets a woman mixed up with a kid," he declared.

"So he told you Libby was pregnant?" Eve asked.

He nodded. "Came by just before he went to see Dale and told me."

"So that's why he went to see Lieutenant Commander Dale?" Eve murmured.

"Who's he?" Violet asked.

"Man I know," Josh supplied. "August came to me after Libby'd gone away and told me all about it. He wanted me to arrange the whaling ship again, but I told him a man's gotta have something more respectable if he's going to get married." He chuckled. "'Course I didn't know about the kid then."

"So you suggested the Navy," Helena guessed.

"I ain't big on the government myself," he snorted. "But if you want to go to sea and you got a family, it's the best option."

"You sent him to this Dale person so he could get a job?" Violet asked. "That was nice of you, Josh."

"Not a job, exactly," said the man. "He ain't no recruiter. But Dale's been in the Navy for a long time and I thought he could steer August in the right direction."

"And did he?" Eve asked.

"Far as I can see," he said. "Told him to go to the Treasure Island recruitment station and he'd put in a good word for him."

"So August and Libby wouldn't have moved far away if they had married," Eve said.

"I reckon they could've set themselves up in San Francisco," Josh agreed.

"And he didn't tell his mother about any of this?" Helena asked.

"I told him not to," said Josh. "So did Dale. Mothers get hysterical when they find out their sons want to join the Navy." He grinned. "I can't see Rosalia throwing fits, though."

"She's an iceberg," Violet agreed.

"Josh, do you think Rosalia knew about August's plans to leave with Libby and join the Navy?" Eve asked.

The man chewed on his pipe, his eyes vacant for a moment. "Well, girlie, I can't say for sure, mind you —"

"But?" Helena prompted.

"But I think she knew something was amiss, if you know what I mean."

"How do you know?' Helena asked.

"'Cause she come to see me one night."

All three sisters sat up.

"Josh!" Violet stared. "Did you tell the police?"

"I don't tell the police nothing unless I have to," he scoffed.

"What night?" Eve asked. "The night Libby was killed?"

"Land sakes, girlie, I don't keep no calendars," he said. "What do I know about the night Libby was killed?"

"It was Friday night," Helena said.

"Before that," he said. "Tuesday, maybe Wednesday. I remember 'cause it was one of those slow days with the fish." He grimaced. "Fish get as tired as we do with the mid-week slump."

"I presume she didn't come to see you often." Helena glanced around. "Not here, anyway."

He burst out laughing. "She don't come to see me at all. Thinks I'm a periah."

"Pariah," Violet corrected.

He raised an eyebrow. "Looks like all that paint on your face don't stifle your brain after all, darlin'."

Violet made a face at him.

"What was it all about?" Eve felt the tension in her chest. "Josh, this might be important."

"Can't see why." He shrugged. "She came to ask questions, of course."

"And you answered them?" Helena asked.

"Well, told you she's got a silky way with her," he said. "She asked me if I got August a job on a whaling ship."

Eve stared. "Why in the world would she ask that?"

"Guess she thought he was thinking of going back to sea," he said. "Which, of course, he was, but not in that way. So I could tell her honestly that I hadn't."

"Nice that you could be honest," Helena mumbled.

"Josh is always honest!" Violet insisted.

He patted her shoulder. "Thanks, darlin'. Wish I'd had you as my lawyer that time in San Berdoo."

"And that was all?" Eve asked.

"Well, I saw my chance, so I gave her a talking to."

"What do you mean?"

"I just arranged the dinner between August and Dale, so I said, 'You got to stop tryin' to run that boy's life. He's a man now. Man's gotta do what he wants on his own.'"

"And what did she say?" Violet asked, her chin in her hands as if she were listening to a bedtime story.

"She said, 'You don't know anything about it.' I said, 'If you don't want to drive that boy away, you'd better welcome his wife with open arms 'cause nothing's gonna stop him.'"

"You told her he was engaged?" Violet stared. "Josh, that was terrible of you!"

"I think she knew already," Helena supplied. "She told us she knew the engagement ring wasn't for Cecilia when Cecilia told her about it. Remember, Eve?" Her older sister nodded.

"He said he was gonna tell his mama once he settled things with Dale anyway," Josh defended. "I tried to prepare her too. I said, 'That boy's got plans of his own.' 'Course, she tried to get me to tell her what they were, but I wouldn't." He thrust his lip out. "Can't shake a confidence out of Josh Kepler, no sir!"

"What did Rosalia say when you told her he was going to marry Libby?" Eve asked.

"That was the odd part." He leaned against his knee. "She said, 'That won't happen. I promised him it wouldn't happen.'"

"How interesting," Helena said. "I don't suppose you know who 'him' is?"

He looked annoyed. "Maybe it was God!"

"Funny thing for a Godless creature like you to say," Violet teased.

His face was grave. "I read my Bible, darlin', just like everyone else around here."

"Did she say anything else, Josh?" Eve asked.

"Not that I recall," he said.

Eve rose. "You've been very helpful." She pressed his hand. "More than you know."

"Long as I don't have to talk to the police," he mumbled as he opened the door for them.

"I'm afraid you might." Helena looked purposefully at her older sister. "Isn't that right, Eve?"

Eve nodded, her head heavy.

CHAPTER 31

It was late when the sisters got home and they went to bed immediately. Even Violet didn't complain retiring earlier than she usually did.

In the morning, Felix slept in so the sisters were alone for breakfast. Surprisingly, Violet showed up at the table on time and dressed in a semi-respectable suit.

"Going to an interview this morning, honey?" Eve asked. "Don't forget they can call us if they need a reference."

"Employers won't put much stock into family references," Helena said, her nose in one of her medical journals.

"They will if they know she was employed with us," Eve argued.

"Employed!" Violet grumbled.

"You got paid, didn't you?" Helena asked.

"Ten cents a week for candy."

"Any more and you would have been spoiled rotten." Her older sister grinned.

"I'm not going to a job interview," she said. "I'm going with you."

"With us where?" Eve stared.

"Wherever it is you're going." Violet sat down and dug into the eggs and bacon.

"How do you know we're going anywhere when we don't know ourselves?" Helena asked.

"That's what we have to decide," Violet said. "Where do we go from here?"

"With what?"

"Really, Helena, you are dense sometimes." Her sister shook her head. "With this murder business. We're on the scent, aren't we?"

"You ain't no bloodhound," Agnes snorted.

"We're the three Sherlockas," Violet said. "I think we ought to storm the citadel."

"Don't talk silliness, Vi," Eve snapped.

"I'm not," she insisted. "Isn't Redbud Manor a sort of citadel?"

"We can't just march in there and say to Rosalia, 'You killed your son's fiancée,'" Helena objected. "We're not the police."

"Then let the police do it," Violet insisted. "We'll tell Oliver what Josh told us."

Eve played with the slice of toast. "And what did Josh tell us? Nothing we can take to Oliver."

"Well, sure we can," Violet said. "We know Rosalia killed Libby. It's a cinch."

"Knowing and proving are two very different things, Vi," Helena said.

"Oh, you and your scientific methods!" her sister grumbled.

"Don't dismiss Helena's methods," Eve scolded. "The police use their method too."

"Josh said Rosalia knew August was going to marry Libby," said Violet. "Isn't that proof enough?"

"That's not proof," Helena argued. "That's possible motive, and even then, a very slim one."

Agnes plucked a plate in front of Violet. The scent of cheese Danishes filled the air. "I told that delivery boy at Gohl's I ain't taking Karl's boxes anymore without paying." She held up a finger. "And it's coming out of your salary once you get hired."

"Don't worry, Agnes, I won't take advantage of his generosity anymore," Violet promised.

"See that you don't," the housekeeper mumbled.

"I don't think it's so slim," Eve said quietly.

"Hm?" Helena looked up from her journal.

"I said, I don't think it's such a stretch that Rosalia would kill Libby." The words left a bitter taste on Eve's lips.

"Careful of what you're saying, Eve," her sister warned.

"I'm not making an accusation," Eve insisted. "I'm only bringing up an idea."

"Forming a hypothesis," Violet added. "Isn't that what you do?"

"I don't form a hypothesis before I've thought it through," Helena retorted.

"Well, I have," Eve said. "I've been thinking of nothing else since I spoke with August."

"Isn't it just a little excessive to kill a woman because your son is in love with her?" Helena asked.

"He wasn't just in love," Violet said. "He bought her a ring and proposed to her."

"Rosalia didn't know that," Helena pointed out.

"Josh said —"

"Josh said he told her Libby was going to marry August," Helena said carefully. "He didn't tell her they were already engaged. You've got to be precise about these things."

"Oh, applesauce!" Her sister sniffed.

Helena looked at Eve. "You said she met the girl and even invited her to spend a holiday in San Diego with them. She must have realized August was getting serious about her. What Josh said wouldn't have been a surprise to her and she probably took it as August making a passionate declaration like a lot of young boys do." She added, "Many don't follow through with those declarations, you know."

"You sound like Oliver," Eve said dryly.

"He ought to know," Violet said. "I'll bet he's made some broken promises to girls when he was young."

"He's not exactly an old man," Helena said.

"What about what Rosalia did to her son two years ago?" Eve asked.

"What about it?"

"She got him that job on the *SS Scotia* knowing he would fail and come home," Eve insisted. "I'm sure of it."

"No one can be sure of something like that," Helena argued.

"Any fool would know sailors resent rich boys," Violet said.

"And just how do you know that?" Eve peered at her youngest sister.

"Because Kitty and I got into a conversation with a couple of those boys last year passing through town on their way to San Francisco."

"Vi!"

"I didn't flirt with them, Eve," she insisted. "We were just spilling."

"You were what?" Helena glared at her.

"Chatting," her sister said emphatically.

"I hardly think Rosalia would know enough about sailors to know that," Helena said.

"Maybe not, but her husband might have," Eve said. "I remember him coming into the funeral home once and trying to convince Papa to join him for the boat races he was trying to organize in San Francisco."

"What would Papa know about boats?" Violet asked.

"He had a friend he went fishing with before he met Mama," she said.

"Oh." Violet looked into her coffee cup. "I never knew that."

"He said he had a friend whose business it was to make ships," said Eve. "I remember it because he promised he would give me a ship inside a bottle if Papa would go."

"And did he?" Violet asked.

"Of course he didn't," Eve said. "Papa had a business to run."

"So you think Rosalia set the whole thing up just to get it out of August's system," Helena said. "But what has that to do with Libby's murder?"

"It has to do with the personality of the murderer."

Helena dropped the cup inside the saucer with an agitated bang. "Eve, don't call her that! Don't convict someone who hasn't even been accused."

"I'm sorry," Eve said. "I just feel it in my gut."

"Gut feeling's just as important as hypotheses," Violet insisted.

"If we're talking about hypotheses, I hate to remind you, but Cecilia is still a suspect," Helena said.

"You can't believe that," Eve insisted. "For God's sake, the girl's still a child!"

"No more than Vi is a child," Helena argued. Violet gave her an exaggerated bow.

"All right." Eve leaned back. "Let me point something out that might appeal to your analytical mind. Would you say Libby's murder was spontaneous?"

"What do you mean?" Helena stared.

"I think, darling, they call it unpremeditated in the moving pictures," Violet remarked.

"If you mean it wasn't planned, I wouldn't say that," Helena said. "The killer brought the rope with him or her, so it was obvious he or she planned on tying Libby's body down to something that would sink it."

"Exactly," said Eve. "Libby was lured to the river where the killer performed the awful deed and then used the rope to tie her ankles to the rock, intending for her to sink to the bottom so the police wouldn't find her." She studied her sister. "Do you think Cecilia would be capable of planning such a thing?"

"She might," Helena said. "Everyone keeps saying she's 'still waters run deep.'"

"They might run deep enough for her to plan such a thing," Violet admitted. "But Josh said Cecilia knew how to tie sailors' knots. She would've made sure they stayed tied. You said that yourself." She crossed her arms, triumphant she had pulled one over on her older sister.

"Even the craftiest murderer slips with the details," Helena said. "It would be perfectly natural for Cecilia to bring the rope and then carelessly tie it. Or she miscalculated how heavy the current would be when she tied it. She's not an experienced sailor, after all."

"Neither was Rosalia," Eve retorted. "She said August would tell her everything. Isn't it possible he was eager to show her how to tie sailors' knots when he got back from sea and she copied what he did?"

"Anything's possible," Helena said. "But the fact remains there is nothing against Rosalia while Cecilia has two strikes against her. No, three. Four even."

"Oh?" Eve looked at her.

"One will suit your way of thinking, I'm sure," said Helena. "She hated Libby. That much has been made clear."

"So she hated Libby," Violet said.

"She has a violent temper," Helena continued. "Even your precious Josh said that." She glanced at her younger sister, who stuck out her tongue. "Those are just as strong motives to kill Libby as Rosalia's."

"Perhaps they are," Eve admitted.

"The police found August's engagement ring —"

"Libby's ring," Eve corrected. "He proposed to her, remember?"

Helena grimaced. "Libby's ring in Cecilia's drawer, wrapped up and hidden away. Now, how did it get there?"

"I don't know," Eve said.

"And, last but not least, there's Mrs. Cinder," said Helena. "She's said all along Cecilia phoned Libby that night and told her August wanted to meet her down by the river. We can agree that phone call was meant to lure her to where the killer — whoever he or she is — was waiting."

"She could have been wrong," Violet said.

"She was very positive about it," Helena insisted. "Eve and I heard her."

"Yes, that's true," Eve said. "But I don't think it was Cecilia."

"Well, for all —" Helena grasped the magazine as if trying to find comfort in it.

"Cecilia's voice isn't very distinct," Eve said. "It could be easily impersonated."

"Especially with the kind of phone service we get here," Violet added warily.

"What are you implying, Eve?" Helena poured herself the last of the coffee before Agnes took the pot. "That Rosalia was the one who called Libby that night impersonating Cecilia?"

"Don't forget to bring more coffee, Agnes," Violet said. "Mother and I are going to the American Legion for their annual shindig."

Both sisters stared at her. It was not the words she said but the way she said them.

Violet grinned and spoke in her normal tone. "Forget about the coffee, Agnes."

"Don't make no sense play-acting that way," Agnes said as she retreated.

"Vi, have you lost your senses?" Helena asked.

"No, dear sister," she said with a twinkle in her eye. "You want proof all the time, so I gave your proof."

"Proof of what?"

"You're very clever, darling, but don't go getting ideas about being in the moving pictures," Eve warned.

"What is this all about?"

"Isn't it obvious?" Violet asked. "I was trying to demonstrate anyone could impersonate Cecilia's sickly-sweet voice."

"Charles couldn't," Helena said dryly.

"Any woman, then!" Violet snapped.

"You did sound like her," Eve said. "Didn't she, Helena?"

Her sister's bottom lip folded inwardly, the same look she used to get when she was a child trying to concentrate. "I suppose she did a little."

"A little!" Violet snorted.

"And Vi was right about the phone reception in Gyver," said Eve. "If she were to call someone and use that voice, anyone who knew Cecilia would think it was her."

"But it wasn't Vi who called Libby that night," Helena said.

"No, but it could have been Rosalia," she said. "She's already lied about several things. Maybe she lied about the dinner in Brenas."

"And stayed home, picked up the phone, called the Cinder house pretending to be Cecilia?" Helena raised an eyebrow. "It's an interesting theory, Eve, but just a theory."

Eve folded the napkin on the table. "Maybe we can show Oliver it's at least a viable theory."

"How?" Violet leaned forward.

"By going to the Shelton house and asking Maisie and Bonnie if Rosalia made a call to the Cinders on Friday night," Eve said.

"What makes you think they'll remember?" Helena asked. "They get a fair number of calls every day and it was some time ago."

"Those two birds?" Violet scoffed. "They have that headset growing out of their ears. They'll remember."

Helena was on her feet. "I suppose there can't be any harm in asking them."

"I want to come with you," Violet said firmly.

"Better not," Helena said. "They'll be gossiping all over town how the two Sherlockas have now become the three Sherlockas."

"Why don't you take the car and go over to Chester?" Eve offered. "I passed by the Chester Employment Office on my way to Madge's house and saw they're looking to employ young women in various positions. The signs were all up."

"You want me working in *that* town?" Violet countered. "They only have clerical work."

"Where were you expecting to work, in Buckingham Palace?" Helena asked.

"It might be a nice change of scenery," Eve said.

"Oh… hell's bells!"

"Don't you go talking to your sisters that way!" Agnes was immediately like a mother lion. "If I catch you using that language again, I'll skin you!"

Violet let out a frustrated screech and stalked off. They heard her yanking her coat from the peg in the hallway and slamming the front door.

"I hope she took the car keys with her," Eve sighed.

"I doubt it," Helena said. "She's probably going to the drugstore to cry on Kitty's shoulder."

"It's better this way." Eve felt a sickness in her stomach. "We don't know what we're going to find."

In spite of her understated demeanor, Helena drove faster than Eve, sometimes jerking too much at the turns. A few times, Eve had to catch her breath.

The Shelton sisters operated the switchboard right out of the house their father had left them in the center of town not far from the main street. As they pulled up, Eve saw the door was wide open, as it usually was in all weather. She peered at the front porch, expecting to find people milling around, drinking Maisie's strong tea and chatting. But there was no one and she sighed with relief.

"I can't imagine how they do their work with people always in and out." She straightened her coat.

"I suppose it gets boring chained to that switchboard all day," Helena said.

The sisters had the switchboard set up right in their living room with two hard wooden chairs side by side. Bonnie turned around and waved at them, the headset tight around her ears and the horn-shaped trumpet through which she spoke close to her lips as if she were going to eat it.

"Morning, ladies," Bonnie said cheerfully. "You still out helping the police?"

"In a manner of speaking." Eve glanced at her sister. "Where's Maisie?"

"Her back's out again," Bonnie said with a sigh. "Been out a week now. Doctor calls it by some fancy name, but I think it's just plain wear and tear. We've been sitting in these chairs day in and day out since we were eighteen."

"You talk as if thirty-four is ancient," Helena said wryly. Both Bonnie and Maisie were only a four years older than her.

"So she wasn't working on Friday night?" Eve asked.

"Sure wasn't." A light blinked on the switchboard and Bonnie pressed a plug in. They waited until she had finished.

"We're trying to trace a call," Eve said.

Bonnie laughed. "You're beginning to sound like the police. A call made on Friday night, I take it?"

"Yes," she said.

"From whom to whom?" Bonnie put on her headset again.

"From Redbud Manor to the Cinder house," said Helena.

The woman whistled. "I thought the police don't think August did it."

"Don't ask questions, Bonnie," Helena ordered.

"All right, all right," the woman grumbled. "I was working that night. There was a call from that number, as a matter of fact. But it wasn't August. It was his mother."

Eve felt her heart beating faster. "To the Cinder house?"

"Now what would she call them for?" Bonnie asked.

The quick beating stopped and Eve felt wary. "I see."

"Who did she call, then?" Helena asked.

"Well, I don't know if I should be telling you that," Bonnie hedged. "That's sort of confidential."

"We're working with the police, remember?" Helena asked.

"I know, but — well, I suppose it can't do any harm since the Winters are out of it now," she said. "She was calling a Mrs. Combs in Brenas."

The sisters exchanged glances. "When was this?" Eve asked.

"Before suppertime," she said.

"So around five or six," Helena guessed.

The woman nodded. "I swear, I woke up that operator in Brenas with a jolt. Nearly tore my head off."

"And there were no other phone calls made from Redbud Manor that night?" Eve asked.

"None that I answered," she said. "Pearl was with me until around ten o'clock. She might have answered one."

"Where is Pearl?" Eve asked.

"She won't be in until after lunchtime," she said. "I'll ask her, though."

"Thanks, Bonnie." Helena patted her shoulder. "I can send over some laudanum for Maisie, if you like."

"That's very nice of you, honey." The woman smiled.

The sun was shining as they descended the porch steps but Eve took each one as carefully as if it were covered with ice.

Helena, as if seeing her sister was dejected, put her arm around her shoulders. "I'm guessing Combs is the name of the people Rosalia had dinner with that night?"

Eve nodded. "Edward and Emma Combs."

"Seems odd she would phone them if she were going to dinner with them in a few hours," Helena remarked.

"I wonder why she phoned them." Eve opened the car door.

"We can find out," said Helena. "We can drive down to Brenas and check Rosalia's alibi."

Eve looked at her. "Wouldn't the police have done that?"

"I doubt it," Helena said. "She's not a suspect, remember. They were focusing on August's alibi, not his mother's."

"Do you really think it will tell us something?" Eve asked.

"It will tell us if she was lying or not," Helena pointed out as she started the car. "And if she was lying, Oliver needs to know about it."

They drove back toward town and over the bridge into Nevada. Neither of them had ever been in that area and they both looked around eagerly as Helena slowed down the car. The landscape was more barren as they got farther away from the river, but Brenas was a town well-manicured for its size. Large houses dotted with colorful gardens and iron gates whizzed by as they passed. They stopped for gas at a filling station and Eve gave the attendant the Combses' address she had heard Rosalia tell Oliver. The attendant gave them a peculiar look but directed them toward the back end of town.

When Helena turned the corner on Prospect Street, Eve could see why the attendant had looked at them so strangely. Of all the mansions they had seen coming in, these were twice and some even three times the size. Each house was grander than the last and large portions of land separated them as if each owner wanted to be as far away as possible from his neighbor. Behind the iron fences were dogs, large dogs that jumped and barked incessantly as the automobile passed.

"Not a very friendly place, is it?" Helena asked dryly.

"People in town have always said Brenas is exclusive." Eve nodded.

"Exclusive!" Helena snorted. "Each house is like a jewel in its own jewelry box."

Eve saw how apt the description was as they pulled up to a yellow house with turrets and towers, making a ghostly image against the slightly cloudy sky. As they both gingerly went up the steps, holding one another's hand as when they were children, the hounds ran to the gate and began their campaign of barking and growling.

"Oh, don't be a goof," her sister snapped. "There's nothing to be afraid of."

A man in overalls appeared, shouting at the dogs, who immediately quieted down. He grinned at them. "They don't receive guests well," he apologized. "You've come to see my wife?"

"Wife?" Eve asked in a dim tone.

"She was expecting some people." He scrutinized them.

Eve felt suddenly shabby in the coat she had bought with such pride last year. But Helena, as always, kept her head and said, "We're here to see Mrs. and Mr. Combs."

"I'm Mr. Combs." He put out his hand. "I beg your pardon about my appearance. I'm rather proud of my garden and I don't let anyone else tend it."

His friendliness immediately put Eve at ease. "It's quite all right. The marigolds are beautiful."

The man was clearly pleased as he led them into the house where a butler with a stiff collar had already opened the door. "It's hard to get them to bloom this time of year."

"I'm sure," Helena said.

"My wife likes to have coffee in the morning room about this time." He put on a well-tailored jacket hanging in the hall. "You're just in time to join us." He glanced at them. "I suppose it's rather unconventional to offer coffee to strangers. You might want to wrangle some money out of me for a church social."

Helena laughed. "We're from Gyver and we're here as friends of August Winters."

They walked along a narrow hallway that echoed with their footsteps and came to one of the largest rooms Eve had ever seen. The woman who sat on the couch at the other end seemed a mile away.

"Did I hear you say you were friends of August's?" She rose. "Did Rosalia send you?"

"Not exactly," Eve mumbled.

"We're helping the police look into the matter." Helena gave her older sister a meaningful look. Eve knew what she was thinking: *Let's hope they haven't read the papers.*

It was immediately apparent they had not, as Mrs. Combs sighed. "That poor boy! Of course he wasn't involved in this murder business. It's silly of the police to think so."

"We understand he was supposed to come here for dinner on Friday night with his mother," Helena said as Mr. Combs offered them coffee.

The man nodded. "Rosalia called to tell us he wouldn't be here. Isn't that right, dear?" He looked at his wife.

"She didn't want us to be disappointed when she came alone." The woman smiled. "We've always thought of August as a son. We've no children of our own, you see."

"What was the reason she gave for August not coming?" Eve inquired.

"She said he had plans of his own," said Mrs. Combs. "Young people often do, don't they?"

"But Rosalia did come that night?" Helena asked.

"Of course," said the woman. "We have the best cook in Brenas and that's saying a lot."

"I imagine," Helena mumbled glancing around the room. "Can you tell us when she left?" At their inquiring look, she added hastily, "It would help to establish his alibi, since he says he was home when she came."

"Was he?" Mrs. Combs blinked. "That's odd."

"Well, dear, the young people could have made an early night of it," her husband pointed out. "They often do when they have to get up early the next morning."

"You mean Rosalia went home early?" Eve asked.

"She had a headache, poor thing," Mrs. Combs cooed. "She used to get them all the time at school. That's where we knew one another, you know."

"I see." Eve glanced at her sister.

"Do you remember when she left here?" Helena asked.

"We don't look at clocks," said the husband. "I know that sounds ironic, considering we have so many in the house. But when you have too much time on your hands —" He sounded almost resentful.

"Would you say it was before, say, eight-thirty?" Helena persisted. Eve saw what she was getting at — it took about a half hour to get from Brenas to Gyver, which would have put Rosalia in town just at the time of the murder.

"I would imagine so," said the man. "I remember remarking to my wife, 'We can take the dogs out after all.'" To the sisters' blank look, he said with a laugh, "We always take the dogs out before bedtime except when we're entertaining. Then Miles — our butler — takes them out."

"And when do you usually take them out?" asked Helena.

"My, but you're persistent, aren't you, Miss —" Mrs. Combs peered at her.

"Mrs. Wright," she said.

"My sister doesn't mean to pry," Eve apologized. "We just want to make sure we have the right information for the police."

"Around eight or so," said Mrs. Combs. "I don't like Edward to be out too late with them."

Eve signaled her sister. "You've been very kind and helpful."

"Tell me, was the boy really involved with this girl?" Mr. Combs asked.

"They were engaged," Helena said boldly.

"Heavens!" Mrs. Combs rang the bell.

"She was a nice girl," Eve insisted. "An honest worker who cared about children."

"Better than some of those young ladies we've encountered, eh, Ella?" asked Mr. Combs with a wink.

"I don't know about that." His wife was haughty. "Some of them are quite nice."

On their way out, Eve's caught something folded on the table. The rich mauve color struck her less than the perfect square. "You fold your linens just like Rosalia does," she lamented.

Mrs. Combs stared at her. "Why, how did you know that?"

"She was working on a tablecloth when we visited her last," Helena supplied. "My sister admires neat linens." She glanced at Eve with an ironic look.

"Neat. Yes, that's what it is, isn't it?" Eve's mind was spinning. "Neat, tidy, nothing uncertain. No loose ends. Like a dead rabbit in the road." As if they heard her, the dogs began to bark.

CHAPTER 32

"I think we ought to tell Oliver."

It was the first thing Helena said as they drove into Gyver.

"Tell him what?" Eve asked.

"Everything," her sister insisted.

"You said yourself it wasn't evidence."

"The lie about Rosalia's alibi is," Helena said. "It might mean something."

"It's incredible!" Eve's hands felt cold. "She would go so far as to —"

"Murder is always incredible," said Helena. "But how many death certificates have we seen with incredible reasons for someone dying?"

Eve was silent.

"All we can do is tell him what we know and let him decide what to do with it," her sister assured her.

When they got to Oliver's office, his secretary told them he had gone to lunch. "Try the drugstore or the diner," she advised. "He usually goes to one or the other when he wants a quick bite."

They didn't find him at the diner and Mrs. Browly told them Oliver hadn't been there. So they went to Rooty Toot Drugstore.

Their younger sister was sitting at the soda fountain, swiveling around on the stool. Two empty glasses were at her elbow while she sipped a third soda, chatting away with Kitty. Eve waved at her. She pressed her finger to her nose, then turned back to Kitty.

"She's doing just what she did when she was a child," Eve murmured.

"She's still angry at us." Helena looked around. "I don't see Oliver, do you?"

Sudie came up to them. "Well, that sister of yours has got the sulks, I can tell you."

"Has Oliver been here for lunch?" Eve asked.

The woman shook her head. "Not yet. Might be in soon, though. I told him about the new roast beef sandwich and he looked interested." She grinned.

Eve's shoulders sagged with the heavy feeling of coming up against a wall. Helena took her arm and led her to one of the tables.

"What are you doing?" Eve blinked.

"We may as well have a bite to eat while we're waiting for Oliver to show up," said her sister. "That roast beef sandwich sounds good."

Eve stared at her. "Food now?"

"Murder or no murder, Eve, we have to eat," Helena insisted. "Besides, food soothes the savage beast."

"We ought to order one for Vi, then." She glanced at the soda fountain. "It might sooth her."

"You know Vi," Helena said. "She's at the petulant stage now. Soon she'll be at the glaring stage, and then it will all blow over, and she'll be chattering away as usual at dinner tonight."

Sudie brought a water pitcher and glasses. "It's getting almost like a café here, Sudie," Helena complimented.

"Kitty's idea," she said. "When I can get that girl's head out of the moving picture magazines, she gets a notion or two that's actually useful." She eyed them. "You two look all done in."

"Didn't Vi advertise it all over the soda fountain?" Helena asked warily. "We've been to Brenas."

"What you going all that way for?"

"We had to see someone," Eve said.

"Well, I'm glad you came here for lunch instead of having it there." The woman hitched up her belt. "They'd have charged you three times more for half the portion."

The water revived Eve. "You're just as convinced as I am that Rosalia was responsible for Libby's death, aren't you?"

"I wouldn't say that," said Helena. "We still don't have anything concrete other than she lied about when she got back to Gyver that night."

"She didn't call the Cinders from Redbud Manor," Eve concluded.

"If she really did kill Libby, she wouldn't risk the police checking calls that night," Helena said. "She's a shrewd woman, Eve."

"I realize that now." Eve sighed.

"I knew it the day we spoke with her," Helena said.

"How?"

"It was the way she talked about Cecilia, as if she were sure she'd committed the crime," her sister said.

"Do you think she was trying to plant the idea in our minds?" Eve asked.

"You mean plant the idea of Cecilia's guilt?" Helena shrugged. "Why would she do that?"

"You heard her make a point of how we were working with the police to find Libby's murderer," Eve pointed out. "She might have thought we would go back to Oliver with it."

"It's possible."

Eve saw Helena was right about their sister. Every time Violet swiveled in their direction, she shot them a glare.

Just as their sandwiches arrived, Dot breezed into the drugstore. She was as opposite to Eve as any friend, tall and lanky, with the joints of her elbows and knees pronounced. She waved to Violet, who gave her a friendly wave back, and joined Eve.

"I went butterflying last weekend," she said.

"Did you find any interesting specimens?" Helena perked up.

"You know I don't look for specimens." Dot laughed. "I only admire their prettiness and leave them on their merry way." She leaned against the back of a chair. "I didn't see any."

"I guess it's too cold for them this time of year," Eve sighed.

"I couldn't help but think how we used to go butterflying in the summer when we were kids." Dot sighed. "It seems like we haven't done that for ages."

"We've been busy, you know," Helena reminded her.

"Yes, I know." Dot's face fell. "This murder business. Awful."

"Your mother and father were very helpful," Helena said. "They steered the police in the right direction. It would have probably taken them a long time to identify the woman if your mother hadn't remembered seeing her around a school."

"I'm glad they were able to help," Dot said.

"Have lunch with us, won't you, dear?" Eve suddenly realized how good she felt to see her friend.

Dot shook her head. "I only came in to make a phone call to Mama. She's at Aunt Ellie's and I promised Papa I would pick her up."

"Why don't you call from the library?" Helena asked.

Dot lowered her voice. "Dragon Andrews is in today."

Eve smiled at the nickname Dot had given the library director, a staunch lady with a tight face who ran the library like a brigade.

"She won't even let you make a phone call?" Helena growled. "That shouldn't be allowed."

"She makes me pay for it if I do," said Dot. "I prefer to call from the phone booth where I have some privacy." She smiled. "Drop by for dinner on Sunday, if you like. And bring the younker with you." She chuckled as she glanced at the soda fountain.

"She would be furious with you if she heard you call her that," Eve said. "She keeps reminding me she isn't a kid."

"She's annoyed at us," Helena added. "We had something to do this morning and we forbade her to come with us."

"Isn't that the way of young people these days?" Dot asked. "They always want to throw themselves into something, no matter what the consequences."

Eve watched her friend slide into the phone booth, closing the door behind her. The booth looked like a cocoon she wouldn't have minded climbing into, perhaps to emerge as a free, beautiful butterfly like the ones she and Dot used to seek when they were children.

"I don't think Oliver's going to show, Eve," her sister said as she wiped the last of the mustard from her fingers.

The bell above Sudie's door rang as two teenage boys came in tossing a football between them. Sudie barked at them and they grumbled but put the football on the floor between them.

She looked at her sister. "Helena, suppose Rosalia did call the Cinders that night, but not from Redbud Manor?"

"From where then?" her sister asked. "Surely not the Combses'."

"Not the Combses," said Eve. "The phone booth."

"You mean that one?" Helena glanced at it.

"Why not?" Eve leaned forward grasping the edge of the table. "She could have come straight to the drugstore from her dinner. Sudie is open here until late."

"But people would have seen her," Helena objected.

"What if they did?" Eve insisted. "We all use that booth to make calls. It's the only one in town."

Helena thought this over as she played with the spoon in the mustard pot. Violet had stopped her glaring and now looked at them with curiosity. The two teenage boys were trying to flirt with her, throwing laughing comments in her direction, but Violet took no notice.

"I suppose it wouldn't hurt to ask Sudie," Helena said at last.

Sudie appeared when Helena beckoned to her, a pencil behind her ear. "If I catch those boys practicing their bullet pass in here again, I swear I'll deflate that damn ball!"

"Sudie, did Rosalia Winters come in Friday night to make a phone call?" Eve asked, her heart racing.

The woman stared. "Well, for crying out loud, how did you know that?"

"Then she was in!" Eve gave Helena a satisfied look.

"I thought it odd at the time," Sudie admitted. "She hardly comes down here, you know. Just sends that maid of hers for anything she wants."

"She came alone?" Helena asked.

The woman nodded. "She was right nice, though. Asked me how I was and how Kitty was and apologized for coming so late —"

"How late?" Eve jumped.

"I don't know exactly," said Sudie. "Probably a couple of hours before we closed."

"That would be about eight or nine o'clock, wouldn't it?" Eve's heart was skipping.

"About that, I guess."

"Did she say anything else other than niceties?" Helena asked.

"Said her phone was out of order and it was lucky we kept ours in shape," Sudie said with a grin.

Now Helena's voice sounded almost excited. "She told you her phone was out of order?"

"That's why she was coming in so late to call." Sudie looked from one sister to the other. "Is it important?"

"It might be," Eve said slowly. "It might very well be!"

Helena pressed her sister's hand with a cautious gesture. "Wait a minute. Sudie, did Cecilia come in to use the phone that night as well?"

"Not that I recall," she said. "Of course, I wasn't here all the time. Kitty was here alone part of it."

"May we ask Kitty?" Eve asked.

"Ask whatever you like." Sudie chuckled. "If you can get an answer out of her. I've tried getting her to see people older than twenty ain't as dumb as she thinks." She threw her head toward the soda fountain. "Kitty, dear! Come here!"

Kitty, who had been giggling over something with the football players, thrust out her lower lip but scurried to her grandmother. Violet followed, hanging over her shoulder. It was clear her earlier annoyance was gone.

"Kitty, you remember Friday night?" asked her grandmother.

"How should I remember Friday night?" Kitty asked.

"The night Libby Cinder was killed," her grandmother said impatiently.

"Oh, that night."

"Yes, that night." Sudie sniffed. "Now pay attention, honey. Eve and Helena want to know if Cecilia Feather came in to use the phone."

"How should I know?" Kitty asked in an agitated tone.

Violet smacked her on the shoulder. "You dumbbell, you know all right!"

"Let me think." The girl shifted from one foot to the other. After what seemed like an hour, she answered, "I'm not sure."

"You're not sure?" Violet snarled.

"Well, I wasn't paying all that much attention," her friend said. "Joe was working the late shift at the cannery that night so he came in —"

"Oh, for Christ's sake!" Sudie grumbled. "I told you to lay off that boy while you're working."

"I'm sorry, Granny." The sulky tone left her and she was sincerely apologetic.

"Did anyone come in that night while you were at the counter?" Helena asked.

"Sure," she said. "Joe and Tommy and Ruth —"

"She means to use the phone," Violet said.

"Two people." Kitty was serious now.

"And neither of them could have been Cecilia?" asked Eve.

"I didn't say that, Eve," she said. "Both of them were women and one of them was about Cecilia's height and size."

"Good observation, dear." Sudie put her arm around her shoulders. "I knew you could get somewhere if you applied yourself." Her granddaughter grimaced.

"Thanks, Kitty." Eve smiled. "That's a great help."

Kitty and Sudie both retreated but Violet plunked herself down in the third chair. "A big help!" She snorted. "She's no Sherlocka."

"Neither are we," Eve retorted. "We're just trying to help."

"What's all this about the phone booth?" Violet demanded.

"So you love us again now, do you?" Helena eyed her.

Violet pinched her cheek. "I've always loved you. You're my sisters. That doesn't mean I can't get mad at you now and then."

"We think Rosalia might have used the phone here to call the Cinders," Helena supplied.

"I don't know if you should say anything yet, dear," Eve hesitated.

"I'm in on the whole thing, remember?" Violet leaned with her chin in her hand. "So Rosalia lied when she said she was having dinner with her friends in Brenas?"

"Not exactly," said Eve. "She had dinner there all right."

"Well, then?"

"She lied about when she got home," she said. "She told Oliver she was home by ten o'clock, but the Combses said she left around eight or eight-thirty."

"So they could walk the dogs," Helena said with a grin.

"What's this about dogs?" Violet frowned.

"Nothing," said Eve. "Eight would have put her in town with enough time to make that phone call."

"Except she didn't make it," Helena reminded her. "Not from Redbud Manor, that is."

"But she did make the call to the Combses in Brenas earlier in the evening to tell them August wouldn't be joining her," Eve pointed out. "Her phone wasn't out of order then."

"Who says her phone was out of order?" Violet asked.

"Sudie."

"I get it now." Violet's eyes were bright. "Rosalia came in here, made some excuse about her phone being out of order so the police wouldn't be suspicious if they checked, and called Libby to get her to come down to the river so she could kill her."

"It's possible," Eve said. "But we'll never be able to prove it."

"Why not?"

"All we know is Rosalia came down here to make a call on Friday night," Helena said. "We don't know who she called, let alone if she called the Cinders impersonating Cecilia's voice."

"Couldn't Maisie or Bonnie tell you that?" Violet inquired.

"Maybe Bonnie could, Helena." Eve looked at her. "Just like she told us about Rosalia's call to Brenas."

"It's a phone booth, Eve," Helena pointed out. "Lots of people call from a phone booth, many of them strangers. It's not like a person-to-person call."

"I'm sure we can find out." Violet pulled her coat around her shoulders. "And don't you dare say I can't come! It was my idea, after all."

"We wouldn't dream of it." Helena rolled her eyes.

Bonnie was having tea and greeted them with a nod. Next to

her sat a young woman with blond hair so bright it almost glared back at the sun.

"Getting on here, Pearl?" Violet leaned against the switchboard. They had been in school together.

"Oh, yes," she said in a spirited voice. "Nothing to it."

"Nothing to it," Bonnie scoffed. In a lower tone, she said to the older sisters, "The girl's got a brain like a cabbage but, lord, she's quick with the hands."

"Sorry to bother you again, Bonnie," said Eve.

"Ain't no bother." The woman rose. "Only I thought you finished with your investigation this morning."

"We need new information," said Helena. "Can you remember if there were any calls made from the pay phone on Friday night, say, between eight and nine o'clock?"

"You mean the phone booth at the Rooty Toot?" The woman waved her hand. "Why, we get calls from them every day."

"I told you." Helena glanced at her sister.

"Kitty said several people made calls from the booth on Friday night," said Eve.

"Kitty the Cotton Kid?" Bonnie grinned. The nickname made Violet wince. The cotton referred to what people thought Kitty had between her ears.

"Please, Bonnie," Eve begged.

"All right, honey." She pressed her hand. "I can't recall any rings on my end from the drugstore that night but Pearl was taking the line also." She flicked her head toward the young woman. "Pearl, you get any calls from the drugstore on Friday night?"

"Drugstore?" The girl stared with wide eyes.

"That one." Bonnie pointed to the jack with a number taped on it.

"We always get calls from there," she said.

"We know that," Violet snapped. "But were there any on Friday night?"

"Why do you want to know?" The girl turned her wide vacant eyes on Violet.

"Never you mind," Violet said. "Were there?"

Pearl studied the jack with narrow eyes.

"Well?" Violet pushed. "It's not a crystal ball, you know."

"I'm trying to think," Pearl said.

Violet rolled her eyes at her sisters.

"Oh!" Pearl sat up. "Tim called from there."

"Tim?" Eve asked. "You mean Tim Hill? Mrs. Hill's son."

"Uh-huh." The girl's tone was almost dreamy. "Wanted to talk to Cathy about some spring social they're doing next month." She looked at Violet with alarm. "You don't think she's sweet on him, do you?"

"No one but a crane could be sweet on Timmy," Violet assured her. "Who else, Pearl?"

"Some girl."

"Girl?" Eve jumped.

"Woman," she corrected.

"And who did she want to talk to?" Bonnie asked. "Come, girl, you can tell the Grave sisters."

"Her voice was sort of whispery," said Pearl. "I thought she wanted to talk to the Cidels at first."

"There are no Cidels in town," Violet said.

"Oh, I know," she said. "I asked her to repeat it and she said Cinders."

"Cinders!" all three sisters exclaimed.

"Yes." Pearl looked from one to the other. "Aren't they nice people?"

"Very nice," said Eve. "Now, Pearl, this is important. Do you know who the woman was?"

"She didn't give a name."

"But was it someone from town?" Helena asked.

"Oh, I don't think so," said the girl.

"Did she sound like this?" Violet imitated Cecilia's voice as she had done that morning.

"I'm sure I don't know," Pearl mumbled.

"I'm sure you don't," Violet snapped.

"Now, Violet, don't go blaming Pearl." Bonnie came to the timid girl's defense. "We're lucky to hear anything at all, and especially from the phone booth. The fuzz you get on the line —"

"We understand, dear," Eve said. "Thank you both. This has been a great help."

"So you think Rosalia had something to do with this murder business?" Bonnie leaned forward.

"Hush hush, Bonnie," Helena said. "Not a word of this to anyone."

The woman was indignant. "I'm no gossip!"

When they were in the car, Violet snorted, "It's going to break her heart one day when someone tells her the truth!"

Eve looked at Helena. "Well, do we have enough now to go to Oliver?"

Slowly, her sister nodded.

CHAPTER 33

But when they went back to Oliver's office, Gladys told them he had been called out to Pilead to help with some problems at the Nevada/California border and he wouldn't be back in the office that day.

"We could have asked her to call him," Violet grumbled as they left the courthouse.

"Call him where?" Helena asked. "There's not exactly a phone on the border."

"I don't want to disturb him anyway," Eve said. "What we have can wait until tomorrow."

"What if this Mrs. Combs calls Rosalia and tells her you've been snooping around?" Violet took out her compact. "Or what if Bonnie blabs?"

"She promised not to," Eve said.

"What about your friend Pearl?" Helena eyed her.

"Pearl won't blab," Violet said firmly. "No one would believe her if she did."

"I don't think Rosalia is going anywhere," said Eve. "The police never checked her alibi, remember? She's convinced they're all wrapped up with Cecilia now."

"And they should be," Helena reminded her. "We still don't know it wasn't Cecilia who made that phone call. Pearl couldn't positively identify the voice."

"Pearl couldn't identify the hiss of a snake," Violet said. "Kitty said she didn't see Cecilia come in to use the pay phone on Friday night."

"Kitty said she doesn't *remember* seeing Cecilia," Helena corrected. "They're two different things, Vi."

Her younger sister's face puckered with stubbornness. "I know my friend. If she says she didn't see her, she didn't see her!"

"I wasn't implying Kitty is lying," Helena argued. "I'm only saying it's not something that would stand up in court."

"We're not in court!" Violet's voice rose.

"Yoohoo! Eve!" The call came from Rosie Peppin, the owner of the stationery store. They were standing not far from her shop.

They crossed the street. "Hello, Rosie, dear." Eve smiled.

"Haven't seen you in ages!" The woman pressed her hands.

For a moment, Eve felt a wave of gratitude. She, Rosie, and Dot had been a trio in school, with Dot being the bookish one and Rosie being the decorative one. Even now in her mid-thirties, Rosie's face was still youthful and her tall, reedy figure fit the new fashions perfectly.

"It's been too long," Eve agreed. "We were just talking yesterday about putting in an order for office stationery, weren't we, Helena?" Her sister nodded.

"Come see the new curtains." She took Eve's arm.

"Didn't you replace them last year?" Violet asked.

"Yes, but they're out of style now," the woman insisted.

"It seems a shame to throw out curtains only a year old," Helena murmured.

"Why shouldn't she?" Violet objected.

"It just seems like a waste of money," Helena argued.

"You're always so judgmental," Violet snapped. "Don't listen to her, Rosie. I think it's grand the way you always primp up your place."

"Thank you, Violet." Rosie beamed.

She took them up the narrow stairs to the small apartment above her shop.

"Aren't they lovely?" Rosie held the edge of the curtain hanging on the window facing the main street.

"Simply scrumptious!" Violet clapped her hands.

Eve felt her gut plummet as if she were falling from a cliff. The curtains were partly pushed back and the window was open so they billowed out like the skirt of a woman swirling between tables.

"Just like the waves of the sea, isn't it?" Rosie sighed.

"You could almost swim in them," Violet agreed.

"Hardly that, Vi," Helena chided.

"You've come at just the perfect time too," Rosie said. "You can see how the sun makes the red shimmer —"

"Burgundy," Eve murmured. Helena gave her a sharp look.

"What, dear?" Rosie asked.

"The color," Eve said. "It's called burgundy."

Violet stared at her sister. "I never knew you to be so interested in curtains, Eve."

Eve jumped as something brushed her hand. She realized it was the curtain, which a sudden burst of breeze had thrown against her. The seams on the edge were sewn with precision and lined up evenly.

"Who did the sewing?" Eve's mind raced.

"Not me." Her friend laughed. "You know I'm no good at those things."

"You ought to learn since you're so fashionable," Violet said.

"Who did it, then?" Eve persisted. "Betty, I suppose?"

"No, her daughter," said Rosie. "She's back from school now, you know."

"We didn't know," Helena said.

Eve suddenly closed the window. "Rather chilly in here, Rosie dear."

"I suppose so," her friend agreed. "I just couldn't resist showing off the curtain."

They went back to the street, waving to Rosie at the window. "She does have pretty things, but my, she did go on so about those curtains." Violet yawned.

"Are you going back to the drugstore now?" Helena asked.

Her younger sister nodded. "The afternoon paper should have been delivered by now, and Kitty always circles the job ads for me."

"Yes, dear, do go," Eve said absently. Her sister gave her a funny look as she left.

"Eve, what's happened to you?" Helena asked with genuine worry. "You look like a ghost."

"Did you notice the curtains, Helena?"

"A little too showy for my taste," her sister said. "That color was giving me a headache."

"Exactly." Eve grasped her hand. "Wine-colored."

"Burgundy," Helena corrected. "What of it?"

"The scarf," said Eve. "It was the same fabric!"

"Oh, for heaven's sake, Eve, what are the odds of that?"

"They had the same pattern," Eve insisted. "Teardrops sewn in so you could barely see them. And Rosalia's tablecloth was the same."

"But that was blue!"

"Azure," Eve corrected. "She was very insistent on that, remember."

Helena was quiet for a moment. "Are you sure?"

"Of course I'm sure." Eve grasped her arm. "I know why Cecilia had it. Rosalia put the scarf with the ring in her drawer."

"There's absolutely no proof of that," Helena insisted.

"I think there is," Eve said. "The scarf was folded in a very special way."

"You said everything was a mess in her room."

"It was," said Eve. "Except that scarf. It was folded from the ends to the middle."

"Ends to the middle," Helena said slowly.

"Like Rosalia's tablecloth," Eve said. "My God!"

"Don't jump to conclusions," her sister warned. "Madge said Rosalia treated Cecilia like a daughter and Rosalia told us herself she taught Cecilia how to do a lot of domestic chores."

"Meaning?"

"Meaning, she probably taught her how to sew and how to fold her sewing once she was finished."

"If that's true, why didn't Cecilia fold all her clothes that way?" Eve challenged. "Why were all the other things in the drawer thrown in, but one scarf was folded so neatly?"

Helena stared at the potted plant outside the shop next to Rosie's. "I don't know." Eve could almost see the wheels of her analytical mind turning. "Maybe we ought to talk to Betty. She could tell us if Cecilia bought that burgundy fabric at least."

"Or if Rosalia bought it," Eve chimed in.

"And if she says Cecilia bought it?" Helena asked. "You realize that will seal her fate. The police might even say she bought it especially to hide the engagement ring."

"Sheriff Warner probably would," Eve remarked.

"It wouldn't do him much good in court," Helena said. "There's no logic in the idea that Cecilia would buy a piece of fabric and sew it into a scarf just to hide something when any scarf or handkerchief would do."

"I leave the logic to you." Eve took her arm. "But if Betty tells us Rosalia bought that burgundy fabric, we've got her."

"We're not out to get anyone," Helena reminded her.

"All right, then, Oliver has her," Eve said with distraction. "We'd have something concrete to take to him. Isn't that what you've been saying?"

"I wouldn't call it concrete," said Helena. "But alongside

everything else we've found, it would probably be enough for him to question Rosalia."

The Bobs and Knobs shop was almost at the end of the main street, a tiny place, cool and dark like something out of the last century. Betty was a slow-moving woman in her late sixties whose back had been slightly bent from her years of sewing.

But she greeted Eve and Helena with warmth, reminding Eve how rarely they visited the shop. "I'm sorry we've neglected you," she said gently.

"The young always neglect the old," she said with a twinkle in her eye. "That's as it should be."

"We're not so young," Helena said with a smile.

"Still young and pretty in my eyes," Betty said. "Why, I remember when you came in here to buy that cream silk for your wedding dress."

Helena blushed.

"Rosie was just showing us the new curtains," said Eve.

"Aren't they lovely?" She beamed. "Wendy's here, you know. My, you should have seen the truckload of fabrics she brought with her!"

"We heard Wendy was back in town," said Eve.

"You must come to us for tea," the woman said. "She'll be glad to see you. She still remembers when you gave her flowers from the funeral services."

Eve laughed. "We couldn't let lovely flowers go to waste, could we?"

"No, certainly not," Betty agreed.

Eve was aware her sister had been studying the woman with what Violet called her "doc eyes" and realized why. Betty looked a little gray and haggard.

She shifted her purse to her other shoulder. "Helena and I went to visit Rosalia Winters the other day."

"Poor woman." Betty heaved a sigh. "Such a relief her son's out of jail now. We've been following the whole thing in the papers."

"You know Cecilia is now the suspect," Helena said.

"Oh, that's just the police being silly." The woman waved her hand. "They'll see reason in time."

"Rosalia was sewing a tablecloth from the same fabric as Rosie's curtains," Eve said. "She told us she bought it from you."

Betty's eyes were as large as an owl's through her glasses. "Well, dear, I really can't say I remember that fabric. But then, my memory isn't as good as it used to be." She gave a small laugh.

"We were curious about it," Eve mumbled.

The woman pressed her hands together, the fingers wrinkled and knotted. "Since Wendy's been home, she's been taking customers, so she might know. She thinks I'm charging too little." She gave another small laugh.

"It's probably best she does," Helena said quietly. "Is Wendy here now?"

"Yes, she's in the office." Betty took her arm. "Oh, she'd be delighted to see you. She's only been home a month, you know."

Wendy was of different stock than her mother. Medium-height but with strong limbs, she sat at the Victorian writing desk in the small, dusty office, looking as diligent as Helena when she was bent over a body at the morgue. Her head bobbed up when they came in and she greeted them with warmth.

"The Grave sisters are here, dear," said her mother. "They have some questions to ask you about that cloth Rosie bought for her new curtains."

"Mama, I told you to go home and rest." The scolding was affectionate but solid as Wendy put her hands on her mother's shoulders, leading her to the door connecting the shop with their living quarters. "I'm handling things, remember?"

"Such a help." The woman looked lovingly at her tall daughter. "Don't overwork yourself, dear. You came home to rest, remember? You don't want to be tired when you go back to Berkeley."

Eve watched Wendy's face as she said in a mechanical tone,

"Yes, Mama." She was gone for a few minutes. When she returned, the despondent look on her face struck Eve.

"You're not going back to school, are you?" Helena asked.

"Of course she is," said her sister.

"Betty has a heart condition, Eve," said Helena. She laid a hand on Wendy's arm. "I'm sorry."

The young woman sat down, shaking a little. "I can't leave her alone. I'm all she has."

"When family we love needs us, we don't abandon them," Eve agreed.

Helena's arm threaded through hers. She knew her sister was thinking of the past and what Eve had done when their parents died.

"Does she know?" her sister asked.

"She knows," Wendy said in the grating tone. "She won't accept it. But she knows."

There was silence for a moment as a noisy fly buzzed around the bare light hanging above them. Then, Wendy pulled a few chairs from the corner, inviting them to sit down. "You wanted to ask me some questions about Rosie's curtains?"

"We saw the same kind of fabric at Rosalia's when we visited her except in blue — azure," Eve corrected.

"You mean you actually got through the doors of that mausoleum?" Wendy asked, amused. "I thought it was tougher to crack open than the safe at the Bank of Italy."

"Oliver asked us to give her the news of August's release," Eve said.

Wendy nodded. "I've been reading about that. I'm glad he's out, but to think Cecilia would —"

"Yes, yes," Helena said quickly. "Have you any other colors of that cloth other than azure and burgundy?"

"Don't tell me you suddenly have a hankering for sewing, Helena." Wendy chuckled. "I always thought you'd rather handle a test tube than a needle."

"I did make my own wedding dress," Helena protested.

"You mean Agnes made it," Eve corrected.

Wendy laughed. "I found only the blue — azure — and the color Rosie bought."

"Who else bought it?" Helena asked.

"The blue?" asked Wendy. "Just Rosalia. She insists any fabric she likes be exclusive to her." Her mouth was set. "Mama stood for that kind of nonsense but I don't intend to."

"Helena meant the burgundy," Eve asked. "Other than Rosie, of course."

Wendy searched her book. "We sold it to two other people. Ida Close bought some." She snorted. "She tried to play the same game as Rosalia — wanted me to put the bolt aside exclusively for her — but I told her nothing doing."

"And who was the other person?" Eve asked timidly. "Was it Cecilia?"

"Cecilia!" Wendy glanced at her. "What are you thinking, Eve?"

"Nothing we can talk about," Helena said. "Was it?"

Wendy was silent, tapping her pencil against the page. "I really shouldn't be telling you this, you know."

"Please." Eve pressed her hand. "This is important. It might help the police see Cecilia is innocent."

"How is burgundy cloth involved in a murder?" Wendy asked.

"The engagement ring August gave to Libby was found wrapped in it," she said. "There, we've told you something confidential the police aren't telling people. Now do you trust us?"

Wendy smiled. "Who doesn't trust the Grave sisters in this town?" She searched her book. "Missy Terril bought the fabric."

"Not Cecilia?" Eve's breath lightened.

"Not Cecilia."

"I don't recall that name," Helena said. "Someone from across the river?"

"I believe she was one of the inmates at the Hatton Farm," Wendy said.

"You shouldn't call them inmates, not even in fun," Helena scolded. "Those girls work hard."

"I've seen a few of them get a little too big for their britches," Wendy declared. "This one said she works for 'the lady in the big house on the hill.'"

"Missy!" Eve said. "Rosalia's maid, Helena."

"Rosalia would certainly fit the description of 'the lady in the big house on the hill,'" Wendy agreed, closing her book.

"Has Rosalia ever sent her maids to buy fabric before?" Helena asked.

"Not that I know of," she said. "Of course, I've been away at school."

"Would Betty know?" she asked.

Wendy tapped the pencil against the page again. "I don't want her disturbed, Helena."

"I know," Helena said. "But we're taking this to Oliver so he would probably need to speak with her anyway."

She sighed. "Wait here and I'll see if she's asleep yet."

When she was gone, Eve turned to her sister with shining eyes. "Well?"

"It would have been stupid of Rosalia to send her maid if she intended to incriminate Cecilia," Helena pointed out.

"She told us Missy has only been with her a month," Eve said. "People in town don't know those girls in Hatton House very well. No one would readily connect her with Rosalia. And she could say she bought the cloth for herself. If Wendy thinks she's become a little conceited, others would think so too and just assume she was copying her mistress."

"Maybe she did buy it for herself," Helena said. "Did you ever think of that?"

"Then why would it have been in Cecilia's drawer unless Rosalia had it?" Eve argued.

Wendy returned with her mother leaning on her arm and Eve's heart went out to her sudden frailness.

"Betty, sit down." Helena pulled a chair closer to her. She pressed her hands and Eve, knowing her sister, realized it was not only from affection. She wrapped her hand around her wrists so she could check her pulse.

"I'm all right, dear." Betty smiled. "I'm always a little light-headed after lunch. I keep telling Wendy she shouldn't make those rich casseroles."

"We won't take up much of your time," Eve promised. "We just wanted to know when Missy, Rosalia's maid, came to buy the burgundy cloth."

"Burgundy?" the older woman echoed.

"The wine-colored one, Mama," Wendy supplied. "Rosalia came in last month and bought the blue one, remember?"

"Of course, now I remember." Betty's voice grew a little irritated. "I ought to have remembered when you first asked me." Her look was almost guilty.

"It's hard to remember something that happened a month ago," Helena said kindly.

"Did Missy buy the wine-colored cloth last month too?" Eve asked.

"That poor girl," Betty sighed. "Just got herself into trouble with the law. Because of a man, of course." Her eyes were sharp. "She's done well with Rosalia, though. She told me herself."

"When did she tell you, Mama?" Wendy asked.

"The day we had the frost," said the woman. "You remember, dear."

"I remember too." Eve met her sister's eyes. The frost had come only about a week ago — just before the police found Libby's body.

"One more question, Betty." Helena grasped the woman's hand. "Did Rosalia usually send her maid to buy fabric for her?"

Betty blinked. "No, not that I recall. She always came herself."

"Is that important?" Wendy asked after she helped her mother back to her room. "About the maid, I mean."

"It might be," Eve said softly. "It just well might be."

~

Eve and Helena had no time to discuss anything when they reached the house, as a young couple from Moody who had lost their child to a riding accident were waiting for them at the funeral parlor. They both spent the rest of the afternoon comforting the grieving mother and father who were clearly beside themselves, death being so foreign to their young lives.

When they came to the dinner table that evening, Violet and Felix were already there, chatting amiably for once. The scent of honey and cloves filled the house and Eve felt the reassurance of the warm spices.

"Looks like we're having honey cake for dessert tonight." Violet dug into the meal.

"You're downing that soup as if you intend to eat the entire pot," Felix joked.

"As a matter of fact, I thought about taking some down to Sudie," she said. "It's her favorite and it's been ages since Agnes made it." She glanced at the housekeeper who came in with soup for her sisters. "How come you're so stingy about the honey, Agnes?"

"'Cause it costs twelve cents a jar," Agnes barked.

Felix rose. "I'm afraid I'll have to miss it, Agnes. They want me there early. Big boss is coming for a visit." He rolled his eyes.

"You'd better go, then," Helena said in a distracted tone.

He shot her a look. "Trying to get rid of me, my love?"

"You know I'm not." She looked at him with her lovely eyes.

He gave her a peck on the cheek. "I know you're not."

The rest of the meal was quieter than usual, as Eve sorted out her thoughts. Violet chattered in her usual way with Helena intervening now and then.

"What's the matter with you two?" her youngest sister complained. "You've both got the blues when you ought to be celebrating."

"Celebrating!" Eve stared.

"We nearly solved the case for the police," Violet said. "What did Oliver say when you told him?"

"We didn't tell him anything yet, Vi," Helena said.

Violet put down the fork and the large chunk of honey cake fell to the side. "I thought that's where you were going when I went to the drugstore."

"We went to see Betty," Eve said.

"Whatever for?" Violet sniffed. "Don't tell me you're thinking of giving Agnes some of that burgundy cloth to make new curtains!"

"Who's gonna make new curtains?" Agnes demanded as she brought in the coffee. "You want it here or in the other room?"

"Here, I suppose," Helena said.

"I hate burgundy!" Eve pushed her plate away.

"Now you're being childish," Helena said. "It wasn't our fault we found out what we did."

"What did you find out?" Violet asked.

Eve smiled at her younger sister. "I'm sorry, dear. You're right. I need to act, but not like this." She rose. "No coffee for me, Agnes. I'm going out."

"Going out!" Violet stared. "At this time of night?"

"You're going to see Oliver." Helena eyed her. "That's what you've been brooding about all though dinner, haven't you?"

"We've got to tell him, Helena," said Eve. "There's too much we know that points toward another guilty party."

"What guilty party?" Violet asked. "Rosalia?"

"Hush and have your coffee," Helena snapped. "Eve, all this can wait until tomorrow, can't it?"

"No, it can't," Eve insisted. "It's like a leech on my mind."

"It's not as if Rosalia is going to run away," Violet pointed out. "She doesn't even know she's a suspect."

"She's not a suspect," Helena insisted. "She may never be."

"That's not what you thought this afternoon," Eve said.

"I've been brooding too," said her sister. "It's not that I don't think we ought to tell Oliver, but I also think we shouldn't get our hopes up about Cecilia."

"I promised August," Eve said softly. "It isn't right."

"Lots of things in this world aren't right," Violet said. "But we try to get them straight all the same. Isn't that what you've always told me?"

Eve looked at her young, pretty sister. She petted her cheek. "That's right, darling. That's why I'm going."

"You're not going without me," Helena insisted.

"Or me!" Violet jumped up. "Take the coffee away, Agnes. We won't be needing it."

"Going to the D.A. when the dinner ain't even been digested yet," Agnes grumbled, taking the tray away.

"I don't know if Oliver will appreciate an entire delegation," Eve said with a smile. But she was grateful she wouldn't have to face him alone.

"He might not be home anyway," Violet said. "Kitty told me there's a big shindig in Moody tonight. Black tie and everything and all the big cheeses are going."

"We have to try, dear," Eve said.

"Speaking of Kitty, don't you need to call her and tell her you're not going out tonight?"

"We hadn't any plans." Violet stiffened. "I'm not going out every single night with my friends, you know."

"I hadn't noticed," her sister said dryly.

"I assume you're not going to tell me to stay home this time?" Violet's eyes flashed at her eldest sister.

Eve sighed. "What would be the good? You're just as involved with this sordid business as we are."

But she refused to let Violet drive, even though she had gotten her license a few months before. Her youngest sister quickly ceased her grumbling when Helena filled her in on what they had discovered at the Bobs and Knobs.

"Why is it so important if Rosalia bought some of that gaudy cloth?" she inquired.

"Because it means Rosalia put that ring in Cecilia's drawer," Eve said.

"We don't know that for sure," Helena reminded her.

"*I'm* sure she did." Eve's tone was stubborn. "You didn't see Cecilia's face when Oliver confronted her with the ring. She really had no idea it was there."

"How could she have gotten it into Cecilia's room?" Violet asked.

"She was like a mother to her, remember," Eve said. "She might even have a key to the house."

"Well, that's one down and one to go," Helena said.

"What do you mean?" Eve looked at her.

"There were two pieces of jewelry missing from Libby's body," she said. "The ring and the pin."

"If Rosalia killed Libby and took the ring, she must have taken the pin," Violet concluded. "I thought someone with your love for logic would have figured that out." She smirked.

"All right, smarty, if she took the pin, what happened to it?" her sister challenged. "Where is it and why is she holding on to it? Why didn't she wrap it in the scarf along with the ring?"

Eve was quiet for a moment. "Because it means something entirely different to her."

"Have you been reading my books on Freud?" Helena asked in a wry tone. "You sound like those new psychoanalysts."

"Freud's a crock," Violet snapped. "I think he hates women."

"Rosalia was very careful when she took the ring off Libby's finger," Eve reminded her. "We saw that ourselves, remember."

"Taking a ring off a dead woman's finger." Violet shuddered.

"But she ripped that pin right off her coat."

"She was probably in a hurry at that point," Helena said. "Time was passing and anyone might come strolling along the river."

Eve shook her head. "It goes deeper than that."

"Oh, really, Eve," Violet snorted. "That sounds like a lot of sap."

"Sap or not, I think it's true," Eve insisted. "The pin was a symbol of Libby belonging at Redbud Manor. Rosalia took it as a way of stripping her of what she thought she had no right to."

"I don't know if I agree with you," Helena said. "But I think we should tell Oliver in case he wants to get a warrant to search the house."

"I wish we could just storm the place and rip it apart," Violet said, her teeth set. "Just like in the moving pictures."

Helena laughed. "Life is more than the moving pictures, Vi."

CHAPTER 34

*O*liver's place was midway between the downtown and Falcon Hill. The two and three-story houses there were not the grand mansions of the upper crust, but they were impressive enough with small front yards and wrapping porches. The pleasant dove gray with sandy blue trimmings was invisible in the dark, but Eve recalled how serene the house looked in the sunlight when she passed it sometimes on her way downtown.

A sour-faced maid answered the door, her lipstick puckered with a deep, irritable red. "Yes?" she practically barked. "Who do you wish to see?"

"The district attorney," Eve answered promptly. "Mr. Clarke."

"I'll see if my mistress is accepting anyone," said the girl. "They're getting ready to go out."

"We asked to see the master, not the mistress," Violet snapped.

"Please wait here." The maid opened the door only a few inches wider to allow them to pass into the hall. "Whom shall I say is calling?"

"You can tell her the Grave sisters," Helena said.

The sour expression did not budge. "One moment."

"Now I know why Sudie says Ellen Clarke is so snooty," Violet snarled.

The maid came back a moment later. "Follow me." The nasty tone had turned condescending.

They were led into the living room, which Eve thought surprisingly opulent and ornate for someone of Oliver's more rugged tastes. Standing by the fire was Ellen Clarke, Oliver's wife. Eve had only seen her once, at the New Year's Eve party a few months ago, and she was struck by the woman's elegance. Everything about her, from her blond hair to her heeled slippers, was polished in a way that caught the eye but shunned gaudiness. Eve felt like a mouse in comparison.

"Should we curtsey to the queen?" Violet snarled under her breath.

"Good evening," Ellen said to no one in particular.

"Good evening, Ellen." Eve stepped forward, feeling her duty as head of the family heavy on her shoulders. "It's lovely to see you again."

The woman gave a conscientious nod. "I understand you wish to see my husband."

"We've got to see him," Helena said. "It's very urgent."

"I'm afraid that's impossible," she said. "Oliver is upstairs dressing. The Moody mayor is giving a dinner party."

"We know that!" Violet snapped.

"I'm sorry we have to disturb him," Eve said. "But as my sister said, this is an urgent matter. It concerns the Libby Cinder case."

"Oh?" Ellen looked from one sister to the other. "Did the sheriff send you?"

"We sent ourselves," Violet said.

"We're helping with the case." Eve suddenly felt as if her tongue were twisted in knots. "Oliver asked Helena and me to help identify her and then it sort of became our affair when August Winters was accused —" She stopped, realizing how idiotic she sounded.

Helena, with her swift manner, took over. "I'm sorry, Ellen, but we must insist. This concerns not only Libby but Cecilia too. In fact, it could come down to a matter of life and death."

The crystal-blue eyes gave her a curdling look. "I take my husband's work as seriously as you do. You needn't be so dramatic about it."

Eve felt her anger boil, though Helena looked more amused than annoyed. Violet, however, had more gumption, as she answered the woman, "My sister is the least dramatic person alive, Ellen. She always tells the truth." Helena gave her an affectionate smile.

"I've no doubt," said Ellen coldly. "But the fact remains if it were that important, the sheriff would come himself."

Oliver suddenly came into the room dressed in a tuxedo but the jacket was unbuttoned and the tie hung undone around his neck. The dark color brought out his features and Eve was struck by how well it suited him. Ellen's blondness and the coral satin dress she wore offset the black and white tuxedo. They looked like a beautiful couple. In spite of their weighty deed, Eve felt her heart pinch.

"Hello, Eve, Helena." Oliver nodded at them with a friendly smile. "Well, youngster, I thought you'd be out with your friends this fine evening. Somebody get a flat tire?"

"I had more important things to do," Violet said briskly. "We know who did it!"

"Oh, you know who did it," he said, amused. "Would you mind explaining who did what to whom for me?"

"The murder, what else!" Violet said impatiently.

"Oliver, maybe we should talk in private." Helena glanced at Ellen.

The woman's acidic look returned as she sat on the lounge chair. "Oliver, darling, we'll be late."

"Is this about the Libby Cinder case?" he asked.

"Yes," Helena said. "We think we might have information you'll want to hear."

"Oliver —"

"Just a minute, Ellen." He leaned against the fireplace. "Go on."

Eve fell silent, frozen in her place. Between Helena's reasoning narrative and Violet's jerking interjections, they told him all they had discovered: Rosalia's lie about the dinner with the Combses, Rosalia's visit to the drugstore on Friday night, the call from the phone booth, and the burgundy fabric.

"You've all been pretty busy, haven't you?" Oliver remarked.

"You got us into this!" Violet insisted.

"Really," Ellen mumbled. She had been sitting examining her bracelets the entire time and even removed one as if she had decided it didn't suit the coral silk after all.

He grinned. "I didn't get *you* into anything."

"Vi's right," Helena said. "That's the truth, isn't it, Oliver?"

"I suppose it is." He glanced at Eve. "And I'm glad I did." She smiled at him.

"Then you believe us?" Violet asked.

"I would never doubt the word of the Grave sisters," he said. "You know, Ellen, these are the straightest shooters in town."

"All of this could have waited until tomorrow morning, Oliver," she hissed.

"Miss Feather wouldn't feel that way," he said sharply. "I'll admit there's some strong circumstantial evidence, as far as it goes."

"But it doesn't go far enough?" Helena guessed. "I warned Eve it wouldn't."

"Why don't you question Missy, Rosalia's maid?" Violet suggested. "Get Sheriff Warner to question her. She'll confess in no time."

"The sheriff isn't as eager to practice police brutality as you think," Oliver said. "And what if Missy did 'confess,' to buying that cloth, which she readily would, since there's a record of it?

What then? Maids run errands for their employers all the time. Don't they, Ellen?" He threw a glance at his wife.

"Now and then," she said shortly.

"She'd say she bought it for herself," said Oliver. "Even if she didn't, she would say so."

"Maids aren't entirely trustworthy," Ellen agreed, glancing toward the stairs where her own maid was ascending.

The superior gaze of those blue eyes finally pulled Eve out of her stupor. Her intimidation left her as she looked squarely at Oliver. "What if we could get concrete evidence?"

"I don't follow you," Oliver said.

"The brooch."

"We haven't been able to find it," he reminded her. "Shreve confirmed they sold it to August but it's disappeared. Probably down the river well into Nevada by now, according to Sheriff Warner."

"Eve thinks Rosalia took it for psychological reasons," Violet inserted.

Ellen cast her eye on Eve like a cat examining a fish in a market window. "What an absurd notion."

"Maybe not so absurd," Oliver said. "Killers often take souvenirs from their victims." His wife shuddered and he touched her shoulder to comfort her. Eve flinched.

"I think I know where it is," she continued. She told him about the hiding place in Rosalia's bedroom.

"It's not unusual for a house that size to have hidden panels and priest holes," he said.

"Well, then, get a search warrant," Violet growled.

"Hold on now," he said. "I can't demand one whenever I get a hankering. There has to be clear justification."

"Haven't we given you enough of that?" Eve asked.

"It's all hearsay, Eve," Helena said. "It's not like the ring they found in Cecilia's drawer. That was concrete."

"That's why Oliver needs the warrant," Violet argued.

"You could at least go to the house and talk to her," Eve suggested. "Maybe confronting her with what we've told you will give you the reason you need to search the house."

"You don't expect her to confess, do you?" Helena asked.

"Sometimes people say enough to incriminate themselves," Oliver said. "She'll call Adkins, of course, but if we take her by surprise, she might say enough —"

"We?" Ellen sat up. "I wasn't aware the Grave sisters were now on the police force."

"They ought to be!" Oliver said roughly as he slid off the tie. "But we have to go as soon as possible if we want to get anywhere."

"You want us to come with you?" Violet could barely contain her glee. "Just like in the detective novels!"

"It's impossible, dear." Ellen rose. "We're late already and Mayor Woodward said he would send the car around at eight-thirty."

"You'll have to go on ahead without me, darling." He took both her hands. "You understand, don't you?"

"Of course," she said but to Eve, it looked as if she felt anything but understanding. "It's just that Mayor Woodward has connections to the people in Sacramento —"

"I'll come when I can," Oliver promised. "Don't tell anyone why I was delayed. Just tell them I had some official business to attend to."

"I always do," she said softly.

"Just give me five minutes to change out of this straightjacket." Oliver grinned as he rushed upstairs.

The living room was silent the few minutes after he had gone, the spicy scent of his cologne lingering in the air. As Eve was about to speak, having thought of a compliment to pay Ellen about the house, the woman turned on her heels and strolled out of the room, leaving them alone.

~~~~~
~~~~~

Helena drove somewhat recklessly to Falcon Hill. Eve could see the lights of Redbud Manor gleaming from the house windows like watchful eyes. Those strung along the pathway leading up to the door gave the shape of the place with its largeness and stretched corridors. Eve thought of how much satisfaction Rosalia must have gotten ripping the pin off Libby's lapel, knowing she would never set foot in the house again.

She half-expected Missy to answer the door but Rosalia appeared in a lavish opal gown, sparking earrings and a necklace that looked as if it were plaited with rubies. Even Violet's eyes widened as she took in the opulence.

"Why, Mr. Clarke." She greeted him with a smile. "I should think you would be on your way to Mayor Woodward's by now." She saw the three sisters standing behind him. Her eyes became slightly more guarded. "Anything wrong?"

"We'd like to talk to you, if we may, Mrs. Winters," he said.

"We'll be leaving in ten minutes," she hesitated. "August is just finishing dressing."

"It won't take long, Rosalia," Eve said quietly.

The woman looked from one to the other, then stepped back to let them in. "I assume this is about Cecilia?" She led them into the living room. "August is quite upset about that. But I told him what Helena said about the police being lenient with Cecilia." She glanced at her. "That *is* what you said, isn't it?"

"It was only a theory," Helena mumbled.

"Even as a theory, it was a great comfort to him," Rosalia said.

"This isn't about Cecilia," Oliver said.

"Oh?"

"There's some new evidence that might prove Cecilia is innocent," he said. "We were hoping you would answer some questions for us."

"Me?" The woman blinked. "What would I know about Cecilia?"

"You used to know quite a lot," Violet said.

"That was months ago." Rosalia nodded at her. "I haven't seen you in a long time, Violet. You've turned into quite a pretty girl." In spite of the grave circumstances, Violet smiled at the compliment.

"I've just discovered you didn't tell the whole truth about what you were doing on Friday night." Oliver gave her an intent look.

The woman stiffened a little. "Don't tell me you've been checking my alibi?"

"We check on everyone who knew the victim, Mrs. Winters," he said.

She eyed Eve. "You mean you had others check for you."

"In a manner of speaking." He didn't bat an eye.

"I don't know why you say I wasn't telling the truth." She crossed her legs. "I was at the Combses' in Brenas for dinner on Friday night just like I said. They can verify that."

"They already have," Helena said.

The woman was quiet for a moment. "I see."

"But you weren't there when you said you were," Violet said.

"Of course I was!" The woman looked annoyed.

"You were there in the earlier part of the evening," Oliver said. "But they told Eve and Helena you left early with a headache."

The woman mulled this over. "I did leave early."

"Why didn't you tell us that when we came to see you?" Oliver asked.

"It didn't seem important."

"Alibis aren't only about where you were, Mrs. Winters. They're also about when you were there."

Eve could see he was getting his temper up.

"I wasn't aware I was under suspicion," she said coldly.

"Where did you go after you left the Combses?" he asked.

"Home, of course," she said. "That's why I saw August. I came home and looked in on him."

"And?"

"And he wasn't in his room," she admitted. "He came a little later."

"Did you question him about where he had gone?" Helena asked.

She glared at her. "I'm not my son's keeper, Helena. When you have children, you'll see that."

Helena's mouth set in anger, but she did not reply.

"You just sat and waited for him?" Violet eyed her.

She gave a sly smile. "Just as your sisters sit up and wait for you, I'm sure."

"You're in no position to make cheap cracks!" Violet snapped.

"What did you do, Mrs. Winters?" Oliver asked.

"I went to bed, of course," she said.

"If you went to bed, how do you know August came home a little later?" Helena asked.

"Because I heard him come in," she said. "I'm rather a light sleeper." She laughed a little. "It used to drive my husband crazy." She half rose. "Does that satisfy you, Mr. Clarke?"

"No, ma'am," he said with respect but resolve. "It doesn't."

"Just as I saw August when he came home, he saw me," she said. "You may ask him when he comes down, and then you really must excuse us —"

"What were you doing at the drugstore that night?" he shot out.

"Drugstore?" She gave a hollow laugh. "What would I be doing at the drugstore? I always send my maid for anything I need."

"I just asked you the question, Mrs. Winters." He looked at her.

"Who said I was at the drugstore?"

"My friend Kitty," Violet said.

"Well, dear, I'm afraid your friend Kitty was wrong or —" she lowered her voice, " — has been drinking some bad bootleg."

"Kitty never drinks bootleg!" Violet flared. Oliver motioned for her to calm down.

"Sudie remembers you," Oliver said. "She said you even apologized for coming in so late to use the phone because yours was out of order."

The woman shifted on the couch. "Now that I recall, I did go in to call the Combses and let them know August wouldn't be coming to dinner because my phone was acting up. I can't imagine what was wrong with the line."

"We checked, Rosalia." Helena's tone was steely now. "Bonnie said you called the Combses from Redbud Manor earlier in the evening."

There was silence for a moment. Then, Rosalia suddenly jumped up. "I see I have to call Hugh Adkins again. First my son and now me!"

"The exchange also traced the call made to the Cinder house from that pay phone," Oliver said. "At about the same time when you were using the pay phone."

"Isn't it obvious?" the woman asked. "Cecilia also went to the drugstore to call Libby and tell her August was waiting for her by the river."

"I didn't say anything about what the call to the Cinder house was for," he said slowly.

Rosalia's features, which had been until now regal and without emotion, crushed with anger. "I'm calling Hugh Adkins."

"Not yet, Mother."

The tone was clear and poised as August descended the stairs, his hands in his pockets, dressed in the kind of tuxedo Oliver was wearing only a half hour ago. "I'd like to hear what else Mr. Clarke has to say."

"It's all as nonsensical as it was when they questioned you, dear," said his mother. Her voice shook slightly.

"I'd like to hear the nonsense," he said. "Sometimes there's more sense in nonsense than there is sophistry."

"I don't know what sophistry is!" his mother snapped.

"It's saying something in order to deceive," Helena supplied.

"August, this doesn't concern you any longer." Rosalia took his arm. "When the car comes, you go on to dinner and I'll come later. Once I speak with Hugh Adkins." She looked meaningfully at the district attorney.

Oliver studied the young man for a few moments and, as if seeing the determined look on his face, continued, "Eve and Helena told me about the blue tablecloth you were so industriously working on when they came to visit you."

The remark took her by surprise. She gave a short laugh. "I didn't know you're interested in linens, Mr. Clarke."

"Is it true?"

"I could hardly deny it, since they told you about it," she said. "I don't see what it has to do —"

"May I see it, please?"

She didn't move. Without a word, August went to a cupboard, pulled the cabinet door open, and took out the tablecloth. He unfurled it and laid it across the table. Again, Violet's eyes again filled with admiration.

"You do fine, careful work, Mrs. Winters," said Oliver.

"The mark of a killer, Mr. Clarke?" she flashed. "And the color is azure, not blue!"

"The ring we found in Cecilia's drawer was wrapped in a similar cloth," he said. "Except it was burgundy instead of azure."

"Eve told me," said Rosalia. "I saw the same fabric at the stationery shop. I can hardly help it if others copy me."

"Eve said the scarf she found in Cecilia's drawer was folded in a certain way," Helena said.

"That's right," Eve said. "The ends toward the middle, like a closed book."

"Just like this one," August said, staring at the tablecloth.

"Well, naturally," said his mother. "As I told Eve and Helena, I taught Cecilia all the domestic arts."

"You said you *tried* to teach her, but she didn't quite catch on," Helena corrected.

"Well, she caught on to this!" The tone slipped a notch.

"Mrs. Winters," Oliver's eyes narrowed, creating an almost menacing darkness, "you realize we can verify all of this with Cecilia?"

"Verify what you like," she said. "Only don't be surprised if the girl lies. She's always lying."

"Mother!"

"I'm sorry, darling." She let out a breath. "They've gotten me so upset that I don't know what I'm saying." Regaining her composure, she said, "As long as you're verifying, why don't you also verify that I only bought the azure fabric with Mrs. Cain?"

"We have." The woman stared as Helena continued, "Betty told us you didn't buy that wine-colored fabric."

The woman's shoulders relaxed. "You see, darling? This is all nonsense, just like I said."

"But Missy did," Violet added.

"Missy?"

"Your maid, remember?" she said in a sly tone.

"As I said before, Mr. Clarke, I can't help it if others copy my good taste." The woman's chin jutted out. "Missy admired the tablecloth, so she probably bought some of the other fabric."

"Why don't we ask her?" Eve suggested.

"I gave her the weekend off," said Rosalia. " She's been working very hard helping with the arrangements for Mayor Woodward's dinner." She cast a meaningful look at Oliver. "I still have a hand in local politics even if my husband is no longer alive, Mr. Clarke. It might do well to remember that."

Eve felt a sting in her eyes as she realized what the woman was implying. Mr. Winters had had a reputation for helping men with their campaigning for local office. Politics and the law, one hand clasping the other.

"I remember it, Mrs. Winters," Oliver said in a dignified tone. "I still intend to have the police fetch your maid for questioning. You wouldn't happen to know where she went?"

A throat cleared and August said, "She went with one of the Hatton House girls to Carson City, Mr. Clarke."

"August!" The color on his mother's face drained.

"Well, Mother?" He looked at her squarely.

Rosalia sat down, slower this time. "I gave her money to buy some fabric for a dress. The poor girl hasn't anything decent to wear for Sunday service."

"Why did she buy burgundy instead of azure?" Oliver asked.

"You'll think me quite vain when I tell you." Her laugh sounded like a shriek "It's really rather ridiculous."

"Why, Mrs. Winters?"

"I couldn't bear the thought of her wearing a dress to church that matched my tablecloth," Rosalia admitted. "So I told her the burgundy would suit her light coloring much better."

Violet piped up, "Missy's ash blond hair is the worst color against burgundy. Too contrasting."

"Missy isn't stylish like you, Violet!" the woman snarled. "She's a hard-working girl."

Rather than get upset, Violet gave her a foxy grin.

Rosalia straightened her dress. "Well, now, if there's nothing else, we have a dinner to go to." She was almost cheerful. "And so do you, Mr. Clarke."

In a tone of finality, Oliver said, "I don't think either of us will be going, Mrs. Winters."

She seemed to hold her breath for a moment before she demanded, "What do you mean?"

"I think you'll want to call Mr. Adkins now."

"But I've explained —"

"Before you do, I'd like to use that phone to call Judge Halifax," he continued. Glancing at Eve, he smiled and said, "While I was changing, I asked him to stand by in case I needed him to sign a warrant."

"Warrant!" August's eyes widened.

"For the burgundy cloth?" Rosalia burst out laughing. "Why,

Mr. Clarke, you can have that without any warrant. I'm sure it's in Missy's room somewhere and as her employer, I have a right to —"

"Not the fabric, Rosalia," Eve said. "The brooch."

"Brooch?" August asked. "You mean the brooch I gave Libby? What would Mother be doing with it?"

"She took it along with the engagement ring when she killed your fiancée!" Violet burst out. "Oh, why does it have to take so long to get to the truth?"

"I would be very careful of making that kind of accusation, Violet," Rosalia said archly. "As your sisters seem to know everything about the law now, I'm sure they will tell you that can get you into a lot of trouble."

"I'm not making any accusations," Violet said boldly. "I'm stating a fact and the police will soon see it."

"Cecilia probably has the brooch somewhere," Rosalia said. "Just like she had the ring."

"If she has it, why didn't Eve find it with the ring?" Helena asked quietly. "It doesn't make any sense."

Rosalia sighed. "My dear Helena, if you knew Cecilia, you'd know not everything she does makes sense."

"We'll ask her that too," Oliver said. "If we don't find the brooch here."

"Of course you won't find it," Rosalia snarled. "Because it isn't here."

"Then you should have no objections to the police searching," Oliver headed toward the hallway. "I promise you they'll be very careful."

August's voice came through the tense room. "You don't need any search warrant, Mr. Clarke. I'm giving you permission to search the house."

His mother looked as if someone had viciously punched her face. Her even features collapsed. "Darling, what are you saying?"

"You heard me, didn't you, Mother?" he asked. "In fact, Mr.

Clarke, I don't think you'll need to search the entire house. Only Mother's room."

"Behind a panel above the fireplace." Eve's throat was scratchy. "In the jewelry box."

The young man looked at her for a moment, the muscles in his neck strained. "I imagine so."

"You're not going near my room!" Rosalia hollered. "I'll call Hugh Adkins. I'll call Ben Blase if I have to!"

"I believe Mayor Woordward is already at the dinner," Oliver said lightly.

The house filled with silence. Then, in a choking tone, August said, "I loved her! I was going to marry her! Mother!" He buried his face in his hands.

Rosalia's face compressed, her body stiff. As if trying to regain her poise, she said, "I want you to believe I had nothing against the girl. I didn't even think the rumors around town about her being a loose woman were true."

"Then why? Why?" He staggered. Oliver caught him by the shoulders.

"I made a promise once," she said. "I wasn't about to let anything or anyone keep me from fulfilling it."

"What promise?"

"To your father." Her mouth tightened. "I didn't hate the girl. Really, I didn't. She was just unsuitable. I said that from the beginning, didn't I?"

"Like the rabbit," he said softly. "You killed the rabbit because it was in the way. You killed Libby because she was in the way of your plans."

Eve felt Violet put her head on her shoulder. She petted the smooth hair, realizing the adventure was no longer an adventure for her. It had been overshadowed by a more brutal reality.

CHAPTER 35

A few weeks later, the trial of Rosalia Winters for the murder of Libby Cinder took place in Gyver's small but impressive courthouse. It was the first murder trial Gyver County had seen in years, and a crowd pushed outside the court-room doors, courteously kept out by Sheriff Warner's young but energetic police force. It seemed as if people from both sides of the river came just to get a glimpse of the wealthy Rosalia Winters be convicted of murdering her son's fiancée.

The Grave sisters had a place in the gallery since they were called to give testimony to some of the evidence they had discovered. Although Eve tried to keep Violet out of the proceedings, her cleverness regarding the phone calls put her in the witness box along with her older sisters.

Afterward, they filed out into the sunny day with the crisp blue sky staring down at them.

"See what a smart lawyer can do?" Violet rubbed her heel, as the new shoes she had worn to the trial hurt her feet. "Hugh Atkins getting her out of the noose like that!"

"He didn't get her out of a conviction," Helena reminded her. "A life sentence is worse than death for someone like Rosalia."

Oliver, who had fallen into step with them as they emerged from the courthouse, nodded. "It's not going to be easy for her."

"She's lost her son," Eve agreed. "That's more punishment than any hangman's rope or jail cell could offer. To think, if she hadn't heard August and Libby in the backyard that night —"

"Heard? She was spying!" Violet spat.

"All right, she was spying," Eve corrected.

"No wonder she accosted Josh with all those questions," Helena agreed as she watched the elderly fisherman, his face sour from being forced to appear in court, hurry away toward the river. "She already had the idea in her mind."

"She did make the phone call to Libby pretending to be Cecilia," Violet said. "And then sneaking into her house to hide the ring in her drawer — a girl she'd treated like a daughter for years!"

"She might have succeeded in getting that poor girl convicted if you ladies hadn't started asking questions." Oliver smiled. "I'll be forever grateful."

"I don't think the sheriff will be," Eve remarked. "He didn't much like it when you told him how you got hold of that brooch."

"He'll just have to learn to trust my decisions in the future," Oliver said in a firm tone.

Rosalia was led out of the courthouse, surrounded by the sheriff, her lawyer, and a few of the sheriff's men. She wore a dark blue dress and a hat with a veil that almost completely hid her face. She took each step as if she were fifty years older than she really was.

August came out with Cecilia on his arm. As the sheriff opened the car door for Rosalia, she saw him. Eve could tell she wanted to break free and run to him, but Hugh Atkins and Sheriff Warner held each arm tightly. August looked at her, his hands in his pockets, as they carefully helped her into the car. He looked much older than his twenty-five years.

The car drove off, leaving silence in its wake. August and Cecilia joined them.

"I'm sorry, August." Eve felt tears come to her eyes. "You didn't deserve this. And neither did you, Cecilia."

"I really thought she cared about me," Cecilia said in a soft tone. "But she was just using me to find out about August and Libby."

"I never knew she promised my father she would see to it that I was the leader of Falcon Hill," said the young man in a vague tone. "I always knew he was disappointed in me — he thought my wanting to be by the river a foolish thing — but I didn't know he made her promise that."

"It wasn't fair," Violet agreed. "Parents shouldn't make plans for their children's futures like that."

"Libby was just another one of her rabbits." August looked at the empty road. "So was Cecilia, for that matter."

"What rabbit?" Violet asked.

"Never mind, darling," Eve said soothingly.

"And all that about the jewelry." Cecilia shuddered. "I understand why she took the ring — she wanted to make the police think I did it — but why did she keep the brooch?"

"She was taking back her son," Oliver said. "Figuratively speaking, that is."

"It's all so twisted!" August cried.

"You'll get through it," Helena assured him. "The human mind has the capacity to forget such things as time goes by."

"At least you're free now," Violet said. "You and Cecilia can start over again."

Cecilia smiled. "We're just friends, Violet. That's all we've ever been and all we will be." Eve noticed her tone, though resigned, was no longer regretful.

"Yes, I'm free," August said. "Thanks to you, Mr. Clarke."

"And the Grave sisters," Cecilia chimed in.

"We hardly did you any favors," Eve mumbled.

"But you did," he said. "It's as Violet said. I'm free now."

"And so am I," Cecilia said. "It's a little frightening, but invigorating."

"And what are you going to do with that freedom, dear?" Eve asked. "You're not staying with your mother, are you?"

Cecilia shook her head. "Mother's been wonderful throughout this whole trial, but I can't live her life anymore. I have a little money my grandmother left me, so I'm taking the train with August to San Francisco. I don't know yet what I'll do, but I'll do something."

"All roads lead to Rome," Violet said cheerfully.

"And you, son?" Oliver put his hand on the young man's shoulder. "The Navy for you?"

"I'm going back to sea," said August. "Josh thinks he can get me a job on a cargo ship sailing out of San Francisco next week."

"Going where?"

"Hong Kong," he said.

"Get as far away from here as possible." Violet nodded with approval. "That's the way to go."

"You have any plans to do the same?" Helena raised her eyebrows.

Kitty appeared on the sidewalk and whistled to her. "I'm only going as far as the Rooty Toot at the moment, but if I change my mind, I'll let you know." She bolted, waving at her sisters. The two young women disappeared around the corner.

"Can I drop you anywhere?" Oliver glanced at August and Cecilia as he buttoned his coat all the way.

"No thank you, sir," he said. "We're going to see if we can cheer Josh up." He chuckled as they started down the steps. Then, he turned around. "Mr. Clarke, I was telling the truth. About Libby and me, I mean. I asked her to marry me not because she was having my child. I loved her."

Oliver smiled. "I never doubted that for a moment, son."

The young man heaved a sigh and continued down the steps.

"Eve, we've got to get back," Helena reminded her. "Mrs. Taper is bringing Mr. Taper's things from the Civil War this afternoon."

"And I'm sure we're in for an earful about this trial from the ladies when they come," Eve said dryly.

Oliver laughed. "I expect you and your sister will be as prudent as you can." He pressed each of their hands. "If they give you grief, you just tell them the D.A. is very grateful you made his job a lot easier."

"Sometimes it's hard to take a new position, especially a small town like this. You have so much to prove," Helena said with sympathy.

"Oliver has proved himself to be a fine district attorney," Eve insisted.

"And you've proved yourself a fine detective." He chuckled. "You be careful or I might call on you again."

His words rang in her ears as she descended the steps with Helena.

~~~~~

Author's Note

Hello fabulous reader!

Welcome to the Grave Sisters Mysteries! This is a brand-new series that follows three close-knit sisters who own the only funeral home in a small town on the California/Nevada border in the 1920s. That background would set anyone up to solve crimes, wouldn't it?

You can read more about the series at this link: https://tammayauthor.com/about-pages/about-the-grave-sisters-mysteries-series.

Why did I choose such a, well, morbid profession for my three sister sleuths?
~~~~~

I was inspired by my new town. In 2023, I moved from a mid-sized city in Texas (about 250,000 people) to a small college town in the Midwest (approximately 13,000 people). I love my new home by the river, but I noticed there are an awful lot of funeral homes here! Yelp lists at least six, and I know of three right on my block. I pass one when I'm out walking, a very quaint and peaceful place in a large Victorian-style house. Another a few blocks from me is known to be one of the few mortuary museums in the country, and while I haven't been there yet, it boasts of death and mourning artifacts which, if you've read my historical women's fiction series, the Waxwood Series (If you're interested in checking it out, here's where you can find out more about the series: https://tammayauthor.com/about-pages/about-the-waxwood-series), you know was very important to 19th and early 20th century life.

Any writer will tell you when something jumps out at them, they start to play the "what if?" game. I started to think, "What if a family owned a funeral home in a small town like mine and just sort of fell into solving crimes because they had access to the dead?"

And, voila! The Grave sisters were born!

What are the Grave Sisters up to next? Violet Grave's old school friend gets himself caught up in a mess when the body of his army buddy is found in the alleyway behind his house. Book 2, *The Missing Witness*, which you can purchase here: https://tammayauthor.com/the-missing-witness-grave-sisters-mysteries-book-2, is up for preorder now, and you get a sneak peak at an excerpt (hot off the presses, as they say) when you turn the page!

Happy reading!
Tam

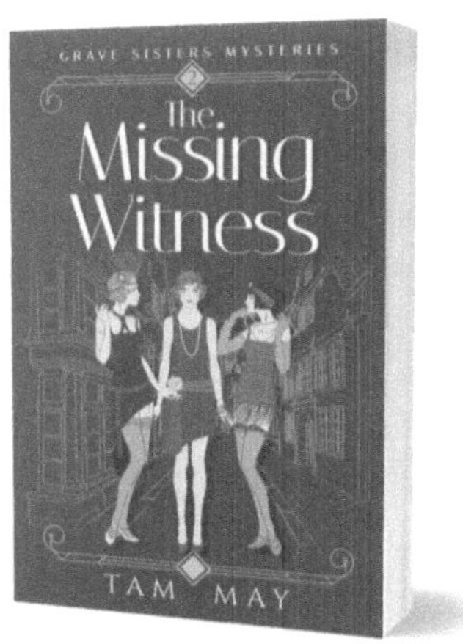

It was an unusually hot summer in Gyver that August of 1921. All of the fans were buzzing in the Grave sisters' living room and every so often, Agnes, the housekeeper, regarded the ornate fireplace with a loathsome stare as if its menacing grate was trying to eat up what little air there was in the house.

Eve, the eldest of the Grave sisters, was in her usual place on the sofa, the *Gyver Bee* in her lap. Helena, the middle sister, had her nose buried in one of her journals. Violet, the youngest, was, as usual, out for the evening, although the sisters had the satisfaction of knowing she was not tearing up the town in Joe Reid's beat-up ford but safely puttering behind the Rooty Toot Drugstore's soda fountain helping Kitty Markie serve sandwiches and sundaes and gossiping with her friends.

Felix, Helena's husband, had stayed home for dinner instead of indulging in his usual "out with friends" meal. He sipped Agnes excellent coffee, patting his stomach with after-dinner satisfaction.

"Maybe I should have dinner at home more often, my love," he threw out at his wife.

"Maybe you should," Helena did not look up from her journal.

He leaned forward, peering at the title. "*Police Science Chronicles.*" His face turned slightly pale with horror. "Good Lord, I thought you were through with that nonsense."

"I've always been interested in crime science, Felix," she said. "You know that."

"And *you* know I'm not interested in having my wife fill her head with such gory details," he snapped. "I thought I made my position clear when you and Eve got involved with the Libby Cinder case."

Eve remained silent, folding the edge of the newspaper.

Helena, as always, remained collected. "As a matter of fact, I'm reading a fascinating article on Mrs. Glessner Lee's Nutshell Studies of Unexplained Deaths."

"Who's what?" he asked.

Helena finally looked up, taking off her reading glasses and rubbing her nose with a little smile. "Mrs. Frances Glessner Lee. She's experimenting with crime scene dioramas."

"You're speaking Greek, my love," Felix said. "We weren't all fortunate enough to indulge our intellects with college learning and eye-opening revelations of rich spinsters like Zadie Hummer who can afford to stick their noses into police business!"

"Helena worked hard for her education, Felix," Eve snapped.

"And *I* worked hard to put bread and milk on the table for my brothers and sisters!" he snapped back.

Eve's voice softened. "I wasn't dismissing that."

Felix flicked his fingers at the coffee cup so it would ring. "I'm simply trying to understand."

"Mrs. Glessner Lee is making miniature crime scene reenactments in order to teach detectives how to look for evidence," Helena said patiently.

"Perhaps she ought to come here and teach Oliver Clarke a thing or two."

"Oliver is no longer a detective," Eve reminded him. "He's the district attorney now, remember?"

"I'm not likely to forget it," Felix snapped. "I expect him to come through the door any minute, flailing helplessly and begging for assistance. And you'd give it to him, wouldn't you?" He eyed her.

Helena tapped her glasses against the journal page. Eve felt a pain in her heart at her younger sister's discomfort. She cleared her throat. "It looks like the veterans are finally going to the help they need."

"Oh?" Felix inquired.

"'Vets will be able to cut through all the red tape, as three government agencies —the Bureau of War Risk Insurance, the U.S. Public Health Service, and the Federal Board for Vocational Training— will merge into one place as President Harding signed a bill today to establish the Veteran's Bureau,'" Eve read.

"Good for Harding," Helena said.

"It's about damn time," Felix growled.

"Disgraceful how those poor boys have had to suffer,

economic depression or no economic downturn," Eve said with a sigh. "All that waiting and paperwork to get what they deserve."

"It's worse than the injuries they suffered in battle," Felix agreed as he rose. "They get blasted in the trenches and then come home to what? Nothing but unemployment and hunger."

"It ain't like you were right there with them," Agnes mumbled, collecting the coffee tray.

Felix glared at her. "I may not have been on the Western Front, but I had friends who were." In a softer tone, he added, "Their letters are the only thing I have left of some of them."

"Felix would have been in the war if it hadn't been for his heart, Agnes," Helena snapped.

"I wasn't saying he wouldn't have been," the woman murmured as she went out.

"Does the article say anything about the men with shell shock or war neurosis?" Helena asked.

"Not specifically," Eve said. "I imagine the bill covers them all."

"I imagine not," Helena grumbled.

There was a clammer and Agnes's voice rose. "Don't you go trailing dirt on my floor, missy!"

Violet rushed in with Kitty and Jimmy, Kitty's beau, in tow. "Eve, you've got to talk to Oliver!"

"Steady there, young man." Felix caught Jimmy by the shoulders. It was clear from the swaying that Jimmy was not entirely sober. "Some bad whiskey on your breath."

"Nonsenth. Betht money can buy." Jimmy's words came out slightly slurred.

"Agnes, get Jimmy a strong cup of coffee. Very strong," Eve emphasized.

Helena glanced at her watch. "You've another hour before the drugstore closes, Vi."

"Never mind that." Violet waved her away. "They've arrested Hank Convoy!"

"Who's he, Jimmy's bootlegger?" Felix asked, amused.

"Don't be a sap," Kitty snapped. For once, she had a somber look on her face instead of her usual pout. "He's a friend of ours."

"He's the one who used to come around and fix the hearse when it was acting up, remember?" Violet said, a little breathless. "He went off to war and came back last year."

"One of the lucky ones," Felix remarked. "He'll benefit from the Veteran's Bureau all right."

"Oh, why don't you scram?" Violet snapped.

"As you wish, madame." He saluted her, and, giving Helena a peck on the cheek, sauntered out.

"Calm down, honey," Eve put her arm around her sister. "Kitty, you and Jimmy sit."

Both obeyed like little children.

"Hank's in jail, and it's all a mistake," Violet insisted.

"Maybe it ithn't a mistake," Jimmy said. "Maybe he really did it."

"Oh, shut up!" Kitty barked.

"Did what?" Helena asked. "Vi, make sense."

"Joe Savage came down to the drugstore tonight and was shooting his mouth off about how the sheriff's arrested Hank Convey," said her sister.

"It's probably nothing more than drunk and disorderly," Helena said. "Lots of soldiers have been letting loose since they got back."

"Joe said Hank murdered someone!"

"Murdered!" Eve stared. "That nice kid?"

"He's not a kid anymore," Kitty insisted. "He was old enough to almost get his brains blown out in the trenches."

"Maybe Joe's just trying to impress you," Helena suggested. "He's always flirting with you."

"That'ths what I thaid," Jimmy insisted. "Noone believeths me."

"Agnes, take Jimmy to the kitchen and get him more coffee," Eve ordered. "You'd better have some too, Kitty."

"I didn't touch a drop of that fire water!" Kitty insisted.

"Nevertheless." Helena rose and pushed both of them at the sour-faced Agnes.

"Eve says coffee and coffee you'll get!" Agnes growled as she seized both of them by the arm.

Violet breathed a little easier when they were gone. "I didn't ask them to come. Honest."

"Now tell us what happened slowly," Eve commanded.

"Joe came in for a sandwich about a half hour ago," Violet said. "He was being his usual pesky self, and I was ignoring him of course —"

"Of course," Helena mumbled.

Glaring at her, Violet continued. "Then I heard him say, 'That friend of yours from the Mold District just got hauled to the station, and Sheriff's got the handcuffs on him.' I said, 'Who in Sam Hill are you talking about?' and he said, 'How many friends you got from Mold District?'"

"Get on with it, Vi," Helena snapped.

"He said, 'Hank what's-his-name. Sheriff says he's going to fry in the electric chair for murder.' Kitty told him he was crazy since there's no electric chair in California." She looked satisfied. "I told her that."

"Brilliant deduction," Helena said dryly. "Now go on."

"Joe said, 'Well, the gas chamber or the noose, then, and serves him right.' I said, 'And who is Hank supposed to have killed?' Joe said, 'Friend of his, I think. And he *did* kill him. He said so to the sheriff and the district attorney.'" She stopped to take a breath.

"I think he was just telling you a story, honey." Helena pressed her hand.

"But it's not just a story." Violet sniffed. "We went down to the police station ourselves."

"Who's 'we'?" Eve asked.

"Kitty and me, of course!"

"And Jimmy?" Helena raised an eyebrow.

"Are you kidding?" Violet stared at her. "In his condition?"

"And the sheriff told you he's arrested Hank for murder?" Eve asked.

"Of course not," said her youngest sister. "He still resents us for solving the Libby Cinder murder case instead of him."

"We didn't solve the case," Helena corrected. "Oliver did. We just helped."

"Oh, applesauce, we solved it and you know it," Violet growled. "Anyway, that old boar of a sheriff wouldn't tell us a thing, but Deputy Elwood hinted Hank was there. He wouldn't tell us anything else."

"Joe Savage could still be wrong," Eve offered.

"That's what we've got to find out." Violet leaned forward, grasping both her sister's hands.

"We're not police women, Vi," Eve protested.

"We're the three Sherlockas, remember?" Violet asked.

"That's your game," Helena said. "I prefer not to think of myself as Sherlock Holmes' sister."

"It's ridiculous for us to go storming into his house and demanding he present the case to us," Eve added.

"I'm not suggesting that!" Violet said. "I'm only saying if we went there and you used a little sweet talk, he'd cough up the whole story."

"Just because he asked for our help once doesn't mean he plans on doing it again," Helena said.

Violet looked from one sister to the other. "All I'm asking for is information about a friend who's been arrested."

"What about Annie Convoy?" Helena suggested. "She's his grandmother."

"I don't think anyone knows about it yet," Violet said.

"More hints from Deputy Elwood?" Helena guessed.

"Eve." Violet appealed to her sister, her fox-like features melting into a little girl's plea. "I know you don't like going to Oliver's house —"

Eve stiffened. "I don't know what you mean, Vi."

"I know Ellen's been a big snob lately, making time with the Brenas people," Violet continued. "I know she's been treating everyone in town as if they're no better than fruit flies, including Mrs. Beaton and her bunch. But she'll probably be in bed already, and we'll have Oliver all to ourselves. If you asked him, he would tell you anything you wanted to know."

"You talk as if I'm one of those vamps from the moving pictures," Eve said warily.

"Well, if Oliver weren't married —"

"Vi!" Eve's voice shook. "I don't want to hear you talk like that!"

Her youngest sister heaved a sigh and turned to her other sister. "Helena, make her go."

"If Eve goes, we all go," Helena said simply. "He can't put us all off."

"He'll think we're all pouncing on him at once," Eve objected.

Violet rose. "If neither of you won't go, I'll storm the citadel myself! Me and Kitty."

"Lord," Helena mumbled.

Eve put her hands on her sister's shoulders. "If it means that much to you, darling, we'll go. But we'll be making fools of ourselves."

"Attagirl!" Violet gave her a hug. "I'll get Kitty and Jimmy out of here." She straightened her skirt. "We've got Sherlocka business to attend to."

"Heaven knows it won't be the first time we've made fools of ourselves for that girl," Helena remarked as her sister scurried out of the room.

"We might do someone else some good, though," Eve said softly as she thought about Hank Convoy, the kind young man who had willingly fixed their hearse.

What happened to land Hank Convoy in jail? Was it really murder? And can the sisters get him out of it? You can find out when *The Missing Witness* comes out later this year. Preorder it here: https://tammayauthor.com/the-missing-witness-grave-sisters-mysteries-book-2

Have you checked out my Adele Gossling Mysteries yet? Read on for how to get hold of my free novella, *The Missing Ruby Necklace*.

Hatfield and Jackson immediately took their positions as lawmen. Jackson used the Abberton's phone to summon Deputy Assistant Edison and other deputy assistants while Hatfield calmed people down and requested everyone stay where they were. Adele joined the Abbertons, leaving Lady Augusta in Nin's care.

Mr. Abberton was holding back Freddie McCarthy, who looked more curious than distressed. "I think she only fainted."

"Take her upstairs," Sheriff Hatfield ordered.

"I'll find Dr. Rhodes," Adele said.

Finding Dr. Rhodes, whom she had seen earlier devouring the *hor d'oeuvres*, proved easier said than done. She finally located him sifting through an abandoned bucket of champagne bottles.

"Doctor, there's been an accident," she began.

"I can see that." He continued searching the bottles. "That man said there was an 1862 here somewhere —"

"An accident in need of a doctor's assistance," she said.

"Smelling salts revive one from fainting spells, as I'm sure even you know, Miss Gossling."

"It may be more serious than a fainting spell," she insisted.

He looked at her with mock amusement. "Are you claiming you have medical expertise now as well as police detection?"

"I know when a woman needs help, doctor," she said.

He went back to searching the champagne bottles. "I'm sure a phone call to Mr. Sanders will do the trick."

Adele lost her temper. "Why should I waste time calling your assistant when you're already here? This may be a party, Dr. Rhodes, but you are still obliged to fulfill the duty of your profession, just as the sheriff and my brother are fulfilling theirs."

The man gave her a sniveling look, but went into the hall and came back with his doctor's bag. "You see, Miss Gossling, I am always fulfilling the duty of my profession, even for swooning females."

She managed to hold her tongue as she led him upstairs.

They found Mis McCarthy in her room still unconscious. Around her were the Abbertons, Sheriff Hatfield and Jackson.

Freddie McCarthy kept tiptoeing toward the bed, peering at his sister.

Jackson took Adele's side as the doctor examined the young woman. "Your friend took Lady Augusta home," he said. "We thought it best." He took her hand. "You ought to go home too, Del. I'm sure Tomas is standing at the open doorway, rubbing his hands, and fretting like a mother hen."

"I think I ought to stay." Adele glanced at Mrs. Abberton. She had expected the woman to be calm, as she imagined she had seen many young ladies faint and looked upon it as little more than a social embarrassment. But Mrs. Abberton was staring down at the girl, her eyes wide and her lips parted. Adele put her arm around the woman's shoulders, guiding her into a chair.

The doctor closed his bag. "You've once again misjudged your powers of observation, Miss Gossling." He cast a stony eye toward her. "Miss McCarthy is merely in a swoon." He looked at Mr. Abberton. "You've spirits of ammonia in the house, I take it?"

"Freddie." Mr. Abberton summoned the boy. "Go and get the bottle marked SPIRITS OF AMONIA out of the cabinet in my study. Here's the key."

"I don't mind." The boy scurried away.

"What caused it, doctor?" asked Mr. Abberton.

Dr. Rhodes threw up his hands. "Who knows what excuses young ladies find for their fainting spells? A tight corset, perhaps."

"That seems likely." The man nodded. "Miss McCarthy is most conscientious about her appearance." He glanced at his wife as if to confirm this. Mrs. Abberton, still startled, nodded.

"Or perhaps she was trying to gain attention." The doctor rose. "It's not uncommon in ladies her age."

"It may not be uncommon," Adele said in an icy tone. "But neither is it necessary for the guest of honor at a large party to feign a swoon to gain attention. If anything, I should think she would have avoided it in order not to draw more attention to herself."

The doctor handed Mr. Abberton a box. "Here's a sedative as well. When she decides she's had enough of this game, you may allow her to take one." He gave a sweeping nod to the room. "I bid you all good night and trust you won't need my services again this evening. Or, shall I say, this morning?"

"You might at least say Happy New Year," Adele mumbled.

He gave her a sour look as he left the room.

Freddie came in with a small bottle. He handed it to Mr. Abberton and retreated to the corner next to Adele. "Why do doctors have to be so awful?" he whispered.

"Not all of them are awful," Adele promised. "Dr. Rhodes is an exception."

"I wouldn't worry, son." Jackson patted him on the back.

"I'm not worried," said the boy cheerfully. "I want to see how long before Eleanor wakes up. Once she went into a faint for five hours!"

Mr. Abberton held the bottle out to his wife. "You ought to do it, Hester. She might be more comforted to wake up to a woman's face."

Mrs. Abberton's hands gripped the arms of her chair. Adele stepped forward. "I'll do it, sir, if you'll permit me."

"My sister worked alongside nurses and doctors in San Francisco's settlement houses," Jackson added. "She knows what she's doing."

The man glanced at his wife, then handed Adele the bottle.

She couldn't help but think Freddie was right, as she barely had time to open the bottle when the girl's eyes flew open. Unlike other women Adele had seen coming out of a swoon, Miss McCarthy's gaze was clear and focused. "Why, what a lot of people!"

"You fainted, dear," Mr. Coldwell said.

"Did I?" Her hand flew to her head, as if checking that the pins and combs were still in place.

"You're all right, aren't you?" Mrs. Abberton spoke softly. "You're really all right?"

"Of course I'm all right." The girl was indignant.

"You gave us all a bit of a fright," the sheriff said.

Miss McCarthy sat up. "I didn't mean to. It was so close in that room."

"Yes," said Mrs. Abberton. "Yes, that was it. That must have been it."

"Freddie, run and tell Mrs. Wells to make a strong cup of coffee and bring it here," said Mr. Abberton. "As quickly as you can."

"Coffee!" Miss McCarthy laughed. "Heavens, no! I haven't had my first taste of champagne yet." She flung her hand out to her brother. "Bring me a bottle of champagne, my good man."

"I don't mind," he said.

Before he could saunter out the door, Mrs. Abberton jumped up. "I'll get it."

"I really think we ought to get coffee," Mr. Abberton mumbled.

"She wants champagne," Mrs. Abberton was almost stern. "It's a celebration, after all!" She practically fled from the room.

Adele followed her and caught her arm. She spoke in a soft tone. "Mrs. Abberton, why did Miss McCarthy faint?"

"She just told you, didn't she?" The woman gave a shrill laugh. "Albert said we ought to open some windows, but it was such a windy night, I —"

"It wasn't the windows," said Adele. "Or the corset."

"Of course it was!" The woman examined some bottles on the floor. "I never could read these labels."

"You were staring at Miss McCarthy as if something more was wrong."

"What an imagination you have, dear," the woman said.

"Miss McCarthy had her hands on her throat when she fell," Adele continued. "You were looking at her throat."

"Nonsense," the woman hissed.

"I noticed she wasn't wearing her ruby necklace," Adele declared.

Mrs. Abberton tore through a row of bottles lying on a table. One rolled onto the floor with a crack and the bubbly drink spilled across the marble. She sunk into one of the chairs. "You've always been very observant, Miss Gossling."

"You saw it too."

"Just before the lights went out," she said. "But Eleanor is one of those girls who gets easily flustered with her jewelry. She says it weighs her down."

"If that's true, why were you so alarmed?" Adele asked.

"I wasn't," the woman insisted. "She has a locked box for that necklace. Albert tried to persuade her to put it in our safe, but she refused."

"That's rather unusual," Adele said.

"Eleanor's a lovely girl, but rather flighty," the woman said in a harsh tone. "I expect Celestine spoils her."

"If the necklace is missing, there might be a theft involved," Adele suggested.

Jewelry goes missing all the time. But does that mean theft? And why is Mrs. Abberton so nervous?

How can you get your hands on a copy of *The Missing Ruby Necklace*, not available in any bookstore? Simple. Go to this link: https://landing.mailerlite.com/webforms/landing/12u0c3. What else will you get when you get this novella? How about fun facts about women in history and true crime classic mysteries, which are just as fascinating, if not more so, as contemporary true crimes?

ABOUT THE AUTHOR

Writing has been Tam's voice since the age of fourteen. She writes stories set in the past featuring sassy, sensitive women characters. Readers experience in her books women struggling to carve out an identity for themselves during eras when their options were limited. Her stories are set mostly around the Bay Area because she adores sourdough bread, Ghirardelli chocolate, and San Francisco history.

Tam is the author of the Adele Gossling Mysteries, which takes place in the early 20th century and features suffragist and epistolary expert Adele Gossling, whose talent for solving crimes doesn't sit well with her small town's conventional ideas about women. Tam also has a new series, the Grave Sisters Mysteries, about three sisters who own a funeral home and help the county D.A. solve crimes in a 1920s small California town.

Tam also writes historical fiction about women breaking loose from the social and psychological expectations of their time. She has a 4-book series set in the 1890s, the Waxwood Series, and a post-World War II short story collection, *Lessons From My Mother's Life*.

Although Tam left her heart in San Francisco, she lives in the Midwest because it's cheaper. When she's not writing, she's devouring everything classic (books, films, art, music), concocting yummy plant-based dishes, and exploring her new riverside town.